GWEILO

Also by Brian Nicholson featuring John Gunn

AL SAMAK

ASHANTI GOLD

FIRE DRAGON

GWEILO

BRIAN NICHOLSON

Trafford
PUBLISHING

Order this book online at www.trafford.com/07-1275
or email orders@trafford.com

Most Trafford titles are also available at major online book retailers.

Note for Librarians: A cataloguing record for this book is available from Library
and Archives Canada at www.collectionscanada.ca/amicus/index-e.html

Printed in Victoria, BC, Canada.

ISBN: 978-1-4251-3356-6

*We at Trafford believe that it is the responsibility of us all, as both individuals
and corporations, to make choices that are environmentally and socially sound.
You, in turn, are supporting this responsible conduct each time you purchase a
Trafford book, or make use of our publishing services. To find out how you are
helping, please visit www.trafford.com/responsiblepublishing.html*

*Our mission is to efficiently provide the world's finest, most comprehensive
book publishing service, enabling every author to experience success.
To find out how to publish your book, your way, and have it available
worldwide, visit us online at www.trafford.com/10510*

Trafford
PUBLISHING™ www.trafford.com

North America & international
toll-free: 1 888 232 4444 (USA & Canada)
phone: 250 383 6864 ♦ fax: 250 383 6804 ♦ email: info@trafford.com

The United Kingdom & Europe
phone: +44 (0)1865 722 113 ♦ local rate: 0845 230 9601
facsimile: +44 (0)1865 722 868 ♦ email: info.uk@trafford.com

10 9 8 7 6 5 4 3 2

GWEILO

'Gweilo' literally means 'white spirit from over the sea', but is used by the Chinese in Hong Kong as a derogatory term for the Caucasian expatriate.

To D, Rugs and Basher

FOREWORD

The theft of a birthright has been the motive for murder since Jacob usurped it from his elder brother, Esau. The birthright to the immense riches of Hong Kong will be stolen at midnight on 30th June 1997 from the descendants of the first settlers on that inhospitable, fever-ridden island of decaying granite, as a result of the signing of the Anglo-Sino Joint Declaration in 1984. Not only the New Territories will be handed back to China - acquired by Great Britain in the 1898 treaty - but also Hong Kong Island which was ceded to Great Britain in perpetuity after the first Opium war in 1842, thus forming the birthright of the descendants of those intrepid traders and settlers who had arrived in Hong Kong - 'a place of sweet water' - under the straining canvas of the triangular sky and moonraker topsails of their lean-hulled trading clippers.

In 1986, two years after the signing of the Joint Declaration, the reactor at the Chernobyl nuclear power station exploded during an unauthorised experiment in low-power output. The subsequent meltdown and escape of radioactive material turned the surrounding area for hundreds of square miles into a deserted wasteland of mutant plants and animals and humans riddled with cancer. The world reeled in horror and condemned the corrupt and decaying Soviet Union for its crass incompetence. But one man in Hong Kong, whose ancestor had disembarked from the first of the clippers to anchor in Victoria Harbour and whose father had died for Hong Kong, tortured to death by the Japanese occupation force in 1943, saw the Chernobyl disaster in a different light. It offered the solution to his all-consuming fury at being dispossessed of his inheritance and betrayed by his own country. He was a 'gweilo' – literally translated from the Chinese as 'white spirit from over the seas'. If he and his descendants couldn't have Hong Kong, then no one would have it - least of all the Chinese.

PROLOGUE

Kwong knew that he was dying because the man had told him that he would die. He hadn't understood what the man was talking about, but realised that if he did what was asked of him then his wife and children would be allowed to emigrate to San Francisco, with American passports and $100,000 to start a new life in the USA. He had considered the proposal and when the man had returned two days later he had agreed to do what was wanted provided that his family was moved to San Francisco first; that had been agreed. The man had come back to the house which he shared with his parents and photographs of his family had been taken.

Three weeks later, the man had returned with the passports and instructions that he should bring his family to the construction site the following night. It had been a bitterly cold night just before the Chinese New Year and the previous two nights there had been frost on the highest peaks of the Pi Chia Shan Hills. There had been no shift working that night and his wife and three children had sheltered from the icy, north-east wind in the construction workers' canteen on the site. The helicopter had come just before midnight and with little time for farewells, his family had been hurried on board and whisked away into the night. A week later, the man had delivered a letter from his wife, which had been written for her and which informed him that she and the children were safe in their new home. There was a photograph of his wife and the children standing outside a small house. The man had kept his side of the bargain and Kwong had agreed to carry out the instructions, which he was given.

All the construction site workers had been given three days holiday over the Chinese New Year. Kwong had been told that he would be required at the site despite the fact that he had been sacked after a spot check at the gates, at the end of his shift, had revealed a coil of electrical cable in his canvas workbag. The man had arrived, dressed in protective clothing, and after giving him his final instructions had sent him in on his own to do the work. It had taken him 4½ hours to do the modifications and when it was finished he had felt very weak and dizzy and it seemed as though his stomach and bowels had turned to fluid. All he had to do was pick up the phone and ask for the doors to be unlocked, but he had no strength left to pull himself across the floor to the telephone. His limbs felt heavier and heavier and so he decided to rest.

Twenty minutes later, the man in protective clothing and breathing apparatus dragged the body out and placed it in a box which was driven off the construction site. The truck was driven eighteen miles to the village of Xiantanling where the man had been instructed to burn the body and throw the box into the sea. Instead of carrying out these instructions, the man had dragged the box onto a sampan and pushed box and body into the sea before returning to his truck and driving back to the town of Shui, ten miles to the north of Daya Bay. As the box fell into the sea, the hasp burst and Kwong's body floated to the surface.

CHAPTER 1

The body was lying on the sand just out of reach of the ebbing tide. The sea was millpond calm and a dappled gunmetal grey in colour, exactly matching the rain-laden sky, which promised an early morning downpour over the South China coast.

A half section of four soldiers stood looking down at the body. All were taking the opportunity of a pause in the first light beach patrol to have a cigarette while the section commander reported the discovery of the body on his radio. The body was that of an Asian, fully clothed in rather threadbare, blue overalls. The feet were bare, the face was buried in the sand and he was definitely dead.

Lance Corporal Williams, the section commander, was speaking into a small, hand-held radio; nothing larger with more range was needed as the island of Ping Chau was only just over a mile long and some 600 yards at its widest part. Williams was talking to his platoon base which was barely half a mile from where he was standing on the beach on the north-east tip of the island, directly opposite mainland China, just over a mile away.

'Hello zero, this is two-two alpha,' and without waiting to check if his platoon base was receiving his signal, Williams continued, 'we've found another floater at grid 430524. He's dead, but the sharks haven't had a go at him, neither have the Chink patrol boats; in fact, he's not in bad nick. Do you want us to bag him like the rest or does the inspector want to see him? Over.'

'Two two alpha, this is zero,' came the reply and Williams recognised his platoon sergeant's voice, 'leave him be. Sunray and the inspector will be with you in five minutes, out.'

Williams clipped the radio back in his belt and tucked his short, SA80 assault rifle rather more comfortably under his right arm. 'Right, you lot,' Williams addressed his half section who had finished their cigarettes, 'Dunston and Phillips, you move off to the left! Harding and Cooper, you go to the right! Go about 200 yards along the beach and see if there's anything you can find belonging to this Chink, like shoes for instance, as the poor bleeder doesn't seem to have dressed for this beach party.' Williams chuckled at his own, morbid sense of humour; 'I'll wait here for the platoon commander and the inspector.' The two half sections moved off with little enthusiasm amidst mutterings of, 'alright for some' and 'just because he doesn't want to grub around in all this crap on the beach.' These remarks were ignored by Williams and treated as an acceptable grumble from soldiers who have just been given a mucky task to carry out some twenty minutes before their two hour patrol was due to finish. The voices gradually faded as the soldiers moved further down the beach. Each man had provided himself with a piece of driftwood to retrieve items of interest from the rubbish which always littered the high water mark of any beach, but nowhere in the world more prolifically than the beaches of Hong Kong and the New Territories.

Very few expatriate residents of Hong Kong would ever leave the chlorinated safety of a swimming pool to go near the polluted water of the popular beaches, which were so important for the tourist trade and the ethnic Chinese population. An army of tractors, bulldozers, tracked monsters of all shapes and sizes and litter collectors fought a losing battle with the rubbish, which was discarded each day or deposited at the high water mark. No such effort was wasted on the beaches of the hundreds of islands around Hong Kong, which justified the lack of enthusiasm shown by the soldiers for the task which they had just been given.

Each day, the number of illegal immigrants from China increased as the British lease approached its expiry date of 30 June 1997. This was exacerbated by the trickle of Vietnamese refugees to Hong Kong becoming a flood when they were turned away by China. This influx swamped Hong Kong and made the task of prevention, control and repatriation almost impossible. The refusal of the Communist Chinese to allow repatriation of illegal immigrants brought the whole situation to a crisis which over-stretched the Security Forces in Hong Kong. This led to the return to Hong Kong of the Gurkha Battalion, which was based in Brunei and the further augmentation of the British Garrison by a battalion from the UK at the request of the Governor and the Commander British Forces.

It was for all these reasons that the tiny island of Ping Chau had been reoccupied as a platoon base to try and stem the rising tide of illegal immigrants and those, in particular, who were prepared to attempt the mile swim from the Chinese mainland. The swim, in many cases, was preferable to tackling the border fence, which was constantly patrolled and topped with razor wire, which shredded any human limb which touched it. The majority of the immigrants would have already overcome the fence put up by the Chinese on the northern perimeter of the Shenzen Economic Zone. This fence ran for about 100 kilometres from Shihchunghin in the west to Tai Mui Sha in the east and prevented the Chinese population from reaching this privileged area. The prospect of facing yet another fence often made the alternative sea route less daunting. The favourite routes were either Deep Bay in the west or Mirs Bay in the east, with the short swim to Ping Chau as another option. The majority of Chinese couldn't swim and so they paddled and floated over, assisted by an assortment of buoyancy aids, of which the inflated condom was the most common.

There were other hazards, which faced the swimmers in addition to that of managing to stay afloat. If they didn't succumb to too many mouthfuls of polluted seawater, then there were always the sharks and barracuda, which had become used to this regular and plentiful supply of fresh meat. Especially as it was offered to them with tantalisingly waggling feet and splashing around in exactly the way that any professional big game fisherman would trail a lure through the water. If all these hazards were overcome, this helpless human flotsam then had to contend with the Chinese patrol boats which would churn through the mile wide channel between the mainland and the island at full speed, zigzagging from side to side using the racing propellers as food liquidisers to shred the bodies of men, women and children into a more digestible meal for the sharks. It was no mean achievement to reach the beach on Ping Chau, but to reach it unscathed was a fairly rare occurrence, hence the remark of the young soldier about the body on the beach being 'in not bad nick'.

Williams looked up at the sound of boots scrunching through the pebbles above the high water mark. His platoon commander, Lieutenant Hutchinson, was approaching with an inspector from the Royal Hong Kong Police. Paul Hutchinson was a sound, if unimaginative young officer, who had been with the 1st Battalion Hampshire Fusiliers for a little over four years. He had gone straight from a moderate public school to the Royal Military Academy at Sandhurst and from there straight to his battalion. His first three years with the battalion had been spent in Germany, based near the town of Munster in Westphalia. The town of Munster was in a staunchly religious part of Germany and its inhabitants disliked the presence of their own Bundeswehr Army, let alone the presence of a large British Garrison. Paul was not a gifted sportsman, nor was he endowed with a very adventurous spirit; he had few absorbing hobbies and therefore constantly found himself away on one exercise after another, while his more enterprising peers were away on sports fixtures or some form of adventurous training with their soldiers. His first three years had been dull; he was a dull person. He longed for his leave back in England where he did little more than spend a large proportion of his time in bed, was cosseted as an only child by over-protective parents and went to his local pub in the evenings. He even succeeded in boring the locals with interminable accounts of his imaginary exploits

11

in Germany, which he had gleaned from listening to the anecdotes told by his fellow officers.

To his delight he had been sent back to England on a course and while he was there, the battalion had come back from Germany to pre-Second World War barracks at Tidworth on the edge of Salisbury Plain. The battalion was part of the brigade, which had come into being after the Falklands Campaign to ensure that the UK could provide forces at instant readiness to cope with operations outside the NATO Alliance.

Whilst he viewed a tour in Northern Ireland with considerable apprehension, he had hoped that the battalion might be sent there so that at last the blank space on his left breast pocket might boast a splash of colour from the general service campaign medal. He had not dared voice his doubts and disappointment when the battalion had been put, first on seven days' notice to move to Hong Kong and then the notice time had rapidly reduced to 24 hours. It was to be a six-month, unaccompanied tour to relieve the strain on the resident battalions of the garrison.

Since his arrival in Hong Kong, Paul had never worked so hard in his life and the battalion had just started its second, six-week tour of duty up on the border. Even the fortnight of light duties and 'R and R' for the battalion back in its tented camp at Sek Kong in the New Territories had done nothing to improve Paul's worldliness. He had found that he had nothing in common with the upmarket, social, hectic and rather artificial world of the international expatriate community of Hong Kong.

Robert Smales had been with the Royal Hong Kong Police for a year after completing three years on a short service commission in the British Army. He and Paul had both been at Sandhurst at the same time where they had only bumped into each other on rare occasions. Despite the uncertainty of the future for expatriate members of the RHKP, Robert had been keen to get to the Far East having never left the UK during his time in the army, except for the occasional exercise. He was considerably more mature than the platoon commander who walked in silence beside him towards L/Cpl Williams and their first week together on the island had not been easy for Robert. The island was a military base and Paul Hutchinson commanded it; he had quickly shown his resentment at having a police inspector foisted on him which had been agreed for all levels of command of the UK battalion to provide experience and give advice to the newly arrived soldiers.

Apart from a short spell in a regional police headquarters, Robert had spent most of his time with the Police Tactical Unit. The RHKP had needed young men with his army experience in preparation for the time when the police would take over all the border duties from the army. After graduating from the Police Cadet School at Aberdeen on the south side of Hong Kong Island, Robert had been sent to the Police Headquarters in Kowloon and from there to his training with the tactical unit. His past experience helped him to excel during his training, where he received considerable praise from the Assistant Commissioner in charge of the PTU training, centre. He had been disappointed to be given the task of Ping Chau Island, wet-nursing an immature and inexperienced officer. He had hoped to be sent to an important position on the border. A position where there might have been a chance to show his skill as a commander. He was keen to make a success of his time with the police before he returned to England to make use of his law degree from Leicester University. He knew that nothing exciting ever happened in this isolated platoon base except the weekly re-supply by helicopter and the daily evacuation of the Chinese illegal immigrants.

'Morning Sir,' L/Cpl Williams acknowledged the arrival of his platoon commander with a perfunctory salute. 'This is exactly how we found him. No one's touched the body and I've sent the lads to scout around for anything else of interest which might belong to him,' this was emphasised with a jerk of William's thumb in the direction of the body.

'Well done Corporal,' Paul Hutchinson commended the young NCO for his initiative to think of looking for additional items rather than confining his interest to the body.

'You said the body's unmarked, but as he - I presume it's a 'he' - is lying face down in the sand, how can you be sure?'

'Well sir, what I meant was, he seemed to be unmarked,' a pause at this point and then, 'not like some of the mangled corpses we have to shovel into black placky bags.'

'Yes, thanks Corporal, I see what you mean,' and Paul then turned to the inspector, 'Robert, would you like to look at this one before we bag it?' He was rapidly losing interest in the whole business.

'Yes I would Paul,' Robert replied, perhaps rather too quickly, because he could detect his colleague's lack of interest and he thought there might just be an opportunity to display his newly acquired police skills. By this time the rest of Williams' section had returned empty-handed except for a collection of flabby, deflated condoms which were no doubt due to be taken back to the barrack room as some form of rather dubious trophy.

'Seem to be quite a few dead fish lying around here,' Williams remarked to no one in particular. 'Look pretty fresh too,' he continued,

13

picking up a three or four pound grouper. 'Might take this back to the cookhouse and have it fresh for breakfast,' he added with a chuckle, but no one paid any attention and so the remark went unnoticed.

'Paul, I wonder if you could ask your men to turn the body over and drag it a bit further up the beach above the high water mark. 'Robert's request was directed at the platoon commander who was more interested in returning to his bed, from which he had been abruptly awoken some ten minutes previously by his platoon sergeant.

'What? Oh sure,' Paul realised that he ought to be paying more attention and was probably not showing up in a very good light in front of his soldiers. 'Corporal Williams, please get your men to do as Inspector Smales has asked. Turn the body over - carefully!' This caution was added as L/Cpl Williams directed proceedings that looked as though they were about to dismember the corpse. The body was indeed unmarked and from a cursory glance, death appeared to have been due to drowning.

'Now see if we can get him a bit further up the beach lads,' directed Williams. 'Harding, you grab his left arm; Cooper, here! Now you grab his right arm. You other two grab a leg each. I'll grab a handful of his hair and when I say heave! We'll drag him up the beach; right?' These instructions were given quickly and decisively by Williams, who reckoned that he should not only be setting his soldiers an example with his own involvement, but also these two officers, who quite clearly had no intention of handling the body, at least, not at this juncture. 'Right then? heave!' ordered Williams and then it happened; nothing terribly dramatic, but it was enough to make them all recoil in horror from the body. Williams didn't recoil, more accurately he fell away from the body, still clutching a handful of hair, having completely scalped the head, leaving it like a monk's tonsure. He gasped, throwing away the scalp in revulsion and then lunged towards the sea and rinsed his hands. The others followed his example, instinctively trying to wash away any contact they had had with the body.

'That's most odd,' muttered Robert as he approached the body for a closer look. He was the first to recover from the shock which all of them had experienced, seeing the cranium of the body scalped with such ease. His recovery was quicker than Paul's, who was staring at the body with his mouth agape, looking forlornly comical. 'I've seen umpteen bodies hauled out of the harbour by their hair after being in the water for days or even weeks, but I've never seen that happen before,' he said quietly, almost to himself, as the others were backing away from the body. Somewhere in his memory a very faint bell was

14

trying to ring, but concentrate as hard as he might, the message wouldn't clarify itself. 'Look Paul,' he attracted the other man's attention as he appeared to be in a trance, 'I think we'd all better move away from this body. Can you get on to your platoon headquarters and tell them to warn all patrols to stay off this sector of the beach and that we will be back in a couple of minutes to make a report.'

Now that someone had given an order, albeit couched as a polite request, Paul snapped out of his immobility and passed the message over his radio. He then ordered Williams to take his men back to base and wait for further instructions. The soldiers required no further encouragement as they wanted to put as great a distance as possible between themselves and the grisly body on the beach.

'Well, aren't you coming?' came from Paul, after he had gone half a dozen paces and then remembered that he probably ought to wait for Robert.

'Yes, sure,' Robert answered in a rather distracted fashion, as he still searched his memory for the information which wouldn't reveal itself. It had been such a long time ago; during his time in the army; something he had seen in Northern Ireland . . . was that it? No, it had been on some course he had gone on . . . yes, that was it . . . yes, and now the little bell started to ring louder. Why should hair falling out remind him of a course in the army? and then suddenly the little bell turned into a deafening alarm. Radiation sickness! of course; it had been the Nuclear, Biological and Chemical Course at the Army's Defence NBC Centre at Porton Down where he had seen the film of the Hiroshima and Nagasaki casualties lying in rows in hospital wards and the most noticeable effect of radiation sickness was the total loss of hair. 'Paul, I could be completely wrong, but I've a nasty suspicion that our Chinese friend was dead before he even entered the water. I think he died from radiation sickness,' Robert added as he caught up with the platoon commander.

'What on earth makes you think that?' Paul blurted out rather too quickly. He felt that he ought to reassert his authority. His lack of self-confidence was beginning to show. 'Just because the bleeding man's hair falls out, everyone starts behaving like a load of zombies and wimps,' his own shock and inability to do anything decisive was now completely forgotten in this immature show of false bravado. 'Christ almighty! if my soldiers had behaved like that on the streets of Belfast we'd have all been in a right pickle.' Paul's bravado was now running away with his tongue as he had never been in Northern Ireland, which was well known to Robert.

'Yes, you may well be right,' Robert agreed, sensing the petulant mood of his colleague, 'but all the same, and of course with your

15

agreement as you are in command here, I would like to speak to my chief superintendent for some information and advice. You see it's not only the body, but it was your corporal who noticed all the dead fish in the area of the body. What caused that? The radiation coming from that body must be enormous. I'm afraid that all of us who were close to it must be badly contaminated and ought to be segregated from the rest of your platoon until we can get a decontamination team here,' he added as they entered the platoon base.

'What makes you so sure?' asked a subdued Paul.

'I'm not sure at all,' Robert answered cautiously, as doubts now started to take place of his earlier confidence down on the beach. 'Could we just have a chat in your room to clear our thoughts before we both speak to our respective superiors, but just to be on the safe side, could I suggest that you issue instructions to keep Williams and his men away from your other men. Make up any excuse; like we think the Chink might have been suffering from some disease or something like that . . . oh yes, and perhaps it would be an idea for them all to go and take a very long shower in those excellent new showers which the army's installed. Sorry, I keep thinking of things Paul! . . . for Heaven's sake get rid of that wretched fish which Williams took back with him!'

'Are you sure this is all necessary,' Paul's confidence was returning now that he was back in his own little empire and this intangible threat seemed so unreal on this beautiful, unspoilt island in the South China Sea. Sergeant Bishop came out of the operations room and approached them.

'Can I get the cooks to fix you two gents with some breakfast?' he smiled enquiringly and then noticing their worried expressions added, 'everything alright back on the beach, Sir?' this he directed at his platoon commander. 'Something fishy about the corpse is there then?' quipped Sergeant Bishop.

'Could be, sergeant,' replied Paul, 'we think he may have been suffering from some form of disease so please keep your distance from any of us and will you see to it straight away that Williams and his patrol are segregated from the rest of the platoon. Tell them to take of all their clothes and burn them in the incinerator and then get them to stand under the showers for a good half an hour. There's no shortage of water. Tell Williams to get rid of that grouper which he brought back with him and when I say get rid, I mean back in the sea, not on the rubbish tip. Please arrange for a meal to be prepared for them - and us - and the inspector and I will deliver it to them. I suggest you tell them to occupy the visitors' accommodation. Is that all clear?'

'Yes Sir.'

'Oh yes, Sergeant Bishop, when all of that's in hand, get everyone else out of the ops room and then give me a buzz in my room where the inspector and I will be eating our breakfast. Oh yes, and one last thing, please get the duty signaller to leave a remote handset at the end of the corridor leading to my room with enough cable to reach my room. Please retune the radio to the battalion net and let our company HQ know what you are doing; clear?'

'Yes Sir, on my way,' and the platoon sergeant disappeared towards the soldiers' accommodation.

Robert Smales was amazed at the transformation that had occurred in Paul's manner and confidence. This was the first time since his arrival on the island that the platoon commander had shown that he was more than capable of doing the job.

'Somewhere in that immature body is a first class officer trying to get out,' Robert thought to himself as the two of them walked down the corridor of the single storey hut to Paul's room.

'OK Robert,' Paul began as soon as they entered the room, 'supposing that you are right about this radiation sickness. Where in the hell could he have picked up such a dose?' Paul got no further because it suddenly dawned on him where the source of that radiation might be. The two men turned to the window which faced towards the distant shore of China, where only some ten miles to the north east were the four, huge nuclear reactors of the Daya Bay Power Station.

'Sweet Jesus, you don't think there's been another of those accidents like the one at Chernobyl?'

'Yes, that's exactly what I was thinking, but don't lets jump to conclusions too quickly. That's why I want to speak to my boss because I know that both the police and fire service have radiation monitoring equipment and the decontamination kit as well. We were all issued with the kit by the government after an incident in the harbour some years ago when a ship was driven ashore and its deck cargo spilt onto the beach. The Corsican captain of the vessel was caught by us trying to make a run for it in one of the ship's boats and admitted, while being questioned, that his ship was carrying containers of nuclear waste which hadn't been declared to the Harbour Authority. So . . .' but at this moment the telephone rang and Paul picked it up.

'Thank you sergeant for fixing all that so quickly. Now as briefly as I can, I will tell you what the inspector and I really think is the problem and what we are going to do about it,' and for the next five minutes he covered all that had happened to them. At the end of the conversation, he left the room and returned with the radio handset.

'I think it's high time I spoke to the old man at battalion HQ and told him what's happening. I'm sure he'll think I'm off my rocker, but here goes anyway; hello zero, this is two two, sunray speaking, please fetch callsign nine, over.'

'Hello two two, this is nine, send, over,' and then Paul explained to the 'old man' what had taken place on the island that morning.

The 'old man' was Lt Colonel Martin Carrington who, at the age of 39, no doubt did seem very old to the 24 year old Lieutenant. His reaction to the message he received from Paul was to summon a Gazelle helicopter. After a number of telephone calls, it was arranged that Robert's boss, Chief Superintendent Charles Mannings and a police sergeant with Geiger counter and protective clothing, would fly with the commanding officer to the island. As soon as the Gazelle's skids touched the concrete of the helicopter landing site, the three passengers jumped out and after removing their life jackets hurried towards the platoon sergeant who was waiting to brief them. The small group moved off immediately towards the body, approaching it from an up-wind direction. They stopped about a hundred yards away from it and the police sergeant donned his protective clothing. He made a couple of adjustments to the Geiger counter and then approached the body. The counter registered immediately, even some eighty yards up wind of the body. Thirty yards away the Geiger screamed in protest, already at its maximum reading. The police sergeant turned and hurried back to the group of three men.

'This island should be evacuated immediately and we must get the decontamination team here as fast as possible, if we hope to give those men who found the body any chance of survival!'

'What on earth can have caused that level of radiation?' the Chief Superintendent asked as they all hurried away from the beach.

'Sir,' the Chinese sergeant replied, 'I've only just returned from my course in England and the instruction is all pretty fresh in my mind. That man,' this was said with a jerk of his head in the vague direction of the body, 'would have had to be inside the core of a nuclear furnace, in amongst the fuel rods, to have achieved that level of radiation count.'

'Right then, there's no time to waste,' this came from the commanding officer. 'I'll get the RAF to bring the decontamination kit up here and also to evacuate the men to hospital afterwards. Charles, can you arrange for the removal of the body and I'll recommend to the brigade commander that we abandon this island as a platoon base until the entire area has been monitored for radiation levels.'

'Yes, of course, we'll take care of that,' and within hours the island was evacuated, the body was removed in a lead container and the platoon base was abandoned. Warning signs written in Chinese and English were planted every ten metres along the beach explaining that the accommodation on the island was for lepers, as that seemed to be the only way of persuading the immigrants or boating fraternity not to land there.

There wasn't a sign anywhere of a leak of radiation and the Chinese hosted a visit of the Hong Kong Government and the International Atomic Energy Authority to the Daya Bay Power Station to dispel any suspicion. All the instruments, which went with the team proved that there wasn't any radiation contamination of the air, land or sea, of anyone or anything. The body of the Chinese male found on Ping Chau was identified as a Mr Chung Ching Kwong who had been employed by one of the many sub-contractors involved in the completion of the nuclear power station. How he had come into contact with radioactive material was a mystery to everyone; everyone, that is except one man in China and two in Hong Kong. The man in China followed Kwong into the sea near Ping Chau, but because he was bleeding profusely when he entered the water, towed behind a small motorised fishing sampan, not even a toe nail was left by the sharks to wash ashore on Ping Chau Island. That just left the two men in Hong Kong.

CHAPTER 2

The Boeing 747 - 400 reached its cruising height of 33,000 feet; John Gunn undid the safety belt, reclined the comfortable, business class seat, and settled down to the boredom of the non-stop flight to Hong Kong. It was a 13 hour flight unless the captain was fortunate enough to find a high altitude jet stream, in which case the flight time could be reduced by as much as an hour or more. He studied the menu, which had just been handed to him by the stewardess.

*

It was nearly eight years since he had last been in Hong Kong on a short visit to see his parents. His father had retired as chairman of Euro-Pacific Construction three years after that visit to settle in Sussex on the farm, which he had bought eleven years previously. John's mother, Mary, was Australian by birth and had had a lifelong ambition to start a racehorse stud. This ambition had been nurtured over many years spent in Hong Kong where she had been unable to indulge in her love of riding, except in a very limited way at the Royal Hong Kong Jockey Club's stables at Beas River in the north of the New Territories. He remembered only too well the weekly visits to the Happy Valley and Shatin racecourses and the excitement as a young boy of being allowed, with his mother and father, into the unsaddling enclosure when their horse was in the prize money. John had two elder sisters and it had always been his father's hope that, as the only son, he would follow him into Euro-Pacific. John had gone to school in England and then to Nottingham University to study civil engineering. He had had a wide circle of friends at university and after his first term in a residential hall, moved out to join three other friends in a flat. The latter was equidistant from the Castle and the 'Trip to Jerusalem' which was reputed to be the oldest pub in the world.

All three of his flatmates had joined 'the University Officer Training Corps for no better reason than it appeared to offer the best social life of all the host of clubs and societies and was the only club in the world, as far as John new, which paid its members. What finally persuaded him to join his friends was his discovery that all the best looking girls in his academic year had joined the UOTC. He had agreed to go along with his friends one evening to give the place 'the once over' and that evening had changed his entire life.

His initial, mildly cynical curiosity was quickly replaced by interest and the UOTC absorbed more and more of his time. He was told by the Head of the Engineering Faculty, at the start of his final year that there was a real risk of him failing his finals if he didn't devote more time to his studies. He had wisely taken heed of the caution, but it had also crystallised an idea, which had been taking shape in the back of his mind. He had no wish to go and sit in an office after leaving university and the army had offered a stay of execution and a way of life which appealed to him.

He was a powerfully built and a shade over six feet three in height. He had a mane of dark brown hair and a swarthy complexion, which had caused both amusement and some embarrassment to his parents who were neither large nor dark. He had served with both the airborne and commando forces, in which, as a forward observer of his commando battery, he had been present at the surrender of the Iraqi Republican Guard in the first Gulf War following the invasion of Kuwait in 1991. He had been considering applying for a regular commission at the same time as he applied, and had been accepted for the SAS selection course.

Gunn had honed his body to a peak of physical fitness in preparation for the gruelling selection. In the event, he had completed the course and had been awarded his SAS wings when he was summoned to the CO's office of 22 SAS Regiment. It took a few seconds to realise what was being said to him by an embarrassed commanding officer. He was told that there had been a most unfortunate mix up of the assessment forms and that sadly, his performance had failed to reach the very high standard required for acceptance into the SAS. He had left the interview bewildered and seething with anger. As the CO's door had closed behind him, the commanding officer of 22 SAS picked up the phone and punched out a number in London.

'PA to the Director.'

'Colonel Graham speaking, please put me through to the Director.'

'The Director's expecting your call, Sir, please hold the line while I put you through.'

'Neville,' was the only response as the connection was made and the Director Special Forces answered the phone.

'Tony Graham speaking, Brigadier. I've just done what you told me to do and I wish to make it clear that if I'm ordered to do that again, you can have my resignation.'

'You must understand...' began the Director, but then realised that the line was dead and he was speaking to no one. 'Damn,' he said quietly and replaced his phone.

Gunn had returned to his regiment in Plymouth and immediately submitted his resignation. His commanding officer had received a phone call from the Director of the Royal Artillery and had told John that his resignation would take effect from whatever date he wished to choose. John had phoned his father who in turn contacted the Chairman of Euro-Pacific Construction. Within 24 hours, a telex had arrived at the London office of Euro-Pacific with the offer of a job as assistant projects manager of the company in Hong Kong, together with a business class ticket on the Cathay Pacific 747-400 flight.

*

'Hello John! What brings you back to Hong Kong?'

He gave a slight start as his train of thought was interrupted. Standing by his seat was a pretty stewardess whose mixed English and Chinese parentage had given her the best of both races. Her height and figure were Anglo-Saxon, whilst her large, oval eyes, golden skin and gleaming black hair were unmistakably Asian.

'Sadie!' John exclaimed, with pleasant surprise, 'so when did you join forces with your father?' Sadie's father was Peter Causland - Cathay Pacific's senior captain. Peter and his wife Jenny and their family of two boys and a girl had an apartment in Peak Tower, a block of luxury flats in the coveted area of the Peak with breath-taking views over Hong Kong Harbour, Kowloon and the mountain of Tai Mo Shan. The Gunns had occupied the company apartment in the same block for nearly fifteen years after moving from a smaller one at The Manhattan on the south side of the Island. Sadie was the youngest of the Causland children and was 16 when John had last visited his parents at the Peak Tower eight years previously.

'Oh, I've been with Cathay for five years Johnny; see,' and she showed him the gold broach indicating that she was a senior stewardess, 'I'm really old now and only allowed to look after the first class section!' The reference to her age was a not too subtle reminder to John that she was no longer 'the little girl in the next door flat'. Certainly the young woman standing by his seat only bore the faintest resemblance to the gawky schoolgirl who had returned to her school in England on the same flight as John eight years previously. 'Are you staying for a little while in Hong Kong, Johnny, or are you on your way somewhere else?' Sadie asked as she removed an imaginary speck of dust from the scarlet skirt of her uniform.

'No Sadie, I'm coming back to work in Hong Kong.'

22

'Permanently?'

'Well, that all depends on whether I make a success of my job with Euro-Pacific.'

'Oh that's great! where'll you be living?'

'I've no idea at the moment; this was all a bit of a spur of the moment decision.'

'I've got my own flat now in Robinson Road - you know, above Central in the Mid-Levels. Why don't you come and stay with me until you find a place?' Sadie hadn't meant the offer to sound quite so brazen, but the passengers around John heard it and were listening with interest to the conversation. Realising what she'd said, Sadie went crimson, 'I mean, the flat's got two bedrooms and . . .'

'I think that's the best offer I've had in years,' Sadie, and of course I accept, but I'll tell you what we'll do. I'll meet you outside Customs, we'll go and dump my things in your flat and then go out and have some dinner while we discuss where I'm going to live - amongst other things! Is La Rose Noire still as good as it used to be?'

'Yes Johnny, it . . .'

'Marvellous, will that be alright with you?'

'Yes, that's fine; I'll see you later then?'

'I'll meet you by the car hire desks outside the Customs area,' John confirmed and Sadie retired through the curtain into the first class section. John closed his eyes and let his thoughts drift back to the strange sequence of events, which had occurred after his resignation from the army.

*

It had been the day after he received the offer of a job with Euro-Pacific that he received a phone call from Humphrey Goldman. Humphrey had been a contemporary of his at university and was one of the three other undergraduates who had shared a flat with John. Humphrey had been the most enthusiastic member of the UOTC and all of them were amazed when he failed to pass his Regular Commissions Board. He remembered that Humphrey had mentioned something about going into the Foreign and Commonwealth Office, but their paths had drifted apart and after a couple of Christmas cards, he lost contact. It was, therefore, all the more surprising that Humphrey had been able to find him at his parents' farm in Sussex and his initial inclination had been to refuse the invitation to have lunch in London. Humphrey had persisted and said that it really was most important that they met before he went to Hong Kong. Since less than a handful of people knew that he was going to Hong Kong, John had changed his mind and agreed to the lunch date at the Army and Navy club in St James's Square. That had also surprised him mildly as

23

he thought that Humphrey hadn't any military connections to qualify for membership, but he then remembered that Humphrey's father had been in the army and presumed that had provided the necessary qualification.

Gunn had managed to find a parking meter free and reversed his much-cosseted classic sports car, a scarlet TR6, into the vacant slot just in front of a Jaguar, which he had overtaken going round the square looking for a parking place. The Jaguar had pulled up in front of the TR6 and the driver's window was lowered. Gunn got out of his TR6 and locked the door. The red, moustached face, which had appeared at the window of the Jaguar saw the size of the driver of the TR6 and decided to swallow ruffled pride and moved on. Humphrey had been waiting for him in the downstairs bar and throughout their pre-lunch drinks and the meal itself, which had been totally ordinary and equally tasteless, the conversation consisted of small talk and university reminiscences. It wasn't until they were seated in the ground floor lounge with their coffee and a very reasonable vintage port, that the reason for the unexpected lunch date had become apparent.

'John,' Humphrey started rather hesitantly, 'I'm sorry to drag you all the way to London for what must seem no better reason than a lot of small talk.' John started to brush off the apology.

'Not a bit . . .' but Humphrey interrupted.

'No please, hear me out first and then events which have occurred recently might start to make some sort of sense.'

'Humphrey, you've got all my attention and not a little curiosity, I must add.' John was hoping that at last the purpose of this meeting was about to be revealed.

'I believe that I told you that I worked for the FCO, didn't I.'

'Yes, that's what I'd always assumed.'

'Well I don't and never have done. I won't bore you with the details of how it all happened, but I eventually ended up working for the Secret Intelligence Service, or MI6 if you prefer to call it that.'

'Quite frankly Humphrey,' John interrupted, thinking that these post-prandial revelations had probably gone quite far enough, 'I've given it very little thought. If you want an honest opinion, I think our intelligence services are a joke.'

'You and many others would be justified in having that view and it's for exactly that reason that I have been sent to speak to you.'

'You must be joking.' Gunn took a handkerchief from his pocket and wiped his mouth, having just spilt some port in his amazement at what Humphrey had revealed. 'What in God's name have I got to do with any of this? And anyway, I've never held an intelligence

24

appointment. Oh, and by the way, if you hadn't heard, my resignation from the army was effective exactly a week ago today and in a fortnight I fly to Hong Kong to start a new job.'

'I'm sorry John, I'm not explaining this very well; please let me start again. It's because of your military training, your knowledge of Hong Kong and, in particular, your fluency in Chinese that we need your help. I expect you read the much publicised litigation over the publication of Peter Wright's book, which gave explicit details of the chaotic state of MI5 and 6 in the post-war years. The Prime Minister had already decided that Britain's intelligence services were a mess and nothing other than a complete reorganisation would repair the damage caused by the leaks, defections and revelations, not to mention the countless MI6 agents who had vanished because of the dreadful laxity in security.'

All of this had been said in a very low murmur which John found difficult to hear as he was being deafened by the snores of two unmistakably retired Generals who had disappeared into the folds of their newspapers at the next door table. He changed places to another over-stuffed leather armchair beside Humphrey, which placed him with his back to the Generals and the long, ceiling length windows, which overlooked St James's Square.

'Go on Humphrey.'

'Please be patient; I'm going to tell you about a strange incident which occurred in Hong Kong earlier this year and why it concerns you. Before I tell you that,' and here Humphrey had paused as a large old club member tottered slowly and majestically past their table to settle with a contented sigh amongst the snoring Generals and Admirals. 'There's something you must know...' but he was interrupted again by the sound of breaking glass.

Gunn glanced over his shoulder at the instant of the sound, expecting to see one of the waiters retrieving a broken glass, but the only waiter was also looking around for the culprit. None of the recumbent bodies in the lounge had stirred.

'How odd . . .' Gunn muttered as he turned back to his friend, but got no further. Humphrey was dead. There was a neat hole above his left eye and the only red stain in that room had not been caused by spilt port, but by the blood seeping from the shattered rear portion of Humphrey's skull onto the pristine, white anti-macassar. John glanced towards the windows. Sure enough, there was the broken pane, low down, indicating a shot from street level. Outside the window, the scene in the square was unchanged.

He picked up the nearest newspaper and placed it over his friend's head, unnoticed by the rest of the occupants in the room. He

25

then emptied his port glass onto the carpet and, almost soundlessly, snapped the stem of the glass with his foot. He walked over to the waiter and led the old retainer over to his table.

'I'm sorry I've made such a mess. Could you clean it up very quietly as I have no wish to disturb the gentleman asleep in that chair. No thanks,' he refused the offered decanter, 'I won't have any more.'

Gunn left the lounge and went out into the hall and then out through the swing doors onto the street. He punched out the number of the SAS Regiment on his mobile. The Regiment's exchange answered and he asked to be put through to the commanding officer.

'Yes John, how can I be of help?' Very briefly, John explained what had happened. 'Where are you making this call?' John had told him. 'Stay where you are and go back into the lounge. Order another port and read the newspaper. Within a very short time everything will be taken care of. Just do as you are told and go along with whatever happens. Got that?'

'Yes Colonel.'

'Well done,' and the connection was broken.

Gunn returned to the lounge and reoccupied his original chair opposite Humphrey. The thought of another port had no appeal, so he ordered a coffee when the waiter appeared and picked up a newspaper. The time dragged by and John found himself scanning every inch of the view of the square. He also felt highly vulnerable until he reminded himself that he had had his back to the window and if they had wanted to shoot them both, nothing would have been easier for the gunman. As it was, Gunn noted, studying the angle from broken pane to armchair, the bullet which had killed Humphrey must have passed his head by no more than a couple of inches.

Three taxis pulled up outside the entrance to the club and disgorged a number of be-suited men, who seemed to be in an extremely jovial mood and soon the sound of their voices, as they gathered in the hall, even penetrated the slumbers of those in the lounge. John could hear them talking to the receptionist and it sounded as though there had been a bomb warning received at the Cavalry and Guards Club in Piccadilly which had been evacuated. This group had no intention of missing their after-lunch port and so had decided to come to the Army and Navy Club. The conversation became louder as the group moved into the lounge, which caused newspapers to be removed from faces and huffing and puffing as the intruders were studied with not a little malevolence. Port was served to the newly arrived group which was moving closer and closer to Gunn's table until it was completely engulfed and hidden from the rest of the room. A glass of port was pushed into his hand.

'Stand up, join in the conversation and follow me when we leave.'

Gunn did as he was told, turned to the nearest man and started discussing what was to be done about the terrorist bombs in London. One part of the group moved towards the bar and it was only as the five men reached the door of the lounge that John realised that Humphrey had vanished. Two of the group went into the bar and he saw the remainder leave the club and gently ease one of their colleagues into the waiting taxi. Two men went with him and the third returned to the bar, collected his colleagues and they all came into the lounge where they rejoined the men standing around John.

'Well, can't spend all afternoon boozing. Must get back to the MOD,' and with this remark John's guide led him out of the club and into a taxi which only the two of them occupied. As soon as the taxi door closed, they moved off towards Sloane Square. Not a word was spoken in the taxi as it threaded its way through the post-lunch traffic around Sloane Square and then into the King's Road. The taxi turned to the right off the King's Road and then took a number of lefts and rights until it disappeared into a multi-storey, concrete car park which was next door to a building called Kingsroad House. The taxi drove round the circuit up to the tenth floor and came to a halt by the lift shaft. John's companion opened the door on his side and got out, so John followed his example and got out of the taxi. As soon as his door shut, the taxi moved away and disappeared down the ramp to the floor below. His taxi companion was waiting for him by the entrance to the lift and John noticed that the call button had been pressed.

'So here we go all the way down to the ground floor again,' Gunn muttered to himself, 'what a bloody joke these spooks are.' The lift arrived, the doors opened and released one occupant and John and his taxi companion entered. There was no one else around. His escort moved over to the control panel and, blocking John's view, pressed the buttons in a set sequence. The lift didn't move, but instead, the other side of it opened. For the first time his escort spoke.

'After you, John,' and he waited for John to go through the door into the passage beyond, then stepped out of the lift and pressed a button on a panel in the wall in the passage. The lift doors closed. 'I'm Simon Peters, John,' and he held out his hand to John who shook it.

'John Gunn, but I think you know that already.'

'Yes, that's right; I only wish we could have met under less traumatic and somewhat theatrical circumstances, however we were left with very little time to react to Tony Graham's phone call,' Simon replied, as he led the way along the passage. At the end of the passage was another door on the right of which was a brushed steel panel. In the centre of the panel was an opaque screen about the size of a piece of A4 paper and under this were touch-sensitive pads, very similar to those on a telephone. Gunn had noticed that there were both visible and, no doubt, concealed cameras which could examine both of them from front, side and from behind. Simon placed his left palm flat against the screen, tapped a number of the buttons below it and then waited. A green light glowed at the top of the panel and then a small flap, rather like that on a litter-bin, opened. Simon removed a small Beretta from an ankle holster and placed it in the receptacle behind the open flap, which then closed. With barely a sound, the door in front of them opened, but not in the way a door normally opens. It divided into two; the top half disappeared into the ceiling and the bottom half into the floor.

'Let me lead the way,' Simon offered.

'Yes, I think I would prefer it that way, just in case there are any poison darts, pits filled with snakes or razor edged pendulums to welcome us.' He followed Simon into what appeared to be a fairly standard, modern office complex.

Simon smiled, 'I've every sympathy with you and I promise that all this cloak and dagger stuff will be explained in a few moments. Incidentally, there aren't darts, snakes and pendulums to greet you as you come through that door, but there are, as you will soon discover, some highly effective measures to take care of unwelcome visitors.'

Simon had stopped at the lifts; there were two on either side of the passage. He pressed the button and the doors opened immediately. They both entered the lift and Simon once again pressed the button. This time the lift behaved like a normal one and a digital display indicated the 11th floor. The doors opened and Simon led the way along an identical passage to the one they had just left. He stopped by a door with a combination lock, pressed the required sequence and then held the door open for John.

'Come into my office; coffee?'

'Yes please.' Gunn looked round a pleasant, modern office with comfortable chairs and a southerly view from the windows towards the river. Simon picked up the phone on his desk, pressed a button and waited.

'Yes it's me, Louise; can you bring coffee for two please. Yes, he's here; well, you'll see for yourself when you bring the coffee,' and he replaced the phone in its cradle. 'Please have a seat. As you might have just gathered, you were expected this afternoon, but it should have been a little later and under slightly different arrival arrangements. Now I've not been given very long to brief you, so please forgive me if I crack on and go fairly quickly.'

'Steady, steady, Simon; you can stop right there,' and John held up his hand. 'I must be talking in a strange language today, because Humphrey clearly couldn't or wouldn't listen to me, and if you haven't got much time that suits me fine because I have neither the time nor the patience for this childish cloak and dagger stuff. I'm a civilian, I've got a job in Hong Kong, I've just had a bloody awful lunch followed by having a friend shot in front of me and so far I think I've kept my patience and my manners pretty well, but all that is about to stop. Will you please show me how to get out of this weirdo's play-park so that I can return to the world of adults and sanity.' Gunn got up from his chair, turned towards the door and walked straight into Louise, scattering coffee cups and spilling boiling hot coffee all over Louise, which was obviously very painful.

He swore, apologised to Louise and then turned to Simon. 'I . . .'

'No, don't worry, John,' interrupted Simon, as Louise disappeared rapidly from the room. 'You said you were on your way out and please don't let me delay you a moment longer. May I just mention that a very brave man who was not one of your closest friends, but who was more concerned for his country than his own life, lost that life in his efforts to try and convince you to help us. It would seem that he made a pointless sacrifice. I'll have one of our security men show you out. Good bye,' and he held the door open for John to leave.

John took a pace towards the door and then stopped and turned. 'Let's, for a moment anyway, Simon, ignore the fact that you or whoever screwed up my whole life by fixing my failure of the SAS course. It was you lot, wasn't it?' and the slight nod of Simon's head confirmed what John had said, 'and instead, let's both confine our hypocrisy to poor Humphrey Goldman. You're quite right. I liked him, but found him to be rather intense and slightly boring. There, at least I've been honest, now let's have the same from you, if that word is ever used in this building. You've got some dirty job you want done and for some unknown reason you need me, God knows why, to help you. So to achieve your goal, unimportant people like Humphrey and me, become totally expendable. Don't give me all that crap about your feelings for Humphrey. I bet you've sent plenty of Humphreys to their deaths with hardly more than a passing thought.' In the middle of this verbal battle, Louise reappeared with a cloth and a very damp blouse, but hastily retreated to her office and picked up the phone.

'Thank you for phoning Louise, I might just pop down to see if I can pour some oil on these troubled waters,' the Deputy Director replied and replaced his phone. He took the lift down one floor, knocked on Simon's door and went in. Both men were sitting down and talking despite an atmosphere of tension in the room.

'Anything you wanted, Sir?'

'No, nothing at all Simon, sorry to have interrupted,' and he backed out and went next door to reassure the worried Louise.

'Right, let me continue,' and so John's briefing had continued from the point when it had been stopped by a gunman's bullet. Having vented his anger about his failure on the SAS course, Gunn had paused, smiled, muttered, 'what the hell!' and had returned to his seat.

Simon Peters told him that MI5 and 6 had become such a farce that they were thinking of putting them both on the tourist guide to London, setting their activities to a score and producing it as a music hall comedy in the West End. The Prime Minister had given the task of a totally different approach to a brilliant army officer who had retired as a Major General at the age of 48. He then in quick succession had sorted out a handful of companies and turned them from near bankruptcy to healthy, profit-making concerns. Within a year of being given the remit to set up an effective, efficient and totally secure intelligence service, the Directorate was in operation. Both the espionage and counter espionage branches were under the same roof and their efforts were complimentary as opposed to being contradictory. Hardly more than a slack handful of MI5 and 6 personnel survived the security vetting initiated by the Director. That handful, of which Humphrey Goldman had been one, now worked in the new building. The two MIs had been left in their original buildings in Shepherd's Market and Vauxhall as an overt intelligence front, but to perform little more than a clerical function for fairly low grade classified material.

The ground floor and next four floors were occupied by the Express Delivery Service plc. It was one of many enterprises that had flourished as soon as the Post Office had lost its monopoly. EDS was part of the Directorate and with its transport fleet, which included twin-jet aircraft, helicopters, motorbikes, vans and lorries all of which were in radio communication with each other, provided the ideal cover, communication and transport for the movement of men and materiel. There were two other office blocks in London and another in Southampton which belonged to the Directorate and which were built on the same lines as Kingsroad House, but possessed subtle variations in case any of the lines of defence were penetrated. There was a skeleton staff in these buildings which maintained the equipment and made the 'unused' part of the building appear to be occupied.

Gunn had been told that there were some ten different ways of getting in and out of the building, which ensured that no one could be followed or 'picked up' on leaving the place. The entire operation in Kingsroad House could be transferred to any of the other two buildings in London within an hour and Southampton in three, without any visible sign of the move.

'Now,' Simon paused, 'that's what this place is, so where do you fit in? But before I go into that, let's have that coffee we never had.' He picked up the phone. 'Yes please, Louise, and John has promised that he will stay seated and has also said that he will buy you something to apologise for knocking the coffee over you,' and he replaced the instrument.

After coffee had been served without any further mishaps, Gunn was told that Humphrey had run the Hong Kong desk and it had been his idea to use him. He was told that the body of a Chinese man had been found six months previously which was giving the same radiation count as a plutonium fuel rod. He was told how it was discovered and that the five soldiers, their officer and a police inspector were still very seriously ill from the effects of radiation sickness. Not only had the MI6 agent in Hong Kong got absolutely nowhere, but had eventually come to a most unpleasant end by committing suicide after the opposition had injected him with Aids-contaminated blood. The Director had closed the MI6 'office' in Hong Kong as it was leaking like a sieve. Fortunately all its operatives still thought that they were reporting to their MI headquarters which, of course, they were and so the new Directorate was not compromised.

'So what've we got?' Simon had summed up. 'A dead radio-active Chinese man on a beach, a determined and totally successful penetration of the Secret Intelligence Service in Hong Kong and lastly a rumour - and that's all it is John - that someone or some bodies are determined to destroy the Anglo-Sino agreement contained in the Joint Declaration.

'What on earth do you expect me to do?' Gunn asked.

'You see, John, the Directorate is closely tied in with the Special Forces for use in the sort of operations at which they excel. Since the Directorate was formed ten years ago, quite a few of the field operatives have been recruited from the SAS and Special Boat Service. Not only is your move to Hong Kong absolutely genuine, but you are almost fully trained for the job; that is, of course, if you are prepared to help us.'

'Aren't you forgetting, Simon, that I was sitting with Humphrey when he was shot. Won't I immediately become linked with him and if I then suddenly turn up in Hong Kong poking my nose around, it shouldn't take rocket science to put two and two together and achieve a total of four.'

'No, not forgotten, John; in fact I spent most of my time studying the angles in that room when we came to collect Humphrey. He was shot from a car or van, which pulled up momentarily. We knew that the opposition had identified Humphrey after the successful penetration of the Hong Kong office. That was the third attempt on his life in two weeks, hence my earlier remark about his courage. It is most unlikely that you could have been identified, particularly as Humphrey often uses that club for his lunch. So, what's it to be? Do you want time to consider or are you happy to say yea or nay now? I think I've placed all our cards on the table.'

'No, I don't need any time, Simon. I'll go and do whatever you want me to do. I only hope I'm not too much of a bloody amateur.'

'Amateurs are often more successful than professionals and anyway, if you agree, we've just got time to give you some training before you leave for Hong Kong.'

'I might have guessed. When do I start?'

'This evening, if you can manage it.'

'Yes, that's OK. May I phone my parents and tell them I won't be back tonight?'

'Yes of course, here, use this one; press 9 for an outside line. I'm just going next door to get Louise moving on the arrangements for your reception at our training centre.'

Gunn had spent ten days at the Directorate's training centre near Maidenhead. Like Kingsroad House, the training centre was purpose built for the job. All the instruction was on a one-to-one basis. The programme prepared for John Gunn started at six in the morning and rarely finished before ten in the evening. Communications, cyphers, codes, explosives, small arms, surveillance techniques, armed and unarmed combat skills and fitness training were but some of the subjects which were taught and then practised over and over again. He had seen no one else at the centre other than his instructors. For an hour every day, he had been coached in the indoor range by an ex-army, Small Arms School instructor.

The 9mm Browning automatic was much scorned by many in the British Army, but Gunn liked it and found that the smaller automatics didn't have the right 'feel' for him. His favourite was the Browning Hi-Power 9mm parabellum. Apart from the fact that he was used to this weapon, it had one or two advantages over other models, like its comparatively long barrel, 13-round magazine and the facility of half-cocking the external hammer.

On the last day at the centre, Simon Peters had turned up to see what progress had been made. Well satisfied, he had given John a final briefing before he left the centre and returned to his parents' farm for the weekend. He caught the Cathay Pacific flight from Heathrow on the Monday evening.

Gunn woke to find that all the lights in the cabin had been switched off while the film was being shown, but one or two reading lights were still on. He had no wish to disturb any of the stewardesses, as he knew that film showing time was their one chance to pause for coffee and a chat. He got out of his seat and helped himself to a paper cup and filled it with chilled water from the dispenser at the rear of the business class section.

'Come and have a coffee or an orange juice!'

Gunn turned, to find Sadie standing behind him. 'That's kind, yes, I'd love a coffee.'

'Follow me to the first class galley,' and she led the way forward through the darkened cabin. The first class section was in complete darkness without even any light from the armrest video screens. There was no one else in the galley.

'How do you like your coffee?' she asked, looking over her shoulder as he followed her into the galley.

'White, no sugar, please, will do fine; where is everyone?'

'Sam - that's Samantha - has gone to bed. We've only got three passengers in First on this flight and I couldn't see any point in us both staying up while they're sleeping. I'll be waking the relief crew in about ten minutes,' she said, glancing at her watch. 'Here you are,' and she gave him his coffee.

CHAPTER 3

'The head office in London has given me the job of investigating the possibility of setting up a Far East headquarters in Singapore,' was Gunn's answer to Sadie's inquiry about his job as he put his coffee down on the stainless steel worktop and reached for a paper towel to wipe off some coffee which he had just spilt on his trousers.

'Here, keep still.' Sadie poured hot water onto a cloth and quickly wiped out the coffee stain. 'There you are; now it looks as though you've wet your pants,' she chuckled. 'Can I top up your cup again?'

'Yes please.' He held out his cup.

'I'll just put a little smear of lipstick on your shirt collar so that your club class companions aren't disappointed and then we'll both get some sleep before we get to Kai Tak.' The lipstick didn't go on John's collar and after a few moments, Sadie readjusted her split-sided skirt, kissed John quickly and disappeared out of the gallery into the darkened first class section.

*

The 747–400 came into Kai Tak on the north-west approach passing over the northern side of Lantau Island where the new Chep Lak Kok airport was nearing completion. The aircraft banked to starboard over Tsing Yi Island and the floodlit tankers unloading their oil, as John heard the hydraulic hiss and thump of the landing gear being lowered and the air brakes being raised. The vast container terminal linking Kwai Chung with Stonecutters Island was followed by the breath-taking approach to the Kai Tak runway. The flight path passed below the cars on the dual carriageway on Beacon Hill and Lion Rock, skimmed over the high rise flats of Kowloon Tong and then, still banking hard to starboard, flared out onto the runway, stretching out into Kowloon Bay. Just before the touchdown, John caught a glimpse of Hong Kong Island, darkly silhouetted by the recently set sun, a blaze of lights on the waterfront from west to east and with lace-like strings of street lights all the way up Victoria Peak.

The roar and shudder of the reverse thrust and John Gunn was back in Hong Kong. He was pleasantly surprised to find that the dreaded hour - or more - wait at immigration was no longer a feature of the arrival process. Computer terminals at each immigration official's booth checked names on passports instantly against a list of undesirables. Then he went through to collect his case off the carousel, a momentary pause at Customs and then Gunn was out and in the relative calm of the meeting area for groups and officials which was separated from the crush and hubbub of the public meeting area. Here, in the official meeting area, were the car hire desks and standing by the Avis desk was Sadie, using the telephone.

Seeing him, Sadie quickly put the phone down, ran across, threw her arms around Gunn and hugged him. 'Welcome back to Hong Kong, Johnny.'

'Wow! That's certainly the best welcome I've ever had, not forgetting that all-to-short, private, little welcome in the first class galley. Are there any more welcomes to come?' he laughed, as he gently put her back on her feet and held her at arms' length.

'Wait and see; come on, we'll go out of the air-crew exit and avoid the crush out there,' and she indicated the teeming mass of humanity with a slight movement of her head which altered the highlights on the sheen of hair. She led the way down a small ramp and out of a side door. The roar of Kowloon's traffic, together with the heat and humidity burst on them as they emerged onto the arrival concourse. Gunn waved down a taxi and then they were soon swallowed in the chaos of the evening rush hour in Kowloon, as the taxi threaded its way at a snail's pace towards the harbour tunnel through the permanent traffic jam. Once through the tunnel, the taxi turned right onto Gloucester Road and then a left into the red light district of Wanchai. The discos, night clubs and massage parlours were just opening for the night. The taxi turned off Queensway and then wound up the base of Victoria Peak on Cotton Tree Drive to the Mid-Levels and Robinson Road.

As the taxi turned off Cotton Tree Drive, Gunn glanced in the driver's rear view mirror and spoke to him in Cantonese. Instead of continuing along Robinson Road, the driver turned right after they passed the zoo and botanical gardens and went back down the hill.

'Why do you want to go this way?' Sadie asked.

'Do you have a rich and jealous boyfriend, Sadie, who drives a black Ferrari?'

'No, why?'

'Because he's followed us all the way from the airport. No, don't turn round,' and he prevented her involuntary move by squeezing her hand. Gunn spoke to the driver again and the taxi turned right into Lower Albert Road and past the Government Offices, then left down Garden Road, across the Queensway flyover, a sharp left and right and into the multi-storey car park of the Bank of America building.

The Ferrari was three cars behind them as they went through the barrier into the car park and up the ramp to the first floor.

'In just a moment I'm going to stop the taxi and get out. You stay in and take the taxi all the way back to the ground floor and wait for me there. Got that?'

'Yes Johnny.'

'Stop here!' Gunn ordered the driver. The taxi driver was enjoying himself hugely. If this daft gweilo wanted to drive all over Hong Kong while the meter was clocking up the dollars, then that was fine by him. He had the door open for Gunn, on its remote lever, which he operated from the driver's seat, before the taxi stopped. He was out and the taxi moving again in a couple of seconds. The tyres squealed as the taxi swung onto the down ramp and Gunn moved quickly towards two large metal canisters. The majority of the skyscraper blocks had a rubbish chute system, with access on each floor and large six by four feet, cylinder shaped, steel canisters bolted to a wheeled dolly, positioned under the chute outlet. Empty, the containers weighed a couple of hundredweight; full, their weight was anybody's guess, but it required a powerful hydraulic mechanism on the back of the purpose-designed refuse lorries to empty them.

Gunn chose the fuller of the two containers and eased it away from the chute to one side of and at the top of the ramp. He then positioned himself beside it, where he could see the approach of cars from the level below. This had all taken less than half a minute.

The deep-throated rumble of the four exhausts and hiss of the squat, low profile tyres on the polished concrete announced the arrival of the Ferrari. Gunn could now see that there were two men in the car and the barrel of what looked like a pump-action gun protruded from the left side passenger window, which would be closest to John as the car came up the ramp.

'Didn't think they were looking for my autograph,' Gunn muttered as he grasped hold of the handles on the refuse container. The Ferrari was being driven dangerously fast in the confined space of the car park and as it turned onto the ramp the back end started to swing out. The driver corrected quickly with more acceleration and opposite lock which rocketed the car up the ramp. The container was already rolling and over the edge of the ramp where it rapidly gathered momentum. The passenger saw him and the barrel of the gun swung round. At the same instant, the gunman saw the container trundling down the ramp towards the car. His mouth opened in a soundless scream of warning to the driver and the shot aimed at Gunn ricocheted its lethal shower of lead pellets off the refuse container. The driver wrenched the wheel over to the right and the back end broke away hurling the Ferrari sideways towards the refuse bin. Gunn threw himself across to the other side of the ramp. The crash of the impact was deafening in the confined space of the low-ceilinged car park. The bin struck the Ferrari, crumpling the passenger's door, killing the gunman instantly and then fell onto its side as it was pushed by the sliding car towards the brickwork of the outer wall of the building. The impetus of the car rolled it over the refuse bin and propelled it, back end first, at the wall, through which it burst in a shower of bricks and concrete. The Ferrari somersaulted through 180° and landed on its roof, forty feet below, on the concrete terrace of the Bank of America building, where it exploded in a mushroom of flame, dense black smoke and searing heat.

There was rubbish scattered all over the ramp from the ruptured refuse bin and to one side lay the pump-action shot gun. Gunn picked it up and wrapped it in a discarded newspaper. He pressed the button for the lift and descended in it to the street level car park. The taxi was parked in a space close to the lift shafts and the driver moved forward as soon as he saw Gunn appear from the lift. Gunn placed the paper-wrapped gun on the floor of the taxi and asked the driver to go to Sadie's flat in Robinson Road.

'Are you alright John? There was such a lot of noise and then a terrific crash and explosion, I. . . .'

'No, it's OK Sadie; I'll tell you what happened back at your flat,' John made an almost imperceptible movement of his head towards the driver.

As the taxi joined the traffic turning into Murray Road, the sound of police, ambulance and fire sirens rose in volume as vehicles converged on the Ferrari's funeral pyre. Back on Queensway, the driver eased the taxi through the evening traffic on the inside lane and then took the slip road by the Pacific Tower up onto Cotton Tree Drive and past the shimmering glass obelisk of the China Bank. Gunn gave the driver a red, $100 note for the fare of $72.50, and a contented man turned his taxi and disappeared down into the labyrinth of Central District. Sadie led the way into the block of flats, where she was greeted by the security guard, which was a feature of the flat-dwelling community of Hong Kong. Gunn carried their suitcases to the lift, where Sadie was waiting with her thumb on the 'doors open' button. Her small, two-bedroom apartment was on the fifth floor and had a spectacular view to the north-east, looking over Wanchai towards Lei Yue Mun and the narrow gap between the Island and the New Territories. The view to the north and north-west was blocked by yet another tower block of flats which, like a thousand others, vied for a foothold on the crumbling granite of Hong Kong Island.

37

Sadie showed John where his room was and then turned and closed the flat door. She rejoined him in the bedroom, saying, 'bathroom's opposite your bedroom, if you want it,' and then she buried her head against his chest. 'Hold me Johnny; what happened back there?' and Gunn told her, but that was later, when she was lying with her head on his chest and the lights of Central reflected changing patterns on her golden skin. 'But why should anyone want to kill you? Unless, for some reason, you have been connected with my fiancé because you're with me.'

'What on earth has your fiancé done to merit that sort of attention and speaking of fiancés - which you were - what are you doing in bed with me if you're engaged?'

'Richard Anderson - do you remember him?'

'No, can't say I do.'

'We got engaged just before last Christmas and would have been married last month.'

'What happened?'

'He was murdered, Johnny . . . possibly by the same people, I think, who tried to kill you this evening; wait, let me start from the beginning as this won't be making much sense,' and Sadie propped her head up on her hands which were folded across his chest. 'Richard had always let me believe that he worked for the Hong Kong Government; he said it was in a branch to do with police matters and was pretty dull, but the salary was good. Well, everything was fine until the New Year - Chinese, I mean - so it must've been about three months ago, when there was all that trouble about the Daya Bay nuclear power station. Did it reach the papers in England?'

'Yes, but only about half an inch of print on the back page,' and the only reason that Gunn knew about this was because Simon had told him.

'Yes, that's about par for the interest shown by the British Press in this place. The only time any interest is taken is when we're flattened by a typhoon, swamped by refugees or visited by a member of the Royal Family - in my book all three of those rate as disasters,' Sadie added bitterly.

'Steady, steady; this isn't the happy, carefree girl I used to know, but I think we're a bit off the point.'

'Possibly; anyway, Richard became busier and busier and I saw less and less of him - now, of course, I know why - but then, I thought he'd gone off me. You know John what they say; a bit of Chinese skirt's alright for a screw, but never marry it.'

'Oh, come on Sadie; yes of course there are people who say that, but they're the same people who'd say that about any race, religion or colour other than their own.'

'I don't know; well, anyway I eventually faced Richard head-on and accused him of two-timing me. Oh God, how stupid I was, but I wasn't to know. He then explained to me in rough outline what his real job was. That the discovery of that dead Chinese man on Ping Chau was but the tip of an iceberg of some scheme, which involved a handful of the most prominent members of the Government, police and British Forces.'

'Did he ever mention any names?'

'No, he said he didn't want to involve me in any way and that's why he'd seen less and less of me, in case I was mistakenly connected with his MI6 set up. It was only about nine or ten days after this, that he'd arranged to take me out to Pierrot's to make up for all the other dinner dates which he'd had to cancel at the last minute. We'd arranged to meet in the top floor bar of the Mandarin - you know, just by Pierrot's - at 8.15. I arrived at about 8.20, or thereabouts, and ordered a drink as he wasn't there. By nine, when he still hadn't turned up, I used my mobile and rang his flat in May Road. The number was unobtainable, which was ludicrous because I'd spoken to him on it at just after seven when we'd fixed up to meet in the bar. I paid the bill and went straight down and jumped into a taxi. I had - and still have - a key to his flat. His flat was right at the top on the 28th floor and nothing seemed to be wrong as I stepped out of the lift. I opened the door with my key and went in. All the lights were out and when I switched them on everything was in its right place - Richard was such a tidy person,' Sadie added as an afterthought. 'I was just about to leave - there seemed to be no point in staying - when, for some reason, I went over to the French windows leading onto the balcony - there was such a magnificent view from that height and we'd spent so many peaceful, happy evenings sitting out there.' Sadie put her arms round Gunn again and continued, 'I pulled the curtains open and, dear God, there he was, hanging, looking straight at me. His face was all bloated and his discoloured tongue was lolling out of the side of his mouth, like some poor, insane moron. I can't remember what I did for a few moments, but somehow I found myself in the next door flat which is owned by a really nice couple, who 'phoned the police for me. After that, everything went past me in a haze. Police came and went, photographers, the body was cut down and removed. I don't know; I suppose I was in some sort of shock. I remember thinking about my wedding dress - silly wasn't it - and we'd just had a letter from the Bali Hyatt, where we were going to

39

spend the first weekend of our honeymoon before flying to Phuket. I remember thinking that I mustn't forget to write to them and cancel the holiday. Oh dear,' and now Gunn could feel the warm tears rolling down his chest.

'Sadie, you don't have to go on,' he said quietly, stroking the cascade of hair, which reached half way down the gentle curve of her back as she lay on top of him.

'Oh I do John; you have to know what monsters these people are and you've heard nothing yet - you don't have a hankie, do you?'

'Sure, hang on a sec,' and he gently lifted her as he got off the bed and produced a handkerchief out of his cotton anorak. He returned to the bed where Sadie was waiting, propped on one elbow and unintentionally displaying the perfect curves of her full breasts and the voluptuous sweep of thighs and legs, shown off to perfection by the contrast with the whiteness of the sheets. As John rejoined her on the bed, Sadie felt him erect against her.

'Ooh yes, that's nice,' and she straddled him, placing him deep inside her before lowering her head down to whisper in his ear, 'go on Johnny, really hard; that's just what I need now.' It was as though Sadie wanted to purge the horror of that night from her memory as she thrust herself down harder and harder onto him. Eventually she lay exhausted and damp with sweat by his side.

'Oh, I did need that,' she sighed very quietly.

'Feeling better?'

'Yes, much, thanks; that's just what I needed. Now I'm going to tell you the rest of what happened,' and once again she lay with her head on his chest.

'There was still far worse to come. Richard had left a suicide note - at least, at the time I believed it was Richard; it certainly looked like his handwriting. In this note he confessed that he was gay and that a recent medical test had confirmed that he was HIV positive He had taken his life rather than face me. I didn't know what to think at the time. I was dazed, confused and shocked and not a little anxious that I might well be HIV positive as well. Then I met someone at our hotel in London - presumably from Richard's organisation - and I still don't know his name to this day, who told me what had really happened. That evening, just after I'd phoned him at seven, these people - whoever they are - had got hold of Richard. He'd been tied to something - there were abrasions on his wrists and ankles - and a power lead had been connected to his genitals. It seems that this torture must have failed to make Richard talk so they threatened him with a hypodermic filled with Aids-contaminated blood. It's uncertain what happened then, but I was told that the autopsy proved that the

Aids virus was present in his body. This man I met in London explained that there was no question of Richard being gay and he also offered me a full medical check up, which I accepted. Everyone in Cathay was very kind and I was offered as much leave as I wanted. In fact, I wanted just the opposite and asked them to roster me on the busiest schedule possible, so that I could immerse myself in the job.'

'You poor thing; you have had a rotten time,' Gunn glanced at his watch. 'Now, what's it to be? Shall we stay here or would you like dinner at La Rose Noire?'

'You're boasting, you couldn't do it again,' Sadie teased, her hand moving down to his groin. 'Oh, I was wrong,' she laughed, 'let's save it 'til after dinner,' and she got off the bed saying, 'you can have the shower after me, as I don't trust you in it with me.'

Sadie telephoned for a taxi and twenty minutes later they both got out of it on Wo On Lane. The lane was a cul-de-sac off D'Aguilar Street. Besides a fruit shop at its intersection with D'Aguilar Street, there was nothing else in this ill-lit lane except rather rundown lock-ups and warehouses, piles of rattan baskets filled with refuse, rows of illegally parked cars and La Rose Noire. The bistro-style restaurant was up a short flight of some seven or eight steps. It was almost ten when the two of them arrived, but it was only a third full. They were shown to a small table, which, like all the tables, had a black rose in a single stem vase in its centre. They both ordered vichyssoise followed by cold lobster and avocado salad. John ordered a chilled Muscadet, which arrived in a silver ice bucket and was accompanied by fresh, French rolls.

La Rose Noire was softly lit, but not so dark that you couldn't read the cordon bleu menu. In the middle of the restaurant was a piano; the pianist and the singer whom he accompanied, invariably judged the mood of the clientele perfectly and matched it with the melodies and songs which never intruded on the intimacy of each table. On the walls, lit by individual lights, were paintings by a French artist and at the far end of the room was a bar.

The food was excellent, the wine at just the right temperature and the atmosphere and soft music in complete harmony, but Gunn could sense that Sadie was distracted and after the second occasion that she failed to respond to a remark of his. He asked, 'what is it Sadie? I'm not the world's most fascinating raconteur, but you're miles away.'

'I'm sorry John; I suppose it's going through all that business about Richard again that's upset me. Perhaps we should have stayed in bed after all,' Sadie laughed, but it was forced. She had left most of her lobster and had only toyed with her wine.

'Would you like anything else? Coffee? Cheese?'

41

'No, really, nothing at all; excuse me Johnny for a moment, I'm just going to powder my nose,' and she left the table with almost undue haste, taking her handbag from where it had been hanging over the back of the chair. Gunn watched her as she crossed the restaurant towards a door with nothing more than a black rose painted on it. He signalled to their waiter and asked for the bill. More on an impulse rather than any need to relieve himself, he walked over to the door leading to the toilets and went through. As he did so, the door with a pink rose on it opened and two American women emerged. Gunn had noticed the foursome at a table near the piano. The two women were chatting and paused in the doorway of the 'ladies' as Gunn came into the small cloakroom area between the two toilets. They smiled at him, which he returned and was turning towards the door with its blue rose, when he realised he could see Sadie beyond them. She had her back to the door and was speaking into her mobile. Puzzled, he went through into the men's toilet. That was the third time he had seen Sadie using a phone since their arrival at Kai Tak. At the airport, he had assumed that she was ringing her parents; in the flat, he had walked unexpectedly out of the shower to get a towel from the bedroom and she was on the phone then. She had said that the taxis were dreadful at coming up to the mid-levels at that time of night and she'd just been checking to see if it was on its way. He'd thought no more about it at the time. They'd been followed from the airport. Was Sadie being followed as a matter of routine because of her known connection with Richard Anderson? But why follow her from the airport, when they knew where she lived, presumably, and could pick her up at any time? Suddenly, again, the scene in the meeting area came back to him, with Sadie hurriedly replacing the phone on the car hire desk and then rushing over and throwing her arms round him. Was it a distraction? Well, it had worked and until now he hadn't given it a second thought. So what did this all mean? It was really quite simple; it was either coincidence or Sadie, for whatever reason, was something totally different from the character part she was playing for him. Simon had told him that there was no such thing as a coincidence in this business, so that only left one alternative. Sadie was with the opposition; they had got to her before Simon had met her at the party during her stopover in London, or perhaps she'd been with them the whole time and had duped Richard as well? John washed and dried his hands and then returned to the restaurant. Still no Sadie; he paid the bill and walked over to the side of the bar nearest to the windows with their draped curtains. His view of the street was fairly limited, but nothing looked any different from when they'd arrived.

Sadie appeared from the cloakroom and saw their cleared and empty table. Gunn was watching her face closely to see what the reaction would be. If he had got it all wrong, then he would expect her to look mildly puzzled, as it was a look of fear swept over her features, until she saw him standing by the bar and the expression was replaced with a smile.

'Sorry John, I didn't do justice to that lovely lobster. It must be jet-lag or your love-making that puts me off my food,' she added with a very forced conspiratorial chuckle, as the waiter held the door open for them.

'Never mind Sadie; let's get you home,' and he led the way down the steps to the street, now convinced that there was something very wrong. He had removed the black rose from their table and as they left the restaurant he gave it to Sadie. 'Compliments of the management,' he said.

As they reached the street, Sadie put her hand up to her ear and said, 'John, did I have both earrings before I went to the loo?'

'Yes, I think so; why?'

'I must've lost one in the ladies' loo. Look, I'll just nip back and have a look. You go on down there,' and she indicated the intersection with D'Aguilar Street, 'and grab a taxi. I'll be with you in a couple of minutes,' and she went back up the steps and into the restaurant.

Gunn looked towards D'Aguilar Street and then quickly up and down Wo On Lane. Was there anything different in the dark lane since they arrived at the restaurant? Would there be any warning? Windows with curtains partially drawn, a parked car with its engine running, anything which might possibly indicate the direction from which a shot might come. Nothing; the lane was dark and deserted. The windows he could identify were so dirty that it was impossible to see if the curtains were drawn or open. No car with running engine, no one and nothing. Nothing, or was that right? Just this side of the fruit shop was a hawker's barrow. These barrows appeared on the pavements, selling everything from cooked chickens' feet to fake Rolex watches and disappeared as soon as the police appeared. Had the barrow been there when they arrived? Gunn was now walking slowly towards the intersection. The owner of the barrow was standing on the far side of it, partially concealed by its ramshackle awning. There was one customer standing on the street side of the barrow. The hawker was holding up the ubiquitous hawkers' scales; an eighteen-inch length of wood with a pan hung on either end and suspended, offset, by a loop of string. In one pan went the weight and in the other went the produce. The scales were about as accurate as holding up a finger to forecast the weather. He was now midway between the restaurant and the intersection. Behind him, voices from outside the restaurant and a car starting up; headlights switched on and a car easing away from the pavement. Was this it? Gunn could feel the sweat trickle down his spine. The car's headlights swung across the street and it accelerated towards the intersection. He was now level with an old, cast-iron lamp post; its lighting capability long since defunct and wires trailed out of the smashed lamp casing, but it was still soundly embedded in concrete. He stooped to retie his shoelaces keeping the lamppost between himself and the car, but it moved on past him and he recognised the American foursome from the table by the piano. The car swerved to avoid a pile of black, plastic rubbish bags and as it did so, the headlights swung across the lane, lighting the hawker's barrow. Gunn was on his feet again. The hawker wasn't holding a set of scales. He threw himself to one side as the crossbow bolt hissed past him. The hawker and his customer disappeared into the crowds in D'Aguilar Street. A sharp crack! And a chip of masonry flew from the wall to Gunn's right. He swore, dropped to the pavement and rolled quickly towards the gutter, turning to face the new threat.

The gunman was standing in the shadow of the restaurant steps, identified by the flash from the muzzle of his gun. The shot was wildly inaccurate and thudded into the bodywork of the car parked nearest to Gunn. The gunman then moved out into the pool of light cast by the restaurant entrance. It was Sadie. In her right hand was a small automatic; her left hand clasped the shaft of the crossbow bolt protruding from her left breast. She sank to her knees and the third bullet ricocheted harmlessly off another car before the automatic fell from her hand as she collapsed on the pavement. Gunn checked over his shoulder to see if there was yet another threat and then moved quickly over to Sadie. She had fallen forward and he gently turned her onto her side. She was still breathing and her eyes opened.

'Why Sadie, why?' Her eyes closed tightly to shut out the pain and a small trickle of blood appeared at the corner of her mouth.

'Richard . . .' she started and then spluttered as more blood came from her mouth. Gunn bent down to hear the almost inaudible whisper.

'It's John, Sadie,' but she shook her head slowly, wincing at the pain in her left side and she feebly tried to remove the obscene bolt protruding from her breast.

'No John,' and her life was ebbing fast. 'Richard broke off our engagement . . .' again she paused as blood seeped from her mouth. 'There was a row; he said . . .' again a pause and now he could hardly hear her. 'Never marry a Chink, but always good for a screw . . .' and she died. Gunr stood up and looked down at her. He bent and quickly picked up the small automatic and removed her flat keys from her handbag and then walked to the steps leading up to La Rose Noire. The road was still deserted and no one had witnessed the incident in Wo On Lane. He glanced back once. Sadie lay on the pavement in a pool of light cast by the restaurant entrance; beside her lay a broken-stemmed black rose.

CHAPTER 4

Since oceanographical records had first been kept, Hong Kong's Royal Observatory had possessed no explanation for the phenomenon of a warm current which had appeared at irregular and unpredictable intervals in the Pacific Ocean to the south-east of Honk Kong. The Gulf Stream drifted north-east across the Atlantic from the warm waters of the Caribbean and created a relatively mild climate for Britain in contrast to the bitterly cold winters of a land-locked country like European Russia which lay on the same latitude. In a similar way, 'El Nino', a Spanish name for the warm current because it always appeared off the coast of Chile, drifted north-west across the South Pacific Ocean through Polynesia and the Coral Sea, to the islands of Melanesia and Micronesia and the south-east coast of China. It had been named the 'child' because, like the nursery rhyme, it behaved just like one:

> 'There was a little girl who had a little curl
> Right in the middle of her forehead.
> When she was good she was very, very good
> But when she was bad, she was horrid.'

The name was appropriate; it brought contentment and prosperity to the shores it washed against with its abundant harvest of fish, but it also brought catastrophic destruction from the typhoons born out of the warm water evaporating from its surface.

That year, El Nino had excelled itself in its 'horridness'; a deep depression had developed to the north-east of Taiwan from which southerly winds blew with ever increasing strength towards Hong Kong. Four hundred miles to the south-east of Mindanao, the largest of the islands in the Philippines, an anti-cyclone had developed with the lowest pressure ever recorded. This was the birth of Typhoon Pamela. Already, the two conflicting low pressure systems had started to compress the sea until the surface rose up into huge waves which grew and grew in size, waiting to be released by the move of one of the low pressure systems.

Raymond Lau was on duty in the Royal Observatory building on the Kowloon waterfront. All the information for the evening weather

46

forecasts had been passed to the media networks in Hong Kong. Weather forecasts in Hong Kong were rarely ever accurate which was hardly surprising as the task of predicting what was going to happen to this tiny pimple, no larger than the Isle of Wight, on the southern extremity of China, was almost impossible. It was quite possible, in an hour's drive, from the Shek O Peninsular in the south to the border with Shenzen in the north, to encounter everything from brilliant sun to a hailstorm.

Raymond's chair in the duty room of the weather forecasting centre placed him in a position from which he could monitor all the radar, computer and weatherfax equipment. A green light flashed on the fax machinery as it started to produce the weather map. He rose from his chair and wandered over to the machine, reaching it as it clicked off. He pulled out the wide strip of paper, glancing at it as he did so to ensure that the print was clear, and then tore it off against the serrated edge. He started to walk back to his chair while he scanned the printout and then stopped. He bent to study the weather map more closely, pushing his glasses more firmly onto the bridge of his nose. Having double-checked what he had seen at first glance, he walked over to the phone which rang just as he reached it. It was the duty met' officer at the Philippine Meteorological Station on Mindanao.

'Yes, I've just received it,' he confirmed to the enquiry. 'Can you confirm that the depression is really only reading 929 millibars?' A pause; 'you can. What's the exact position? 350 miles south-east of you, crossing the Palau Islands at a speed of 10 knots with wind speeds of 170 mph recorded. Thank you. Where did this one suddenly spring from for God's sake? Developed in the last hour! But that's impossible - well, yes I know that it is possible, but it's so rare. Thank you very much and the same to you. Good luck and keep your head down,' and Raymond replaced the phone. For a moment he considered the bleak outlook for Mindanao if it was hit by the typhoon which had just been christened Pamela. With wind speeds of 170 mph, nothing would be left standing in the path of the typhoon. The damage, loss of life and livestock, destruction of crops, severe flooding and subsequent outbreaks of cholera and typhoid, would devastate the southernmost island of the Philippines.

Raymond Lau picked up the phone again and rang his director. Twice the latter asked for the information to be repeated. Raymond then went through the laborious business of going through the checklist of all the numbers, which he had to ring. It started with the Police followed by the Security Branch of the Government, Fire Services, Military Duty Officer at 'Polmil' - the joint police/military headquarters in Central Police Station - the Marine Police, Public Works Department, radio and TV stations and so on. Pamela was too far away for the track to be predicted accurately in relation to Hong Kong, but using computer-stored data, it seemed that the typhoon would pass some 300 miles to the south-west.

Lau had learned from experience that tropical typhoons were notoriously unpredictable, particularly as they swept across the islands of the Western Pacific. Their speed over the surface varied from 3 mph to 30 mph. Some would follow a reasonably typical curving path to dissipate their colossal energy and its ensuing havoc over Vietnam. Others would swing sharply north to create mountainous seas on the coasts of Taiwan, Korea and Japan, and twice in the last 24 years they had come straight over Hong Kong. Lau had still been at university in the New Territories when 'Rose', the first one, had struck in 1971 and had been with the Observatory for five years when the second one, 'Hope', had struck in 1979. Neither of these had been of the intensity or ferocity of Pamela which was now sweeping across the Pacific Ocean, siphoning up millions of cubic metres of warm, evaporating sea water into its cauldron of accelerating winds and thermal currents. On the late evening news summary, on all four TV channels, the first indication of a typhoon, 1550 miles to the south-east, was announced. It was forecast to move north-west at 10 mph towards Hainan Island on the South China Coast, 160 miles to the south-west of Hong Kong. Hong Kong paid little attention and life continued as normal.

*

The police had arrived within five minutes of John Gunn's call on his mobile from the restaurant. After all the paraphernalia of photographs and establishing identities, Sadie's body was unceremoniously placed into a black body bag and driven away to the police morgue. Gunn went with the police to their headquarters in Central. Before making his statement, he was given permission to phone Sadie's parents. By this time it was nearly 2 am. Gunn explained to Sadie's father what had happened and Peter Causland arrived at the police station within 20 minutes. Gunn gave him rather more detail of what had happened and, in return, was told by Peter Causland that Sadie had become a changed person since the engagement had been broken earlier in the year. She had shunned her father's company and eventually the family rows became so intolerable that she had moved out into her own flat in Robinson Road. He asked John if he could think of any explanation for her murder in such a bizarre fashion. There seemed little point in adding

48

to a father's misery by explaining that he had been the real target. Nor was there any need to tell Peter that he had been set up by Sadie, which would have compromised his own position. Gunn suggested that it was probably a tragic case of mistaken identity, but Peter Causland shook his head wearily.

'No John; we knew she was mixing with a pretty strange circle of people and there was absolutely nothing that we could do to warn her of the consequences. She wouldn't speak a word to me and on one occasion when I attempted to reason with her, she spat at me. Her brothers - you remember Andy and Tim?' and John's nod allowed him to continue. 'Both of them returned to Hong Kong and tried to help, but with no success. No, John, I didn't lose a daughter tonight; I lost my daughter six months ago. Oh God! What happened to her?' and he buried his head in his hands to hide the tears of grief which had been bottled up for months. The police offered to drive him home, but Peter Causland shook his head, thanked them for the offer and forgetting that Gunn was there, walked out of the police station into the night.

The police asked Gunn to return to the station at eleven o'clock the same day and asked him where he was staying. He confirmed that this was at the Mandarin and made a phone call to the hotel to ensure that his room had not been reallocated. The hotel assured him that his room was the suite which was always booked by Euro-Pacific and was available whenever he cared to book in, despite the hour. John had no wish to spend the night in Sadie's flat, and so once again he was dropped outside the flat in Robinson Road, where he paid the taxi to wait for him while he went up to collect his suitcase.

He had slept well on the flight from Heathrow and the combination of that and the eight hour time difference with the UK, made Gunn feel as though it was still only six in the evening as his body clock hadn't had time to adjust. He nodded to the man at the security desk and walked into the lift. His finger was just about to press the '5' button when he paused and then pressed the '6'. It was now some three hours since Sadie's murder. She had made two phone calls, one from the flat and then another from the cloakroom at the restaurant. On the sixth floor he got out, opened the fire door, which led to the stairs beside the lift shaft and went quietly down the stairs to the fifth floor. He opened the fire door slowly and as he did so, the door of Sadie's flat, which had been fractionally ajar, closed.

How many were in the flat? Gunn reckoned that he had to expect a minimum of two. He removed the flat key from his pocket and checked Sadie's small Beretta. It was .22 calibre and the magazine had four rounds in it; that gave him five, counting the one in the chamber. The automatic was no man stopper, but a .22 bullet in the right place made the target just as dead as one hit by a .57 magnum slug and had the advantage of making considerably less noise and mess.

Gunn slid the key silently into the lock with his left hand, holding the automatic in his right; he placed his right foot against the door and as the catch of the lock released it, his leg straightened out and drove the solid, hardwood door open. There were three of them. One took the full impact of the door on his head, which acted as a doorstop. The second man was in the short corridor which led to the two bedrooms and the first two bullets from Gunn's Beretta hit him; one through his open mouth and the other in the neck. The third man was on the right of the door and the blow from his baseball bat glanced off Gunn's shoulder, numbing it and knocking the automatic along the corridor towards the dead Chinese man who was still clutching a meat cleaver - the standard Triad execution weapon. Just to the right of the front door, was an umbrella stand. Between May and September, everyone carried umbrellas and every flat, house and shop had an umbrella stand near the entrance. Still in the stand and unnoticed by the killers who had broken into the flat, was the newspaper-wrapped, pump-action, 12 gauge shotgun. As Gunn rolled with the blow from the baseball bat, he reached out and grabbed the gun with his left hand. A grin spread across the face of the Chinese man wielding the bat. He was still grinning as the 12gauge cluster of lead shot hit him in the stomach at point blank range. The blast drove him back against the wall where he sank to the floor, gazing in horror at the gaping hole in his abdomen.

At this point, the man who had provided his head as a doorstop regained consciousness, decided that it was time to leave and made a dash for the stairs by the lift shaft, as the lift itself had returned to the ground floor. Gunn dropped the shotgun, grabbed Sadie's automatic off the floor in his left hand, swung round and fired, greatly hampered by his numbed right arm. The Chinese 'doorstop' had just reached the fire door when the small, .22 bullet entered his skull just in front of his left ear. 'Maidenhead would've been impressed with that,' Gunn muttered before returning to the gut-shot man in the hall. He held the barrel six inches from the man's groin and spoke to him in Cantonese. 'Who sent you?' The man tried to spit, but was unable to raise the necessary saliva. The fourth .22 bullet went into the carpeted floor a fraction of an inch below the man's genitals. Gunn brought the automatic even closer to the man's crutch. He gasped two indistinct words in Cantonese and then died.

Gunn paused to see if the noise of the shotgun and automatic had produced any reaction from the other tenants of the apartment block. There was no sound from either the stairs or lift shaft, which was not surprising in Hong Kong as barely any sound carried through the reinforced concrete of the high-rise buildings. This lack of reaction was due, partially to the construction of the buildings and partially to Chinese culture, which discouraged involvement in any form of 'Good Samaritan' behaviour because superstition dictated that the 'do-gooder' then became responsible for the soul of the person rescued.

Gunn collected his suitcase and took it out to the lift. He dragged the two dead men out of the flat over to the lift where the two bodies were united with the third body of their companion. John returned to the flat and cleaned up the worst of the mess left by the night's activities and then went out into the lift area and cleared up the mess by the fire door. He had pocketed the Beretta, but the pump-action gun joined the three dead men after it had been wiped clean of any prints. He summoned the lift and descended to the basement with its grisly load. In the basement were the large metal refuse canisters. Into the empty one went the three men and the pump-action gun. Gunn removed the canister from under the refuse chute and replaced it with the body-filled one. He went back up to the first floor and walked down the stairs to the ground floor with his suitcase. In the stairwell was the fire alarm. He broke the glass with the butt of the Beretta and pressed the alarm button. The security guard leapt from his semi-comatose state at the desk and disappeared into the office to the main switchboard to turn off the power to the lift - a standard and well know procedure in every high rise hotel and apartment block. Gunn picked up his suitcase and walked out of the building unnoticed. He roused his taxi driver and directed him to the Mandarin, where he was dropped a little before 4 a.m. Ten minutes later, after a shower, he was asleep.

*

He was woken at 9.30 by the buzzing of the phone beside his bed. It was Peter Wyngarde, the chairman of Euro-Pacific Construction. 'Welcome back to Hong Kong, John; flight alright?'

'Many thanks; yes Sir, the flight was fine. When would you like me to come into the office?'

'Oh, there's no hurry for that. Graham Freeman, your Projects Manager, has never had an Assistant Manager before so what he's never had he won't miss. No, I've told him to leave you alone until next Monday to give you a chance to find a flat and so on. Now, where was I? Ah yes; Josie and I would like you to join us this evening at a reception we're going to, that is if you're not too jet-lagged.'

'No Sir, I'm fine and thank you.'

'Good, good; that'll make us a foursome as we've persuaded Candy to go out with her parents for a change.' Candy was the

51

chairman's only daughter, Candida. Gunn hadn't seen her for many years and he supposed that she must be in her mid twenties or so. She had been a pretty girl at the age of 18, when he'd met her at some function, which his parents had given just before leaving Hong Kong. Gunn viewed the prospect of escorting Candy to a reception with mixed feelings. If she ran true to the form of the majority of wealthy expatriate daughters, she would be spoiled and self-centred. Gunn paused in his train of thought as his chairman was talking to ponder on the possibility that his assessment of Candy and the other expatriate daughters could, just as appropriately, have applied to him before he had left the territory to go to university.

Graham Freeman had occasionally visited their flat in Hong Kong and Gunn had played tennis with him on a handful of occasions. Graham was some years older than him and had gone straight into Euro-Pacific Construction after graduating from Cambridge with a first class honours degree in civil engineering. Graham had not been blessed with an overdose of male hormones and Gunn, by instinct more than anything else, had chosen to avoid him. Graham was a person who held onto another man's hand just that fraction too long after a handshake. All in all, Gunn had considered him to be gay and had been most disappointed to hear that he was going to have to work for him for six months.

Peter Wyngarde, on the other hand, was a wiry, energetic and thoroughly dynamic chairman. He had steered Euro-Pacific through the property boom and the slump which followed in the late seventies and early eighties, squared up astutely to the tremendous competition from the Japanese construction firms and he now owned the most powerful, Far-East-based construction firm operating out of Hong Kong. He and Gunn's father had been great rivals in Euro-Pacific, but had also been good friends, each respecting the other's not inconsiderable ability. When Peter Wyngarde had achieved the chairman's appointment, Gunn's father had wisely decided that retirement would probably lead to a happier and more peaceful existence than all the hassle of boardroom intrigues.

Peter Wyngarde had succeeded in securing contracts for, or a controlling financial investment, in nearly every major construction project in Hong Kong in the previous ten years. These had included the main contract for the supply of material for the Daya Bay Nuclear Power Station in China, the new airport at Chep Lak Kok, three new tunnels under Victoria Harbour, the Taite's Cairn Tunnel through the Lion Rock from Kowloon to Shatin and the extension of the Kwai Chung Container Terminal, which had made Hong Kong the world's largest container port operator. Josie was Peter Wyngarde's wife, Josephine.

'Yes, that's fine Sir, thank you. What time shall I meet you?'

'Oh yes, sorry; can you meet us at Queen's Pier at 6.15 this evening? I'll have the company boat come and pick us up there and that'll take us out to that vast, ostentatious gin palace which is anchored just off Lantau Island, near Discovery Bay.'

'Who's giving this reception, Sir?'

'Of course, I was forgetting that you've been away for so long, otherwise you'd have known who owns Middle Kingdom; it's Yung Shue Wan's latest toy.'

'Can you say that again,' Gunn prompted.

'What, YS' toy?'

'No, just before that.'

'Oh, the name of his boat - it's not a boat, it's a damn great liner. It's called Middle Kingdom; you remember, John, the Chinese proverb about them being the chosen race from the Middle Kingdom.'

'Yes, I remember, Sir. I'll see you at 6.15 at Queen's Pier; presumably black tie.'

'Yes, it's DJs and you'll need the jacket inside the boat; he keeps it air-conditioned like a fridge,' and Peter Wyngarde rang off.

Gunn checked his watch and then asked the hotel operator to get him a call to Express Delivery Services. It would be about 1.30 am and he would probably be put through to the duty controller. To his surprise it was Simon Peters who answered.

'It's about the opening date of our new Hong Kong office,' Gunn explained. 'Our competitors have made two attempts to discourage this project. Does our American office have anyone out here I could call on if necessary?'

'Understood; I'll see if there's anyone available from the New York office to strengthen our negotiating team. He'll contact you at the Mandarin,' and the connection was broken.

When Gunn arrived at Central's Police Station, he was taken to see Charles McBain, who was the Assistant Commissioner responsible for all police operations. His parents had known the McBain family very well. Charles McBain had risen very rapidly through the officer ranks, being one of the few officers to survive the purge of the police force by the ICAC after the corruption scandal of the early seventies. He was of medium height, with neatly barbered dark hair and tended to be slightly overweight. His wife Aileen was eight years his junior and they had two young boys aged 10 and 12 who were at school in Hong Kong. He greeted Gunn civilly and then asked him to explain what had happened the previous night. Gunn did just that, but confined his account to the incident outside the restaurant, having explained that he and Sadie had met on the flight.

'The police officer who took your statement, John, says that you think it was a case of mistaken identity,' McBain said, scanning the statement in front of him on his desk.

'Well, for the life of me, I can't think of a more plausible explanation Charles. Sadie is a sweet person, so who on earth would want to kill her? I would have understood a mugging assault, although those are so rare here, but a deliberate murder defies reason.'

'Do you think that you might have been the target?'

'Anything's possible Charles, but there are a number of facts that make that a pretty far-fetched theory. Although the street is generally badly lit, the scene of the murder is well lit by the lights from the restaurant. So, point one; either they were appallingly poor marksmen - and that's most unlikely as it looked like a professional job; you know, a hawker's stall, two of them and a car parked in D'Aguilar Street - that's what the police inspector told me had come from witnesses' statements. No Charles, they meant to kill Sadie, or as I've said, someone who looks like Sadie. Anyway, why kill me? I've still only been in Hong Kong for about 18 hours and have been away for over eight years. I don't recall leaving any bad debts behind me or making any enemies who would want to kill me. No, I wasn't the target.' Gunn wondered how convincing he sounded and the next question did nothing to dispel his doubts.

'They did a paraffin test on Sadie, which proved positive. Any ideas about that?' McBain was twisting a pencil in the tip of his fingers. He was well aware of Gunn's service in the army and his experience of terrorism. He would be expected to know what a paraffin test was and to deny it would be amateurish in the extreme.

'If I'm right, Charles, that test proves that someone has either fired a gun or been in very close proximity to one?'

'The former, John.'

'When would she have done that? Did she have it on her?'

'No, strangely enough, it wasn't in her purse. Neither were any keys for her flat.' John had been waiting for this and hoped that his explanation would sound plausible.

'Damn; I've got those, Charles. How bloody stupid of me,' Gunn apologised, producing them out of his pocket. McBain accepted the keys and placed them on the desk.

'Perhaps you would tell me how these came to be in your possession?'

'Yes, that's very simple. I told the inspector in my statement that Sadie and I had gone to her flat for a drink before we went to the Rose

Noire. As we left the flat she gave me the keys, as the plan was to return after our dinner.'

'And presumably, John, it was after this 'drink',' and McBain emphasized the word, 'that you both had sexual intercourse.' Gunn had been expecting this one too, knowing that the autopsy would have revealed their energetic love making of the previous evening.

'No, as it happened, the drink never took place. We just made love and then went out to dinner. Now unless you consider that these questions are absolutely vital, I would particularly like to go and see Sadie's parents, who are great friends of my parents, as you will remember,' Gunn purposely injected a tone of irritation into his reply.

'No, John, I won't keep you much longer. Just this business of the positive paraffin test which is puzzling. The test showed that the weapon had been fired within the last hour before her death. Now I believe I'm right in saying that she was with you all the time in that last hour?' again the pencil being twisted between carefully manicured fingertips.

'Correct up to a point, but there were two occasions when we were not together - it's all in my statement. The first occasion was when Sadie went to the 'ladies' in the restaurant. The second occasion was just as we left, when she asked me to go and get her earrings, which she'd taken off during dinner - she had recently had her ears pierced, at least that's what she said, and they were irritating her. I went back into the restaurant and picked them up off the table. I suppose we must have been separated for about two or three minutes. When I came out of the restaurant, she was dead.'

'Did anyone see you when you returned to the restaurant for her earrings?'

'I really haven't the faintest idea. You know how dark it is in La Rose Noire and anyway you've been to the restaurant to question the staff, so you tell me; did anyone see me return?'

'That's our problem, John. You see the staff can't remember whether you returned or not.'

'What about the other clientele?'

'Oh, don't worry, we're working on that. So you think that Sadie fired her automatic at a person or persons unknown while you were inside the restaurant?'

'How, as a matter of interest, do you know that she fired an automatic, if you haven't found it yet,' John asked calmly, avoiding the very clumsy trap set by McBain.

'We know that it was an automatic because a revolver leaves a very large and distinctive powder deposit on the hands, whereas the enclosed breach and chamber of the automatic leave a smaller, but equally distinct deposit on the hands.'

'Since it's most unlikely that she let rip with this automatic in the toilet - there were certainly other women in there with her - then that's the only plausible solution I can offer, but I still don't see what happened to the gun. Presumably someone removed it?'

'Yes, that's rather what we'd come to think. Well, thank you John for coming in to see us. We'll let you know how things go, but I must ask you not to leave Hong Kong without checking with us first.'

'Yes, of course,' Gunn assured McBain as he stood up, 'you can always find me at the Mandarin,' and he left the office wondering what a paraffin test would have shown had it been done on him. He had sent all the clothes he'd worn the previous evening to the laundry and had used after-shave lotion on his hands to remove the powder traces. He took a taxi to the Peak and spent a somewhat harrowing half-hour with Sadie's parents before returning to the Mandarin and its Chinnery Bar for an ice-cold St Miguel beer and a plate of rare beef.

CHAPTER 5

The 56 foot, ketch-rigged, motor yacht American Pie turned slowly through the wind onto the starboard tack as it changed course towards the sheltered cove. The jib and staysail, together with the main and mizzen, swung across the boat in unison and soon the swish and gurgle of the sea below the leeward rail rose in volume as the boat picked up speed on the new tack. Dan Grant, the owner and skipper of American Pie, leant forward from where he was standing at the boat's wheel to check that both engines were out of gear and then pressed one of the starter buttons. Below, in the engine compartment, the first of the two 80 horsepower diesels fired and rumbled into life, quickly followed by the second one, and a spurt of cooling water appeared out of the twin exhausts at the stern.

In the spacious deck cockpit outside the wheelhouse, the Grant's charter guests relaxed over a leisurely breakfast. The delicious aroma of freshly ground coffee and hot rolls drifted back towards the skipper. With appetites sharpened by the sea air and a night sail down from Cebu, the eight people seated round the oiled teak table were doing justice to Amy Grant's cooking.

Dan signalled to his two Filipino boat boys, who were sitting on the pulpit, that he was about to anchor. The two young men quickly winched in the two furling headsails and then carried out the same procedure with the in-mast, furling main and mizzen sails. In less than four minutes all the sails had vanished and the two men unshackled the large anchor from its stowed position on the short bowsprit. Bending over the chart, which he had clipped on a board beside the wheel, Dan identified the small pencil ring, which he had placed there the night before, marking an ideal anchorage in a lagoon which was in the lee of the high north-east peninsular of Mindanao. He decided to anchor in eight metres of water. Both boat boys were looking towards him awaiting the next order. Dan held up one hand and opened the fingers five times to indicate 25 metres of chain - three times the maximum depth of the water at high tide. They switched on the electric winch at the bow which brought up the chain from its locker and laid it out neatly in fathom loops so that it would run straight out once the anchor was dropped. As soon as this was all completed, the senior boat boy turned towards his skipper and raised his hand. Not a word had passed between the skipper and his crew during the preparation to anchor, and the peaceful, paradise island scene of palms, white sand and clear blue water was undisturbed for the charter passengers on the motor yacht.

Dan disengaged the combined gear and throttle levers and American Pie gracefully slipped through the water under her own momentum towards the shore. He watched the digital readout of his depth meter as it slowly clicked down and then steadied at 8 metres. He reached out with both hands and pulled the levers towards him engaging astern with both engines. The boat stopped and then slowly gathered way astern. Dan raised his arm above his head and then dropped it to his side. The Filipinos immediately released the anchor, which splashed loudly into the clear water, the chain racing and rattling after it over the stainless-steel bow-roller. He eased the levers forward into neutral and waited for American Pie to settle to the chain. Once she had done this, he re-engaged astern on both engines and increased the revolutions to make the anchor bite deep into the sand on the seabed. He then pressed the decompressors and both engines stopped; apart from a small flock of parakeets, which had risen from the beach palms, nothing else stirred to spoil the beautiful anchorage. Dan signalled to his two boys to join him in the stern.

'I want you to put the kedge anchor out as well, boys; the glass has fallen over the last few hours and I think we're in for a bit of a blow, which I reckon'll come from the south-east. That's why I've tucked her right in close to the lee of this high ground,' and he indicated the changing shades of green as the ground rose until it turned deep blue just before the bare rock pierced the skyline. The boys smiled, nodded their approval of the skipper's seamanship and immediately got on with the task of lowering the tender in its davits so that they could row out the heavy kedge anchor. Dan walked forward to the cockpit where breakfast was nearly finished.

'Well folks, I think we'll stay here for the next 24 hours or so. It's a nice sheltered anchorage and I'm pretty certain that any wind will be offshore, which'll keep us clear of the beach. I'm just a little concerned about some shallows over there,' and he indicated to seaward with a wave of his arm, 'which we had to avoid coming in, but I think we're OK. I think we might be in for a bit of a blow later, so if you want to do some diving and board sailing, now's the time while it's still calm. The boys'll be finished with the anchor in five minutes and then they'll help you with the air-compressor, scuba gear and sailboards.' He then sat down to enjoy a peaceful cup of coffee and one of his wife's excellent croissants, which had been made that morning.

58

One headland away to the west, where the lush vegetation reached right down to the sea, American Pie was being studied closely through a pair of powerful binoculars. The prolific vegetation almost totally concealed the lines of a Second World War, American, motor-torpedo-boat. The boat was now painted with a black hull and a disruptive pattern of matt green, brown and black on the topsides and superstructure, which made it virtually invisible when moving close in to the shore.

'What d'you reckon?' this came from one of the two men studying the boat through binoculars.

'We wait,' was the curt reply. 'There're too many people on board,' added Manuel Arturo who was the captain of the converted boat. For as many years as the Caribbean had played host to pirates of all nationalities, so had the myriads of islands of the Thai, Malaysian, Philippine and Indonesian Archipelago. The drug traffic from Colombia and Cuba to the Florida Peninsular had increased the spoils for the modern Caribbean pirate. In the same way the exports from the 'Golden Triangle' of Burma, Thailand and Cambodia, together with the pathetic plight of the Vietnamese refugees, provided rich pickings for the pirates of the South China Sea. The refugees were still taking to the sea in their thousands in boats which were unfit to sail across a child's paddling pool, let alone the typhoon-swept seas of South East Asia. The refugees fell easy prey to the pirates, who stripped them of all their possessions, jewellery - if they had any - and money. They would then murder all the men, rape all the women and those worth keeping were then sold into vice rings for large sums of money. If they were too old, then they too would be murdered once the pirates had finished with them. In the South China Sea, the pirates had become so audacious and well armed that many a large cargo vessel had been attacked. Now, private and charter yachts in the Caribbean had taken to carrying weapons and more than one attempt by pirates to take on what looked like an easy target had resulted in the massacre of the pirate crew. This had also happened in the cruising grounds of the Western Pacific. Men like Arturo made their money from anyone and anything. He supplied guns for the communist terrorists, more guns for anyone attempting a coup, drug trafficking, slave trading, stealing from private and charter yachts and if they were really at a loose end, stealing from Filipino fishing boats and coastal traders.

The ugliness of the converted boat was only exceeded by the ugliness of its crew. Manuel Arturo operated with a crew of eleven men, all of whom looked like grotesque imitations from a Rambo film, but there was nothing comic about the armoury of weapons, which they carried. These ranged from M16 and AK47 assault rifles to machine pistols, magnum calibre pistols and an assortment of machetes and knives.

*

The Grants were not totally unaware of the dangers of cruising in the islands of the South China Sea and Western Pacific. Their yacht was registered in San Francisco, but more and more frequently Dan Grant had been lured to the other side of the Pacific by the very lucrative charter fees being paid by Japanese tourist agents. His guests were four Japanese couples, all in their thirties, who had chartered American Pie for a three week cruise round the Pacific Islands. The party of eight had flown from Tokyo to Manila where they had transferred to a small plane which had flown them to Cebu Harbour - the centre of the yacht charter trade in the Philippines.

The four men were totally absorbed in the task of preparing the scuba gear, while two of the wives swam and the other two had the sailboards. Dan gave Amy a hand with clearing away the breakfast things and then went up to his navigation cubby-hole in the wheelhouse to check one or two calculations and plan for the rest of the cruise. He sat down in the comfortable rotating chair, in which he could swing round to see the radar scope, GPS display, HF and VHF radio and his pride and joy, Amy's gift to him when American Pie was launched, a highly polished, antique brass chronometer and barometer. It was the latter instrument, which pulled him up short.

'Must be something wrong with it,' he muttered to himself as he examined it more closely, and then broke the golden rule of a lifetime and gently tapped the glass face of the instrument. He recoiled as though the barometer had given him a shock as it plummeted a further two millibars down to 931. However hard he tried to convince himself that the instrument had gone haywire, he knew that it was merely doing its job and doing it very accurately. It was also spelling out a clear warning to him which is what it was designed to do and which he was trying to ignore.

'Sorry old fellow,' Dan grimaced as he patted the instrument gently. 'Thanks for the warning; now let's get to work and take advantage of it.' He immediately switched on the radio and tuned it to the local forecast frequency.

'Did you say something?' asked Amy from down in the galley, as she gave the surfaces a final wipe down.

'Talking to myself again, love. I'm sorry to say that we're about to have one hell of a storm. Can you get round and batten down everything that can possibly move, particularly in the galley. This one

60

is going to give us a real hammering. I've never seen the glass go so low in all my life.'

'Will we be all right, honey?'

'Yes, of course, provided that we take some precautions. I'm now going topsides to do just that. You do as I suggested and batten down everything below decks,' and with that Dan disappeared on deck. As soon as he reached the deck, he summoned the two boat boys who were helping with the scuba gear.

'That blow I warned you about is going to be a real bastard. Take the tender out again and the third anchor with all the heaviest warps from the lazarette. Take it out along the main anchor chain and two thirds of the way along it, I want you to bend on the heavy warp for the third anchor. Take the anchor well out to port,' and Dan pointed to the spot, 'and drop it there. Then come back and ease out another thirty metres of chain and warp on both the other anchors. Got all that?' They both nodded, smiled and dashed off to complete all the tasks which they had just been set. The urgency of their skipper's voice was encouragement enough for them both.

Dan Grant walked over to the four Japanese men who had been listening to all the instructions. 'I'm sorry guys, but we'll have to leave the diving for another day. The weather is going to give us all a bit of excitement shortly. The forecast is for some very strong winds in this part of the Philippines before too long. Perhaps you could help us by stowing all that diving gear. I'd also like you to get your wives back on board and then go below and stow away all your possessions and anything movable in your cabins. Amy's down there and will tell you exactly what to do.'

They responded with alacrity and soon all were involved in preparing themselves and the boat for whatever might happen. Dan hurried back into the wheelhouse and carefully tuned the radio. The static was dreadful.

'. . . imminent, I say again, imminent. Typhoon Pamela is now moving towards Mindanao at a speed of 15 mph. Wind speeds of 180 mph have been recorded. Everyone should take shelter immediately and . . .' Dan switched off the radio as another deafening roar of static interrupted transmission.

He swore to no one in particular, but it startled the eldest of his male Japanese guests. 'Sorry about that,' he apologised, smiling, 'but I think we're all in for an experience we'll not forget for some time.'

'It's very serious?' was the anxious enquiry.

'Sir, you have the credit of the understatement of this century, but hell, don't you worry. Pie and me've been through rougher stuff than this before,' which was completely untrue, but there seemed to be no point in frightening the guests, as he explained to Amy when he bumped into her down below.

Dan went back on deck to find the boys lashing down the two sailboards. The two younger wives were already below helping with the re-stowing of everything movable. He looked up at the sky; the sun was now shielded by a halo formed from high altitude, jet-stream stratus clouds. Out in the Mindanao Channel he could already see the waves building up with the rising wind strength. He wished that he could see over the protective escarpment which was shielding the boat, to get an idea what was coming and then decided that perhaps it was better not to know. Would Pie survive such a blow? He thought probably not, but there was little he could do about it, which he hadn't already done.

*

On the bridge of the converted MTB, Manuel Arturo had also been watching the sudden activity aboard American Pie and wrongly deduced that she was making ready to put to sea. He hadn't missed the presence of the four slim Japanese women and had been dwelling on various forms of sexual perversion to which he might submit all of them after he had stripped everything off the boat. All of the women should fetch a good price from the vice ring in Manila. Most of the trade done by this vice ring was for US servicemen and the Western tourist trade from Scandinavia and Germany. By the time their pimps put them on the street or in the brothels, the women's minds were so blown by drugs that the poor creatures had no idea who they were or what was happening to them. So intent was he on his sexual fantasies that Arturo failed to turn his binoculars towards the channel. Had he done so, from the better but exposed anchorage where the MTB was moored, he would have seen the awesome sight of the approach of the leading edge of Pamela.

*

Gunn finished his plate of beef, baked potato and sour cream and had just caught the barman's eye to order another ice-cold beer, when a voice behind him said, 'make that two barman!' Gunn turned to see a man of almost the same height as himself with the same sort of build and with unmistakably Mexican blood somewhere in his ancestry.

'Doyle Barnes!' he exclaimed, 'what the hell are you doing in this part of the world?' The last time that Gunn had seen Doyle was during a six month attachment to Fort Benning, when he had been doing an exchange with 82nd Airborne. He and Doyle had become close friends.

'Well you see John, it's like this,' and his long Southern drawl cut through the mixture of dialects and languages in the Chinnery Bar

62

like a hot knife through butter, causing heads to turn. 'I'm from the New York office and was on my way to Hong Kong. When I arrived a couple of hours ago I was given new instructions and they told me that an old friend of mine couldn't hack it on his own, so they sent in the cavalry - airborne, of course - to come and give some advice.'

'Excellent; where are you staying?'

'Right here, John; I just finished booking in and came up here on the off-chance of finding you.' Their silver tankards of beer arrived.

'Here's mud in your eye,' Doyle toasted and sank his beer in one. 'Ah! I needed that.'

'So it would seem,' Gunn laughed. 'I'll just finish mine and then we'll go for a walk and discuss old times.'

'You're on,' Doyle replied and when the beer was finished they both left the bar and took the lift down to street level.

They crossed over Connaught Road by the pedestrian walkway, along the harbour by the Star Ferry Terminal towards the British Military Headquarters in the Prince of Wales building and then round and back towards the Mandarin via the Furama Hotel, the Hong Kong Club and the Legislative Council Building. The frenetic and constant hubbub and roar of Hong Kong would have made it impossible for anyone to eavesdrop on their conversation.

'And that brings you right up to date, Doyle. I've only the slimmest lead, which I intend to follow up this evening, but judging from the reception I've just had, you'll realise that 'they' don't waste time or wear kid gloves. When I say that I need someone to watch my back, I mean that we both need to take that precaution here. You clear on my movements tonight?'

'No problem, John; you go ahead and I'll be around. Incidentally, I've got a small present for you which was sitting awaiting collection in our Consulate.'

Back in the Mandarin, Gunn collected his present from Doyle's room; this was his 9mm Browning Hi-Power and two holsters, one strapped on his ankle and the other fitted on the waist band in the small of the back. There were three full clips for the magazine and a full box of 9mm ammunition.

Gunn then went to his room and had a long hot shower, which he turned to cold for the last two minutes. He changed into his white dinner jacket, clipped the holster in position, worked the cocking mechanism on the Browning and chambered a round. He removed the magazine, inserted one extra round from the box and then replaced it. With thumb on the hammer, he pulled the trigger and eased it into the half cock position; a final check to ensure that the safety was off and he slipped the automatic into its holster. He checked his watch; just before six. He left the Mandarin and followed the same route, which he and Doyle had taken earlier that afternoon. The sun was now setting over Lantau Island in a blaze of colour reflected off the gold, green, blue and opaque glass of the waterfront skyscrapers. As he passed the entrance to the Stock Exchange Building its employees were only just beginning to leave, having been at work since eight in the morning. Making money was an all consuming passion of the Hong Kong Chinese and few of them resented working long hours to assuage that passion. Then it was down the steps off the walkway, past the fountain in the little piazza opposite the main post office and then Gunn had to weave in and out of the crowds hurrying to the Star Ferry Terminal on their way over the harbour to Kowloon. Once past the City Hall he reached the paved area opposite Queen's Pier and parked there was Peter Wyngarde's Bentley. John could see the chairman and his wife Josie sitting in the back of the car, making the most of the air-conditioning before stepping out into the oppressive humidity; not so Candy. She was leaning against the bonnet of the car, well aware of the many curious and admiring glances directed at her. Gunn had to admit that even from fifty yards away, the effect of the low evening sun on her cascade of titian hair, perfectly set off by an Armani creation with matching shoes, was pretty stunning. The final touch were her designer sun glasses, which were removed as soon as she spotted Gunn.

'Johnny!' her voice echoed around City Hall plaza and Queen's Pier, as she removed her very attractive backside from the Bentley and ran towards him. Her perfume preceded her by a few milli-seconds and then she flung her arms round him.

'Candy, I didn't think it was possible, but you're even more beautiful than the last time I saw you. Mind you, you were only a schoolgirl then, so I suppose that might account for it!' John greeted her, laughing as he disentangled himself from her embrace and led her towards her parents' car.

'Still the perfect officer and gentleman,' teased Candy.

'I'm not sure about the gentleman part Candy, but I'm certainly no longer an officer.'

'Hello Sir,' John greeted Candy's father, 'good to see you again, and you Josie, looking so well. I can't decide which of the two, mother or daughter is the more beautiful!'

'That's enough, you flatterer,' Josie laughed, 'you may not be an officer any longer John, but you've certainly lost none of your charm.'

'Come on, Johnny,' Peter Wyngarde interrupted, 'otherwise we'll never get out of these women's clutches and anyway, the boat's waiting for us.'

They walked over to the pier, and at the precise moment when they reached the steps, a gleaming, 55 foot Bertram cruiser, belonging to Euro-Pacific, snubbed up against the fenders and was held in place at bow and stern by two junior boat boys. From her stern flew the Red Ensign and from the radar mast on the flying bridge, flew a pennant with the company logo, which was in the form of a monogram of the letters EPC.

Gunn jumped aboard first and then assisted Josie and Candy over the dipping side of the boat. Peter Wyngarde brought up the rear and once aboard, nodded towards his coxswain, who had never taken his eyes off his boss ever since the moment he had stepped out of the Bentley. The two, heavily muffled, 500 hp turbo-charged, Perkins diesels gave a deep throated roar and the cruiser eased astern from the steps to allow another boat, waiting impatiently, to come alongside.

'Come on everybody,' urged Peter Wyngarde, 'let's all go up to the fly bridge and have a quick drink up there before we get to YS' boat.'

'What about my hair,' complained Candy as they all headed up to the exposed bridge.

'Good heavens above girl' Peter Wyngarde shouted over his shoulder, 'you spent an hour and a half mucking about with it to give it that 'windswept, casual look' or that's what you said. Now I'm offering the perfect solution to you and all for free, except about 20 litres of diesel,' he added as a business-like afterthought. It took only 15 minutes for the powerful cruiser to reach the huge yacht and as the engines throttled back, Peter Wyngarde waved his hand towards her saying, 'there she is, Middle Kingdom, in all her vulgar glory.'

Middle Kingdom had been the last two words uttered by a gut-shot Triad assassin as his life-blood seeped onto the floor of a flat in Robinson Road.

CHAPTER 6

'Cast off!' shouted Manuel, in the Spanish-originated, Tagalog patois of the Philippines, 'let's go grab ourselves a Yankee sail boat.' This command was greeted with a chorus of approval from his crew of thugs, who were eagerly looking forward to the spoils of a successful raid, not the least of which would be the orgy of sexual delights to which they would submit the helpless and terrified women.

The converted MTB had two, 600hp petrol engines and carried nearly nine tons of fuel. When first built in 1942, this mark of boat had been capable of speeds in excess of 50 knots in reasonable sea conditions, but its Achilles heel had always been the large quantity of petrol required to feed the thirsty, supercharged engines which, in effect, turned the boats into floating petrol bombs. Many of these MTBs had disappeared without trace in the Second World War after an explosion of the fuel tanks. Since all of Arturo's crew smoked anything and everything from tobacco and cannabis to any available drug that could be stuffed into a pipe or wrapped in a cigarette paper, it was only chance that had prevented the boat being blown to pieces on many occasions.

The boat's engines roared into life as Manuel Arturo took command of the boat himself. Between his boat and the lagoon in which American Pie was anchored, was a long sand spit surrounded by very shallow water which Arturo knew well. It meant that he would have to take the boat in a wide sweep out into the Mindanao Channel and then approach the narrow entrance to the lagoon on exactly the same course that he had watched the ketch take. He pulled the port throttle lever to slow astern and pushed the starboard one to slow ahead. The light-hulled boat gathered way quickly, leaving the concealing vegetation behind. He brought both throttles together at half ahead as the boat moved from the shelter of its mooring into the rising seas of the channel. Then with an exclamation of delight, he pushed both throttles to full ahead and the boat leapt forward with spray flying in every direction. Greed and lust overrode any thoughts of caution or seamanship and Arturo didn't even glance at the eastern horizon - or what little could be seen of it - as his boat careered out into the rough water.

*

Another trip into the wheelhouse showed Dan that his barometer had now fallen to 929 millibars. He hurried back on deck where everything was stowed or lashed down. He quickly moved to the stern and removed the Stars and Stripes, which was straining in the down-draught of wind from the high ground inshore. He hauled the flag down and then started his minute check of everything on board. Both the boat boys were still on deck and needed no encouragement to check everything again and again to ensure that it was properly lashed and secure. Dan went all round the boat doing his checks and when he reached the stern again he looked around to see how the yacht was holding. As he glanced towards the Mindanao Channel, a puzzled frown creased his forehead. 'What the hell's that boat doing out there,' he muttered to himself, hardly daring to answer his own query as he rushed towards the wheelhouse to get his binoculars. He grabbed the binoculars and then went back on deck. He steadied himself against the mizzenmast and focused the glasses on the boat in the channel.

'Sonofabitch! As if we haven't enough problems without those bastards finding us.' He went back into the wheelhouse and summoned everyone into the large wheelhouse saloon.

'Listen everyone and listen good because I won't have time to repeat this,' which ensured that he had everyone's attention. 'Not only have we got one God-almighty storm about to descend on us, but worse still, we're about to be visited by some of the local pirates!'

'Oh no!' gasped Amy.

'These guys mean business and bloody dirty business at that,' Dan's language helped to get the message through to the Japanese. 'Salvador and Pedro, come with me to get the weapons. While I'm getting the weapons, this is what is going to happen. All you ladies get into your swimming costumes and put a change of clothing, shoes and some food and water into a plastic bag. Amy will show you what you need and how to do it. As soon as you're ready, all the women are going to swim to the shore - it's only about a seventy yard swim - once there, you're to get into the undergrowth and stay still. Amy, you take your little pistol and if the very worst happens you know what to do with it. Understood? Right, you've got no more than three minutes to do it, so get going,' and the four women led by Amy disappeared down below. 'Now then, how many of you can use a gun?' All of the Japanese nodded in unison. 'Good,' said Dan with relief, 'I'll be back in two minutes to tell you what's going on; in the meantime, please help me by launching the tender again and tie it up on the starboard side. Got that?' and again the nods. 'Right, get going!'

67

Dan Grant went down to the engine compartment and the boys helped him lift back the floorboards over the port diesel tank. He then depressed an innocent looking switch, which was but one of a whole bank of switches on the master switchboard, and along the line of a weld on the diesel tank, a compartment opened revealing a collection of neatly stowed weapons and ammunition boxes. Dan removed two M 16 rifles, two pump-action shot guns and two, US Army, Colt automatics. These and the ammunition boxes he handed to Salvador and Pedro. 'Quickly, boys, get this lot up to the wheelhouse and load them.' Once they had disappeared, Dan pressed another switch, which revealed a different compartment, in which was stowed his main line of defence against just this sort of attack. Again, neatly stowed in this compartment were four, 60 mm, light anti-tank rockets. The small missile and launcher were self-contained as one unit, which was designed as a fire-and-throw-away weapon. It had a range of 500 yards and the hollow charge warhead could pierce up to ten inches of hardened armour. It had been specifically designed to cope with the front glacis plate of the Soviet T72 tank. He removed two of these, closed the compartment and went up to the wheelhouse where he found five very nervous women and four, equally anxious Japanese men. He glanced out of the wheelhouse towards the open sea; the MTB was just at the northern extremity of the shallow water and was starting to make its turn to starboard into the channel leading to the lagoon where American Pie was anchored.

'In about thirty seconds, we'll be shielded from those bastards by that spit of beach and coconut palms,' and he pointed. 'Now, as soon as that happens, Amy, you and the girls go over the starboard side so there's no chance of them seeing you and swim like hell for the shore. I'll get into the tender with these,' and he patted the anti-tank missiles, 'and head over to that spit I've just pointed out to you. Just as we did, that boat must come within twenty yards of that spit before turning into the cove. I'll attempt to finish them there. If I fail, then it's up to all of you. Stay out of sight until the very last moment and then let them have it with everything at the same time, but aim for the flying bridge first and kill the helmsman. Have you got all that?' again a series of nods answered him. 'Right, Amy honey, off you go,' Dan sent the women on their way after a glance had confirmed that the spit now blocked the pirates' view of the yacht. The five women disappeared over the side of the boat and swam strongly towards the shore. Dan slid over the same side of the yacht. Salvador and Pedro handed down the two missiles and the M16 rifle to him. The outboard fired as he pressed the starter and he guided the small, fibreglass tender under the bow of the yacht and then at maximum speed to the spit of sand. As soon as the boat touched the sand he was out and dragged it up the beach to ensure that it was not seen by the MTB as it came close inshore. He quickly moved into the low vegetation. The MTB was about half a mile away and approaching at maximum speed.

Dan Grant steadied his breathing as he selected the best position from which to engage the MTB. 'I sure hope the sonofabitch slows down for the turn,' he muttered as he extended both the launcher tubes. Each launcher was now some 1½ metres in length. Fitted below the launcher and with identical ballistic characteristics as the missile itself, was a 9mm spotting rifle. Each launcher had a magazine of five, 9mm, long tracer rounds with flare tips. The sight image showed a grid pattern of five horizontal lines - the top one was 100 yards and the bottom, 500 yards. There was a centre graticule and lead marks left and right for moving targets. These graticules were lit by a Tritium light source, which enabled the missile to be fired in very poor light. He pulled out the safety locking-pin, and selected the spotting rifle with the change lever. With relief, he saw that the bow wave on the MTB had subsided as it came into the narrow inshore channel and then only a hundred yards to his right it turned a couple of points to starboard to make the run along the offshore side of the spit. Dan sighted along the launcher. The missile had to go into the fuel tanks which would be fitted just forward of the engines. He must give enough lead for the boat's speed. All these thoughts raced through Dan Grant's head as he brushed the sweat out of his eyes. Closer and closer loomed the MTB and now he could see the crew and all the weapons, which they were carrying. He held the blade of the sight on a point level with the bridge and just above the waterline. Now; he pulled the trigger and the flash of the spotting round only preceded by a split-second the satisfying woosh as the initiator motor carried the missile clear of the tube and the firer before the main rocket propellant fired and accelerated it to Mach 2. Dan immediately picked up the second launcher. The first missile struck true, but too far aft and exploded in the engine room. Both engines stopped and a fusillade of bullets thudded into the palms and shredded the leaves around Dan Grant. The MTB started to slew to port and headed towards the spit, rapidly losing way. He pulled the trigger and the ignition of the rocket motor and the enormous explosion, which followed split-seconds behind, were almost inseparable. Dan Grant was lifted bodily and hurled some fifteen feet back to the other side of the spit, where he landed face down in the sand next to the yacht's tender. Half a dozen or more of the palms and the vegetation around them were on fire. With the exception of a few indistinguishable items floating in the sea, there was not a trace of the converted MTB. Dan got slowly to his feet, and spitting sand from his mouth, retrieved the M16 from his fire position. His attention was drawn back to the yacht by a cheer, which came from six figures dancing up and down by the wheelhouse. He waved wearily and dragged the tender to the water and launched it. Again the outboard started immediately and Dan steered the boat towards the five women swimming back to the bo

'Oh well,' Dan said to no one in particular, 'let's hope we've as much success in dealing with the typhoon.' Once everyone was back on board, Dan Grant gave the weapons to the boat boys and directed that they should be cleaned and stowed quickly. The tender was lashed on board once again and then Dan broke out the brandy and toasted everyone.

'Well done all of you; having survived a human onslaught, let's see how we cope with the worst that nature can throw at us. Here's to all of us and American Pie!'

Pamela raced across Mindanao, destroying almost everything in its path. Uprooted palm trunks flying through the air removed both main and mizzenmast on the yacht and snapped the third anchor warp, but the crew and the charter passengers survived. They were battered and bruised and very frightened, but alive, and although the tangled mess of masts and rigging on the decks looked chaotic, neither the hull nor engines were damaged. In her well-sheltered lagoon, American Pie had survived the onslaught of the worst typhoon in the Western Pacific in living memory. As Pamela swept out to sea again, regenerating some of the energy dissipated over the land, little was left standing in its wake. There were two hundred people dead and thousands of injured and homeless on Mindanao, but life in Hong Kong still carried on as normal.

*

Middle Kingdom was 280 feet in length, with a hull and superstructure of the highest quality aluminium and designed and built in the renowned Baglietto Yard in Italy. She had twelve staterooms in addition to the owner's state suite which occupied the full 45 feet of the ship's beam and included two bathrooms. It had accommodation for a crew of fifteen in conditions that would be considered luxurious for an owner on smaller yachts. She was powered by four MTU, twelve cylinder, turbo-charged diesels, which developed a shade over 10,000 hp. The latter were connected to four Kamewa water-propulsion jets, giving her a top speed of nearly 40 knots. This yacht possessed its own gym, operating theatre, jacuzzis in every en-suite bathroom, satellite communications, two helicopters and four fast motor tenders. At the stern was a large hydraulically-operated platform which formed the yacht's own sea-level swimming pool wherever she anchored and an ideal water ski platform. Each motor boat deposited its passengers for the reception onto this platform, which then raised them up to the deck. There were six stewards waiting with silver salvers carrying crystal glasses filled with champagne and plates of chilled caviar in napkin-wrapped earthenware jars.

Two boats reached the platform just before the Euro-Pacific motorboat eased alongside. As soon as the Wyngardes and John Gunn had disembarked, the platform rose up towards the deck.

'Not bad for a weekend runabout, John,' Peter Wyngarde remarked as the platform drew level with the deck. 'Come on. I'll introduce you and then I'll leave the two of you to look after yourselves. I'm told there's a disco, a night club or you can use the swimming pool if you're not too fussed about what you wear.'

Yung Shue Wan and his daughter Mandy were receiving their guests as they stepped off the platform onto the deck. There had been a Mrs Yung Shue Wan, but she had certainly not been seen in public for some eleven or twelve years. She had held onto the traditional Chinese way of life and YS - as Yung Shue Wan was known worldwide - had discarded her as he pursued his climb among Hong Kong and the Western World's pseudo-social elite. YS had been born in Harbin, the capital of Heilongjiang Province, in the north of China. Like many of the men from this part of China he was unusually tall for an Asian and his slightly hooked nose and high cheekbones were typical of the people from the Manchurian Plain, which had been under Russian influence until the end of the Second World War. When he was still only an infant his family had moved south to Beijing where his father, who had been a foreman at a steel foundry, had hoped to earn a higher wage. YS' father had held strong nationalist views, which he had not concealed and which led to the destruction of the family in 1937 when Mao's revolution swept through China. His father had been garrotted, his mother had been raped and then bayoneted to death while still pregnant and his two elder sisters had been raped and murdered, even though they were only eleven and thirteen years old. YS was at his grandmother's house and escaped with her, as a terrified eight year old, to Taiwan and from there to Hong Kong. The horror of the persecution of his family and the determination to seek revenge had been the driving force behind YS' acquisition of enormous wealth. How this wealth was acquired was a matter of speculation in Hong Kong and the world money markets, but it was certain that drugs, gambling casinos in Macao,

71

prostitution and Triad protection rackets in Hong Kong and Middle East arms deals had all played a part. There was, of course, no proof. Now that YS had devoted himself to the acquisition of respectability by handing out enormous sums of money to charity, it was considered to be only a matter of time before his Knighthood was announced in the New Year or Queen's Birthday Honours list.

That had been the prediction prior to the signing of the Anglo/Sino Joint Declaration in 1984. The UK not only agreed to honour the Treaty of 1898 by handing back the New Territories to China on 1 July 1997, but decided to give away both Kowloon and Hong Kong and a number of associated islands, as well. YS' feeling of betrayal by the UK Government was shared by many of the expatriate, British community in Hong Kong, particularly those who were descended from the first commercial settlements in the territory.

This feeling of betrayal was made worse by the refusal of the UK Government to let the Hong Kong Chinese have British passports and then on 4th June 1989, the encouraging signs of the birth of democracy in China were snuffed out by the massacre of demonstrators in Tianenmen Square. What had been a steady exodus of educated, middle-management business men from Hong Kong, as the clock ticked towards 1997, turned into a flood of tens of thousands a year. YS' hatred of the Communist Chinese was almost equalled by his dislike of the British. Now that the handover date of the Territory to China was only a matter of days away, the Briish Garrison had been reduced to little more than a a token force capable of handling the ceremonial aspects of the handover.

'Ah, Peter and Josie,' YS greeted the chairman and his wife effusively, 'how nice of you to come, and bring your beautiful daughter,' he added, noticing, as had many other men, the arrival of Candy. Gunn's unexpected presence as Candy's escort momentarily ruffled YS. 'Ah, I see your daughter has brought her own knight in armour to protect her from the inscrutable Chinese.'

'Yes, that's right YS,' replied Peter Wyngarde, with just a slight edge of frostiness in his voice, 'you will no doubt remember that I discussed that with you at the party at Government House last week.'

'Indeed you did,' YS acknowledged, 'but I had no idea that we would be honoured by the presence of one of Her Majesty's Army officers as Candy's escort.'

'High time you improved your information services YS,' Peter Wyngarde smiled innocently, 'John Gunn left the Army nearly two months ago and is now my Assistant Projects Manager. Come on my dear,' as he turned to Josie, 'mustn't cause a traffic jam at the reception line.' At that moment, there was no one waiting behind them and so the barb in the comment struck its target as Peter and Josie moved to join the cocktail party hubbub of the self-styled glitterati of Hong Kong society.

What Peter and Josie missed, but Gunn saw, was the look of anger that twisted YS' face as he turned to whisper something to his daughter, who gave a very slight shake of her head and quietly slipped away towards where the reception was taking place. Gunn and Candy had both collected a glass of champagne and now moved over to speak to their host who had once again recovered his composure. 'Do enjoy yourselves,' he encouraged them, 'we hope the younger guests will make use of the disco. I've just asked Mandy to go and check that it's all ready to go,' and he smiled and turned to his next couple of guests.

'Come on John;' Candy grabbed him by the hand, 'let me introduce you to some of the people here.' When they were out of hearing of YS she added, 'Christ, that slimy toad gives me the creeps. I sometimes wonder why my father accepts these invitations, except, of course, that it's so important in his line of business to be in with this crowd, otherwise the contracts and all the graft and back-handers that accompany them will go to the most unscrupulous tenderer.'

'Yes, I can see that, Candy. Nothing much changes in Hong Kong except its steel and concrete facade. I shall have to get used to all of this if I'm going to work out here,' Gunn added as they made their way amongst the guests. He recognised a reasonable proportion of the guests; they squeezed past Daphne Tang, a loquacious and outspoken member of the Legislative Council and reputed by cocktail party gossip to have carved so many notches of past conquests onto her bedstead, that it was a miracle that it was still standing. Chatting to her was Sir Peter Butler, the Chief Secretary of the Hong Kong Government, whose young, vivacious and much-gossiped-about wife was currently in a secluded corner of the beautifully decorated saloon, in deep conversation with the newly appointed Head of the Independent Commission Against Corruption, James Taylor. He was bright, good-looking, ambitious and tipped for high office, even if that was to be achieved via a shared bed with the Chief Secretary's wife. YS had now given up his position on the aft deck receiving his guests and was dancing attendance on the 28th and last Governor of Hong Kong, whilst his daughter Mandy had reappeared and was introducing the Governor's wife to selected guests. Everybody who was anybody was at the party that night and Gunn estimated that there had to be between two and three hundred guests. In mess kit, were the last remaining officers of the British Military hierarchy. He recognised the Commander of the British Forces, Major General

73

Patrick Rogers who had spent most of his life with the Gurkhas and most of that had been spent in Hong Kong and the Captain-in-Charge, who was the senior naval officer in Hong Kong. Gunn did not know the man, but had no doubt that he would be introduced before too long. Removing a drink from a waiter's tray was the Chief Justice who was in earnest conversation with the Chairman of the Hong Kong and Shanghai Bank and the Chief Executive of the Royal Hong Kong Jockey Club, a retired British General. There were senior policemen, headed by the Commissioner, Sir Peter Aldridge. Talking to him was the Chief Fire Officer, Hamish Walker, who was reputed to drink so much of the lubricant with which he shared his name that he was a liability at the scene of any fire. It was supposed to be unsafe to come anywhere near his breath with a naked flame - or so went the jokes on the cocktail party circuit. The rest of the guests were made up of both Chinese and expatriate millionaires, film and TV personalities, fashion designers, a visiting Swedish pop group and a small collection of British military officers from all three Services. On the periphery of this 'social elite' of Hong Kong society were the press, media and the usual acolytes who thrived on the gossip columns and being close to the rich and famous.

Gunn picked up snippets of conversation as Candy guided him through the guests. Peter Wyngarde had been right about the air-conditioning; it was beautifully cool despite more than 200 bodies radiating a kilowatt of heat each.

'. . . you can't be serious? Surely not? Dennis is working for the Hong Kong Government? I don't believe you. Dennis is a really switched-on guy who knows exactly what's what. Why does it surprise me to hear that he works for the Government? Well I have to admit that I had always thought that the Hong Kong Government was full of retired, passed-over army officers, failed UK civil servants or the drop-outs from red brick universities. That's all a thing of the past you say? You work for the Government as well! Oh dear, I'm so sorry, I . . . Hello Candy,' and then in a loud stage whisper, 'please rescue me darling, I've just made the most awful bish, but who's this gorgeous creature with you, whom I haven't met yet.'

'Johnny, this is Cynthia Styles who writes for the newspaper gossip columns. Cynthia, this is John Gunn; he's just left the Army and is now working for my father's company.'

'What a frightfully macho name for such a hunk of a male,' cooed the ghastly, flat-chested social parasite.

'Sorry, Cynthia; company orders, I've got to introduce John to Robin Henshaw, our MD. See you later perhaps, bye,' and Candy whisked John away from Cynthia's clutches.

74

'John,' Candy said, pulling him forward by the sleeve of his dinner jacket, 'this is Robin Henshaw, whom you won't have met before. Robin is the managing director of Euro-Pacific; Daddy head-hunted him off the Japanese construction company, Mitsui Taka.'

'How do you do, Sir,' John said, shaking Henshaw's hand which was just like picking up a piece of cold, wet cod off a fishmonger's marble slab and, involuntarily, he let go of it immediately.

'How do you do, you won't have met my wife Martha,' Henshaw offered, moving his galleon-like bulk to one side, to reveal a thin and uninspiring looking woman who peered rather myopically at John from behind an ornate pair of Yves St Laurent glasses.

'Nice to meet you,' volunteered Gunn, but as no hand was offered nor any other effort made to acknowledge the introduction, he realised that this was going to be hard work. Meanwhile, Candy had been quickly surrounded by a group of admirers and was thoroughly enjoying being the centre of attention.

'Are your children out here with you,' Gunn started, thinking that he was on fairly safe ground.

'No,' was the abrupt reply, 'we don't have any children. Perhaps you'd excuse me as I really must find the ladies' room.'

'Heads,' John couldn't resist the correction.

'What on earth do you mean?'

'Ladies and gentlemen's rooms are called heads on a boat, Mrs Henshaw.'

'Well, really!' and she vanished in a direction where, no doubt, she hoped to find her ladies' room.

'Thank God for that,' muttered Gunn as he realised that Robin Henshaw had disappeared in hot pursuit of a plate of canapés. Gunn helped himself to a delicious seafood canapé as it came past him.

'John Gunn isn't it?' a voice queried from behind him. Gunn turned with his mouth full of crabmeat and caviar. He held up his hand in an apology, indicating his rather over-full mouth, but it also gave him time to study the man whom he now faced. He was nearly the same height as Gunn and the overall impression was that of an archetypal English aristocrat. He had grey, slightly receding hair, good bone structure and a long, straight nose; the sort of man that one might instinctively trust on first acquaintance and what a mistake that would have been. 'Geoffrey Winchcombe,' he volunteered. 'I'm an assistant commissioner with the police,' and then he added, 'I'm the Head of Special Branch.' Before Gunn had a chance to say anything, he added, 'my boys tell me that you had a spot of trouble down town last night. Nasty business; must've been a great shock to Peter Causland and his wife. One or two slightly odd aspects to the case -

75

the automatic for instance - now what was a girl like Sadie doing with an automatic and where did it go?' and he finished with a mild inflection of his voice.

'Geoffrey?' and the slight tilt of the head confirmed the name to Gunn's inquiry, 'I've been in Hong Kong exactly 24 hours of which eight have been spent in bed and another three of those at your police station telling them all I could about Sadie's death, which was precious little, as I don't have the faintest idea what it's all about. Now, I'm off duty tonight; I've no idea in what capacity you're attending this reception, but if you want to know about the incident last night, everything that I know is in that statement. If you'll excuse me now, I'm rather neglecting the lady I brought tonight.'

'Yes, of course; you certainly haven't wasted much time in finding another lady to escort.' Gunn displayed no reaction to this attempt to make him lose his composure or throw him off balance.

'Good evening, Assistant Commissioner,' and John turned his back and made his way towards Candy.

'I wonder,' the Assistant Commissioner said to himself as he sipped at his mineral water, 'just how much, if at all, Mr Gunn, you were involved in all the incidents that occurred last night. Your arrival in Hong Kong and the immediate death of three people and a further three, missing, presumed dead, could just be a coincidence, but I think not. No Mr Gunn, I don't think that you're the innocent ex-army officer that you purport to be. A phone call to London is called for,' and after that self-deliberation, Geoffrey Winchcombe made his way to the reception area where he could use his mobile without being overheard.

John Gunn's path to Candy was suddenly blocked by the appearance of YS' daughter, Mandy. 'Hello John, I wonder if you'd be my escort to the disco?'

'Well, I was trying to do my duty to Candy, but I rather think that she's doing very well without me. Yes, of course, Mandy, I'd like that and thanks for asking me.' Gunn couldn't fail to admire the 'Suzy Wong' style of long, gleaming black hair, high split cheongsam and pale golden skin.

As they moved through the guests towards the forward saloon, Mandy encouraged someone here, a couple there and a group of young officers surrounding three girls from a Swedish girl band and so on. By the time they reached the disco they were followed by twenty or thirty of the younger guests at the reception. The music was loud, but the saloon was well air-conditioned and seemed to be totally sound-proofed, as none of the noise could be heard through the double set of doors leading into the disco. The disco was quickly filling up and the coloured lighting reflected off the white dinner jackets set the ideal scene as the dancers swayed and gyrated round the dance floor.

'Can I get you a drink Mandy?'

'Please John, a whisky and soda; lots of ice and soda.' He eased his way through the crowded room to the bar and ordered Mandy's drink and a beer for himself. When he got back to their table, Mandy was already on the dance floor. He took a drink from his glass and then, unnoticed, left the disco. The main saloon was still packed with guests and the younger exodus to the disco seemed to have barely dented the number of people thronging the saloon and the deck outside, where the lights of the Hong Kong waterfront formed a colourful backdrop to the party. John removed a pen from his inside pocket and took off the cap. The pen was a neat, miniaturised Geiger-counter, which he'd been given at Kingsroad House. It looked exactly like an ordinary fountain pen, but once the body was unscrewed, it revealed a little digital display; twist the nib through ninety degrees and the counter became active. He did this and held the nib over his watch. The counter immediately registered the minute amount of radiation given off by the luminous paint. He closed the pen and returned it to his pocket. The party had been going for about forty minutes and was due to go on until the small hours of the morning, but many of the senior guests would leave long before then.

Gunn left the main saloon and went forward, using the port side of the yacht, which was less populated than the starboard one as it faced away from the lights of Hong Kong. Even at this early stage of the evening, there were one or two couples locked in passionate embraces in various dark corners of the boat deck. As he sauntered along the deck, he noticed that one couple had wasted no time at all as the woman's dress was hitched up round her waist and there were unmistakable noises of an approaching climax to the situation. No one, and certainly not that couple, paid any interest to John as he reached the companionway leading down to the lower decks.

The companionway was either a fire escape or stewards' access to the various decks. At the foot of the first flight of stairs, John opened two glass-panelled doors into a softly-lit corridor which extended across the full beam of the yacht and was bisected midway by a wider corridor running fore and aft. The decor was lavish and Gunn presumed that this was the guest stateroom deck. He let the doors close quietly behind him and then descended to the next deck. The colour scheme on this deck was the palest of green, and a quick check revealed a surgery, operating theatre and four private rooms for patients. Not a sign of anyone; in the other direction was a small

77

gymnasium and workout room with every possible contraption for pulling, stretching, distorting and generally torturing the muscles of the human body. Again, he closed the doors silently, and started to descend to the next deck and then stopped. There was the sound of two people talking at the foot of the companionway, but out of Gunn's sight. He went down two more steps and could now hear what was being said; the dialect was Cantonese. One voice was telling the other that he had been sent down to get more stewards up to the saloon. The other voice argued that he'd been told to stay at the foot of these stairs to make sure that none of the guests, or any unauthorised person, went down to the deck below. The steward who had come down from the saloon seemed to be senior to the one guarding the companionway, won his argument and the next moment John saw them come into view as they headed towards the foot of the stairs on which he was standing. He went quickly up the steps and through the swing doors, steadying them after he'd gone through to prevent any residual movement, which might attract the stewards' attention. They came past, still arguing, and went on up the companionway. Gunn went down the stairs again; on the next deck the decor changed radically; it was now all painted metal, conduits carrying electrical cable, fire points, coloured pipes carrying salt water, fresh water and steam in various directions and instead of a swing door there was a watertight metal one.

Gunn eased the locking levers down slowly and the door opened; one glance was enough to reveal that this was the galley, stores and crew area of the yacht. He closed the door and went down again. The shape of the hull on this deck indicated that he was either on, or very close to, the lowest deck. Subdued machinery noises came from behind the watertight door. Again he eased it open, whereupon the noise increased a hundred-fold. The door led onto a metal catwalk; down below him were the four huge twelve cylinder diesels and aft of them the compressors for the water jets. These monsters were silent; the noise was coming from auxiliary generators providing the yacht's power. There appeared to be two duty engineers in spotless white overalls, fluorescent yellow safety helmets and ear-protectors. These two men were engrossed in their task of doing their checks; both of them had checklists, clipped to a board, which they carried around with them. Gunn turned to his left and went along the catwalk. Running the full length of the engine room was a robust gantry crane, which presumably had the lift capacity to remove an entire engine, 'but what happens to it then?' John thought, as he moved cautiously forward. The answer was at the for'ard engine room bulkhead; there was a clear space with rails set into the floor on which was a dolly to move heavy pieces of machinery forward, through two large steel doors, into a lift. Gunn presumed that this lift would also service the galley and stores facility, where, no doubt, there was a side hull aperture, through which items could be both loaded and unloaded. As he reached the bulkhead, he removed the Geiger counter. There was a minimal reading of ambient radiation, which barely registered on the counter. He unscrewed the body of the pen and switched on the counter. He turned the nib through another ninety degrees, which activated a small, audible alarm and then stuck the counter in the outside, breast pocket of his dinner jacket.

In front of him was an open, watertight steel door. Very slowly, he moved round the door. This was the engine control room and all the walls were completely filled with dials, switches, levers and what looked like the engine and steering control panel, in front of which was standing another duty engineer. There was a corresponding bulkhead door on the starboard side of the compartment and another door leading for'ard in the middle of the engine control room. Gunn wasn't prepared to push his luck too far by trying to get through the next door without alerting the duty engineer, so he quietly went back onto the catwalk. There was certainly not a sign of anything unusual. The whole area was state of the art marine machinery and being maintained in perfect condition. He went back along the catwalk, past the door through which he had entered the engine room. At the aft end of the catwalk was another closed door. It seemed as though this visit had been a complete waste of time. He retraced his steps towards the door. The traveller on the 'I' beam of the gantry crane, with its hook, block and reduction pulleys, was lashed to a tie down point just to the right of the catwalk. John had had to turn sideways to avoid the large, grease covered hook coming the other way and now had to repeat the manoeuvre on the return trip. As he turned sideways, he became aware of another noise, in addition to the constant din of the auxiliary generators. He stopped to try and identify it; it was on a much higher octave and he couldn't recall hearing it when he had been at the for'ard end of the compartment. It was at this moment that he saw one of the duty engineers, down below him, walking towards some metal steps giving access onto the catwalk where he was standing. 'What the hell was that noise?' He looked down to watch the progress of the engineer; as he did so he saw the tip of the Geiger counter sticking out of his top pocket. He removed it and glanced at the LCD readout. 'No wonder the little bugger was squealing,' he muttered. The reading showed a count of 80 to 85 roentgens which was well above any safety limit. The man had now reached the foot of the steps. Gunn twisted the nib back to shut off the alarm. 'Where the hell was the source of this radiation?' he wondered as he leant forward to see how much longer he had before being spotted by the engineer. As he leant forward, the reading on the counter raced up to 120. Right in front of him was the hook for the gantry crane, which he had been using to conceal his presence. He held the little counter out towards the hook; the reading went up to 160. On the outside of the hook was what looked like a smear of dull aluminium paint, but when he looked at it closely, it appeared to be more like lead. His counter was now at maximum reading and the engineer was climbing the vertical steps up to the catwalk. He pushed the pen into his pocket, went out through the steel door and closed the levers. Above him he could hear the voices of two people who were descending the companionway. He looked round; there was nowhere to hide and then he noticed that the top lever on the watertight door was moving towards the open position.

CHAPTER 7

Like the engine room, YS' conference room, which adjoined his personal suite of rooms in the yacht, was fitted with state of the art equipment to keep him constantly in touch with his worldwide business empire. There were computer terminals, telephones linked to the satellite network, every audio and visual gadget to facilitate any conference presentation and the entire room was sealed in a metal 'cage' which prevented any form of external electronic eavesdropping or the inadvertent emission of any electronic signals from within the room. At the entrance to the conference room, which was through two sets of doors, both protected by electronic combination locks, was a piece of equipment, similar in outward appearance to that at airport security checks, but which checked every person entering the room for electronic bugs, explosives and weapons. Both sets of doors at the entrance were constructed of armoured one-way glass; every arrival for a meeting could be studied at leisure, but the latter could see nothing of the interior of the room.

Most of the room was taken up by a large, glass, oval table around which were six stainless steel and black leather upholstered chairs. In the centre of one of the long sides of the oval table was YS' place. His chair was only slightly different from the others, but in front of him, set into the table, were both a TV monitor screen and a computer VDU with keyboard. There was also an array of buttons, switches and joysticks for controlling all the gadgetry, which would not have been out of place on the flight deck of an aircraft. In the middle of the table was the small, red, blue and white Chinese Nationalist flag on a marble stand. Five men sat at the conference table; three in white dinner jackets, one in the mess kit of the Royal Hong Kong Police and one in the 'mess undress' of the Royal Navy. YS' chair and one other were empty.

At the door leading into YS' suite of rooms was a member of the yacht's crew, armed with an Uzi machine pistol. YS paused as he reached the door and spoke with the guard. He was informed that all those requested to attend the meeting had arrived. YS nodded and went through the private drawing room and dining room to the conference room. As he appeared, the guard at the conference room pressed a switch, which released the combination locks on the doors.

YS entered the room and took his place. It was now nearly eight thirty and all YS' senior guests, who numbered some twenty or so couples, had departed. Their departure made no difference to the party on the yacht. On the sun deck, around the swimming pool, was a night club and all the tables were full. The disco was packed and even the original reception area in the aft saloon was still moderately full. No one would have noticed the absence of YS and five of the guests who were seated around the conference table.

YS looked at the five men seated on the other side of the oval table. On his extreme left was Sir Peter Butler, the Government's Chief Secretary, next to him was the Head of the RHKP Special Branch, Geoffrey Winchcombe and on his left, sagging over both sides of his chair, was Robin Henshaw, the MD of Euro-Pacific Construction. The next chair was empty. By the empty place was George Balmain, a somewhat eccentric High Court Judge of the Hong Kong Judiciary and, last of all, on YS' right, was Commander Peter Molyneux. All of them would have preferred to be anywhere but seated at that table.

The Chief Secretary had resigned from the Royal Navy as a Lt Commander twenty years previously to join the Hong Kong Government. He had lost his wife twelve years later from a rare appearance of cerebral malaria in Hong Kong, which had claimed half-a-dozen lives. Less than a year after this bereavement, he had married Susan who had been the result of an extra-marital relationship between an Australian expatriate and his Filipino maid. She had provided him with two children and then considered that her wifely duties were finished. Not only did she spend most of her time away from Hong Kong, visiting the most expensive shops in London, Paris, Rome and New York, but also succeeded in having a number of sordid love affairs which had been hushed up with great difficulty. Peter Butler was finally tipped for the appointment of Chief Secretary and it was at that point that he had been invited to a meeting with YS. At the meeting he had been shown photographs of his wife in bed with two men, one of whom was a very large West Indian. The photos he was shown depicted both men having sex with his wife in every imaginable position. He was also shown documents that proved that he had used insider information to make large sums of money on the Hong Kong Stock Exchange to finance his wife's very expensive travel and shopping habits. Little further persuasion was required to ensure his co-operation in YS' plans.

The Head of the Special Branch was an easy target for YS. He had extremely expensive tastes and was unscrupulous. No government flat was adequate for Geoffrey Winchcombe. He had a luxury apartment on the Peak. The occasional raised eyebrow questioning how he afforded it on a policeman's salary was allayed by hints of a considerable private income. This was true, but the income did not come from family sources, but from bribes and payoffs. With YS' domination of the Triad gangs, which had now been dispersed from the 'Walled City' in Kowloon, he had enough evidence to put Winchcombe behind bars for the rest of his life.

The Managing Director of Euro-Pacific had probably been the easiest of all to blackmail into submission, with the possible exception of the High Court Judge. Henshaw had indulged his gay tastes to the full when he was in Japan as the Projects Manager of Mitsui Taka Construction and his susceptibility to blackmail was known to YS long before he knew how useful it was to prove. He was currently having an affair with Graham Freeman, the present Projects Manager of Euro-Pacific, which had kept YS well supplied with incriminating evidence. Balmain, the judge, lived in a schizophrenic world of halucination and imagined grandeur, which was induced by his addiction to an assortment of drugs. Since the latter were all supplied by YS, the former's co-operation was assured. That only left the Naval Commander and the empty seat. The empty seat had an absent occupant, but it was never occupied when any of the others were present. Those present had been told that the absentee was in service with the Hong Kong Government, but would never be known to, or seen by, them in order that their full co-operation was one hundred percent guaranteed. Whatever plans each of them might have conceived in the past to disentangle himself from the irremovable sinews of YS' web of conspiracy, extortion and corruption were always negated by fear of the unknown member.

The presence of the Naval Commander was very mundane. YS needed detailed knowledge of everything happening in the harbour and access to the movements of every ship. He also needed unimpeded movement for Middle Kingdom, particularly when it was carrying a cargo like the one earlier in the year. The Naval Commander, Peter Molyneux, was a semi-alcoholic; not a bad case of addiction, but he was quite unable to moderate his intake of beer and spirits which invariably resulted in his being carried to bed to sleep it off. He had been easily targeted by YS' men and the Commander and a number of fellow officers had been followed on a 'run ashore' in Wanchai'. They had done a circuit of the usual haunts, Red Lips, Sex Unlimited, The In Spot and one or two others, where the Commander's drinks had been systematically fixed. Peter Molyneux had been carried to a taxi, conveniently positioned by YS' men, and his less inebriated companions gave the driver directions to get the poor old soak back to his quarter at Mount Austen Mansions on

Victoria Peak. Once the taxi was out of sight of the other officers, it pulled into the kerb and stopped. Molyneux was in a comatose state in the back seat. A car pulled up behind the taxi. The slumped body was transferred to the other car and driven away by the two men. When Peter Molyneux came to his senses, encouraged by the injection of a stimulant, he was sitting at the wheel of the car. The car had smashed into a lamppost and there was an old Chinese woman, who was quite dead, pinned under the front wreckage of the car. All the necessary photos were taken, the Commander was then removed and unceremoniously dumped by his quarter, where he was found by the night security man. The hard evidence of the whole faked incident assured YS of the Commander's full co-operation.

'Good evening, gentlemen, I shan't keep you long,' YS opened the meeting. 'For a year or so now, you have all assisted me in achieving my life's ambition, but I don't suppose that any of you have any idea what this was all about?' and he now indicated the Nationalist Chinese Flag in the centre of the table. No one volunteered a comment. 'Your part in the plan is finished. As you know, it's been my intention to do everything I can to bring down the Chinese Communist Party. My assistance to the students in their fight for democracy and the overthrow of the old guard, came close to success and then was crushed in a welter of pulped human flesh, bone and blood under the bullets and bulldozer blades of the Communists and the PLA soldiers. I almost despaired of being able to destroy the Communists who raped and murdered my family. Believe it or not, it was that very Chinese Communist leadership which gave me the idea for my plan and even more ironically, it was the Russians who supplied all the rest of the information I needed.'

'I shall only keep you a little longer and then we must rejoin all the guests before our short absence is remarked upon. This is the last time we'll meet as this plan comes to fruition next Monday, in exactly five days time on 30th June, the day before Hong Kong is handed over to the Peoples' Republic of China. You will all have just enough time to withdraw the large sums of money, which have been credited to your accounts and make the necessary flight arrangements to leave Hong Kong before Monday. No questions at this stage,' which was said as the Chief Secretary made to interrupt. 'Thank you; now the plan, but preceded by a little background to ensure that you all fully understand the significance of your involvement and what I am about to do.'

'Some five or six years ago, a particularly stupid General in the Chinese Peoples' Liberation Army stated that the Chinese Homeland could survive a first, or pre-emptive nuclear strike. It was his view that the combination of the landmass and well over a billion inhabitants would leave enough surplus Chinese humanity for a counter-strike. There was also the suggestion in his statement that a few million deaths caused by a handful of nuclear explosions would certainly solve the nation's population explosion.'

'On the 25 April 1986, the Russians showed me how to achieve my goal. On that day, some scientists at Chernobyl Nuclear Power Station decided to conduct an experiment using minimum low output from the reactors. There was no authority for this experiment and in order to conduct it all the automatic safety devices were disconnected. Only one reactor was used and as the experiment proceeded, large quantities of gas were produced containing ions and protons, which further fuelled the heat of the reactor and its graphite core. No cooling water could get into the system because it had been disconnected. By the time the director discovered what was happening, it was too late. The core went critical within four seconds, despite the efforts to reinsert the control rods, which took a full eighteen seconds. The number four reactor went into a melt down and released hundreds of kilograms of radioactive material into the atmosphere. One hundred and twenty people were killed immediately, thousands, a little later, died from massive overdoses of radiation and tens, if not hundreds of thousands, are predicted casualties from radiation induced diseases.'

'Please look, gentlemen,' and YS removed a remote device from a compartment in the table and turning his chair, pressed a button. A coloured map of Southern China and Hong Kong appeared on a screen measuring some fifteen by nine feet. 'This is the year's weather pattern over this area,' he explained as the screen changed and bar charts appeared of rainfall, winds and temperature. 'I can assure you that the Royal Observatory had nothing to do with the production of these charts,' but none of his audience were inclined to see the humour of this remark, so horrified had they been by the realisation of what YS was about to reveal as his plan.

'You will see that from July until the end of September, the prevailing wind is almost exclusively from the north-east. The prevailing wind in the Ukraine was from the south-east and carried the radioactive plume north-west to Scandinavia and then over the North Pole to Canada and thence to disperse worldwide. The land, which lay in the immediate shadow of this plume was made uninhabitable and will remain that way for at least 150 years. That land extended for 200 kilometres from the Chernobyl Power Station and is now a deserted wasteland, filled with horrifying mutations of nature which hardly bare thinking about if related to the human body.

I am now going to superimpose the Chernobyl plume over the Daya Bay Power Station so,' and the picture appeared on the screen.

'You can see that this will mean that a large portion of Shenzen, the whole of Hong Kong and the New Territories and Macao would be completely uninhabitable. Hainan to the south-west will probably be much the same and Vietnam, Cambodia, Laos, Thailand and, to a lesser extent, Malaysia will all get a pretty hefty dose of fallout. After that, it will spread across the Indian Ocean until it reaches that country of peace and racial harmony, South Africa.'

'On Monday, the entire Communist and PLA leadership are parading at the Daya Bay Nuclear Power Station when the fourth reactor is brought on power for the first time and the nuclear power station is officially declared open to coincide with the return of Hong Kong to Chinese sovereignty. In number four reactor the control rods have been replaced with fuel rods, of which five are of weapon grade, enriched uranium as opposed to fuel grade. All the safety mechanisms have been altered to give every indication of the correct function, but in fact will either do nothing or the exact opposite function. It will take less than five seconds for a slightly larger melt down than that of Chernobyl to commence. Within thirty seconds the entire Communist and PLA leadership will be dead and within a week, Hong Kong, the golden prize for which the Communists have waited sixty years, will be deserted, never to be inhabited again for at least 150 years. I will destroy everyone and everything in Hong Kong and make the place uninhabitable, rather than let the Chinese Communists get their hands on it.'

'The man on Ping Chau Island . . .' and the voice of the Chief Secretary faded away.

'Yes, Mr Chung Ching Kwong who baffled everyone with the level of radioactive contamination of his body which was discovered on Ping Chau earlier this year. His body should have been burned, as he requested, but the man detailed to do the task couldn't be bothered and thought the sharks would save him the trouble. I couldn't disappoint the sharks which seemed to have disliked the taste of the radioactive Mr Kwong, and so the miscreant was cut all over his body to make the blood flow and then he followed Kwong into the same stretch of water. I can assure you that not even a scrap reached the abandoned Ping Chau Island. Mr Kwong was sacked from Euro-Pacific's construction force after the discovery of shoddy workmanship and corrupt handling of contracts. Right Henshaw?' and YS raised an eyebrow in the direction of the obese lump overflowing his chair, from which came an unintelligible noise, which was a mixture between a belch and a grunt. 'Kwong had already been messing about too close to radioactive material and his life expectancy was limited to a few years at the most. It was not difficult to persuade him to do a little job for me when he saw the amount of money his family would receive and, of course, their relocation to San Francisco, which was so neatly handled by Sir Peter. After the modifications he did in the core of the fourth reactor, he was virtually a fuel rod himself and death was fairly quick. Now gentlemen, you have five days to get out of Hong Kong. I leave tomorrow for the Philippines to avoid any possible unpleasantness from this approaching typhoon. I suggest you remove yourselves with equal haste. One last reminder; if the team keeping an eye on all of you is given one hint of a suspicion that you may have let something slip, you will also go for a quick dip near Ping Chau Island.'

'I have one piece of information to add, YS, which you ought to be aware of,' volunteered the Head of Special Branch.

'Does it directly affect the successful execution of my plan?' prompted YS harshly.

'It does indeed.'

'Very well, please be brief, Assistant Commissioner.'

'At our last meeting, nearly six months ago, I submitted a report which gave the details of our success in penetrating the MI6 cell in Hong Kong. Since then, we've believed that all the intelligence going back to London has been carefully engineered by our own intelligence network.'

'And what gives you cause to believe that's not the case?'

'Bear with me a moment longer, Sir. We received a windfall when Miss Causland came over to us and led us to Mr Anderson. She told us that she had been approached by MI6, after Anderson was killed by us, with the offer of a free medical check to make sure she wasn't HIV positive, which, of course, she had to accept.'

'Yes, I'm well aware of all this,' snapped YS.

'Mr Gunn was with Goldman just before the assassination team killed him. The two men were at university together, but there was no evidence to suggest that Gunn was connected with MI6. Barely a week after that lunch where Goldman was killed, it was discovered that Gunn was booked on a flight to Hong Kong. The team in London decided that this was more than coincidence and sent a message to Miss Causland to roster herself onto the same flight. She and her family have known the Gunns for a long time and she was given the task of identifying Gunn for our surveillance and assassination teams here.'

'So what happened?'

'We're not absolutely sure.'

87

'What do you mean?'

'As you know, Sir, a team operates completely independently, only reporting to you or me when the mission is complete.'

'Geoffrey,' YS said with icy calm, 'why are you repeating rules to me which I made?'

'Bear with me a second longer, Sir. Our surveillance team had a car at the airport, which was contacted by Miss Causland on arrival, confirming that Gunn was on the flight and would be going to her flat with her. The two men in the car were found burnt to a cinder at the foot of the Bank of America Building at 1920 hours last night. Miss Causland was killed, instead of Gunn, with a crossbow bolt - the assassination team's weapon - outside a restaurant in Central, just before midnight. The three remaining members of the team have vanished, although traces of blood in Miss Causland's flat seem to indicate all of them are dead as well. Miss Causland went to the restaurant with Gunn, whom you met tonight, and presumably is still on board this yacht. She knew him and his family well for many years before Gunn joined the British Army and we can only assume that she was suspicious and passed information to the assassination team. The two of them had dinner, having met on the flight from London - incidentally they had sexual intercourse as soon as they reached her flat that evening and before they went out to dinner. She contacted the team before leaving the flat, giving our men the name of the restaurant.'

'So, Assistant Commissioner, it would seem that Miss Causland was doing exactly what she had been told to do; go on.'

'I made a phone call to London a little earlier this evening, to our contact in MI6. Gunn appears to be clean; this was then confirmed by another call I made, through which I've a direct access into the MI6 building. The only information I was able to get hold of was his failure to pass the SAS selection course which led directly to his resignation and application for a job with Euro-Pacific.'

There was a cough and splutter from Henshaw who then blurted, 'yes, I can confirm that.' There was absolute silence in the room and not one of the five men raised his eyes to meet those of YS. The Assistant Commissioner's immediate neighbours, Sir Peter Butler and Robin Henshaw did their best to distance themselves from the policeman.

'How was it that our bungling idiots killed Miss Causland instead of Gunn?'

'I've no idea, Sir, as all of them have vanished. It was Gunn who contacted the police from the restaurant and his account of the incident has been accepted by the police.'

'See that he is killed,' and YS stood up and left the room.

*

The two stewards stopped on the deck above Gunn. The second lever on the watertight door swung down and the door opened. Gunn waited behind it, as the engineer emerged, wiping his hands on a rag and then reached up to remove the ear protectors before turning to close the door. The blow caught him behind the ear and he collapsed soundlessly as Gunn eased him onto the metal flooring. He removed the man's overalls and hat and picked up the ear protectors. He struggled into the overalls, which pinched him horribly in the groin and left a clear three inches above his shoes. The hat just fitted with a squeeze, even with the tape inside slackened right off. He carried the man back into the engine room and then through the aft watertight door, which led to the steering flat. He dumped him unceremoniously on the gridded decking and then returned, closing the door behind him. The other engineer was still engrossed in his checks. Gunn went back through the door into the companionway and placed the protectors over his ears. The stewards were still chatting on the deck above. In very coarse Cantonese, Gunn made a remark about getting some fresh air, as though he were talking to his colleague in the engine room and then went up the stairs.

The stewards shouted a derogatory remark after him as he went up the stairs, which he didn't catch, so he shouted back an equally unintelligible response, which aroused no suspicions. When he got to the boat deck, he took off the overalls, hat and ear protectors and threw them into the sea. John glanced at his watch; the party had been going for two hours. He made his way back along the port deck. The number of couples in dark corners had increased, but the couple who had just reached the short strokes the last time he passed, had disappeared. He went back into the reception area, which was still a hubbub of conversation, flashing camera lights and stewards circulating with trays of drinks and canapés. He removed a glass from a tray and eased his way through the guests towards the disco. He spotted the Chief Secretary's wife who was still being closely escorted by the Head of the ICAC. James Taylor was looking slightly dishevelled and when John Gunn glanced at the rumpled state of Susan Butler's dress, the identity of the fornicating couple on the boat deck was revealed. John smiled and moved on through the chattering crowd. He saw Martha Henshaw, who was talking to a very smartly dressed and heavily made-up woman, whom he presumed was Geoffrey Winchcombe's wife as he had last seen her when accosted earlier by the policeman. Just before he left the room, Gunn glanced

89

around once again, taking in as much of the aft saloon as he could see. No sign of Butler, Winchcombe or Henshaw, but there was still the disco - most unlikely, John considered - or the night club. He looked into the disco, which was packed solid. He squeezed a passage to the bar, where he exchanged his champagne for an ice-cold beer. He saw Mandy on the dance floor and smiled in return to the cheery wave in his direction. He put his beer on the bar and slipped out of the disco again and went up the companionway to the sun deck and the night-club. At the night-club everyone was seated, as the cabaret was in full swing; the latter consisted of six, very scantily clad girls going through a particularity gymnastic and energetic dance routine, which gave the audience ample opportunity to admire every conceivable part of their anatomies. The lights were up and so John Gunn was able to see the audience clearly; no sign of the same three men. For'ard of the swimming pool was the entrance to YS' private state suite; two stewards stood by the door.

At that moment the doors swung open and YS strode out into the relative shadow, in contrast to the bright spotlights directed at the cabaret. Thirty seconds later, Geoffrey Winchcombe appeared and went down the companionway to the aft saloon.

'Interesting,' Gunn murmured to himself. The door opened again and his MD appeared in deep conversation with George Balmain. The latter, John only knew by reputation and the number of times the Supreme Court Judge had had to uphold appeals against the inappropriate sentences handed out by him. Shortly behind them came Sir Peter Butler who was followed by a naval officer, whom John had never met. 'Now what were all of you doing in there?' John muttered, as he followed them down the companionway.

In the aft saloon, YS was once again the charming host, drifting amongst his guests. The Head of Special Branch walked over to his wife; what was said was self-evident as she immediately departed for the ladies' room. Henshaw and Balmain appeared and John could easily gather from watching the group, that a collective decision to leave the party had been made. Other couples moved towards the aft platform, where mobiles were much in evidence as owners summoned their boats, which had been at anchor in Discovery Bay. Gunn saw Peter and Josie Wyngarde on the platform and walked over to join them.

'Hello John, you don't have to return with us; it's only time for the wrinklies to depart before we turn into pumpkins or something even worse,' Peter added. 'I'll get Chan to bring the boat straight back and he'll wait for you.'

'Many thanks, Sir, but that jet-lag's catching up on me now and I think I'd like to call it a night.'

'Oh, fine, we'll drop you off at the Mandarin.'

'No, please don't do that, as you'll have to go all round the one-way system; it only takes two minutes from Queen's Pier to walk.'

'John's right, darling,' Josie intervened. 'Are we leaving Candy?'

'She said she wanted to come back with us,' her father replied.

'I know where she is,' and Gunn headed towards the disco. As he entered the aft saloon, he saw Winchcombe and his wife coming towards him.

'Leaving so soon, Mr Gunn? I don't think you've met my wife Celestine. Darling, this is John Gunn, who is now working for Peter Wyngarde's Euro-Pacific.'

'How do you do,' and Gunn shook hands.

'Don't tell me that you've mislaid another of your girlfriends Mr Gunn?' came the mildly goading comment from the policeman.

'No, I don't think so Assistant Commissioner. I've been with my partner for most of the evening and wasn't offered a place at the private meeting you had with YS, the Chief Secretary, my MD, Balmain and the Naval Commander.' It had been a gamble, but even the practised composure of the Head of Special Branch cracked for a moment, particularly when the over-painted Celestine added, 'you told me that your office wanted you on the phone Geoffrey.'

'What meeting was that, Mr Gunn?' was Winchcombe's flustered and ill-considered retort.

'The meeting you had in YS' suite, from which you emerged by yourself directly behind YS and in front of Henshaw and Balmain exactly six minutes ago; that meeting, Assistant Commissioner.'

'You'll discover that it doesn't pay to be quite so inquisitive Mr Gunn,' was the policeman's rather feeble rejoinder.

'My! You do change your tune quickly, Assistant Commissioner. At the beginning of this party, you wanted me to tell you all about my movements since arriving in Hong Kong twenty-four hours ago. Perhaps you were given a new orders by your boss at the meeting. Was that it?' Just how close John Gunn's jibe was to the truth, was again evident in the expression of discomfort on Winchcombe's face.

'What on earth's this all about, Geoffrey?' demanded Celestine imperiously.

'Nothing, my dear, I'll explain later,' and he retreated with his wife out of the saloon.

'How very interesting,' Gunn said to no one in particular. 'This night has produced some surprises.' He found Candy at the entrance to the disco, where she was trying to avoid an invitation from two young army officers to return to their officers' mess at Stanley Fort.

'Ah! Johnny, there you are; I was just explaining to Gerald and . . . er . . . I'm sorry, I've forgotten your name,' she apologised to the shorter of the two officers.

'Cecil.'

'Ah yes, Cecil; John's taking me home in the company boat.'

'Right Candy, if you're ready to go, I think you'll find that the boat has just arrived. Sure I can't leave you to these two gallant young men?' he added as they made their way aft.

'You rat, Johnny; you wouldn't do something as mean as that. I've seen those two at a number of parties. They're either gay or they're sharing a brain; they certainly haven't got one decent chin between the two of them!'

They rejoined the Wyngardes on the aft platform and it sank to sea level. Immediately, gleaming white cruisers appeared out of the night, rather like huge whales coming to feed, Gunn thought, as they came alongside the platform. Chan, as usual, was in first and the junior boys held the cruiser steady with their boat hooks while the four of them clambered aboard. The night was hot and sticky and they all went up on the flying bridge. Before joining the family on the bridge, Gunn used his mobile to the number given to him by Doyle Barnes. It was answered immediately.

'All well?' asked Gunn.

'Sure, no problems; we'll speak at the hotel. I'm about a hundred metres behind you right now.'

'Many thanks; see you in about twenty minutes,' and Gunn went up onto the bridge

CHAPTER 8

Typhoon Pamela was now on a nor-nor-westerly course some eight hours after it had devastated the island of Mindanao. The destructive track across the island had starved the typhoon of evaporating seawater and the Royal Observatory in Hong Kong had downgraded it to a severe tropical storm. The moment Pamela reached the west coast, the spent energy was regenerated from the Sulu Sea between Mindanao and the island of Palawan. In less than an hour, the turmoil of destructive winds had reached its previous ferocity and was heading for Puerto Princessa on the east coast of the island of Palawan, where the inhabitants made a futile attempt to tie down everything in sight and prayed for deliverance.

*

Dan and Amy Grant stood on the stern of American Pie looking at the tangled mess of standing rigging, snapped masts and booms and a heap of radar, radio and GPS antennae, mixed with an assortment of foliage and vegetation deposited by the typhoon. The charter guests were all in the wheelhouse saloon.

'Well, that's that,' muttered Dan with a resigned sigh, 'I suppose we'd better heave all this lot over the side and then limp back to Cebu for repairs. I'm sure our guests can't wait to get back on dry land and civilisation in Japan.'

'Rubbish!' what a defeatest you are Daniel Grant,' countered Amy, 'we all - that is, we women - have just been saved from the proverbial 'fate worse than death' and have all survived the typhoon.'

'Yes honey, but. . . .'

'Quiet Dan; I haven't finished. Where was I? Oh yes; American Pie is perfectly alright, but minus her masts. We have an obligation to our guests who have paid for a three weeks' cruise. I reckon that if you stick your head into that wheelhouse and ask for volunteers, they'll all be out to help us tidy up. I can't see why we shouldn't continue the cruise as a motor boat; American Pie's got two engines and a cruising range of over 2000 miles on engines alone - at least that's what you've told me - so let's get this mess cleared up and get on with the cruise!'

Dan smiled; Amy's resilience to the 'downs' of their married life had always been stronger than his. 'Very well Ma'am,' and he

93

disappeared into the wheelhouse. He reappeared less than thirty seconds later almost being trampled over by the eight Japanese who, in the euphoria of their recent survival of both a pirate raid and a typhoon, considered this charter to be the most exciting adventure of their lives. After instructions had been given and tools and cutting equipment had been issued, all of them set to work to clear up the debris. Lunch and their fears of a couple of hours previously were completely forgotten.

Apart from one or two scratches to the paintwork, American Pie appeared to have survived the typhoon remarkably well. Both of the masts were deck-stepped in tabernacles so had done no damage to the deckhead when they had snapped at the height of the typhoon. They unbolted the broken stubs of the main and mizzenmast and threw them over the side. The top thirty feet of the main mast was then drilled and inserted into the tabernacle once the radio, GPS and radar antennae had been replaced. The stainless steel rigging was shortened with bolt cutters, spliced to the bottle screws and tightened up. Both the main and mizzen sails had been badly damaged when the masts broke, but Dan had removed the roller foresail before the typhoon had struck. The Japanese women set to work with needles, terylene thread and sailmakers' palms and produced an almost professional mainsail and a shortened roller foresail, so American Pie had the ability to sail in case of an engine breakdown. By early evening the task was complete. The two additional anchors, which Dan had put out and which had certainly saved the boat from being smashed to pieces on the beach, were brought back on board. The main anchor was weighed just as the setting sun turned the heavens into a vivid palate of crimson and copper hues.

For the last hour of the work to repair American Pie, Dan Grant had retired to the wheelhouse and his chart table to replan the cruise. He had charted a passage that would take American Pie north to the islands of Leyte and Samar and then to Catanduanes Island, or Cat Island as it was known locally, which was some ten miles off the south-east coast of Luzon. The course he had plotted ensured that there would always be land close at hand to the west of their track so that they could run for shelter should Pamela decide to double back on her north-westerly course. Under the power of her twin diesels, American Pie had a comfortable cruising speed of eleven knots which was exactly the speed she was doing as Dan Grant set course for Leyte and then handed the wheel over to his senior boat boy. Amy Grant was determined to make supper that evening a very special occasion to celebrate their survival. She was working in the galley assisted by two of the Japanese women while the other two were decorating the table in the salcon. On deck the men finished the last of the repairs. The sea was almost unnaturally calm in the wake of the typhoon and the setting sun had turned it to the hue of molten copper as American Pie headed north on the new course.

*

The prayers of the people of Puerto Princessa had been heard because fifteen miles out into the Sulu Sea, Pamela decided to jink onto a more northerly course. This took the typhoon to the north of Palawan Island into the Mindorro Strait, just south of Mindorro Island. From there it went out into the South China Sea across the North Danger Reef, an area almost as notorious as the Bermuda Triangle and the Sargasso Sea as a graveyard of ships. The typhoon was now 900 nautical miles south-east of Hong Kong and still out of range of the 700 mile radar coverage of Waglan Island off the south-east tip of the Island. The meteorological station on the east coast of Mindanao had managed to make contact with the Royal Observatory in Hong Kong by radio despite the electronic interference being caused by Pamela and had reported the new track, renewed intensity and the devastation caused by the typhoon. On the late evening news on TV, Hong Kong was warned that the Number 1 typhoon signal was likely to be raised in the next 24 hours if Pamela continued on its current course and speed of 15 knots. Not a large proportion of the population listened to the late evening news and even those who did paid no attention to the warning of the Number 1 signal, as this went up and down like a fiddler's elbow during the typhoon season. A great deal more attention was being devoted to the various ceremonies connected with the celebration of the return of the Territory to China and the planned monumental firework display as the Union Flag was lowered and the Chinese flag raised one minute after midnight on 30th June. The British Army had handed over the boder to the Hong Kong Police and was now preparing for its evacuation on the final day as was the Royal Navy with its remaining patrol craft and the Royal Air Force from its base in Sek Kong in the New Territories. There had been a daily flight of Hercules C130 transport aircraft to the airfield in Sek Kong taking materiel and stores back to the UK.

*

'Telephone call for you Mr Gunn,' announced Chan, who had just appeared on the flying bridge of Peter Wyngarde's boat.
'You seem to be in demand tonight, John,' Peter Wyngarde remarked as Gunn turned to follow Chan down to the Saloon.

95

'Gunn speaking.'

'Ah! Commander Molyneux here . . . er, we haven't met, but I saw you at YS' reception. I wondered . . . that is, my wife and I wondered, if you and Miss Wyngarde would like to come and have supper with us at Lamma tonight. You see, we've booked a table for ten and one of the couples we invited has had to drop out so I thought if we caught you while you were still on the Wyngarde boat, you might be able to use it for the evening. So sorry about the short notice, but it seemed too good an opportunity to miss to make up our numbers again.'

Gunn's immediate reaction was to refuse as he had no wish to go and have supper with the owner of the voice at the other end of the phone. The story of the couple dropping out was, of course, rubbish as it didn't matter how many times you altered the booking at a restaurant in Sok Kwu Wan on Lamma Island. Gunn had only seen one Commander at the reception; he had, in fact, seen him twice, once at the start of the reception when he was hovering around his Captain and the second time was when he emerged from the meeting with YS. So why invite him to Lamma? Even as the question went through his mind, he was fairly certain he knew the answer. Provided that there were other couples, he considered that the risk to Candy could be kept at an acceptable level. All of these thoughts had been racing through his mind as he listened to the disembodied voice on the phone.

'Thank you for the invitation, Commander; could you hold on while I go and ask Candy.'

'Yes, yes . . . of course.' John went up to the bridge and asked Candy.

'Yes, I'd like that Johnny,' and she then saved Gunn asking her father for the use of the boat by adding, 'can we have the boat for the evening, Daddy?'

'Yes of course, Candy; can you just drop your mother and me off first and then she's all yours. Perhaps you'd like to warn off Chan, John.' Gunn returned to the saloon and picked up the phone.

'Yes, that's fine, thank you; which restaurant and what time would you like us to join you there.'

'Oh good! So glad you can join us; I've booked a table at the Wan Kee and we hoped that you might join us there about 9.45. Is that OK with you? We'll be on our way from Middle Kingdom as soon as our boat returns from HMS Tamar after dropping off CAPIC.' John glanced at his watch.

'Yes fine; are you using CAPIC's barge?'

'Yes, as a matter of fact we are; why?'

'Oh, just curiosity; I've been away from Hong Kong for some time and I wondered if it still existed.'

'Yes, I knew you'd been away for . . . I mean someone mentioned it when they suggested that you might like to make up our numbers at supper tonight.'

'Oh really; who was that Commander?'

'Er . . . it was Geoffrey Winchcombe, I think.'

'Will he be there tonight?'

'On no, it's all Navy and Army tonight.'

'Worse and worse,' thought John and then out loud added, 'fine, please forgive us if we're a bit late as we've got to drop off Peter and Josie Wyngarde. We should be there just before ten.'

'That'll be fine. See you both at the Wan Kee at ten,' and the Commander rang off.

'So it would seem that my name may well have been mentioned at the meeting this evening,' John said to the empty saloon and continued, 'and the Commander is travelling in CAPIC's barge which has a maximum speed of about 15 knots, if I remember rightly.' John Gunn dialled Doyle Barnes on his mobile .

'Change of plan,' he said as the phone was answered, 'please join me as quickly as possible at Queen's Pier and I'll brief you.'

'On my way,' was the reply and the phone went dead.

Gunn went forward to where Chan was steering the large motor cruiser and spoke to him in Cantonese, explaining the change of plan for the evening. He then asked Chan what the boat's maximum speed was as he picked up a pair of dividers and swung them over the course from Queen's Pier to the pier in Sok Kwu Wan on the south side of Picnic Bay, which lay in the centre of Lamma Island. He did the same with the course from Discovery Bay to Picnic Bay. Gunn thanked Chan and made his way slowly back to the bridge. Both distances were identical - give or take a cable or two - at eleven nautical miles. It would take CAPIC's barge about an hour at cruising speed and forty-five minutes at maximum speed to get to Picnic Bay from Middle Kingdom. The Captain had left the reception at about eight, so his barge should be arriving back at Middle Kingdom any minute now. Chan would have their boat alongside the pier in about another five minutes, John reckoned, as he glanced out of the large expanse of toughened glass in the saloon scuttles. Provided that Doyle was punctual, it would be just possible to get to Picnic Bay before the Commander's party and to see if any 'special arrangements' had been made by YS. By the time he had reached the flying bridge, Gunn had the makings of a plan for their evening at Picnic Bay.

Chan brought the boat through a throng of others returning from the reception and put it neatly against the steps leading up the side of the pier. Candy had said that she would remain on board when Gunn had told her that he would see her parents safely to their car.

He helped Peter and Josie off the boat and then followed them up the steps to the car, which was waiting for them. Just as the car pulled away towards HMS Tamar – the now almost deserted headquarters of the British Forces - there was a whistle from the deep shadow of the covered arcade in front of him. A figure moved forward out of the shadow and Gunn checked the movement of his hand to the gun, holstered in the small of his back, as he recognised Doyle.

He quickly recounted what had happened on Middle Kingdom and the invitation from Commander Molyneux. 'Doyle, I'll be at the Wan Kee Restaurant and on my mobile. Henshaw and Balmain are together and are using Euro-Pacific's other boat; they can't be more than five minutes behind us. Henshaw lives at Shek O and there's just a chance that both of them may go there together which may give you a chance for a bit of eavesdropping.'

'You're quite sure you don't need me to cover your back for this party on Lamma Island,' Doyle queried.

'Nothing I'd like better, but I don't think we can afford to miss the chance of trying to find out what's going on, from what appears to be the three weakest links in whatever YS' scheme is. I'll see if I can get anything out of Molyneux while you have a go at the other two.'

'OK, if that's what you want, but shout for help if you need it. I'll get my boat to go round to Aberdeen so that I can make a quick dash across the East Lamma Channel if you call for help. Watch your back John,' and Doyle vanished once more into the shadows of the arcade.

Gunn hurried back to the pier just in time to see the Henshaws and Balmain leave their boat. He sat on the harbour wall where his prominent height was concealed by the Chinese who were watching all the activity caused by the boats returning from the first part of YS' reception. Henshaw's BMW pulled forward as the three of them reached the top of the steps. Neither of the men saw Gunn nor noticed another BMW which pulled out into Harcourt Road behind them.

John waved to Chan who had had to move away from the pier steps to allow other boats to disembark their passengers. Diesel smoke instantly appeared at the stern of the powerful motorboat as she eased through all the filth and flotsam on the water surface to the steps. As soon as the fenders touched, John jumped aboard and Chan swung the cruiser out into the harbour. 'Well done Chan,' John greeted him as he came into the wheelhouse.

'Drink Johnny?' Candy offered who was standing by the bar in the saloon.

'Yes thanks, I'd love a cold San Mig, Candy.

'Right Chan, as soon as we're clear of all these boats, take her up to twenty knots and at Green Island increase to thirty knots as you turn south for Lamma Island. OK?' The senior boatman's grin was answer enough as he pushed both the throttles together and then switched the radar down from a five mile to a one mile scan.

'Hey! what's the hurry Johnny? I've just spilt your beer,' came from Candy in the saloon as the big cruiser dug its stern into the water and threw a sheet of spray away on either side of the bow as the deep 'V' hull sliced into the sea.

'Sorry about that Candy, but our hosts for supper tonight are well ahead of us and I was taught that it was impolite to be more than ten minutes late.'

'Liar, you're up to something; incidentally, what did you get up to while we were all in the disco tonight? I saw you sneak out.'

'I wanted to get my bearings, Candy. I've been away so long I feel I hardly know anyone and if I'm to be of any use to your father's company I must know who wields the clout in the business and financial circles here.'

'And did you?'

'Did I what?' answered Gunn, as he watched Chan weaving expertly past one of the Star Ferries plying between the Island and Kowloon.

'Find out who wields the clout, as you put it. No Johnny, you're up to more than just joining Daddy's company, but I won't ask again. Please take care if it's dangerous or risky.'

'Candy, I'm involved in a very minor way in a UK Government investigation into what is thought to be some fairly irregular business deals. I think that this man, Commander Molyneux, might have something to do with it . . . er, on the periphery, as it were. That's why I was prepared to accept the invitation tonight as long as you wanted to go. It could be that I may ask you to do something that might seem a bit odd or I might say something equally odd this evening, so will you just go along with me please?'

'I thought so, John Gunn; yes of course I'll go along with whatever you say or do, but the only periphery that Peter Molyneux has ever been involved with is the one round the neck of a bottle. He really is an alcoholic; no, if Peter's involved then you can bet that he is very small fry and, I should imagine, totally expendable,' Candy added as an afterthought.

'I'm sure you're right, but I think for all those reasons you've just given, he might be one of the weakest links in whatever is going on, so perhaps it's a good place to start.'

'Yes, you could well be right. Now you realise that there's a speed limit within the harbour and dear old Chan is exceeding it by quite some margin, which means that if he's stopped by the Marine Police he's likely to lose his licence. Apart from making my father very annoyed, the delay caused by a confrontation with the police might well upset your plans for tonight.'

'Thanks for the reminder, Candy; yes I did know that there was a limit, but I've got to take that gamble if we're to get to Picnic Bay before Molyneux.'

'Why's that so important?'

'Guesswork really; I think that this invitation was set up at a meeting while we were on Middle Kingdom. If there is some form of reception being planned for me - not you, I hasten to add - then it would be very useful to have a preview of what's going on. I've told Molyneux that we won't be at the restaurant until ten, which he will have passed on. I could be totally wrong, of course!' The boat heeled hard over as Chan avoided a small sampan with no navigation lights which was left bouncing around alarmingly in their wake. Gunn could see Green Island in the glow of the lights from Kennedy Town and the high rise flats on Mount Davis. He pointed out the course to Chan, south of Green Island through the Sulphur Channel. 'In just under a mile we should be clear of the harbour limit,' John said to no one in particular as he studied the radar display for any signs of an approaching or pursuing boat. Gunn had kept Chan on a course close inshore where the motorboat would not only be masked by the myriads of on-shore lights, but it would have taken a very attentive officer on a police launch to identify them amidst all the shore 'clutter' on a radar screen. The powerful motorboat heeled slightly to port as Chan brought her onto a southerly course and then the bow lifted further as he pushed the throttles forward. The turbo-charged diesels now made a deep-throated roar as the boat leapt across the small waves, scattering the phosphorescence like a million, minute precious stones. Gunn spoke again in Cantonese to Chan and told him to hug the coast all the way to the light off Ap Lei Chau Island, going inshore of the dangerous and minute Magazine Island, before swinging to starboard on a course for Picnic Bay. By doing so, it would look as though they were approaching Lamma from Aberdeen Harbour and could mix with the majority of water traffic, which came from that direction. Fortunately for Gunn, it was a busy night for shipping and there was a constant procession of large container, cargo and tanker ships heading north and south in the East Lamma Channel. Twice now, he had been out onto the stern of the boat to see if he could identify the lights of CAPIC's barge. Even the first time he had checked as they swung south after Green Island, when he had calculated that the two boats would be closest, it was impossible to identify specific lights. The area of sea round Green Island was the confluence of the two major shipping routes into Hong Kong Harbour, which turned round more than a hundred ships every twenty-four hours. It was the intensity of this traffic on which John Gunn had relied to mask the speeding Euro-Pacific boat from CAPIC's barge.

Gunn glanced at his watch as they came level with island on which the power station had been built; 9.25. The power station had long gone. He tapped Chan on the shoulder and immediately the boat swung to starboard as he pointed the bows at Picnic Bay. The old power station had been built with five chimneys. One of the chimneys was completely false, but the Chinese in Aberdeen had insisted on it being built because of the superstition connected with the figure four, which in Cantonese had the same tonal sound as 'death'.

When the sun moved round to the west, the chimneys cast their shadows across the town and so the fifth chimney had had to be built. Gunn smiled as he recalled this example of the intensity of Chinese superstition - 'Fung Shui' - but turned back quickly to watch their progress as they were now crossing the main shipping channel at close to forty miles an hour. Without the slightest adjustment in speed, Chan timed his course perfectly. The boat went past the stern of a 20,000 ton container ship with some 50 metres to spare and in front of an oil tanker in ballast leaving a gap of about 100 metres, but which still drew a series of strident blasts from the irate pilot. Then they were into Picnic Bay, following the lights marking the deepwater channel for the tugs and barges, which came in to collect their cargo from the cement works on the north shore of the bay.

In the sea, just off the south shore, were all the fish farms in the middle of which was the village of So Kwu Wan with its ferry pier sticking some fifty metres out into the bay. The ferry from the 'Outlying Districts' pier in Central District called at two hourly intervals and was now about a cable ahead of the motorboat. At a word from Gunn, the throttles were eased right back, the boat settled into the water and the roar of the diesels changed to a muted rumble.

'All lights out please, Candy,' John said and then in Cantonese to Chan, 'no, leave the navigation lights on please.' Again he looked at the luminous dial of his watch; it was 9.36. The ferry was only fifty metres in front of them and completely hid their approach. The pier stuck out at right angles from the centre of the one and only street of So Kwu Wan, which ran along the waterfront. All of the premises on this street were restaurants; all had the shop and kitchen on the shore

101

side of the street and restaurant area on the seaward side, built on piles driven into the seabed. Each restaurant displayed its seafood in glass tanks, from which the clients chose their evening meal. The dining area for customers was covered by a canopy and the view for those eating was highly picturesque with the lights out in the bay. Picturesque as long as they were not treated to a sight of the sleek, fat rats which abounded in the raw sewage which flowed straight from the restaurant toilets into the sea.

The Wan Kee Restaurant had been well chosen if it was to be a repeat of the incident outside La Rose Noire. It was the last restaurant at the far end of the street and could, therefore, be easily identified by someone on a boat in the bay. Beyond it were derelict outhouses and disused shacks and then the thick vegetation along the shoreline. It was doubtful if any attack would come from the direction of the other restaurants or the street. It was far more likely to come from a boat anchored in the bay or from the buildings on the other side of the restaurant. This would give the attacker an ideal escape route into the hills to the south of So Kwu Wan and from there to any one of a number of places to be picked up by boat. Gunn had been considering these options ever since the invitation had been accepted and now as the ferry turned to port to come alongside the pier it was time for a decision. There were at least twenty boats at anchor and any one of them could have someone on board with the appropriate weapon and sight to pick him out in the Wan Kee.

'Stop Chan; now please bring the boat into the first of those small jetties over there,' and Gunn pointed to a collection of flimsy structures in front of restaurants at the opposite end of the waterfront street to the Wan Kee. 'I want you to tie up there. If you have to move to let other boats drop off or collect passengers, always come back to that jetty. That's where I'll expect to find you, OK?'

'OK, Sir,' Chan replied and turned the boat towards the jetty.

'Candy, do you keep any clothes on this boat?'

'Yes; Mum, Dad and I keep swimming things and some casual clothes on board; why?'

'Would you go and change into whatever you've got as quickly as possible.'

'Yes of course; on my way,' and Candy disappeared down the companionway to the cabins on the lower deck. As soon as she had gone, Gunn went into the saloon and removed his jacket. He then unclipped the holster from the waistband of his trousers and removed the Browning. He removed the magazine, eased back the slide and a 9 mm round was ejected onto the saloon table. He replaced the round in the chamber, depressed the magazine catch and let the slide go forward. He then replaced the magazine. He put the holster in his jacket pocket, removed his bow tie and rolled up his sleeves. He pulled up the right trouser leg and clipped the Browning into its ankle holster.

He then pushed his jacket under the cushions of the fitted seats round the saloon table. 'That's much more comfortable and less conspicuous,' he muttered to himself as Chan brought the boat gently alongside the jetty. Candy reappeared in a blouse and short skirt.

'Won't they all be in mess kit still, John?'

'Yes, I hope so.'

'Oh well, I said I wouldn't ask questions; what now?'

'Come with me,' and Gunn helped her off the boat onto the jetty and along the narrow little causeway to the shore. They turned right into the street and made their way through the dogs, children, occasional rat, tourists and waiters. Despite it being a weekday, all the restaurants were doing well and the majority of tables were occupied. The humidity was higher than ever, particularly after the air-conditioning on the boat and after only a short distance, Gunn could feel the sweat trickling down his back. Dishes piled with grouper, red snapper, lobsters, crabs and prawns were whisked in front of them from the shop fronts to the tables. John led the way to a restaurant, two away from the Wan Kee, which delighted under the name of the Lamma Hilton. Whether Conrad Hilton objected to this infringement of copyright of his multi-national hotel chain was of little concern to the Chinese owners or the tourists who flocked to the restaurants for a little bit of pseudo-local colour. It was only when there was a cholera scare that the tourists deserted the local restaurants for the sterilised havens of their five star hotels.

Most of the tables were round, in the Chinese tradition, and could seat anything from six to sixteen people, but there were one or two small tables and one of these was free in the Lamma Hilton. The table was right in amongst all the other tables which was the reason Gunn had selected it. Once seated, he blended in with all the other gweilos and Chinese, but Candy's hair, good looks and figure always attracted attention, as they did tonight. There was a group of Australians at the Lamma Hilton and their fair skins, hair and the loud noise they made were just what Gunn wanted.

'So what happens now,' Candy asked. Gunn looked at his watch again; 9.45, and there was no sign of their host although John had already spotted the reserved table at the Wan Kee. The table was one of three nearest to the sea.

'We'll have a beer and wait. When they arrive and we join them, you must get a seat on the far side of that round table,' and he pointed out the table to Candy. 'Do whatever you have to, but don't accept a seat that places you with your back or front facing the sea.' John noticed the expensive Chanel scarf tied round the strap of Candy's handbag. 'Don't laugh, but can you put that scarf on your head somehow to cover up as much of that lovely hair as possible.'

'I expect so; I'll just pop into the loo and fix it.'

'Thanks; be as quick as possible and don't bump into our host as you come out.' The waiter placed a bottle of San Miguel beer and two glasses on the table and then handed the menu to Gunn who told him that they would order in a few minutes. Candy reappeared having worked wonders with her scarf. John Gunn dropped a HK$20 note on the table, picked up the beer and led Candy towards the Wan Kee. There was still no sign of Molyneux. They walked straight to the reserved table and John placed Candy in the seat he had identified from the Lamma Hilton. The restaurant owner appeared and told them that the table was booked. The moment John spoke to him in Cantonese explaining that they were the Commander's guests, there was no further problem. 'Change of plan; I've decided that we'll move first. Don't let anyone move you from that seat and I shall be right here beside you. Make up anything you want, but don't let them move either of us; clear?'

'Absolutely, and if I'm not mistaken, here comes the Commander now.' The arrival of Commander Molyneux and his party had caused quite a stir as all the men were in mess kit and the women in cocktail dresses. Cameras appeared, flashlights lit up the restaurants and a barrage of ribald comments and whistles came from the Australians in the Lamma Hilton. Peter Molyneux was leading his party and stopped short when he saw John and Candy seated at the table.

'I'm sorry, but this table's reserved for our party,' he blurted, clearly not knowing Gunn by sight and failing to recognise Candy with her hair concealed by the scarf. Gunn stood up.

'Peter Molyneux? I'm John Gunn and this is Candy Wyngarde. I'm sorry that we've arrived before you, but we made rather better time than I expected, so please forgive us for ordering a drink.'

'Sorry . . . er, we haven't met,' and the Commander shook hands with Gunn and then Candy, adding, 'didn't recognise you with your hair done up like that.' There was a naval Lieutenant and the two army officers, from whom Candy had been rescued on Middle Kingdom and four women, one of whom was presumably Peter Molyneux's wife. 'That's marvellous, so we're all here. Now let me sort out the seating plan. John, I'd like . . . .'

'Peter,' this came from Candy, 'I haven't seen John for nearly eight years and if you think that you're going to split us up I shall go straight back to the boat. Now come on, be fair, let me sit beside the most eligible bachelor in Hong Kong for one night.'

'I quite agree, Peter, don't be so bossy,' interrupted his wife, 'and what's more, I'm going to sit here,' and with that she planted herself on John Gunn's left.

'Looks like a free for all, so we'll come round here,' and the naval lieutenant and his girlfriend moved round the table to sit on Candy's right. The arrangements were not going according to the Commander's plans, but there was nothing he could do about it.

'Oh, very well; everyone sit where you want. I'm going over there,' and the seat he chose positioned Molyneux with his back to the sea, 'and the army can have that side of the table.' The Commander then introduced everyone and ordered beer. Like many visitors to the Lamma restaurants, they had brought their own wine as the variety sold at some of the restaurants bore a strong affinity to a feline effluent. The girls with the two army officers had been bred from very similar loins to those of the officers' and the conversation on the other side of the table to Gunn centred round parties in London, weekends in the country and current gossip and scandal from the Guards Polo Club. John chatted with Pat Molyneux, wine was produced from cool boxes and bottles of beer were placed on the 'lazy susan' in the centre of the table. The men wearing mess kit went pinker and pinker in the face and perspired freely. All in all, the evening seemed to be very much the same as any other one that Gunn had spent on Lamma and he found himself wondering whether he hadn't been something of an alarmist.

The tables behind Gunn were all full and so close together that the back of his chair was touching the back of another, which made it a co-operative effort if either person wished to go and inspect the non-existent plumbing. From the other side of the street, their waiter appeared with a large serving dish piled with fried prawns. He made his way nimbly through the other tables until he reached theirs and then suddenly fell forward onto the table, burying his head in the prawns. Instantly Gunn dragged Candy down below the table as one of the glass fish tanks disintegrated and he heard the roar of big outboard motors out in the bay. Keeping Candy down he sat up. Fish were flapping around all over the floor of the restaurant and the manager had rushed forward to see what he could do to repair the damage caused by his clumsy waiter. Everyone was concentrating on either the waiter or the fish and no one was looking in the other direction where their host was leaning back in his chair, dead.

Gunn let Candy sit up again. 'Take care of Pat,' he whispered, 'Peter's been shot, but she doesn't realise yet.' He then climbed out of his chair, walked round to where the waiter was still sprawled over the table, lifted him up and carried him through the tables to the shop. Now that the focus of interest had been removed, people's heads turned. Gunn heard Pat's scream as he carried the waiter into the manager's cubbyhole at the back of the shop. The same bullet that had smashed the fish tank had gone clean through the waiter's heart, killing him instantly. The second bullet had killed Peter Molyneux.

John dialled Doyle's mobile. It rang three, four times . . . 'Answer! damn you Doyle,' John cursed in frustration.

'Hi! What do you want pal, you've just saved me calling you,' came Doyle's calm voice.

'The Commander's been shot and there's chaos in the restaurant. Anything at Shek O?'

'The two guys we're interested in have both gone to the Shek O place. I heard enough to send them both to the electric chair. I'm on my way to pick you up and was just crossing the Tai Tam Dam when you called. Some maniac almost drove me off the road so I couldn't answer. You know the jetty at the north side of Deep Water Bay?'

'By the sailing club?'

'That's the one; I'll be there in five minutes; I've got a friend from our place in Central who'll meet us there and send messages home. I'll wait for you.'

'See you there,' and Gunn disconnected and then called the police. Out in the restaurant, there was pandemonium. Pat Molyneux was hysterical, very understandably, and the crowd of voyeurs was growing by the second, fuelled from the other restaurants. Gunn forced his way through the people until he caught Candy's eye. Pat was being consoled by Susan, whilst the army contingent was looking after one of the girlfriends who had fainted. Candy joined him and they eased their way back through the crowd, no one paying the slightest bit of attention to them.

'Isn't it against the law to leave the scene of the crime?'

'You're damn right it is, but I haven't got time to spend the rest of the night answering police questions. Chan will drop me in Deep Water Bay and then take you back round to Central or you can grab a taxi when I get off and go home that way. Which is it to be?'

'Where are you going?'

'To check out something else?'

'Can I. . . .'

'No, you can't, Candy; it was stupid of me to take you to Lamma. Please go back home and I'll be in touch tomorrow,' but it was a refusal, which he was going to regret.

CHAPTER 9

I thought you might say that, John, in which case I think I'll stay here and see if I can help Pat Molyneux. Could you ask Chan to come back with the boat when he's dropped you?'

'Fine, that's a better plan,' John agreed. 'Take care of yourself.'

'Yes, I'll do that, but I'll come and see you off first,' and Candy and Gunn headed for the wooden jetty. Chan had been forced to move and as Gunn appeared he was just returning to the jetty. Gunn and the motorboat reached the jetty simultaneously and after jumping aboard and waving to Candy, he explained the plan to Chan who immediately swung the boat out into the bay. Once they were clear of the fish pens, Chan opened up the throttles and the boat surged forward across the calm and sheltered water of Picnic Bay towards the East Lamma Channel.

The bright lights of the fun fair at Ocean Park on the Sham Shui Kok Peninsular acted as a beacon to lead them into Deep Water Bay and fifteen minutes after leaving the jetty in Picnic Bay, the boat was alongside the short stone pier of the sailing club. Gunn had retrieved his jacket which was looking very much the worst for wear and as soon as he was clear of the boat, Chan put her astern and then headed back to Lamma Island. It was just before eleven and the traffic on the coast road was still quite heavy. He had only moved a few paces along the pier when Doyle appeared and led him to a metallic grey BMW in the car park between the road and the beach. 'I've given our guy from the Consulate as much as we know and that will be going back to London and Washington in the next quarter of an hour,' he told Gunn as they reached the car.

'Well done; who's paying for this machine?'

'Your lot in London,' was the reply as the fuel-injected engine sprang to life on the first touch of the ignition key. Doyle selected a small break in the traffic and they were soon heading east on the tortuous coast road to Shek O.

There was very little traffic on their side of the road and even when they joined the road, which crossed over from the north side of the Island, through the Wong Nai Chung Gap, the traffic was still quite thin. Repulse Bay was ablaze with lights from both the hotel of that name and all the apartment blocks around it.

'What happened at Henshaw's place tonight?'

'I followed them to Shek O where I found a convenient place to get over the wall, which surrounds the entire property. By the time I got to the house, there was an argument going on between Henshaw and his wife. The argument seemed to be about a trip he's just planned and she knew nothing about. I didn't have to make an effort to listen as they were on the veranda, and you could have heard the shouting down on the road. Anyway, this female . . .'

'Martha.'

'That figures; well, she stormed off to bed leaving the two men standing in the hall. Things got tricky at this point because they lowered their voices. Getting the door open was a cinch, but I had no idea if it was connected to some sort of alarm and just gambled that if it was, they wouldn't have had time to switch it on. The two of them were standing at the entrance to the lounge. Hang on a second, I'll just get past this idiot,' the offending car had indicated right at the turning to Chung Hom Kok and had then gone straight on. They followed it down the hill to the 'T' junction with the road to Stanley Village, where it gave no indication and then turned right. There was a muttered oath from Doyle who accelerated down the gradient past The Manhattan and the American Club and then up the hill towards Tai Tam. Doyle continued, 'I had missed some of the conversation, but it seems as though the two of them are involved in something,' and here Doyle paused. 'I know this sounds crazy, but what I heard suggested that unless they're out of Hong Kong by Sunday, they and all the rest of the people in Hong Kong will be dead.'

'What!' exclaimed Gunn, just as Doyle swung the car onto the road over the Tai Tam Dam.

'Well, this ties in with you finding those radio active traces in the engine room of that yacht. It seems that these men have got themselves a nuclear bomb which they're going to explode sometime around Sunday.'

'And that radio-active body was in some way involved in getting the weapon grade uranium for this device?'

'Could be; it fits. So where do we go from here?' Doyle asked as he swung the BMW round the sharp right-hander at the other side of the dam and then accelerated again up the gradient to the crossroads at Tai Tam Gap where they would turn right onto the Shek O Peninsular. Neither of them attempted to answer that question until they were approaching the hairpin bend on Shek O Peak and then Doyle said, 'his place is just down here on the right by the golf course.'

'You included all this in your signal?'

'Sure.'

'Can you begin to imagine the panic and chaos if this guesswork of ours is correct and it leaks to the public? Thousands will die in the stampede to get away, let alone those who'll die when this bomb goes off. Those two must be made to talk . . . tonight.'

'We're here. I'm going past and I'll then turn round. I'll park here,' and he pointed to a spot in deep shade under wide-canopied flame trees. He turned the BMW and then with lights off cruised silently to a halt under the trees. He switched off the interior light so that it wouldn't come on as the doors opened.

Doyle locked the car and put the keys behind the spring-loaded flap covering the petrol filling cap. 'Just in case we don't both get back at the same time,' and he led the way back along the road. Gunn could see the wall through the undergrowth; it seemed to be about six feet high and although an obstacle, was certainly not a difficult one to overcome. Doyle had paused at a point along the wall where a large clump of bamboo was growing on both sides of it. 'This is for uninvited guests,' and he reached up got hold of a thick bamboo trunk.

Just as Doyle started to climb the wall using the bamboo, a flurry of light rain started to fall. Gunn followed him quickly before the rain made the bamboo too slippery. As he caught hold of the bamboo, the movement brought down a spray of rainwater from the leaves onto his head and shoulders. If it had not been for this distraction, he might have noticed the thin yellow snake, just over a foot long, which dropped soundlessly off a bamboo stem into the left hand pocket of his dinner jacket. The species was well known in Hong Kong, but much smaller than its South American cousin and rarely reaching a length of more than eighteen inches. It lived in trees and bamboo and was quite erroneously known as a 'fer de lance'; the genuine fer de lance only existed on the island of Martinique. The species had accounted for more deaths in South America than any other snake, but its kill rate in Hong Kong was uncertain as it was frequently incorrectly identified as either a krait or bamboo viper. Its correct name was the 'barba amiralla' or 'yellow beard'.

Gunn reached the top of the wall, went over it on his stomach to avoid silhouetting himself on the top and then swung his feet over and jumped. He landed in a dense herbaceous border beside the drive leading to the house. Doyle was just to his right and immediately led the way through the border onto the grass and then along the edge of the border towards the house.

The house was built in the Spanish style, with heavy orange pantiles on the roof and arched colonnades, which overlooked a sweep of lawn and a paved terrace surrounding a swimming pool.

Doyle led the way up to the front door and then turned and whispered to Gunn, 'the door's been shut, but I can still see the lights at the edge of the lounge curtains, so my guess is that the two men are still there. That means that there's a good chance they haven't switched on any alarm system. Worth trying the door?'

'Yes, give it a try,' replied Gunn as he removed his sodden jacket. The lock proved no problem and no alarm sounded as Doyle eased the door open.

'There's a safety chain. Wait a second,' and he went over to the nearest flower bed from which he returned with a thin stick broken from some species of hibiscus. The rain had started to fall steadily now and promised to turn into the inevitable sub-tropical torrent before long. Doyle slipped the stick through the four-inch gap between door and frame and after three attempts the chain slipped out of the grooved lock. He led the way into the large hall from which a wide staircase with a wrought iron balustrade curved up to the first floor. Doyle pointed to the left; 'dining room and this is the lounge,' he whispered, as they both walked carefully over the highly polished terracotta tiles to a pair of heavy, panelled doors on the right of the hall. Gunn put his ear to the door and listened. He took hold of the door handle and gradually increased the pressure; it made no sound and the door opened slightly. He turned to Doyle and indicated that he should stay outside the lounge so that his presence in Hong Kong would remain unknown as long as possible. Henshaw was sitting with his back towards them. Balmain was sitting in an armchair; a glass of brandy on a small table beside him. Both men had discarded their jackets on the arm of one of the chairs. Smoke curled up from Henshaw's cigar. It was a large room, filled with dark, rosewood furniture, which detracted from its spaciousness and in the subdued light, cast by two side lamps, gave the room a depressingly monastic atmosphere. Heavy curtains were drawn across all the windows and at the far side of the room was a fireplace with an empty, wrought iron fire basket.

'Good evening,' Gunn said sociably, as he walked into the room. 'Sorry to arrive uninvited - no, please stay seated,' this was added as both men started to get up from their chairs. 'I think that we might all benefit from a frank discussion to ensure, if for no other reason, that we don't join the ranks of Peter Molyneux who, incidentally, was murdered about forty minutes ago.' Neither of the two men was able to conceal an expression of alarm on hearing this information. 'I do apologise for my appearance,' Gunn continued, as he moved round the two men until he was facing the door. He then sat on the arm of a chair and dropped his jacket where the other two men had put theirs.

'How dare you break into my house! You've finished your career with the Company before it even started. I'm going to phone the police now,' and Henshaw started to raise his bulk out of the armchair. Gunn made no attempt to stop him.

'When you get through to the police, and I presume that will be Geoffrey Winchcombe, why don't you suggest that he join us here and picks up Sir Peter Butler on the way. I doubt if you'll get YS to leave his yacht, but we could reconvene your earlier meeting of this evening when somewhat catastrophic plans for the future of Hong Kong were discussed.' Rather like a punctured balloon, Robin Henshaw sank back into his chair.

'I've no idea who this hooligan is or what he's talking about, Robin. He's nothing more than a common felon, like the ones I deal with every day at the Courts of Justice. If you don't call the police, then I shall,' blustered George Balmain and with slightly more agility than Henshaw, got out of his chair and started towards the door.

'Do you really believe that YS intends to let you all live? He's already killed one of you and that was barely within an hour of your meeting.' George Balmain stopped. 'You're all planning to leave Hong Kong by Sunday, or perhaps before, but there isn't one of you who was at that meeting who'll leave this place, other than in a wooden box,' Gunn was guessing, but neither of the men had contradicted him. He had noticed a slight movement of the door and knowing that Doyle would never be so clumsy, he continued, 'tell me Henshaw, how much does Martha know of these plans? Have you discussed this with her?

'Shut up! You interfering idiot; I'll. . . .'

'What's going on, Robin?' demanded Martha, who was now standing in the doorway. 'What's that man doing here?' and she pointed at Gunn. 'Wasn't he at the party on the boat? What's going on George?' and she now confronted Balmain who had retreated and was leaning against the back of his chair.

'Robin and I were just having a night-cap, as you know, when this man burst into the room. I was just on my way to the phone in the hall to call the police when you came in, Martha,' murmured Balmain silkily, moving from the back of the chair and once more heading for the door.

'Sit down George; I've got a lot more questions to ask before anyone phones the police. Now, young man; I've forgotten your name. . . .'

'John Gunn.'

'Thank you Mr Gunn, now what plans were you talking about which Robin hasn't told me?'

111

'My dear, I can . . .' blurted Henshaw.

'Quiet Robin; please remember that this house belongs to me and my family. I wish to know what is going on. Mr Gunn doesn't appear to be a burglar. Now what's all this about plans for leaving Hong Kong by Sunday. If you're up to your old tricks and have let me down again, then I gave you fair warning in Japan that if it ever happened again we were finished.'

'Oh shut up! You stupid bitch; you and your bloody house and your bloody family can get stuffed. Yes! I am leaving Hong Kong on Sunday. For ever, thank Christ; away from you, away from this house and away from everything that I hate about this Chink-ridden, God-forsaken part of the world,' during this outburst, Henshaw had been edging round to Gunn's left towards an attractive Queen Anne writing bureau against the wall.

'Stop it Robin, for Christ's sake; don't say anything else,' George Balmain almost shouted. Martha stepped quickly towards the door, turned the key and then removed it and put it in the pocket of her dressing gown.

'No one leaves this room until I know exactly what's going on, George. Go and sit down. Where do you think you're going?' This question was directed at Henshaw who was now within about six feet of the writing bureau. Gunn had been watching his progress, had assumed that the bureau was his target and that in it was some form of weapon. The question triggered Henshaw's great bulk into action and with surprising agility an old Webly revolver appeared in his hand from the top right drawer of the bureau. Two shots sounded simultaneously. Gunn had dropped to the floor as the Webly appeared in Henshaw's hand, but the second bullet hadn't come from his Browning. Henshaw's bullet had gone harmlessly through the curtains and the French window behind. The bullet from Martha's small automatic had entered her husband's head, just behind the left eye, as he turned towards John Gunn: he was dead before he hit the carpet and the Webly fell from his hand.

At the sound of the shots, Gunn had expected the doors to burst open and Doyle to appear, but there was no sign of him. George Balmain launched himself at Martha Henshaw, grabbed the small automatic out of her hand and swung her body in front of his; the automatic was pressed firmly against her neck.

'Put that down Mr Gunn, or I shall have no hesitation in shooting Martha.' Gunn put the Browning down on the armchair in front of him. 'Now we're all going to leave the house slowly and carefully. Where are the keys to your car Martha?'

'I'm not go . . .' Martha's scream and the report of the small calibre bullet sounded as one. The bullet had sliced through the fleshy part of her neck and blood poured down over her dressing gown.

'The car keys, Martha; the next bullet will be even more painful. One move from you Mr Gunn and you die first and Martha follows instantly afterwards. Is that quite clear?'

'That's quite clear Balmain. Mrs Henshaw, please tell him where the keys are,' John said quietly to Martha, whose head had now sagged forward. Her head came up slowly.

'I have a set in my bag in my bedroom,' and her voice was barely audible.

'What about him?' and he indicated her husband with his foot.

'Yes, he usually has one on a ring with his front door key. It should be in his pocket.'

'Gunn, move very carefully towards Henshaw and take the key ring out of his pocket. Make any move at his gun and you're dead. Now start moving, slowly,' he added as Gunn stepped across an overturned pedestal table to reach the body. Where the hell was Doyle? Something had gone very badly wrong the other side of the lounge door, which worried Gunn more than the situation he faced this side of it. He felt in the pockets and found the keys, which he removed carefully from the left pocket.

'Good; now throw them across so that they land just on front of Martha. Don't try to be clever.' Gunn threw the keys and they landed as directed. By now the drumming of torrential rain outside could be heard. 'Throw my jacket over here.' With his eyes never leaving Gunn, Balmain forced Martha down as he stooped to pick up the keys and jacket. Martha was barely conscious and had lost a considerable amount of blood. Balmain stood up with her, put the keys into his left pocket and swung the jacket over his shoulder.

Balmain had removed the key from Martha's pocket and now started to back towards the lounge door. Gunn was pretty certain that once through the door, Balmain would shoot Martha - he couldn't afford to leave her alive, or him for that matter. The same thought process must have been going through Martha's mind, despite the pain from the bullet wound in her neck. As the two of them backed through the door, Martha struggled and the shot aimed at Gunn disappeared into the sofa as he dropped behind it. The door slammed shut and the key turned in the lock. No reaction from Doyle; Gunn rushed over to the curtains and pulled them aside; long French windows and every one with a security lock on it. He picked up his Browning and walked over to the door. He aimed the automatic at the lock and was just about to fire when there was a dreadful scream from

113

the hall. Gunn cursed and fired. The heavy steel-jacketed bullet smashed through the lock and crouching low, he wrenched open the door, to be faced with a most bizarre scene.

Of Doyle there was not a sign; Martha Henshaw was crawling away from her captor on hands and knees. George Balmain lay on his back by the front door and coiled on his chest was a small snake, which made it look as though he had just grown a whispy, yellow beard. Gunn bent down and retrieved his dinner jacket.

*

Doyle Barnes had been standing with his back to the door of the lounge, listening to the conversation inside and keeping an eye on the stairs. He had heard Martha's approach as soon as she opened her bedroom door and had gone through an arched opening to the right of the staircase which led to the cloakroom and toilets. He was concealed behind this archway as Martha Henshaw crossed over to the lounge doors and paused to listen. She listened for only thirty seconds and then pushed the door open and went in. Doyle came out of his hiding place and went back to the door. So intent was he on keeping his eye on the exact moment when he might have to assist Gunn, that he never noticed the front door open. Henshaw had just begun his tirade at his wife, when Doyle's world exploded in momentary pain and then black oblivion.

The two men carried Doyle out of the house and closed the front door only seconds before Balmain backed out of the room with Martha Henshaw and slammed and locked the lounge door. The car was parked near the entrance to the drive. The night watchman lay across the table in his little shelter and both gates were wide open. Doyle was carried through and the gates, which were closed behind them by a third man who had been waiting with the car. His hands and feet were firmly bound, a handkerchief was stuffed in his mouth and then duck tape was stuck across the lower part of his face. The driver of the car opened the boot and Doyle was unceremoniously dumped inside and the lid closed. The driver reversed the car out of the driveway onto the road and headed back towards the north side of the Island.

At the 'T' junction at Tai Tam Gap, some very wet and bedraggled Highways Department workers, wearing bright yellow hard hats were setting up a diversion sign and lights. The driver of the car paused to speak with one of the workers who had waved him down with a red light. They spoke for a few moments and then the driver was waved in the direction of the right turn to Shau Kei Wan and the Island Eastern Corridor route into Central. In Causeway Bay the driver turned south onto the elevated road through Happy Valley and then left onto the slip road to join up with the Wong Nai Chung Gap Road, but at the foot of Mount Nicholson he turned right onto Stubbs Road and headed for the Peak. The car pulled up outside black steel gates where there were two guards armed with long night-sticks. The driver got out and spoke to one of the guards, neither of whom made any move to let the car through. One of the guards then came out through a side gate and examined the occupants in the car with a heavy, high-powered torch. He went back through the gate and only then did one of the steel gates start to slide back into its recess in the left side of the wall. The car went through the gate, turned hard left and then hard right as the drive zigzagged up a steeply terraced garden to a large white Georgian-style house with a pillared portico.

The driver took the car round to the back of the house and stopped. Doyle was now semi-conscious and vaguely aware of being blindfolded and then being removed from the boot of the car and carried into the house. He was made to stand up in a small lift, which went up to the second floor. From the lift he was carried along a corridor to a bedroom which looked out on the back of the house and a sheer escarpment of granite from which sprouted clumps of vegetation. The bedroom was sparsely furnished, but clean. Doyle Barnes was placed on the bed and handcuffed to a purpose-designed ring bolt set into the wall. Just as the cuffs snapped shut, someone else came into the room. Doyle could sense the deference accorded to the new arrival. The voice was strong and the English without accent. 'Is he alive?'

'Yes, Sir, he still lives.'

'Show me!' and Doyle heard the movement of feet.

'Is this some sort of joke?' the 'voice' thundered. 'Who's this?'

'Mr Gunn, Sir,' came the apprehensive response.

'Was he in Henshaw's house?'

'Yes, Sir.'

'Armed?'

'Yes, Sir.'

'Show me!' and Doyle presumed that his Colt Mustang was being examined. 'You imbeciles! You've got the wrong man. Get rid of him. No traces! Understood?'

'Yes, Sir.'

'Are the road works in position?'

'Yes, Sir.'

'Well that should deal with Balmain. Get rid of this one, once you know who he is and what he knows. Don't waste any time; use sodium pentathol. Understood!'

'Yes, Sir.' The door shut and the noise of footsteps receded towards the lift.

'Hope my life insurance is paid up,' Doyle muttered to himself as he started to work at getting his blindfold off.

*

The venom from the yellow beard attacks the nervous system, causing paralysis and kills the victim by asphyxiation when the lung muscles cease to function. Death occurs between one and three minutes after the bite. George Balmain was dying. Martha Henshaw had disappeared into the lounge and Gunn had removed the snake and killed it with the long handled poker from the fireplace in the lounge.

'Can you hear me, Balmain?' Gunn asked, pulling a chair over and sitting beside the prostrate figure. A slight movement of his head acknowledged John's question. 'You are dying and you and I know that neither of us can do anything to stop that. Try and show a vestige of remorse and tell me what YS is planning to do. Surely you can't go to meet your maker with the guilt of thousands of deaths on your hands.' Balmain was finding it increasingly difficult to breathe. Gunn went into the lounge and returned with a cushion, which he placed under the judge's head. He was trying to speak, but the venom had already started to paralyse the muscles controlling his vocal chords. Gunn bent down to try and catch any word. 'Come on man, try,' urged Gunn, with very little compassion for the drug-addicted bigot who lay on the hall floor.

'. . . not a bomb,' the words were so indistinct that John nearly missed them. '. . . like Che . . . Che . . .' 'Chinese?' Gunn prompted, but the minute shake of the head contradicted the prompt. 'Try, come on, try; what are you trying to tell me?' but he was talking to a dead man.

CHAPTER 10

Typhoon Pamela was approaching the Paracel Islands, which lay some 200 miles to the south-east of Hainan Island. After leaving the Mindorro Strait in the Philippines at 15 mph, its speed had now reduced to 8 mph, much to the consternation of those who were plotting the track on radar. A fast moving typhoon followed a reasonably predictable track, but the moment it lost its momentum, not only did the depression tend to deepen and the wind speeds within the typhoon increase in ferocity, but its track could vary erratically. The winds were rotating round this depression at an average speed of 160 mph with some gusts recorded at 180 mph.

At a position of 130 nautical miles to the south-east of the Paracel Islands, Pamela changed course to a track which was slightly west of north and headed straight for Hong Kong 600 miles away. The typhoon was now within the radar coverage of the Waglan Island tracking station, where the change in course was immediately noted and the number one signal re-hoisted. The population of Hong Kong was asleep, but all the duty officers of the government, military and emergency services were alerted. The departures of ships in the container port and harbour were brought forward so that they could put to sea and get clear of the path of the typhoon.

*

The weather in the area of the Southern Philippines was as near perfect as could be imagined. The night sky was ablaze with stars, the sea was flat calm, particularly in the sheltered waters of the narrow channel between the islands of Samar and Leyte, through which American Pie was now passing. With the assistance of the north-west setting current, Dan Grant's GPS fix at midnight put American Pie just to the north of the two islands; this meant that they had covered 150 miles since leaving the anchorage off Mindanao Island. Flicking his dividers across the chart, Dan measured the distance to Catanduanes Island; 156 miles to go, Dan thought to himself. That would mean an ETA of about midday the following day.

Amy and the guests were sitting in the cockpit enjoying a night-cap and the magical scenery, as American Pie made her way through the myriad of islands and atolls that dotted the sea in this popular cruising area of the Philippines. Dan Grant had decided to press on through the night, taking watches with his two boat boys, for no other reason than to put as great a distance as possible between their last anchorage and the boat. Having checked the course carefully, he sent his boat boy to his bunk and sat behind the polished teak wheel in the outside steering position. Amy got up and came to sit beside her husband who was about to make inroads into a well-aged Bourbon.

'May I come and join the officer of the watch?' she asked as she sat down beside him at the aft end of the cockpit. He put his arm round her and kissed her

'Thanks honey for everything you did today to help me. I'd have been lost without it.'

'Do you know, Dan, I've just been wondering what it would have been like to have been raped by all those hairy pirates. You never know, I might've been able to show them a thing or two.'

'You brazen hussy, just wait until I come off watch and then I'll show you a thing or two!' and the two of them laughed as American Pie cruised northwards through the calm, starlit sea.

*

Gunn stood up and looked down at the body of Balmain and the dead snake beside his head. 'Not a pleasant death, but then I doubt if anyone will mourn your departure.' Gunn spun round at the sound of a shot. He drew the Browning and kicked back the right hand door of the lounge. There was no need for caution or the gun; Martha Henshaw was kneeling on the floor in front of an armchair with her head buried in a pile of cushions. Her right arm hung limply at her side and the small automatic lay on the carpet just out of reach of her fingertips. He walked over to the armchair; there was hardly any blood; she had shot herself in the head and ended the misery of a marriage to a gay husband and the sadness it had brought to one of the oldest and most respected families of Hong Kong.

Gunn glanced round the lounge at the two bodies, both shot in the head by the same weapon. He walked out into the hall and said aloud to the empty house, 'I wonder what the police will make of this mess?' and went out through the front door. There was still no sign of any of the house staff, not that there was anything unusual about that, as they had probably locked themselves in their rooms the moment the first shot had been fired. The dead night watchman at the gate, the hasp of the heavy padlock sheared by bolt cutters and the tyre-marked gravel at the drive entrance were all clear enough evidence of Doyle Barnes' disappearance from the house.

118

Gunn walked along the road to the flame trees; the rain made the darkness under the trees so impenetrable that he was only a few paces away from the BMW before he was able to distinguish it. 'Thank God for that,' he murmured as he retrieved the ignition keys from inside the petrol flap. He checked all round the car for bombs and booby traps; there were none. He got into the car and glanced at his watch; nearly ten past two. At that moment, the rain, which had eased over the last few minutes, once more became a blinding deluge. 'This'll make the job for the police even harder,' he thought as he eased the car out from under the trees and onto the road. With the wipers at full speed, he drove slowly up the road without any lights. He waited until he was a couple of hundred yards beyond the house before he flicked on the powerful twin headlights. He drove back up the hill to the hairpin bend at the southern end of the Dragon's Back, the Chinese name for the spine of rock, which ran the full length of the Shek O Peninsular. As Gunn made his way northwards along the Shek O Road, he considered what might have happened to Doyle.

It was reasonable to suppose that it was some of YS' men who had visited the house, with the intention of removing Henshaw, but had bumped into Doyle instead. It would be almost impossible to discover where he had been taken - presuming, of course, that he was still alive. He arrived at the 'T' junction at Tai Tam Gap and saw the diversion sign directing him to turn left for the road over the Tai Tam Dam. John Gunn had been going to turn left anyway although he could have gone by the eastern route back to the Mandarin Hotel in Central.

As soon as the BMW turned left, the 7½ litre turbo-charged diesel of an eight wheel earth-moving truck from the Shek O quarry, which had been parked out of sight behind the diversion barriers, rumbled into life. The truck steered on both sets of front, five foot diameter, earth-mover tyres and, with the assistance of power steering, these now turned as the truck rolled slowly out onto the road, belching black diesel smoke from an overhead stack. The torrential rain dissipated the exhaust immediately. The man beside the driver raised a small radio to his mouth and spoke into it. All the crash barriers, lights and signs were loaded into a panel van, which had been parked behind the truck.

In a lay-by, carved out of the rock on the other side of the dam, another identical truck started up and moved forward onto the road, well concealed by the deluge of rain, which had reduced visibility to less than fifty yards. The road along the top of the Tai Tam Dam was just wide enough to take two cars, side by side. Anything bigger had to wait at either end until its access to the road was clear. The dam

119

road ran virtually north-south; on its eastern side was a sheer drop of 220 feet down to Tai Tam Bay and its small fishing village of shanty-built structures and flimsy bamboo pontoons which stretched out into the sea. On the west side of the road was the reservoir, with its backdrop of thickly jungle-covered hills and deep ravines, all of which were now filled with a turbulent mass of storm water cascading down to the reservoir. The reservoir was three-quarters full after a summer of above-average rainfall. The height from the road to the surface of the reservoir was some 45 feet.

Gunn peered through the water streaming off the BMW's windscreen, only momentarily being cleared by the wipers. The road down to the northern end of the dam was steep with hairpin bends alternately twisting left and right. The surface of the road acted as a sluice for the rainwater which rushed all round the car towards the storm water drains on either side of the road at the point where it went onto the dam. As he cleared the last of the bends, Gunn noticed with relief that there were no lights at the other end of the dam - not that he had expected to see any at this time and in such foul weather. The road followed the same graceful curve of the dam and in any form of reasonable visibility there was nothing to obstruct a driver's view from one side of the dam to the other - a distance of about 450 yards.

Gunn took the BMW onto the dam at 20 mph, its tyres throwing out sheets of water all round the car. He stifled a yawn as he strained his eyes to concentrate on the road, turning the air-conditioning de-mister up to full to clear away the misted windscreen. Even inside the well-insulated interior of the BMW, Gunn could hear the crash of the thunder as it rumbled and rolled around the rain soaked hills. The next instant he was half-blinded by an explosion of light as lightening flooded the whole scene with brilliant strobe-like light. It was followed almost instantly by an ear-splitting crash of thunder, which shook Gunn out of his lethargy, focusing his attention on the huge yellow truck, which was bearing down on the BMW from the other side of the dam. 'Bloody half wit, he hasn't got any li . . .' but the oath died, as his brain switched from dead slow to full ahead. 'I must be half-asleep. No one in his right mind would've diverted all the traffic over the dam, not even in Hong Kong!' He braked the BMW, flicked the selector into reverse and looked over his shoulder. The same scene repeated itself behind him. Less than fifty yards away and roaring towards the BMW was the other truck. At that instant, on a command given over the radio, both trucks switched on their lights on high beam, including the cab mounted spot-lights, swamping the BMW in blinding, quartz-halogen light.

Gunn flicked the selector into low and moved forward with the truck behind him only some 15 yards away. He could see nothing in front of him but blinding light, so he was only able to act on guesswork. The truck behind was driving him towards the one in front, which appeared to have turned across the road and stopped, judging by the lights in front which had swung over to his right. The plan for his execution was very clear; the angle of the truck in front and the bulldozing effect of the truck behind would hurl the BMW over the left parapet and down into Tai Tam Bay.

Holding the wheel firmly with his left hand, he opened his door and held it with his right. The truck behind the BMW had reached it and rammed the rear bumper. The one in front was less than 20 yards away. Gunn threw the door open and dived out of the car, continuing to roll quickly towards the parapet as the great, fat, earth-moving tyres of the truck churned past barely a foot away. He never paused, but vaulted onto the low stone wall and then hurled himself as far out as possible to avoid the outward curvature of the dam. The BMW continued partially under its own impetus and partially shunted by the truck until it crashed into the side of the stationary truck. The fuel tanks of the BMW and the truck exploded simultaneously; the car was blown over the parapet into Tai Tam Bay and the force of the explosion hurled the truck through the right hand parapet into the reservoir. The truck that had rammed the BMW braked, skidded to the left and despite the desperate efforts of the driver to regain control hit the parapet at 20 mph. It demolished the stone wall as it careered out into the abyss, turning end over end and exploding on impact at the foot of the coffer-dam.

Gunn surfaced, gasping for breath, split seconds before the blazing truck struck the water 20 yards from where he struggled to stay afloat. The impact of the truck swamped him as pieces of the disintegrating vehicle landed all round him. The surface of the reservoir appeared to be boiling with the torrent of rain, which was striking it. Gunn had little idea of where he was and swam in what he hoped was the direction of the south end of the dam. After what seemed an eternity, he reached the bank, where he paused for a few seconds before dragging himself up the mud bank to the line of vegetation where there was a path used by fishermen. The rain was still a deluge and the surface of the path was like grease. Gunn crawled along it for a few yards and then stood up and walked precariously away from the dam towards some steps which led up to a car park. He slowly made his way up them and as he reached the top, the rain appeared to ease a little; he was about two miles from the

Stanley Village 'T' junction and a little less from the high rise apartments just before that junction.

His white dinner jacket had been shredded when he threw himself out of the BMW so he stripped it off and threw it into the thick vegetation on the side of the road. Of a car, there was not a sign and John Gunn very much doubted if one would have given him a lift in his present, dishevelled state. He set off along the road towards Stanley Village. To take his mind off the walk in soaking wet clothes and no shoes - these had vanished in the plunge into the reservoir - he continued to analyse the events which had led up to the attempt to kill him on the dam road.

Some of YS' men must have gone to Henshaw's house to kill him, as he, like Molyneux, was of no further use to YS' plan. On arrival, they had found Doyle and had removed him. Why? Why not just kill him? Was it possible that they had mistaken Doyle for him? That was a possibility. So who was the expected victim of the dam incident? That had probably been set up for Balmain. He had taken a lift in Henshaw's chauffeur driven BMW, which was almost the same colour as the one lying at the foot of the dam. In the torrential rain it would have been impossible to tell the difference between the two cars or to have seen how many occupants it had. Presumably, whoever had been watching the house at Shek O, had seen someone come out of the house and then drive away in a BMW. Did that reasoning make sense? Well, some of it did, Gunn thought as he saw the lights of the American Club and the Manhattan come into view.

During his sock-footed trudge up the road not a single vehicle had passed him. He looked at his watch; it was now just on half past three. Five minutes later he had reached The Manhattan. Every apartment block in Hong Kong had security staff manning the entrance to the place to prevent unwanted visitors reaching the residents. The entrance drive to the Manhattan rose steeply from the road and, sure enough, there was the security guard's office at the closed barrier. Gunn moved closer until he could see inside. The security guard had just taken a kettle off a stove and was pouring a cup of tea. At the rear of the office was a 250cc Kawasaki motorbike on its stand. Gunn moved quietly round to the door; the guard had poured the cup of tea and was standing with his back to the door as he drank it. The cup fell to the table and broke as Gunn hit him and then lowered him into his chair. The ignition keys for the Kawasaki were in the man's left trouser pocket; the machine seemed to be almost brand new and it started first time. He rode the motorbike carefully down the entrance drive of the Manhattan and out onto the road. He had no money on him so would have to go over the Wong

Nai Chung Gap road rather than the Aberdeen Tunnel where he would have to pay the toll. The rain had almost stopped and it only took him fifteen minutes to get back to Central where he parked the bike by the Furama Hotel and then walked to the Mandarin. Gunn stopped at the reception desk to collect his key and to see if there were any messages. No news of Doyle; just one message - would he contact Assistant Commissioner McBain - 'that can wait,' Gunn muttered and thanked the young man at reception who hadn't batted an eyelid at Gunn's appearance.

His room number was 682; the lifts were all free and he rode up quickly to the sixth floor and stepped out as the doors slid quietly open. His room was only about five yards from the lift and as he stepped out into the corridor, the door of 682 closed with a soft click. Without a pause he walked straight past his door and stopped at 681 and noisily tried to put his key into the lock, hoping that it was either unoccupied or that its occupant was a sound sleeper. He kicked the foot of the door with his toe, yawned loudly and thumped the edge of it with the flat of his hand in a passable imitation of it being closed. He returned to his own room and listened. Nothing; not a sound, and then the door handle started to turn very slowly. He stepped back to the left of the door and flattened himself against the wall. The door opened and an arm appeared. Gunn reached out, locked both his hands onto the arm, just short of the elbow and using his own body as the pivot, accelerated the intruder's exit from his room, spinning the Chinese youth who now erupted through the door through 180° and slamming him face-first into the wall. As the man slumped, Gunn hit him first in the kidney, which spun the youth round to face a clenched fist in the larynx. He instinctively ducked and the baseball bat thudded into the wall where his head had been. Judging that his second assailant would have to be off balance, Gunn launched himself backwards. His head struck the second man in the midriff, winding him and knocking the bat out of his hands. Gunn rolled clear, grabbing the bat as he did so and coming up into a crouch position, he used the bat like a piston, which he drove into the man's chest, just below his heart. Instinct and the training he had been given in the last fortnight before he flew to Hong Kong probably saved Gunn again. He lashed backwards with the bat, only too aware that he had his back to the open bedroom door. The move saved him from having his skull split in two by the butt of a Heckler-Koch sub-machine gun, which glanced off the side of his head and he felt himself falling into a roaring whirlpool of darkness.

*

123

Candy Wyngarde watched the motorboat and its broad wake disappear into the darkness and then turned and walked back to the Wan Kee Restaurant. Gunn's phone call had produced a Marine Police launch and a young, Chinese inspector was attempting to restore some form of normality into the situation. His two police constables had sent the crowds back to their restaurants, photographs and statements had been taken and a scenes of crime section was on its way over from Aberdeen.

Candy went over to Pat Molyneux who was close to a state of collapse. She offered everyone a lift back to Aberdeen in the company boat, which was readily accepted. All of them had made statements to the police except for Candy. She was approached by the inspector. 'Miss Wyngarde, isn't it?' he asked courteously. Candy turned from making small talk with Pat Molyneux.

'Yes, I'm Miss Wyngarde.'

'May I ask you some questions please, Miss Wyngarde?'

'Yes, of course,' and Candy moved to another seat at the table to save Pat Molyneux the unpleasantness of hearing, yet again, a repetition of the shooting incident.

'I believe I'm right in saying that you came here with a Mr Gunn, who left immediately after the shooting took place?' the inspector inquired as he checked his notebook.

'Yes, that's right inspector. I came here with Mr Gunn at the invitation of Commander Molyneux. After the shots which killed the commander and our waiter, Mr Gunn asked me if he could borrow the Company boat to try and catch, or at least identify, the boat from which the shots came.'

'You know that it's an offence to leave the scene of a crime, Miss Wyngarde.'

'Yes I do inspector, but tell me something; do you have any idea what sort of boat was involved, how many people were in it or in which direction it went?'

'We still have a number of witnesses to question, Miss Wyngarde, and I'm sure we'll find out who did this.' The Chinese policeman was becoming increasingly irritated at the possibility of losing face to a gweilo, and worse still, a female, in front of his subordinates and an audience.

'Inspector, I can assure you that no one saw that boat except Mr Gunn, which is why he went after it. I know that he'll be in touch with you and I'm sure will provide you with some very helpful information.'

'Possibly, Miss Wyngarde; and where can we find Mr Gunn? I'll have to report his disappearance from the scene of the crime.'

'He has a room at the Mandarin; he'll no doubt contact you with anything he's found out. I'm sure when you submit your report, that you'll find Mr Gunn will do everything possible to help you. Now, with your permission, I would like to take Mrs Molyneux home, as I don't think she can take any more of this questioning,' Candy added, getting up from her chair.

'We'll have to ask you some more questions, Miss Wyngarde,' the policeman persisted doggedly.

'Yes of course, I fully understand, but not now inspector,' and Candy moved over to Pat Molyneux. With the assistance of the Lieutenant's girlfriend, Candy led the exodus from the restaurant, trailing the two, army officers and their girlfriends. The inspector realised that he had very definitely lost face, but was too inexperienced to know how to reverse the situation. He therefore resorted to shouting at his subordinates who were doing a very efficient job in keeping the onlookers out of the way and identifying those who believed that they had something to volunteer as witnesses.

By the time that they reached the wooden pier, Chan had returned with the boat. They all boarded the motorboat and at Candy's direction, Chan headed for Aberdeen. She then spoke on the phone to her father, explaining what had happened and asked if their chauffeur could bring the car to the marina at Aberdeen so that she could give Pat Molyneux a lift to her naval quarter at Mount Austen Mansions. 'Is John there?' her father asked.

'No Dad, he's not. I'll explain everything to you in the office tomorrow.'

'Where's he gone then?' persisted her father.

'Dad, I can't say on the phone; don't worry, I'll explain everything tomorrow.'

'Very well, my dear,' and Peter Wyngarde rang off.

Candy took Pat Molyneux to her quarter where she left her with another naval Commander and his wife who had a flat on the same floor and immediately offered to have Pat to stay for the night. As she left, a phone call was being made to the Captain at HMS Tamar, so Candy felt confident that the military system would now take over the task of caring for Pat. All the other members of the ill-fated supper party had taken taxis from Aberdeen. Candy got back into her father's Bentley and asked the chauffeur to take her to her flat at Tregunter Path in the Mid-Levels. The Bentley climbed the steep, corkscrew ramp to the apartment block and the night security guard let Candy into the lobby and called the lift for her. She pressed the button for the

21st floor; the flat came with her job as personal secretary to her father in Euro-Pacific Construction. She had achieved this job on merit, not nepotism, but needless to say, it provided her father with a very high level of loyalty and confidentiality, which was vital in the never ceasing battle to win contracts against the competition. She found her key and opened the door to the flat, instinctively reaching for the light switch. Her wrist was grabbed and she was pulled into the dark hallway; at the same instant a black cloth bag was placed over her head and she quickly lost consciousness from the sickly, cloying fumes of a chloroform pad which was pressed over her mouth and nose.

*

The debate at the Legislative Council Building had concerned a number of amendments to the Basic Law, which had been proposed by the Communist Chinese delegation to the Basic Law Drafting Committee. Ever since the hard-liners had re-exerted their out-moded influence after the massacre in Tianenmen Square, all the negotiations with the People's Republic of China had achieved little headway and, indeed, many had regressed. Even at the end of the debate, just before one in the morning, reason and patience had lost to rhetoric and alarmist speeches. Every single amendment was defeated with a large majority.

The Governor had returned to the 'Legco' debate from the reception on YS' yacht, and now wearily left the building and got into the waiting Daimler. His wife, had returned to Government House to have supper with their two daughters, who were both on holiday from their schools in the UK. The Daimler swept through the gates of Government House and the car door was opened as soon as it came to a halt by the pillared entrance, where the Governor's Private Secretary was waiting.

'Hello Martin, not more problems I hope,' the Governor said anxiously.

His secretary waited until the front door had been closed and then said, 'I hope not, Sir; the Prime Minister put through a call about five minutes ago. I explained where you were and that you would return the call within twenty minutes.'

'You've no idea what it might be, Martin?' the Governor queried as he followed his secretary into the 'box'. The latter was a free standing, 'container-like' room-within another-room, which permitted bug-free conversation. 'Which line was it on, Martin?' the Governor queried as his secretary swung over the steel locks on the door. A green light appeared as soon as the locks were fastened and the hum of the air-conditioning increased in volume.

'The 'box' is secure, Sir,' the secretary said, following the routine procedure.

'What? Oh, thank you, Martin.'

'It's that 'phone, Sir,' and his secretary pointed to a black plastic attaché case. 'The codes are all inserted, ready for your call.'

'Oh hell!' muttered the Governor, 'it's never good news on that machine. Oh well, let's get on with it. My wife and the girls around, Martin?' he asked, as he sat in front of the case and opened it.

'Yes Sir, they're in your private lounge. Your wife said they would wait up for you. Right Sir,' his secretary added, 'the Prime Minister should be on the line in a few seconds. Shall I stay?'

'Yes please, Martin,' and then, 'good morning from Hong Kong, Prime Minister,' and the Governor then listened for nearly five minutes, interjecting with only an occasional affirmative or negative. At the end of the call he quietly replaced the phone inside its cradle in the attaché case and closed the lid. His face had drained of all colour.

'Bad news, Sir?' came the quiet and hesitant enquiry from his secretary.

'Our Intelligence Directorate has uncovered a plot to wipe out Hong Kong and the majority of Southern China with some form of nuclear device,' the Governor said in a voice barely louder than a whisper.

'What!' gasped his secretary. 'I mean how do they know? . . . when will . . .'

'By Monday,' the Governor interrupted. 'Martin, there's no time to lose. I want CBF, the CP and the Chief Secretary here,' and he glanced at his watch, 'by 2.30 and I want my Security Committee meeting brought forward to nine, but I want minimum attendance - only the principals, understood. Oh yes, Martin, and please tell the Chief Secretary that his appointment with me at eleven still stands.'

'Yes Sir,' his secretary was taking notes.

'I'm going up to see my wife and the girls, have a shower and I'll be back in half an hour,' the Governor said, undoing the door of the box. He went up to the lounge, mentally ticking off in his mind all the points which he would need to discuss with the Commander British Forces and the Commissioner of Police. He could hear the sound of the late night horror movie coming from the lounge as he approached the door. 'Hello everyone . . .' he started as he opened the door and then stopped. The room was in a chaotic mess; overturned tables, chairs and broken pictures were scattered all over the floor. His wife was lying bound, gagged and strapped to the sofa; of the girls, there was not a sign. The Governor rushed to his wife and removed the gag.

'The girls,' his wife sobbed, 'they've taken them!'

CHAPTER 11

Unable to see his watch, Doyle Barnes guessed that he had been left for about half an hour, when he heard footsteps approaching the door. He had failed to remove the blindfold. He had been told at Langley, in Virginia, that when the end came, it was usually in a seedy hotel bedroom or to be discovered floating head down in some polluted backwater and never in a heroic gunfight, as so often portrayed in novels. They had mentioned sodium pentathol, so presumably that would be done now and once they considered that they had learnt as much as they needed, it was the long drop for Barnes. He had no idea how many people had come into the room.

'Well, Mr Barnes, if that really is your name, there is a slight change of plan for you. We have just removed your colleague, Mr Gunn, who has been incinerated in a BMW, which is lying at the foot of the Tai Tam Dam. We are going to take you to Mr Gunn's room in the Mandarin, where we will inject you with sodium pentathol. After hearing all you have to tell us, we will substitute another drug, which you will probably know as LSD, and then you, most unfortunately, will decide to jump from the balcony of Mr Gunn's hotel room. That little problem will certainly occupy the police for some time.' It was the same voice and now it was directed at whoever else was in the room. 'Have you spoken to our contact at the hotel?'

'Yes, Sir, we'll be taking him up in the service lift; it's all arranged. We'll be given a pass key to get into his room.'

'Right; see that there are no mistakes; understood?'

'Yes, Sir.'

'Very well, get on with it!' and the owner of the voice left the room. Doyle's handcuffs were unlocked from the ring bolt in the wall and he was lifted to his feet where his other wrist was then locked into the cuffs. He was guided back to the car and once more, unceremoniously dumped in the boot. He tried to judge where the building was, but the closest he got was somewhere on the Peak. The car stopped and he was lifted out of the boot. Noise around him confirmed that he might well be in the service area at the back of the Mandarin or any hotel for that matter. The conversation around him was Cantonese and spoken too quickly for him to understand what was being said. The rain seemed to have stopped because his feet went through puddles but he couldn't feel the rain on his face. He was led into the building and heard lift doors opening. As the lift started to move, a handkerchief was forced into his mouth and covered with adhesive tape. The lift stopped and the doors opened; he walked onto a thick pile carpet and his escorts brought him to a halt after what seemed about twenty yards. No one spoke; a door was opened and he was led into what he assumed was Gunn's room.

There was a sudden flurry of urgent whispers amongst those escorting him and he was hastily dragged into the bathroom. He heard the click as the bedroom door was shut. He was dragged over to the bath and a handcuff was undone from one wrist and locked onto what appeared, from touch, to be a water pipe. Everything went quiet and then he heard a late returning reveller banging his door shut. Even if he was able to make some sort of noise, the person next door would probably pass out in a couple of minutes and would sleep through an earthquake.

Doyle's thoughts were interrupted by a crash outside the door into the room, followed by all sorts of noises from the hotel corridor. They were unmistakably the noises of a scuffle or fight, but who in the hell was fighting whom? Doyle wondered. John was dead - or so the 'voice' said so who had bumped into his captors? And then everything went quiet.

*

'Was there any note left by the men? I mean any sort of threat or demand?' asked Major General Rogers, having been told of the most recent development. He and Sir Peter Aldridge had arrived within a minute of each other just before 2.30am at Government House. The Chief Secretary arrived at 2.35; his apology for being five minutes late was ignored by the Governor. All three were given a summary of the Prime Minister's telephone call and the abduction of the Governor's two children. It was at this point that CBF had asked his question.

'No, Patrick; all my wife can remember is that suddenly about six - she's not even sure of the number - men burst into the lounge. The girls put up a hell of a struggle, but both were eventually bound and gagged. It's a disgrace that they managed to get through the security of this building. Peter, I shall want a full explanation of how this was achieved and the steps being taken to remedy the situation by the time we meet for my Security Meeting at nine this morning. I shall not need you there at nine, Sir Peter; Martin will have told you that I would still like to see you at eleven; that concerns another matter which we've discussed before.' Both the CP and CBF were well aware what was going to be said at that meeting. The scandal surrounding the Chief Secretary's wife had become the main topic of the gossip

129

columns of the press and now the ICAC had produced a report that provided irrefutable evidence of Sir Peter's involvement with insider dealing on the Stock Exchange. The director of the ICAC, James Taylor, had also been invited to Government House half an hour later at 11.30 and would be asked to submit his resignation for his scandalous behaviour with another senior government official's wife. It was for all these reasons that the Governor did not want the Chief Secretary to attend his Security Committee at nine that morning.

'Did the Prime Minister divulge the source of this information?' asked the Commissioner of Police.

'No,' replied the Governor. 'Sir Peter,' he continued, 'I shall want a full brief from the Secretary for Security at my meeting. I would be grateful if you would go and brief him now so that he has time to produce a report. Thank you for turning up at this hour of the night; I'll see you later this morning.' That was the Chief Secretary's dismissal and he rose from his chair, bid the men in the room goodnight and left.

'Was it wise, Sir, to have let him know the context of the phone call?' asked the CBF.

'I had no choice, Patrick. He must go and brief Security Branch and until I remove him from office, officially, tomorrow - sorry, later this morning - he is my Chief Secretary. He's being carefully watched, isn't he Peter,' the Governor added turning to the CP.

'Yes, Sir Charles; my head of Special Branch is supervising that personally.'

'That's Winchcombe, isn't it?'

'Yes, that's right, Sir.'

'Very well; thank you, and now I'll answer your question about the source of this information. Our Intelligence Directorate has an agent who's been in Hong Kong for no more than 48 hours and it is he who has provided them with this information. Another report is expected this morning. Once we have had the content of that passed to us, we must be prepared to use every possible resource to confirm if this nuclear device exists, and if it does, neutralise it.'

'The typhoon will hamper us, Sir,' the CBF quietly reminded the Governor.

'And I strongly suspect that you will very shortly receive a form of ransom note that will prevent us making any overt move to track down this device. Do we have any names yet, of those thought to be involved?' asked the CP.

'No names yet, Peter, and yes I'm sure you're right about the ransom note; I'd also temporarily forgotten about the wretched typhoon. Gentlemen, we don't appear to hold any quality cards;

please go and find something that gives me a hand to play. I mustn't keep you any longer; Heavens knows, you've little enough time as it is. Goodnight gentlemen; I'll see you both in a few hours time,' and he turned and went upstairs to comfort his distraught wife.

*

Mr and Mrs Hiram J. Bronowski, from Illinois, were thoroughly enjoying their week in Hong Kong in room 681 at the Mandarin Hotel. The holiday was a reward from the Ford Motor Company for his outstanding sales record. There were fifty or more couples like him on this 'incentive holiday', not only from the States, but from Europe as well. They were all due to fly to Bali the next day to stay at the Bali Hyatt for a further four days before returning, via a night in London, to the USA. Hiram Bronowski had overeaten at the Jumbo floating restaurant in Aberdeen Harbour; he and Mrs Bronowski, with three other American couples, had tucked into Peking Duck and a host of other dishes, all washed down with copious quantities of wine and lager. As a result of this overindulgence, he had woken at three in the morning with chronic indigestion, heartburn and a mouth, which tasted like the bottom of a parrot's cage.

Hiram was standing in front of the bathroom mirror surveying the ravages of his excesses during the evening, when to his horror he heard someone inserting a key into the lock of his bedroom door. This was followed by a kick and then a thump on the door panel which was clear enough evidence to Hiram that someone was trying to force an entry into the room. A firm believer in making full use of all the security arrangements in a top international hotel, Hiram stumbled back into the bedroom, picked up the phone on his side of the double bed and considerably exaggerated the situation to the hotel security staff. The immediate result of this was a rapid exodus from the hotel reception area of the duty security officer and no less than five of the hotel staff. They were expecting to have to deal with at least a slack handful of 'goddam drunken maniacs' who were trying to beat down Mr Bronowski's door.

Hiram Bronowski appeared out of his room like an enraged bull just a fraction of a second before the lift door opened and retreated, if anything more rapidly, as a burst of five rounds from the Heckler-Koch sub-machine gun missed him by a fairly wide margin. As the man holding the sub-machine gun swung back to the lift, the night stick of one of the hotel security staff landed on the back of his head with such force that his skull was shattered, killing him instantly.

At this point, John Gunn started to regain consciousness, but wished he hadn't as the pandemonium in the corridor was only now

131

exceeded by the appearance of Mrs Bronowski with hair in curlers and something which resembled a mud pack on her face. Her husband was explaining to the security staff how he had faced them all single handed and was not satisfied with the level of security in the 'best goddam hotel in South-East Asia.' Gunn's return to consciousness had not been noticed, until he pulled himself up onto his knees and then to a standing position. Hiram's courage suddenly deserted him and both he and the horrific, mud-packed Mrs Bronowski disappeared and slammed the door of 681. Gunn explained in Cantonese to the hotel security staff that he was the occupant of room 682. He told them that he had been attacked as he returned to his room. He suggested that the police should be called and if there was a duty hotel doctor, he would be grateful for a plaster on the side of his head where he had been hit by his attackers. The security officer left two of his men in the corridor to guard the three bodies and Gunn assured him that he would be available when the police and doctor arrived. He then went into his room to have a shower and change. As he switched on the bathroom light, he instinctively started to go for the Browning as he was faced with the trussed, blindfolded and gagged character, handcuffed to the pipes behind the bath taps. 'Doyle! Hey, you don't have to go to all that trouble to have a shower,' Gunn laughed as he removed the sticking plaster and gag.

'Wise guy! Just get me out of these things.'

'Keep your voice down, there are two of the hotel security staff out in the corridor. At the moment they believe, I think, that this was some sort of hotel mugging, but your presence, chained to the bathroom pipes, puts a different complexion on the whole matter. Wait a second,' and Gunn left the bathroom and retrieved his room key from his pocket. He then walked out into the corridor and told the two men that he would like to have his room key back which his attackers had taken, and without waiting for their approval, Gunn bent down and started searching the men's pockets. After a momentary hesitation the security staff shrugged and let him continue. Sod's law made it the last of the three bodies, which had the key for the handcuffs. Holding this in his closed left hand, he produced his room key, which he held up for inspection. He returned to his room and closed the door. As soon as Doyle was released from the water pipes and sipping a whisky from the mini-bar in the room, the two men exchanged accounts of what had happened that night. 'I wonder who this character is who speaks English with no accent; you didn't get any indication of his height or anything else?'

'Sorry, no help there; it's damn difficult to judge anything when you're trussed up like a turkey.' There was a knock on the door. Doyle headed for the bathroom, but Gunn diverted him to the fitted wardrobe. If this was the hotel doctor he would probably want to use the bathroom to wash the dried blood off the side of Gunn's head. It was the doctor and he did use the bathroom. Hot on his heels came the police to whom Gunn gave an account of the assault. Photographs were taken of the bodies and they were then removed. It was just on ten to six as Gunn wearily dug Doyle out of the wardrobe and told him that it was clear for him to return to his own room in the hotel.

'We'll meet for breakfast at ten, OK?'

'OK,' and Doyle returned to his room after collecting his key from reception.

*

Geoffrey Winchcombe was woken by the phone beside the bed. He glanced at his watch; 3.16. 'Now who the hell is that?' he muttered, picking up the phone; 'Winchcombe,' he said.

'Peter Butler here, Geoffrey; I must speak with you most urgently.'

'How many times have I told you not to ring me here, Peter,' Winchcombe almost hissed down the phone. 'Now what is it?'

'May I come to the house, Geoffrey? It really is desperately urgent that we speak.'

'Oh, very well; I'll meet you in that lay-by, fifty metres short of the entrance; you know the one I mean?'

'Er, yes; I think so. Why can't I come to the apartment?'

'I'll tell you when I meet you; how long will you be?'

'Ten minutes, at the most.'

'Right,' and Winchcombe slammed the phone down. 'Stupid bugger,' he swore and punched out another number and gave a series of curt instructions. He then got carefully out of the double bed.

'Problems dear?' came the sleepy query from the other side of the bed.

'Yes, as usual; sorry to wake you Celie. Go back to sleep,' which is exactly what Celestine Winchcombe did. Geoffrey Winchcombe dressed and went down in the lift to the lobby. The security guard was asleep in his little office and hadn't heard the lift. Winchcombe checked that he had his keys and went cautiously across to the security barrier, ducked under it and walked down the short entrance drive to the road. He turned right and walked down the hill. The lay-by was conveniently situated round a corner and out of sight of the apartment block. These lay-bys were at every quarter mile on the Peak roads to allow overloaded buses and lorries to pull in and let the stream of frustrated traffic overtake. There was no traffic on the road and not a sign of anyone. The torrential rain, which had only just stopped, had left the Peak swathed in mist which deadened all sound and which was dyed orange by the sodium street lamps. Winchcombe stood back in the shadows of the lay-by; there was no sign of Peter Butler yet.

Even as he did so, the Chief Secretary's car appeared and after a momentary reduction in speed, pulled into the lay-by; there was no one following him. Sir Peter Butler got out of the car and looked around in a bewildered manner, failing to see Winchcombe in the shadows as the mist drifted with the fitful gusts of rain-laden wind.

The head of the Special Branch walked out of the shadows and called to Peter Butler, who turned, startled at the sound of the voice. 'Calm down, Peter; you go on like this and you'll land all of us in trouble.'

'That's just it,' blurted the Chief Secretary, 'the Governor had a call from London about an hour and a half ago,' he continued after a glance at his watch. 'MI6, or whatever, has briefed the Prime Minister on the general outline of YS' plan. It can only be a matter of time until the Governor knows all our names. I. . . .'

'Stop, Peter; did the Governor say how MI6 got this information?'

'No, I was asked to leave to go and brief Robin Masefield so that he can have a report ready for the Security Committee meeting which the Governor has called for nine this morning. The Governor has asked me to see him at eleven and has said he does not want me at the Security meeting.'

'Do you know what the meeting at eleven is about?'

'Unofficially, yes; I'm going to be asked for my resignation.'

'Oh, Peter; you stupid bastard! Why didn't you give that tramp the push ages ago.'

'I love her, Geoffrey.'

'Dear God, give me strength; do you realise that the CP has told me, personally, to keep you under constant surveillance. If I hadn't made a call after you phoned me, you would have one of my men watching this meeting.'

'Oh no!' gasped Sir Peter; 'what do we do now, Geoffrey?'

'You go home, get some sleep if you can - you look awful, incidentally. I'll get hold of the other three and the sooner we all disappear from Hong Kong, the better. Be ready to leave anytime from mid-day today. Is that understood?'

'Yes, but what do I tell Sus. . . .'

'You tell that bitch nothing; is that quite clear, Peter?'

'Yes, of course.'

'Go into work as normal, Peter, and wait for a message from me. Now go home and for Christ's sake get a grip of yourself. Go on, off you go,' this was added after the Chief Secretary had got into the car and had started to wind down the window. The head of Special Branch watched the tail lights of the car disappear round the next corner and then swore as he turned to walk back to the apartment block.

As he turned, his face was lit up by the sodium lamp and gave the officer from Special Branch a perfect photograph of his boss, taken by the image-intensifying camera. 'The CP will be most interested in that photo,' he muttered as he hurried back down the road to his motorbike.

CHAPTER 12

Gunn was woken shortly after 9.30 by the phone ringing. It was Charles McBain, the Assistant Commissioner. 'I've just glanced at the reports about the mugging in the Mandarin last night and the Marine Police account of that shooting on Lamma Island. I'm sorry that you seem to have had such bad luck since returning to Hong Kong. Aileen has chided me for not inviting you round for a meal, so I'm trying to make amends. Unfortunately, both of us are tied up with evening engagements connected with the handover ceremonies for the rest of this week and the weekend, and then I'm off with the whole family on Sunday evening to UK to start the boys off at their boarding school. Could you possibly come and have a sort of 'brunch' with us at about 9.30 tomorrow morning?' At that very moment, brunch was the last thing which Gunn felt like; at 9.30 or any other time of the day, however it was a kind offer and he and Aileen had been close friends of his parents.

'Thanks, Charles; that's kind of you and Aileen. Yes, of course I'll come. Is it the same apartment?'

'No, we moved a couple of years ago, when they promoted me - to Tower Court; do you remember it?'

'Yes, I think so; off the Peak Road, around Magazine Gap?'

'That's right; after the junction at Magazine Gap, take the first right into Barker Road and Tower Court is about 200 yards along on your left.'

'Oh yes, I remember.' The building belied its name; it could hardly be described as a tower as it was only three storeys high and was reserved for the senior grades of the Government and police. 'Many thanks again,' and he replaced the phone. His head was still painful from the blow, which he'd received some hours previously and his right arm had come up in a multi-hued bruise from the blow in Sadie's flat, but a hot and then cold shower worked wonders. At two minutes after ten, Gunn walked into the coffee shop of the Mandarin and spotted Doyle in a chair by the windows, which overlooked Connaught Road.

'How's the head?' Doyle greeted Gunn.

'Fine thanks; those pills the hotel doctor gave me worked wonders. Have you ordered and what about your head?'

'Head's OK and yes, I've ordered; I'm having fruit juice, coffee and rolls.'

'I'm feeling hungry,' Gunn muttered as he studied the menu. 'The last time I had a proper meal must've been at lunch yesterday. I'll have everything that you've had, but I'll start with a plate of bacon and eggs,' this was directed towards the waiter who had appeared to take his order.

'OK, so what's your plan for today?' and Doyle broke open a fresh, warm croissant.

'Time is running out fast, Doyle; counting today, we've only got five days till this disaster occurs and at the moment we haven't the faintest idea what or where it is, except that it's not a bomb - according to Balmain. From what you overheard at Henshaw's place, all those involved in the plot - for want of any better word - are getting out of the place on or before Monday.'

'That's about it.'

'Now that Molyneux, Henshaw and Balmain are all dead, it only leaves Butler and Winchcombe. Of those two, I think there's more chance of getting something out of Butler and that's what I propose to do this morning. Could you go to your Consulate and send another signal to Washington and London, with a summary of what happened last night and all the characters involved in the conspiracy - including those that are dead - and tell them to stand by for requests for assistance. By now, my Directorate should have signalled with instructions; specifically, who is going to inform the Governor of this plot, and when? Got all that? Gunn paused as a TV screen in the corner of the coffee shop caught his eye. 'That's all we needed.'

'What's that? Doyle asked, turning round towards the TV. 'Oh no, not a typhoon. What're the chances of it hitting this place?'

'From what I can see, very high. That's really going to mess things up and will probably suit YS' plans perfectly. The more confusion and chaos there is, the better. Add the news of the typhoon to that signal, Doyle, and see if you can find out where YS' yacht is. That radioactive trace seems to be our only lead at the moment. If I have no success with Butler, then I'll have to have a go at Winchcombe.'

'Better let me give you a hand with that snake, John.'

'You're right; we'll keep in touch using mobiles or by leaving messages here, at the hotel,' Gunn glanced again at the TV; 'if that's moving at the speed they say it is, we really do have very little time. C'mon Doyle, let's get going,' and after signing the bill, the two men left the coffee shop. As they headed for the main entrance, a Chinese youth put down his comic and followed them out of the hotel. At the hotel entrance the youth with comic met with another man who had been flicking aimlessly through brochures at the excursion counter.

'We've got company, John.'

'Thanks; I'm going through Hutchinson House and then up onto the walkway. If you take the street level to Garden Road and your Consulate, I think we can give both of them an interesting morning.' They had reached Hutchinson House, which was another multi-storey office block, with shops and the Bull and Bear pub on the first two floors. Doyle turned right onto Murray Road and Gunn went through the automatic doors of Hutchinson House. Each of them was followed.

The majority of the large office blocks and shops were all connected by a walkway at first storey level. In Hong Kong this was an absolute necessity rather than a sensible innovation as the pavements at street level simply couldn't cope with the mass of humanity that thronged them throughout the day. These walkways led through split-level mezzanine floors, interior piazzas, restaurants and every type of shop from a fast order sandwich bar to the top designer and couturier shops in the world. They provided the tourist with total air-conditioned protection from the Hong Kong climate and ensured that he or she was relieved of the maximum amount of money possible. The whole of this area in Central was a maze of wide corridors with glass-fronted shops which made the task of following an unsuspecting quarry very easy, but impossible if he was alerted to the tail. Gunn rid himself of his tail before he was out of Hutchinson House by using a combination of escalators and lifts and then crossed over to the Bank of America Building and picked up a taxi at street level. The taxi took him to the Central Government Office in Lower Albert Road.

Central Government Office was a plain and uninspiring building in every possible way. It's dull design was only marginally improved by a portico bearing the heraldic coat of arms of the Hong Kong Government. The Governor's large black Daimler was parked outside. Beside it, looking very much the poor relation, was Commander British Forces' Ford Granada. This would soon fall into the veteran car category unless it was replaced, but then like many other things, it probably had to last until the Territory was handed back to the Chinese in a few days time.

Gunn went up to the reception desk on the right of the entrance hall and asked for the Chief Secretary' office. He was told that it was on the fifth floor. He would be directed to the office by the girl at the reception desk on that floor. He was met on the fifth floor and asked by the receptionist if he had an appointment.

138

'I've come from Police Headquarters with a most urgent message for Sir Peter Butler from the Head of Special Branch,' was Gunn's answer to the receptionist's enquiry.

'And your name, Sir?'

'Balmain,' this was a gamble that the receptionist would not know Balmain by sight and anyway the Chinese were just as prejudiced as the Caucasian. To the latter, all 'chinks' looked alike and to the former all 'gweilos' looked alike.

'Would you follow me Mr Balmain, please,' and Gunn followed the bespectacled receptionist to the Chief Secretary's office where he was handed over to a dour Scottish PA whose appearance was almost as offensive as her manner.

'Do you have an appointment?' was snapped at him as he entered the outer office.

'No I don't, but would you tell Sir Peter that I will only take a moment of his time; the subject is the meeting which we were both at last night and the matter is extremely urgent.'

'There was no meeting last night,' was the officious retort as the tight-lipped harridan consulted her appointment book.

'Sir Peter was at the reception on Yung Shue Wan's yacht last night where he, I and three other gentlemen had a meeting. I have a most urgent message from the Head of Special Branch who was one of the men at that meeting.'

'I very much doubt if the Chief Secretary can spare you the time, Mr Balmain; he's extremely busy today.'

'May I suggest that you let him be the judge of that.' Reluctantly, the intercom was pressed and the message passed.

'Please show Mr Balmain in straight away,' was the response from the intercom.

'Can I remind you, Sir, that you have an appointment with the Governor at eleven and that's in eighteen and a half minutes' time,' the lips were even tighter.

'Janet, please show Mr Balmain in; I'm well aware of my next appointment so please waste no more time,' and the intercom went dead. Puce in the face with frustrated rage and radiating her loathing of the male species, Gunn was led towards the door to the Chief Secretary's office by the humiliated PA, who only just succeeded in controlling her anger in time to remember to open the door.

'Mr Balmain, Sir Peter;' the introduction might have been chipped off a block of ice. Gunn walked in and quickly closed the door behind him. Sir Peter was standing with his back to Gunn, looking down at the screen of a small, portable TV set; he was watching a report on the

139

progress of Typhoon Pamela. Gunn stooped quickly and removed the Browning from the ankle holster.

'No doubt the typhoon will interfere with your plans for leaving Hong Kong before YS' plan reaches fruition, Sir Peter,' Gunn remarked quietly. The reaction was instantaneous; the Chief Secretary spun round, almost losing his balance as he did so, and was forced to grab the edge of the desk to steady himself.

'Who the hell are you,' he swore, reaching for the right hand drawer of his desk. Gunn took two quick paces forward and brought the barrel of the Browning hard down on his wrist.

'Please don't do anything like that again, Sir Peter. Sit down in that chair - no! Not the one behind your desk - that one,' and Gunn indicated with his left arm an easy chair with its back to the windows where the Chief Secretary would be separated from both his desk and any form of communication to his outer office.

'Who are you,' Sir Peter gasped, clutching his wrist as he sat in the chair.

'My name's John Gunn.'

'So Winch. . . .' Sir Peter began and then checked himself.

'Were you going to say, Sir Peter, that Assistant Commissioner Geoffrey Winchcombe, who was present with you at your meeting with YS last night, might have mentioned my name?'

'I've got nothing to say to you whatsoever.'

'Wrong again, Sir Peter; you've got lots to say to me. Whatever the outcome of YS' holocaust, you're finished. Molyneux, Henshaw and Balmain are all dead,' the reaction this information produced confirmed that it was news to the Chief Secretary, 'which puts you and Winchcombe pretty high on the disposable list, wouldn't you say?' There was no reply and it seemed as though Sir Peter Butler was barely paying attention to what Gunn was saying. 'Even if you get out of this place with your life before Monday - that is the date isn't it? - enough is known about your complicity in this conspiracy to put you away for the rest of your life. What is it that motivates a man like you, Sir Peter? You've totally destroyed the trust of the high office you've attained in the Government by dishonest dealings on the Stock Exchange, and the nymphomania of your wife has made you the laughing stock of Hong Kong. I'm giving you one opportunity to do something decent and stop YS' conspiracy. If you don't co-operate, I'll see that you suffer the full public humiliation which you deserve.'

The Chief Secretary's response took Gunn completely by surprise. After a pause of no more than five or so seconds, during which time he said nothing, Sir Peter suddenly leapt to his feet, took one quick stride to the window, threw it open and dived head first out of it.

Gunn moved quickly to the window and saw the Chief Secretary lying on the concrete fifty feet below with a very obviously broken neck. He then re-holstered the Browning and opened the door to the PA's office. 'Many thanks indeed Sir Peter; yes, I'll pass that on to your PA,' and then turning to the delightful Janet said, 'Sir Peter said he wasn't to be disturbed for a couple of minutes. Goodbye.'

'Goodbye, Mr Balmain,' came the frosty reply as he left her office. He walked quickly to the lifts, both of which were indicating that they were on the ground floor. He took the stairs and met up with the lifts on the second floor. No alarm had been raised yet. The lift stopped on the ground floor, the doors opened and the lobby was as dull and uninviting as always, but somewhere in the distance, Gunn could hear shouting, which was getting louder. He walked out of the building, turned left and at the junction with Garden Road, turned left again and was soon swallowed up in the crowds in Central.

Gunn cursed; every source of information was snuffed out as soon as confronted with complicity in the conspiracy. That only left Winchcombe and he had to be the hardest and most dangerous one to crack of all.

*

Captain Raoul Bueno arrived on the bridge of Middle Kingdom at about the same time as Gunn had received his phone call from the Assistant Commissioner. He was barely five feet eight inches in height, with a barrel-like chest supported by an equally large abdomen. The top of his head was totally bald and a monk's tonsure of long, straggly black hair grew over his collar, which matched the unkempt state of his heavily bearded face. He had not been employed by YS with a view to winning any beauty competition, but because his knowledge of the Western Pacific, South China Sea and all their associated islands was second to none. This knowledge had come from nearly twenty years of preying on the fishing and sea community of South-East Asia, having started life as the illegitimate son of a notorious Filipino pirate. Natural disasters, such as earthquakes, floods, volcanic eruptions and typhoons had always produced rich pickings for unscrupulous scavengers like Raoul Bueno. Even more profitable were the pickings to be had from man-made disasters such as the wars in Vietnam, Kampuchea, Laos and Cambodia and the weeping sore of communist terrorism in the Philippines. These wars had set in train a constant stream of refugees which flowed east towards China and Hong Kong and south-east down the chain of islands from Malaysia to Papua New Guinea. His escapades and reputation reached YS' intelligence network and resulted in him accepting employment as the bosun on YS' previous yacht. He very quickly came to the attention of his employer as an individual who was totally devoid of any morals, compassion or any pleasant attribute and was utterly ruthless in his handling of the crew of Middle Kingdom.

On entering the bridge, Raoul went across to the weather forecast facsimile and tore off the hard copy, which was protruding from the front of the machine. One glance told him enough and he moved to the command console at the front of the bridge where he picked up a telephone, which connected him to YS' suite of staterooms and offices. It was Mandy Yung Shue Wan who answered the phone, which she then handed to her father.

'Mr Yung Shue Wan? . . . ah, the typhoon has changed course and is heading for Hong Kong. May I recommend that you consider leaving this anchorage within the next hour.'

'You may indeed, Captain Bueno; how long will it take us to reach Luzon?'

'At cruising speed, we'll be in sight of Luzon by dawn tomorrow and in the lee of the island by midday.'

'Thank you Captain Bueno; please make arrangements to leave as soon as you are ready,' and without waiting for any acknowledgement, YS replaced the phone in its bracket. 'How very convenient,' he continued, 'it would seem that even the weather has contrived to intensify the panic and chaos of my little plan.'

'Aren't you taking a risk that one of those men who've helped you will talk?' Mandy asked her father.

'No, my dear, that was never a risk which I had any intention of taking. Three of them are dead and the remaining two will follow shortly.'

'What about the sixth man,' she asked.

'There's no need to worry about him, my dear; he is the architect of this plan and sometimes the intensity of his loathing of not only the Chinese Communists, but the government of his own country exceeds mine. No, we have no worry in that direction,' and feeling the movement of Middle Kingdom, he added, 'let's go on deck, my dear.' As they both reached the deck, Middle Kingdom was heading for Victoria Harbour and the Lyemun Channel beyond it.

'Take a good look at your birthplace, Mandy; neither you nor I will ever come back here,' and YS added, 'and nor will anyone else after Monday.'

*

Dan Grant had anchored American Pie in a sheltered cove on the west coast of Cat Island. The yacht had reached the anchorage shortly after midday and he had decided to have lunch after they had anchored, having been assured by the boat boys of the quality and variety of seafood available from the fishing village which was just visible through the coconut palms. The yacht was anchored in six metres of crystal clear water 150 yards from the beach. Along the beach was an assortment of brightly coloured fishing canoes with their 'crab claw' sails furled and the fishermen perched on the outriggers mending their nets. While Amy prepared the lunch, Pedro had taken the Japanese ashore in the dinghy to buy some prawns, lobsters and crabs. After the 300 mile run on the engines from Mindanao, Dan retired to the engine compartment to give the diesels a thorough service. As soon as the Japanese charter guests returned, the fresh seafood was cooked and then they all sat down to a meal of freshly baked rolls, seafood, mayonnaise and a chilled, dry white wine. As soon as the meal was over, everyone retired to secluded areas around the yacht for an afternoon siesta.

*

Typhoon Pamela was heading straight for Hong Kong and nothing short of a miracle was going to divert this raging vortex of high velocity winds. Since ten the previous evening, the typhoon had covered another hundred miles. The Royal Observatory was predicting a direct strike on Hong Kong between ten and midnight on Saturday and the number three signal was quickly replaced by the number eight. All loading and unloading of ships had been stopped, hatches were sealed, derricks stowed and lashed and there was now a constant trail of ships leaving the harbour to get well clear of the typhoon.

The fishing junks and sampans were all jostling with each other to find space inside one of the typhoon shelters. In the squatter villages of the New Territories, Kowloon and Hong Kong, the residents were lashing down the roofs of the shacks with chains and rope in the vain hope that this might prevent them from being blown away. In the police and military headquarters all duty personnel manning emergency appointments were on eight hour shifts around the clock. Every remaining army unit had at least a company-sized sub-unit on standby. In the duty battalion and the engineer regiment, these sub-units were on half-hour's notice to move and so slept in full combat uniform. All the military earth moving and lifting plant was fuelled and ready for deployment. The marine police launches were scouring all the bays and coves around the Territory to chase the more ignorant amateur boating enthusiasts into the typhoon shelters. In military headquarters and units, all those not involved in manning emergency posts were sent home to their quarters to assist in the procedure of preparing for a typhoon. Everything had to be removed from balconies, shutters were lowered, carpets were rolled back from the windows and baths were filled with fresh water to provide a reserve for cooking and drinking if supplies were cut off. Those who had ignored instructions to maintain a reserve of tinned food and bottled-gas cookers, rushed to the supermarkets to remedy this oversight, only to find the majority of the population doing the same. This led to empty stores, traffic jams, minor rioting, accidents and increasing panic as Hong Kong prepared itself for the worst typhoon in its history which immediately put on 'hold' all preparation for the handover ceremony.

CHAPTER 13

Geoffrey Winchcombe was back in his apartment just after four in the morning. He returned to bed, but was unable to get back to sleep. He had been told that the removal of Molyneux had been successful and another telephone call had informed him that Gunn and an American called Barnes, who was probably CIA, had been dealt with. Henshaw and Balmain were both liabilities and he was certain that it wouldn't be long before they joined Molyneux. Butler was a disaster and had to be dealt with sooner rather than later. So where did that leave him? It seemed as though a tidy-up operation was in progress to remove any possible chance of a leak or blackmail. It was high time he was out of Hong Kong. He glanced at his wife who was fast asleep. They were booked on the Friday night Cathay Pacific flight to London. Should he bring it forward? It would make Celestine highly suspicious and she would probably refuse as it would no doubt interfere with her bridge, golf or charitable works. All these thoughts turned over in his mind until his alarm went off at six. He got out of bed and quietly got dressed in his running shorts and trainers.

Geoffrey Winchcombe went jogging every morning without fail and had two or three routes which he used. Today would have to be the short one as there was a great deal to get organised before their departure from Hong Kong. Celestine Winchcombe knew nothing of her husband's involvement with YS.

He left the apartment and ran down the road past the lay-by where only a couple of hours earlier he had met the Chief Secretary. Just round the corner beyond the lay-by, he crossed the road and turned onto a tarmac path, which wound across the face of the jungled escarpment of the Peak and was very popular as a jogging track. After the rain of the previous night, the air was cleaner and clearer and a breeze had swept away the mist.

Winchcombe prided himself on both the slimness of his figure and his fitness. He kept up a steady pace and it was only occasionally that anyone would overtake him. All the regulars were out whom he saw every morning. It was pleasantly quiet and as the path curved around the inside of a re-entrant in the hillside, he heard and then saw that there was another jogger following him. Winchcombe had always been a highly competitive man, whether it was in his job or in any of

145

the sports which he played. He had noticed that the man following him was Chinese, who, as a race, were not yet noted for their long or short distance running prowess. He gradually increased his pace and soon the sweat was pouring down his bare torso. After half a mile, he decided to ease off the pace, convinced that there would be no sign of the runner behind him. As his pace slowed and his breathing eased, he could hear the runner behind him and a glance over his shoulder proved that he was less than twenty yards away and now gaining ground quickly. There were two joggers coming towards Winchcombe. He recognised the two women and returned their smiled greeting. Ahead of Winchcombe, the path went round a spur, which concealed any view of the rest of the route. The pace of the man behind him increased and he was obviously going to overtake Winchcombe. 'Bloody Chink trying to prove something,' he thought childishly which was, in fact, the very last thought he did have, because a split second later his head was blown apart by a .357 magnum, soft-nosed bullet. His killer pushed Geoffrey Winchcombe over the side of the path, down a forty-foot drop, into thick undergrowth and then returned the silenced gun to its holster inside the track suit. The runner's pace barely faltered as he continued his morning exercise along the path. By chance, Winchcombe had fallen into the thick vegetation at the back of a squatter's tin and cardboard shack, which resulted in the arrival of the police just before nine o'clock. His body was in the morgue half an hour later.

*

By 8.55, those who had been summoned to attend the emergency session of the Governor's Security Committee were all seated in the ante-room of the Executive Council Room in Central Government Office. In addition to the CBF and CP, there was the Head of the Fire Services, Hamish Walker, whose reddened eyes indicated an excess of whisky the previous evening and Robin Masefield, the Secretary for Security. The Governor's Private Secretary, Martin Holmes, entered the waiting room and invited the four men into the Executive Council Room. The Governor was seated at the head of the rectangular table and had been reading the brief prepared by the Secretary for Security. He removed his reading glasses; 'please be seated, gentlemen, and we will get on with the meeting as quickly as possible.' He had noticed Walker's reddened eyes and wondered whether it had been wise to include him, but it was impossible not to as the Fire Service possessed all the radiation monitoring equipment and the protective clothing.

The Governor opened the meeting with a summary of what had been said to him by the Prime Minister, the break-in to Government

House and the abduction of his two daughters. He concluded by turning to Hamish Walker and said, 'this will all be news to you Hamish as the four other people in this room were involved with all this in the small hours of this morning. Very well; your brief please, Robin - no, please remain seated,' he added. It was the standard practice for those required to brief 'Exco' to stand.

The Secretary for Security was a young and highly intelligent Honours graduate from Oxford who was tipped to replace the Chief Secretary. He was a 'workaholic' and had succeeded in producing a brilliant position paper on the crisis which clearly and briefly explored every eventuality, but which, in conclusion, he frankly admitted after some twenty minutes, meant very little until they had heard from the kidnappers of the Governor's children. The Governor then opened the meeting for discussion and all the while every detail was recorded in Martin Holmes' shorthand.

Just after 10.30, a red light came on by the door and Martin Holmes got up and went out. He returned immediately and walked over to the Governor and bending down, produced a black attaché case from under the table which he placed beside the Governor. 'The Prime Minister, Sir,' he said, lifting the phone out of its cradle. The Governor pulled a notebook towards him as he listened and then started to write. At the end of the conversation, he informed the Prime Minister of the abduction of his daughters and confirmed that there would be a report every eight hours, or sooner. It was now 10.42. As the Governor looked up from his notebook, he appeared to have aged ten years in the same number of minutes. 'I suppose it could have been worse, but I'm not sure how. These are the men known to be involved in this plot. Yung Shue Wan, the Chief Secretary,' he paused at the audible intake of breath around the table. 'Your head of Special Branch, Peter; your Commander Molyneux, Patrick; George Balmain, one of our High Court Judges and Robin Henshaw, the MD of Euro-Pacific Construction. Of those men, only Yung Shue Wan, the Chief Secretary and Winchcombe are alive; the remainder have all been murdered.' He smiled ruefully at the CP, 'it seems you set a thief to catch a thief, Peter.' The Commissioner of Police pushed a photo across the table.

'That was taken at 3.47 this morning by a Special Branch policeman. I had my suspicions, but no proof until this was handed to me at 7.30 this morning. My apologies, Sir, I . . .' but he was interrupted by the red light.

Martin Holmes hurried to the door. He returned, ashen faced and whispered to the Governor who then addressed the meeting. 'I'm sorry, gentlemen, I'll amend that list. The Chief Secretary has just

147

committed suicide - or been murdered; someone came for an unscheduled appointment just before Butler was discovered on the concrete below his window, so whether he jumped or was pushed is not known. Winchcombe's body was found in the last hour on Chatham Path. He had been shot. As yet we have no . . .' again the red light came on, 'I expect I spoke to soon; what is it, Martin?'

'Your wife has received a phone call, as has Peter Wyngarde, the Chairman of Euro-Pacific, whose daughter has also been abducted. The call has been recorded. There are instructions to collect a tape from a video rental shop in Central, but the warning was clear. Any action taken against Yung Shue Wan will result in the immediate death or mutilation of one of the hostages.' The private secretary turned to the Governor, 'I'm so sorry about this, Sir,' but the Governor waved him back to his seat.

'Does anyone in this room have the slightest idea who the British agent is who has discovered all this?' There was no response. 'Martin, please come back with me to Government House and get Peter Wyngarde to come and meet me there - with his wife Josie,' he added. 'I must ensure that my wife is all right and I want you to put a call through to the Prime Minister. I want to see that British agent,' and he left the room.

*

Peter Wyngarde had arrived at the office at 8.30 and was mildly surprised to see that Candy was not in the outer office. He thought no more about it as he sorted out various papers from his brief case and tapes from his recorder. At ten to nine, he went into the outer office expecting to find Candy, but the office was still empty. He picked up the phone, pressed the button for an outside line and rang her apartment. There was no answer. He rang his wife to check if Candy was there or whether she had had any phone calls. His next call was on the internal system to the receptionist to get his car round to the front entrance. Twenty minutes later he got out of the lift and rang the bell outside Candy's apartment. After the third ring, he went down in the lift again to the lobby, showed the security officer his identity card, carried by everyone in Hong Kong, and the two of them returned to the apartment with a set of pass keys. The security officer opened the door and they both went in. Peter Wyngarde went straight to the bedroom where he saw the untouched bed. He headed towards the amah's quarters at the back of the apartment, shouting, 'Susanna!' as he went . He opened the amah's bedroom door, took one look and came out retching. Susanna was on the bed and her throat had been slit from ear to ear. The security officer looked in and came out just as quickly. Peter Wyngarde staggered to the phone in the lounge and rang the police and then his office. The receptionist told him that a letter had just arrived by special delivery for him marked 'personal and urgent'. Mary, please get it delivered immediately to my daughter's apartment, where I am at the moment,' he instructed and then rang his wife. The police arrived four minutes before the delivery of the letter. Peter Wyngarde opened the letter and read the typed message.

*

Gunn dialled Doyle Barnes who answered immediately, 'get here just as fast as you can. Things have started to move and there are instructions for you from London. There'll be someone waiting for you at the gate.'

'I'll be there in five minutes,' and Gunn broke the connection and left the hotel. The taxi dropped him outside the fortified entrance to the US Consulate in Garden Road. Ever since a lorry bomb had been driven through the US Embassy entrance in Beirut, killing scores of Marines and Embassy staff, the Americans had adopted something of a siege mentality in the security arrangements for their diplomatic premises in the capitals of the world. Stretching the full width of the entrance was a three-foot high metal barrier, held in place with hydraulic rams which was reputed to be able to stop an Abraham's tank. All the windows were fitted with reflecting glass, allowing the occupants to see out but no prying cameras or other surveillance devices to see in.

Gunn walked up to the pedestrian entrance, which was guarded by a Marine Sergeant. The entrance was evidently being observed from within the building because instructions were issued to the guard through a small radio as Gunn approached. He was allowed through the turnstile and given directions to the chancery section of the Consulate. At the door to this section, which was out of sight of the street, Doyle Barnes was waiting for him. They both went up to the electronically 'swept' briefing room. 'You can cross Winchcombe off that list, Johnny; he's dead. Shot through the head at about 6.30 this morning, while out jogging. Always did believe that jogging was bad for your health! So that only leaves YS - and that slinky daughter of his,' Barnes added. 'Sir Peter did a high dive out of his office window - incidentally, the police are looking for someone who might bear a strong resemblance to you. What happened?' Gunn quickly explained what had happened in the Chief Secretary's office. 'Right,' continued Doyle, here are your instructions from the Directorate,' he handed a signal to Gunn, but continued. 'You're to go and brief the Governor immediately on your assessment of the crisis and to present him with a possible solution,' the latter was said with a strong note of cynicism. 'I'm still a member of the team and we can both call for extra assistance from either or both of our agencies should we want it. All the facilities of your Armed Forces, here in Hong Kong, are at your disposal and the President has ordered USS Abraham Lincoln and the 7th Fleet to move towards Hong Kong. In essence, that's what that signal says,' he concluded. While he had been talking, Gunn had scanned the signal. 'Oh yes, there's one thing not on that signal. The Governor's children and Candy Wyngarde have been kidnapped,' he paused as Gunn swore, 'and any interference with YS will mean mutilation and then death of the hostages; tends to make things difficult for us.'

'How long have we got before I'm expected at Government House?' Gunn asked.'

'From the Governor's point of view, you should've been there ten minutes ago.'

'That's very understandable; our only source of information now to find this nuclear device is YS and his daughter, Mandy. Is the yacht still in Discovery Bay, incidentally?'

'No; it cleared the Lei Yue Mun Channel an hour ago, heading for Luzon, according to CAPIC's staff.'

'Ah, that might just be to our advantage.' The germ of a plan began to form in his mind.

'If you've got any ideas, I'd like to share them with you because don't forget that there must still be a person or people in his outfit around here who are watching what we do. Bear in mind those who've been murdered; all members of the government and security forces. If he had them, Johnny, who else has he got and who was the man who wanted to shoot me full of sodium pentathol and lysergic acid?'

'No, I hadn't forgotten that one, in particular. I've a plan which might work as long as it's known by the minimum of people; how does this sound?' and for the next ten minutes Gunn explained his plan, but whether the Governor and his security committee would accept it or not was another matter. On the way to Government House, Gunn remembered that he'd been invited to 'brunch' at the McBains' the following morning. He rang Aileen McBain on his mobile and cancelled the invitation.

'Couldn't you manage Saturday morning, John?'

'Possibly, Aileen, but bear in mind that we're getting very close to the arrival of Pamela and the chaos that will cause the handover ceremonies.'

'Oh damn, I'd forgotten that wretched typhoon; I hope it doesn't stop our flight on Sunday with the boys.'

'I'll ring you, Aileen, if I can make it; otherwise it will have to be when you return to Hong Kong.' He broke the connection. The taxi halted at the gates to Government House and Gunn got out. Having paid the taxi, he was asked for his identity card, which he was unable to produce, having just arrived in the Territory. The policeman on the gate contacted the house by phone. He was allowed in and escorted by the same policeman up the drive to Government House. At the door he was met by Martin Holmes who introduced himself.

'John Gunn,' replied Gunn, shaking hands.

'Wasn't your father one of the Directors of Euro-Pacific Construction?' Martin enquired as he led Gunn towards the Governor's private lounge.

'Yes, that's right, but all the family have been away from Hong Kong for some time. Thank you,' this was said as Martin held the lounge door open for Gunn. In the lounge was the Governor and his wife and Peter and Josie Wyngarde. After meeting the Governor and his wife, Gunn went over and kissed Josie Wyngarde and apologised for not having seen Candy back to her apartment.

'Not your fault, John; they would've got her later,' was the pragmatic response from Peter Wyngarde. 'Now, what's more important is what you're going to do about it; any ideas?' and Gunn outlined the plan which he had discussed with Doyle Barnes.

*

Five hundred miles to the south of Hong Kong, typhoon Pamela's speed over the sea had decreased slightly, but the wind speed within the typhoon had increased. Those ships, which had been the first to complete loading were already feeling the effects of winds which one report had confirmed as gusting to 200 mph. What made the effect of the typhoon even worse was the combination of hurricane force winds and abnormally high equinoctial tides which had created mountainous seas to the south of Hong Kong and three large container ships were in serious difficulties. 'Maydays' had been received by the RAF Search and Rescue, but all attempts to go to the assistance of these ships had been defeated by the hurricane-force winds. Exhausted aircrew had returned, giving reports of conditions at sea which none of them had ever experienced before. The community of Hong Kong was now paying serious attention to the typhoon reports and the Hong Kong Police were faced with numerous disturbances as fights broke out over dwindling stocks of food in the shops. In the Eastern Harbour anchorage, a 17,000 ton cargo ship, the Yorktown, had suffered an engine failure as it was leaving Hong Kong via the Lei Yue Mun Channel. The Captain of the Yorktown was

151

a Sicilian and the crew was a mixture of South Koreans, Malay-Chinese and Hong Kong Chinese. The engine room had partially flooded and the pumps were not working. The ship had been towed to a temporary anchorage and the senior engineer officer was trying to repair the damaged engines.

*

Warrant Officer Kennedy was a Loadmaster with the Hercules C130 crews based at the RAF Station at Sek Kong in the New Territories. Since the final run-down of the British Garrison had started, there had been a daily C130 flight to Hong Kong to air-lift stores and spares back to the UK. The crews had a 24 hour stopover in Hong Kong and then returned on the next C130 to RAF Lyneham in Wiltshire. Dave Kennedy's wife, Sharon, had particularly expensive tastes and he was well overdrawn on his bank account having bought a house-full of rosewood furniture for their RAF married quarter back in England. This was in addition to the acquisition of expensive designer dresses for his wife from the up-market boutiques in Central and an array of photographic and electronic equipment, which he had bought for himself. All of this had been freighted back to Lyneham as 'indulgence' cargo on the now daily flights at no or insignificant cost.

Sharon had a wandering eye and Dave Kennedy went through agonies of jealousy whenever he was rostered for aircrew duties. He had already overheard one conversation at 'happy hour' on a Friday evening in the sergeants' mess at the base in Lyneham, which had ceased abruptly as he approached. He was justifiably convinced that someone was knocking off his wife as soon as his back was turned on these trips to Hong Kong.

A message had been passed to him at the bar in the mess at Sek Kong that he was wanted in the 'Ops Room' immediately. When he got there, the briefing room was filled with the C130 crew. They were briefed for a sortie that evening, leaving at 20.45 hours, which would have two passengers plus one container; all requiring parachutes. He swore as he left the briefing room, 'just my luck and a trip to the 'Wanch' laid on for tonight.' Dave Kennedy's view was that if his wife could play around in UK while he was away, then why shouldn't he take advantage of the massage parlours in the Wanchai. As he left the building he was stopped by the Pakistani 'Cha Wallah' who provided the Wessex Squadron with a twenty-four hour service of food, drinks and every commodity under the sun, including pimping for the tarts in Kam Tin, a village just outside the military base in Sek Kong. He was told that there was a man at his little stall by the main gate who wanted to speak to Kennedy Sahib. The title rather pleased Dave Kennedy and he expected that it was one of the many men who came to the camp selling everything and anything. When they reached the stall, he was ushered into the back premises, where there was a threadbare military camp bed, two rattan armchairs and various other items that didn't bear to close an inspection. A young Chinese man stood up from one of the chairs and Fuseini, the cha wallah, hastily departed into the front of the stall, pulling a curtain behind him.

'Warrant Officer David Kennedy?'

'Yes, that's me. What d'you want?'

'I believe that you are going on a trip in your plane tonight?'

'I may be; so why's that of interest to you?' Kennedy had a nose for money and somehow there seemed to be the smell of it here.

'I have two cases here Mr Kennedy,' and the man pointed to two black leather brief cases. 'There is half a million dollars in each of them; about one hundred thousand pounds sterling. I want you to do something for me.'

'What's this; drugs or something?'

'Oh no, nothing like that.'

'Let me see the money.'

'But of course; silly of me,' and the man opened the two cases which were both crammed full of yellow thousand dollar notes. 'Go on, have a look. It's all there, but you're welcome to count it if you wish.'

'No; that looks about right,' Kennedy muttered as he rifled through the piles of notes. It was more money than he'd ever seen in his life, and he had no idea whether it looked 'about right' or not, but it was all a question of maintaining his cool in the presence of this little short-arse Chink crook. That'd show Sharon when he came home and bought a Porsche, he thought. 'So, what am I expected to do for that lot?'

'Oh, very little, really; you will make sure that the two parachutes for your passengers on tonight's flight will not open.'

'Now wait a. . . .'

'No, Mr Kennedy, I cannot wait. This is not a request; I'm telling you what you will do. Perhaps these photos, which might be seen as a souvenir of your last trip, might help to convince you,' and a handful of colour photos of his last trip to a massage parlour in the Wanchai were laid out in front of him. 'You will, of course realise that you were in an 'out-of-bounds' area. One set will go to your commanding officer in England and the other will go to your wife at 17, Bader Crescent in the village of Stapleford. I don't think that either your career or marriage will survive, do you?'

It was the mention of the address of his house, which really shook Kennedy. So what difference did it make if a couple of stupid 'pongos' from the army bought it. Plenty more where they came from. The vision of a gleaming silver Porsche kept flitting in front of his eyes.

'So what's the deal then? Do I get one case now and the other on return?' he asked, already having made up his mind to do it.

'Better than that, Mr Kennedy,' he was assured by the Chinese man. 'You get both cases now and both sets of photos and the negatives.'

'So how do you know I'll do it?'

'Oh, Mr Kennedy, that's very simple. You will take both cases now. This one,' and the man picked up one of the cases, 'you can start spending the money now. This one, and you will see that it is slightly larger than the other one, has a cunning little mechanism in it which will release an acid that will totally destroy all the money. You will take it with you and if you do exactly as you are told you will find that on your return a specific radio frequency sent by me will secure the mechanism, release the locks and you will have all your money.'

'But why take it with me?'

'That is a good question; this case also contains a small, but very powerful beacon which will enable me to keep track of your progress,'

'But. . . .'

'You were about to say that it might interfere with the electronics of your aircraft.'

'Yes, well. . . .'

'Don't worry, Mr Kennedy; that has all been taken care of. Now as I close the case . . . so,' and the lid was closed, 'we have our guarantee that you will complete your task. Simple really, but quite ingenious.'

Kennedy could see the Porsche parked outside his married quarter and could imagine the envious remarks of all the other members of the mess who lived around them. He picked up the photos and negatives, which he replaced in their envelope and then placed that in the smaller case. He picked up both cases and left the cha wallah's stall without a backward glance. He was already driving along the M4 motorway into London at 150 mph for an imagined night on the town.

Fuseini reappeared through the curtain. 'Thank you Mr Singh for helping me sell those two brief cases. This is for the use of your premises and, of course, for your silence,' and an envelope was handed over before the Chinese man departed.

*

Martin Cowley was a successful solicitor in Hong Kong and that Thursday afternoon was at the wheel of his 36 foot, Grand Banks motor cruiser, just over 160 miles to the east of Hong Kong. He and his wife, Sonia, had been for a cruise to the Philippines with another two couples as guests and were now making best speed back to Hong Kong having found themselves beyond the point of no return when the typhoon warning had been picked up. The weather was still fine and there was almost no wind at all except for that caused by their passage through the water. Martin swore by the reliable, six cylinder Volvo Penta diesels, which throbbed away steadily below him, but the moment he had picked up the typhoon forecast sneaking anxieties haunted him. Martin found himself looking frequently at the engine oil temperature gauges and he had been down twice to the lazerette at the stern to check that the grease compressors in the stern glands of the two prop shafts had been turned down.

He gave a shout for his boat boy, Tony Lam, to come up to the fly bridge and as soon as he had handed over the wheel, he went below and switched on the radio again as it was coming up to the hour. Hong Kong was now broadcasting an hourly typhoon report and he felt that he must hear if it was doing anything unexpected. With relief, he heard that the typhoon had slowed down slightly and, if everything went alright, they should be tucked up in their berth at the Royal Hong Kong Yacht Club in Causeway Bay in the early hours of Friday morning. That would be almost 36 hours before the predicted strike of the typhoon. 'What's the matter, darling? Why don't you join us for a drink? Peter's made the most marvellous dry martini and you haven't had a sip of yours yet,' Sonia chided her husband.

'Just coming darling, once I've done all my checks,' he replied as he went forward to the inside steering position and checked the gauges again.

'Good Heavens!' remarked Peter's wife, Alice, 'anybody would think that we were actually going to have a typhoon hit Hong Kong at last!'

'Yes, well perhaps that's my fault everyone,' Martin admitted. 'You see,' he continued, 'this typhoon is not only going to hit Hong Kong, but it's already been confirmed as the worst typhoon in living memory - anywhere in the world,' he added somewhat lamely. 'I didn't want to cause anxiety unless it was necessary; so often in the twelve years that Sonia and I have been in Hong Kong, these typhoons have either just fizzled out or gone away. The radio is reporting that three container ships have already vanished without trace and not one of them was less than 20,000 tons. Makes one feel a little vulnerable in good old Tradewinds at a shade over 15 tons.' All of a sudden, the dry martinis didn't seem so enticing.

CHAPTER 14

The Security Committee fully appreciated that the salvation of Hong Kong was the first priority and the safety of the hostages had to come second, but had vetoed CBF's request for a full military operation to arrest YS. As the latter had succeeded in penetrating the government, police and armed forces with his intelligence, preparation for such a military operation was almost certain to leak to the kidnappers. Now that the Royal Marine raiding squadron had left Hong Kong, there was no one with the specialist skills possessed by Gunn and Barnes. It was, therefore, hardly surprising that the Security Committee voted 3:1 in favour of Gunn's plan.

The plan which John Gunn and Doyle Barnes had devised was a simple one. There were three remaining patrol craft in the Royal Navy Squadron based at HMS Tamar; at any one time, barring mechanical breakdown, there would be one alongside and two on deployment; one to the west and one to the east of Hong Kong. The patrol craft covering the eastern sector was a hundred miles to the west of the Babuyan Islands; a small group of islands lying about fifty miles to the north of the Island of Luzon; the second largest of the Philippine Islands on which was the capital city of Manila.

Making use of this patrol craft, Gunn's plan was to fly out in the RAF C130 and get ahead of Middle Kingdom, drop into the sea and use the sea-raider RIBs of the patrol craft to board YS' yacht. Once aboard, Gunn and Barnes would destroy the yacht's communications, neutralise its crew and then persuade YS, using any means necessary, to divulge the location and nature of the device he intended to use for the destruction of Hong Kong.

While this plan was put into operation, the Commissioner of Police was to use every discreet facility he possessed within the Force to locate the three hostages. The video tape had been collected from the hire shop, but revealed nothing to help the police. The three hostages had been filmed, seated in a white-painted room with the Governor's daughters holding up a copy of that day's edition of the South China Morning Post. The message on the tape announced that all three would be released unharmed at midday on Monday, provided that there was no interference with YS or his plans. Should

156

there be any attempt to do so, then Miss Wyngarde would be the first to be killed, followed by the Governor's children. The decision for the Governor was agonising, but very simple; do nothing, get his children back and see Hong Kong destroyed; approve Gunn's plan and risk the lives of his children and Peter Wyngarde's daughter and save Hong Kong - possibly. Neither course could guarantee the safety of the hostages or Hong Kong. Gunn had told the Governor bluntly that there was a very slim chance of seeing the hostages released, even if the instructions on the tape were obeyed.

He had left Government House with a taciturn CBF who had given him a lift to the Headquarters of the British Forces in the naval base at Tamar. He was joined there by Doyle and they were both taken up to the eleventh floor of the Prince of Wales building where the three heads of Services and two principle operational and logistic staff officers were waiting in the briefing room. CBF had been directed by the Ministry of Defence in London to provide the Governor with whatever military resources he requested. The briefing by Gunn was short and other than the CBF, none of the officers knew what the real purpose of the operation was. They were told that it was all connected with a joint operation with the USA to break the Burmese and Asian drug cartels. The position of the patrol craft was confirmed and from this the intercept point decided. Gunn and Barnes would leave RAF Sek Kong at 2045 hours that night, by which time a reconnaissance flight from the Hong Kong Auxiliary Air Force would have pinpointed the position of Middle Kingdom. The two men left the building just before mid-day and returned to their hotel to get some sleep. They would be back at six that evening to be flown by helicopter from the North Arm of Tamar Harbour to the RAF base at Sek Kong

Only half an hour after they had walked through the entrance of the Mandarin Hotel, the plan was known and instructions were given to ensure that neither Gunn nor Barnes reached the target area alive. The threatened action against the three hostages would not be implemented because this would divulge knowledge of the plan to intercept Middle Kingdom and thereby focus attention on only a handful of people. Holding the hostages was an extra precaution, which had been planned to ensure the impotence of action of the Hong Kong Government. The absentee member of the conspiracy smiled, replaced the phone and then walked out of the Hilton Hotel.

*

Middle Kingdom was cruising at twenty knots and was seventy miles to the east of Hong Kong. The course was west-south-west to the Babuyan Islands and then due south down the east coast of Luzon. YS was sitting at a table beside the swimming pool; the level of water had been lowered while the yacht was under way. Mandy was lying on a sun-bed reading a book. Captain Raoul Bueno appeared and informed YS that there was a call on the secure link to Hong Kong. YS rose and went into the conference room, which served as his centre of communications. He took his seat behind the banks of switches and lights; one red light was flashing. He flicked the HF radio link and paused; the sophisticated transmitting and reception equipment both in Hong Kong and on Middle Kingdom had removed any carrier signal or background interference. HF was being used to make the task more difficult for RDF equipment; the voice was clear. 'Hello Yankee Sierra Whiskey, this is Golf Whiskey Echo; after countdown of figures five, switch to code Alpha Sierra 53; acknowledge, over.'

'Yankee Sierra Whiskey, roger; start countdown, over,' YS replied.

'Golf Whiskey Echo, countdown; 5 . . . 4 . . . 3 . . . 2 . . . 1 . . . activate!' YS had already punched out the code and on the command flicked another switch. 'Hello, Yankee Sierra Whiskey, this is Golf Whiskey Echo, radio check, over,' the voice now sounded as though it was coming from a voice synthesiser.

'Hello, Golf Whiskey Echo, this is Yankee Sierra Whiskey, OK, over.'

'Yankee Sierra Whiskey, this is Golf Whiskey Echo, OK. You need to know of some recent developments to our plans,' came the voice from the loudspeaker in front of YS. 'I have implemented Precaution One and the three hostages are all secured. Despite our threat, Gunn and his CIA friend, Barnes, are being flown out at 2045 hours this evening to intercept your yacht, however I have ensured that they will not reach you. I am not taking any action against the hostages, at present, as my knowledge of Gunn's movements would place me under suspicion immediately. When you are within helicopter range of Manila Airport, I want you to fly there and board the next China Airlines flight to Shenzen Airport. Move to the safe house at Shui where I will join you before the typhoon hits Hong Kong; I will have the hostages. I suggest that you leave your daughter on the yacht and we can then rejoin her at the RV to the south of Pinghai as planned, over.'

'Yankee Sierra Whiskey, roger to all of that; I have no questions. I will see you at the safe house, out,' and YS flicked the switch off. He then went to the bridge and studied the chart of the Philippines. 'Captain Bueno, what's the maximum range of our helicopters?'

158

'Remember, Sir, that yours can have extra fuel tanks fitted,' Bueno replied, 'with those, the maximum range is 250 miles or a round trip of about half that without refuelling.'

'Thank you, Captain. Now, from your experience of this area,' and YS circled an area to the east of Luzon, 'what would be the best place for Middle Kingdom to anchor which puts her in helicopter range of Manila Airport. Somewhere you can wait until it is time to sail and make our RV at Pinghai?'

'Cat Island, Sir,' was the immediate response, with barely a glance at the area of the chart being identified by YS.

'Where's that?' YS asked, bending lower over the chart and unable to find an island of that name.

'Catanduanes Island, Sir, is the real name, but everyone talks of it as Cat Island; here,' and he pointed to the island on the chart.

'Very well, Cat Island it is; please contact me when you have our arrival time.'

'If you can wait one minute, Sir, I will have that information for you,' Bueno suggested, tapping co-ordinates into the satellite navigation system.

'Very well, Captain,' YS agreed, as a whole series of figures appeared on the display unit.

'We will be at the Cat Island anchorage at 1558 hours tomorrow. At that point you will be 203 miles from Manila Airport; it will take the helicopter one hour twenty minutes to fly that distance, depending on tail or head winds. Are you taking a flight from Manila, Sir?'

'Yes, Captain: please find out the departure times for the China Airlines flight to Shenzen.'

'Very well, Sir; I'll contact you as soon as I have that information.'

YS left the bridge and returned to the swimming pool. 'I shall be deserting you, Mandy, for a few days. I will be leaving tomorrow afternoon and we will meet again on Monday. Captain Bueno has found a nice anchorage and you know that you can use the second helicopter if you wish to go shopping or sightseeing.' Mandy looked up from her book.

'Where will you be meeting us, father?'

'Just off the coast of our homeland, Mandy; near a place called Pinghai.'

'Very well, father; what are you going away for; business?' she asked.

'Yes my dear, just business.'

*

159

Gunn had asked for a call at 4.45. After a shower, he dressed and went down to the coffee shop where he ordered a steak. He was joined by Doyle Barnes. They both left the Mandarin at a quarter to six, as it was getting dark, and walked to Hutchinson House and then crossed over Connaught Road on the pedestrian bridge to the military headquarters. There was a young naval Lieutenant waiting for them at the gate with a Landrover. He drove them round the south side of the base and out onto the North Arm, where a Scout helicopter was waiting with rotor turning.

'Johnny, that should be in a museum,' Doyle laughed as they saw the helicopter.

'That's probably where that particular machine came from, Doyle. Eight or so years ago, the pilots described them as a few thousand rivets flying in close formation, so God knows how they keep them airworthy. There was a joke that the aircraft museum at Worthy Down in Wiltshire was the base workshop for these machines. Anyway, let's hope they've tightened the 'Jesus Nut'.' They got out of the Landrover and moved to the front-right quadrant to the pilot who lifted up his thumb. All four doors of the Scout had been removed as standard procedure in a hot climate, which encouraged a passenger to pay particular attention to fastening the safety harness. The two men got in and did up the safety straps. As soon as the observer had checked them both and returned to his seat beside the pilot, the rotor was wound up and the Scout lifted clear of the harbour, dipped its nose and climbed towards Stonecutters Island, Lantau and Tuen Mun. The sun was setting on a very hazy horizon.

Fifteen minutes later the Scout landed at Sek Kong and the two men undid the safety harnesses and stepped out of the helicopter. The C130 was parked on the hangar apron. A small minibus pulled up beside them with a driver and an RAF warrant officer in it. 'Welcome to RAF Sek Kong, gentlemen. I'm your Loadmaster for the flight tonight. The name's Kennedy.'

'Thank you, Mr Kennedy; we've got some bits and pieces to check before the flight,' Gunn replied to the welcome

'Right, Sir; you can do that first and then there's a briefing in the ops room. Can I assume that you'd both like to check your own chutes?'

'Yes please, that'd be fine.' The mini-bus drove through a partially open hangar door and stopped beside a trolley attached to a small tractor. The place was deserted and Gunn noticed that there were armed RAF Regiment guards at all entrances to the hangar.

'Your equipment is there, Sirs, and the parachute packing tables over there,' and he indicated the large smooth surfaced tables just to

160

the right of their equipment. 'I'll leave you in peace now and I'll be back in thirty minutes to take you for a cup of coffee or tea before the briefing,' and Kennedy saluted and left them. The two men started to check the equipment.

For the free-fall and parachute descent into the sea, there were black, neoprene survival suits. In the container, which would go out just ahead of them, was a homing beacon for the patrol craft sea-raiders to lock onto and solid fuel, rocket-propelled grappling hooks with rubber-muffled tines. There were two, silenced Stirling sub-machine guns, each with four magazines taped together, a small wooden crate of ten hand grenades which were already primed and a satchel of plastic explosive and shaped charges with detonators and fuse cord in separate packages. The container included a self-inflating dinghy and food and water to last 48 hours, in case they were not picked up by the sea-raiders.

All of this equipment was checked carefully, which included the firing mechanisms of the weapons, the loading of the magazines, the altitude-operated release mechanism of the container parachute and lastly, both men unpacked their own parachutes, checked them thoroughly and then repacked them. Everything they had asked for was there. 'That's it then; I think it's time for that coffee,' Doyle said, straightening up from a close examination of the laced elastic cording of his parachute pack. Right on cue, Kennedy appeared with a young corporal.

'If you're ready, Corporal Simms will take you to the crew room for a coffee. I'll get on with loading this lot now,' Gunn and Barnes followed the Corporal out of the hangar. Once they had gone, Kennedy picked up the two parachutes, placed them on the trolley and then climbed up onto the driver's seat of the tractor and drove it out to the C130. Once there, the ground crew loaded everything into the aircraft and then left the Loadmaster to do all his checks.

Once the briefing was over Gunn and Barnes were taken to the crew room again where they dressed in black flying suits and were then driven out to the C130. As soon as they were aboard the door was closed and the engines were started. Gunn strapped himself into the canvas seat, which was one of a row, either side of the Hercules. The Loadmaster was doing his pre-flight checks and had disappeared up the ramp into the tail of the aircraft to check something, which required the use of a torch. He then returned, reported to the pilot and strapped himself into his seat, which was on the opposite side of the fuselage to Gunn and Barnes. Underneath his seat was a leather briefcase. The noise of the engines increased and the C130 moved off down the runway, before it turned and braked. The flight was due to take one and a half hours; the last thing that they had been told at the briefing in the ops room was that a positive identification of Middle Kingdom had been made and HMS Swordfish, the patrol craft, was waiting at the rendezvous.

The engine note reached a crescendo, the brakes were released and the C130 rapidly picked up speed. It climbed steeply from the runway, banking hard to the right to avoid the Tai Mo Shan range of hills and then headed south-east over the town of Shatin and out over the bay of Port Shelter to the South China Sea as it climbed to 18,000 feet. Speech in the rear of the C130 was virtually impossible and both Gunn and Barnes were content to sit with their own thoughts as the Hercules droned on into the night sky. Gunn must have dozed because it only seemed a moment later that the co-pilot handed him a headset on a trailing lead and spoke to him. 'We'll be over your target area in about twenty minutes. I suggest that you get into your survival suits and parachutes now. The Loadmaster will help you. We have started our descent and will level off at 8,000 for your jump. The ramp will be lowered and you will both jump simultaneously after the container has gone; any questions?' There were none. 'OK, then; all the best of luck, whatever it is you're doing,' and he shook both men's hands and climbed back up to the flight deck.

The briefing completed, the Loadmaster appeared to help them prepare for the free-fall. Once they were all set and John and Doyle had checked each other, they moved to the rear of the fuselage. The Loadmaster strapped a safety harness round his waist and stood between them by the container. He glanced at his watch and then looked up at the lights. He received a message over his headset, moved to a control panel and pressed a large button. The rear of the fuselage started to open and all of them could feel the buffeting of the slipstream. The ramp levelled off with the floor of the fuselage and in their 'wake' John Gunn could see nothing but a mass of stars. The fuselage was flooded with the glow of the red light. Red to green! The Loadmaster pushed the container on its runners and it disappeared over the lip of the ramp, quickly followed by Gunn and Doyle.

The Loadmaster went over to the control panel and pushed the button, which closed the rear of the fuselage. He then undid the safety harness and went up onto the flight deck to report that all was clear. Having done so, he returned to his seat by the starboard, mid-fuselage door, poured himself a coffee from his flask and then bent down and picked up the brief case from under his seat. The C130 banked slightly to port and headed back for Hong Kong.

*

On the 36 foot motor cruiser Tradewinds, Martin Cowley and his guests had recovered some of their spirits as the boat had made good progress towards Hong Kong. They were now only 23 miles to the east of the Lei Yue Mun Channel and the three couples were up on the flying bridge enjoying a drink under a beautiful starlit night. There was no hint of the maelstrom of wind and water that was approaching Hong Kong from the south. The latest weather forecast had said that Pamela's speed over the sea had increased slightly and the typhoon was now expected in Hong Kong any time from midday on Saturday. The engines were running as smoothly as silk and Martin's confidence in his boat had returned. Beside him, in a suction cup container, was a malt whisky, which the number two boat boy had just replenished for him. He heard an approaching aircraft and glanced up at the winking navigation lights. The sound of the turbo-prop engines was quite distinctive and unfamiliar amongst the never ceasing stream of jet aircraft pouring in and out of Kai Tak Airport.

'That's unusual . . .' he began and then stopped as a vivid orange fireball engulfed the aircraft. For some split seconds, Martin Cowley stared at the rapidly descending fireball, refusing to believe what his eyes told him. All the others followed the direction in which he was staring and saw the blazing aircraft fall into the sea about five miles away on the starboard bow. Martin jumped to his feet and took the wheel from Tony, his number one boat boy. He glanced over the compass and noted the bearing to the point where the aircraft had hit the sea and then opened both throttles wide.

Sonia, his wife, went over to her husband; 'what on earth was that, Martin?'

'That,' he said, emphasising the word, 'was an aircraft, which has just been blown out of the sky poor sods. I don't think anyone could've lived through that, but we must go and look. Tony, take the wheel please. Your course is 350°; the log is reading 15,706 miles. When it reads 15,710, we should be approaching the area of wreckage. Switch on the spotlights and slow down to eight knots. Understood?'

'Yes Sir.'

'Right Sonia; dig out some blankets just in case . . . Christ! What was that?' Martin exclaimed as something fell into the sea barely a hundred metres away on the port bow, followed quickly by two parachutes. 'Steer towards them, Tony, and make the speed ten knots,' he ordered as he switched on the spotlights. 'Get on with it girls, don't stand there in a trance. These guys are going to need help.' This galvanised the women into action and they disappeared off the bridge and went below. 'Right,' and Martin addressed the other two men, 'let's get these men aboard.' They followed Martin down into the well

163

deck at the stern and Tony skilfully brought the boat alongside the first of the men in the water. The man had a lifejacket on and was conscious. 'How badly are you hurt?' Martin asked anxiously.

'Apart from a good ducking, I don't think I can claim sympathy for even a scratch,' came the cheery reply.

'Thank God for that; right, come on, let's get you aboard,' and with the help of the other two they got him onto the swimming platform at the stern and then over the side into the well deck. Martin shouted to Tony that all was clear and the boat immediately moved towards the next man who was illuminated by the spotlights. All three men were brought on board; the worst injury appeared to be the last man who had suffered a blow to the side of his head, which was developing into a multi-coloured bruise. All three men were taken to the saloon where they were presented with hot cups of tea, towels and dry clothing. 'I've told the Marine Police that we've picked you up,' Martin said, coming into the saloon from the forward steering position, 'and are continuing to look for survivors. They've got a boat on its way and the SAR chopper is also coming.' There was a squawk from the boat intercom and Tony told his boss that the boat was now in the area where the spotlights were illuminating what little wreckage there was. The pilot held up his hand as everyone started to make a move towards the deck.

'I think I might be able to save you all some trouble. Thank you for such a professional rescue Mr, . . .'

'Martin Cowley.'

'Mr Cowley; there were only four of us on the C130; myself, Jeremy, here,' and he pointed to the co-pilot, 'Dick, who's my navigator and our Loadmaster, Mr Kennedy. The explosion took place in the rear of the aircraft where Kennedy was sitting. He would have been blown to bits. The old 'Herc' is so tough that all three of us on the flight deck were able to get clear.'

'Thanks for that; we'll just have a quick look round the area and then stand down the SAR,' Martin replied. He took the other two men on deck and left the women to fuss over the three survivors. Less than five minutes later they returned to the saloon; Ronnie, one of Martin's guests on the cruise, was looking distinctly pale. 'You're quite right,' Martin said, 'only a few bits and pieces left.'

'What's up with Ronnie?' asked Sonia, 'he doesn't look at all well.'

'One of the pieces we saw was the headless and armless torso of their Loadmaster,' Martin said quietly.

'Oh dear . . . I didn't . . .'

'No, of course you didn't, love, but it confirms what the pilot told us. I'll radio the police and get them to stand down the SAR. We're now back on course for Hong Kong. Funny thing . . .' he paused.

'What's that darling?' Sonia asked as Martin started to leave the saloon for the flying bridge.

'The poor man must have taken the full force of the explosion.

'Don't Martin, I'd rather not know.'

'No, Sonia, I'm not being morbid, but there seemed to be quite a large amount of remnants of yellow, thousand dollar notes imbedded in the torso,' and he left the saloon.

*

Dan Grant was on his own; he had sent everyone ashore sightseeing or shopping. He had now fully serviced the boat's diesel engines and the generator. He tidied up the work on the jury-rigged mast and then went below and serviced the air-compressor for the sub-aqua gear. Having done all of these jobs, he went into the engine room and opened the two compartments containing the boat's self-defence weapons. He took each one out in turn and thoroughly cleaned and then re-oiled it. He was never going to pay lip service again to the warnings, which he had been given about the piracy in South East Asia. Having cleaned the weapons, Dan went up on deck and studied the anchorage again, carefully.

Luck had been on their side on Mindanao Island in that he had, by chance, selected an anchorage, which had allowed him enough warning of the approach of other boats. Now that he was on his own he undertook a thorough appraisal of every approach to the yacht. Having done this, he went into the deckhouse and sat in front of his chart. American Pie was anchored in the middle of a bay which, being on the west coast of the island, resembled a reversed capital 'G', providing, at its southern end, a natural harbour with shelter from any wind. The hook of the 'G' was a line of razor toothed rocks which went some distance out to sea under the surface of the water. With interest, Dan Grant saw that there were two channels into the southern part of the bay, one close inshore and the other, close to the rocks where the action of the sea had scoured out a narrow channel. In between these two channels, the chart marked sandy, shoaling ground with a maximum depth of 1.5 metres. Dan opened the chart, and once again checked the date of the latest correction and the Notice to Mariners on the back of the chart with even more recent amendments. The latest amendment was just over a year old. There was little doubt that the best anchorage was to the south of that shoal, well sheltered from every direction. There was only one drawback; the present position of American Pie gave him a commanding view of approaches to the bay and would afford him plenty of time to prepare the defences of his yacht, should there be a repetition of the Mindanao incident. The southern anchorage would considerably limit his view of the approaches, but likewise, he argued to himself, it also hid American Pie from the view of those sailing past the bay. 'Come on, Dan,' he cajoled himself, 'make a decision man. The only reason why we were attacked before,' he continued the conversation out loud, 'was because we were seen. They must've been anchored out of sight somewhere and watched our approach to the anchorage. No, the southern anchorage it is, and no time like the present.'

Decision made, Dan made preparations to move American Pie. He could easily manage the yacht by himself and with the two powerful diesels ticking over, he went for'ard and started to bring in the anchor on the hydraulically powered winch at the bow. He had given the yacht a quick thrust forward from the main engines to take the strain off the winch and the anchor chain now came in quickly. The anchor broke free cleanly from the seabed and he was able to slow the pace of the winch as he saw it come up through the clear water. The last of the chain came up through the hawse and the anchor self-stowed against the stainless steel bow plate. Dan Grant walked back to the wheel, adjusted the brilliance of the depth meter and turned the yacht towards the narrower, but deeper channel by the rocks. There was a gentle on-shore wind, which had little effect on American Pie, with her shortened masts. He took the yacht into the channel at barely two knots, watching the reading on the depth gauge. American Pie had a draft of eight and a half feet; Dan Grant always allowed three metres. The gauge dropped rapidly from six metres to four and Dan's hand moved instinctively to the gear and throttle control, but the reading steadied and held at four and then went back up to seven. The yacht was through and now completely sheltered from both severe weather and from the view of anyone at sea. Ensuring that the boat had plenty of room to swing the anchor chain, he brought her to a stop in a depth of seven metres. He then went forward pulled out five times the calculated maximum depth of the inlet at high tide. He pushed the anchor out of its stow and it splashed into the water. After putting the boat astern to make the anchor dig in, he decompressed the diesels and switched off.

Time was on Dan Grant's side, so he lowered the dinghy into the water and followed it with the kedge anchor which was made fast for'ard. Using the little 3hp outboard, he took the dinghy out to his chosen position and heaved the kedge over the side. The sun was blistering hot, so he returned to the boat and the shade of the bimini awning stretched between the repaired main and remnants of the mizzenmast. He glanced at his watch; a shade before 3.45. The shopping expedition should be back in about quarter of an hour. He broke open a can of cold beer and waited for them to appear on the beach.

CHAPTER 15

Seven thousand . . . six, five, four, three, two, fifteen hundred feet and Gunn pulled the release; nothing . . . one thousand feet; he pulled the release on the reserve chute; nothing. Below him he saw the drogue start to deploy the main chute on the container. He adjusted his position and side-slipped towards the container. 'Don't open yet!' Gunn said through gritted teeth. Suddenly Doyle appeared, but he had misjudged his move towards the container and was going to overshoot. The main container chute appeared, rather like a furled umbrella, being dragged out of its pack by the drogue.

Gunn grabbed Doyle's arm and then both of them thudded into the container, which was decelerating rapidly. They locked their arms through the webbing straps holding the parachute pack to the container and waited for the wrench as the chute deployed fully. When the jolt came, there was a shouted oath beside Gunn and he saw that Doyle's left arm had come away from the webbing and was hanging in an unnatural way. The shoulder appeared to be dislocated and the pain that it was causing Doyle was plain from the gritted teeth and tightly shut eyes. His right hand was losing its hold on the container. John Gunn reached over the container and locked his hand round Doyle's forearm. The sea was coming up fast towards them; some ten feet above the water, Gunn let go of both Doyle and the container. The two men and the container plunged into the warm sea. Gunn surfaced almost immediately and pulled the cord on the CO2 bottle of his life jacket. The container bobbed in the sea ten yards away; there was no sign of Doyle. Gunn swam towards the container and using it as a reference point, began to swim in widening circles in search of Doyle. He found him after one circuit. As Gunn reached him, Doyle lost consciousness and slipped below the slight swell. Gunn grabbed him by the hair, reached down, inflated his life jacket and then swam with him back to the container

Hopefully, the patrol craft had picked up the beacon's signal and so the wait to be picked up should not be too long. Who had fixed those chutes? John Gunn wondered. There had been nothing wrong with them when they had been packed. The only person to handle them after that was the Loadmaster, or possibly one of the ground handling crew. So how had the information about this flight got to Sek

Kong so quickly? It had to be one of the people at the Governor's EXCO meeting, or someone very close and totally trusted by a person at that meeting, Gunn thought, as he, the container and Doyle rose over the swell. A message would have been sent to YS telling him of the flight and the plan to board Middle Kingdom. He would have also been told how this was to be stopped by fixing the parachutes. So an attempt to board the yacht would not be expected. Who was this person in Hong Kong? Was it the man whom Doyle had heard when he was blindfolded? These and other thoughts raced through Gunn's mind as he refused to let his mind dwell on the possibility of sharks.

The beam from a powerful torch swung onto them and they were greeted by a cheery voice; 'you two going to stay there all night or can we give you a lift?' The sea-raider throttled back and came to a rest beside the two men.

'We'll take the offer of a lift, but please get him over the side first; he's unconscious and, I think, has a dislocated shoulder.'

'Right Sir; here, you two give me a hand to get him aboard,' and Doyle was eased into the RIB. 'Now you, Sir,' and slightly less gently, Gunn was heaved over the side of the boat. The container was tied to the sea-raider and the coxswain spoke into a small, hand-held radio. Out of the night appeared the patrol craft's second sea-raider, which came alongside. Gunn spoke to the coxswain; 'how far away is the yacht?'

'Five miles and closing fast,' was the instant response.

'Right; please take my companion back to the ship. I'll load what I need into the pack,' and Gunn removed the parachute and reserve. 'Will you please lock these two chutes away somewhere; no one is to touch them until I can examine them properly; is that clear?'

'Yes Sir.'

The container was now open and Gunn quickly transferred the equipment into his pack. As soon as the grapple and its mortar tube appeared, the sea-raider crew started to set it up in the bow. Once they were satisfied with its position, the rope was attached to the shaft. The engine on the other sea-raider came to life and it returned to the patrol craft. Gunn was out of his survival suit and was dressed in the black flying suit, black cotton balaclava and black, high sided trainers. He slung the pack of equipment on his back; the silenced Stirling sub-machine gun hung from its sling across his chest and a wide-bladed diving knife was in a sheath attached to the flying suit on his right leg. Gunn's Browning was in the pack on his back.

'Ready Sir?'

'Yes thanks; lets go,' and the sea-raider leapt forward under the thrust of the two, large 100 hp Mercury outboards. The coxswain had the radio to his ear again.

'She's two miles away...over there!' and he pointed to some lights, which could be seen as the RIB went over the top of the swell.

'Right, we get one try and one only. You men ready?' they nodded. 'What speed does this boat do?'

'A shade over thirty knots, Sir.' It was going to be a very close run thing. Middle Kingdom's speed had been estimated at twenty-five knots and they had to come in over the bow wave and get close enough for the mortar to be fired. Gunn was thankful that the climbing rope attached to the grapple was knotted which would make the climb up to the deck less of an effort. He could now make out the starboard and masthead lights of Middle Kingdom and even at that distance, could see the bone of white water boiling round her bow. The coxswain chose his angle of approach carefully and then opened up the engine to two-thirds throttle. The little boat came up onto the plane and skimmed over the calm sea. It would have taken a very sharp-eyed lookout to have spotted the small RIB and there was no danger of being picked up by radar. They rapidly closed with the yacht and the two men in the bow with the mortar braced themselves as the boat approached the steep bow wave. Gunn was seated amid-ships of the craft in front of the coxswain's position. The sea-raider soared over the bow wave and jumped clear across twenty feet or more of sea before it hit the water with a jolt that jarred everyone. They were over the bow wave and about thirty feet from the hull of the yacht and in a position just aft of the yacht's bridge. The petty officer on the mortar depressed the trigger mechanism and with a muffled thump, the grapple streaked into the night and over the side of the yacht, the climbing rope snaked up behind it as the coils whipped out from the box in the boat. Gunn didn't wait to follow the flight of the grapple, but quickly began taking in the slack on the climbing rope. The sea-raider was now in a position some ten feet away from the hull of Middle Kingdom; this was the most dangerous moment. Too close to the yacht's hull and the light RIB would be sucked under the yacht and jettisoned at the stern; too far out and Gunn would swing into the sea rather than against the hull.

The grapple had hooked onto something and held tight. Gunn gave it a hard pull, but it didn't move. It was extremely difficult to maintain any sort of balance as the sea-raider was behaving just like a roller coaster as the coxswain fought to keep the craft in exactly the right position. Gunn signalled with thumb up to the coxswain. Now came the crucial test of his skill as a helmsman. He had to chose

170

exactly the right moment to come as close as he dared to the wall of steel beside him. Gunn reached down, removed the knife from its sheath and severed the rope from the surplus, now lying in tangles in the bow of the sea-raider. He quickly tied the rope round his waist and then poised himself, ready for the instant that the coxswain chose his moment. The sea-raider swung in towards the hull of the yacht, cork-screwing over the turbulent, boiling water; fifteen feet, ten, five. Gunn reached as high as he could and jumped. He crashed into the side of the hull and hung there, his feet inches from the surging maelstrom of water. Knot by knot, he pulled himself up the rope, his pack feeling like a few hundred-weight of lead on his back. He glanced back and saw the sea-raider veer away from the yacht and disappear astern. There were only a few more feet to the deck. With his muscles shaking with the strain, he eased himself up so that his head was just over the edge of the deck. Not a sign of anyone, but Gunn found it hard to listen for any sound because of the pounding of his heart and his laboured breathing. Holding onto the stanchions at the deck edge, he swung over the side of the yacht, underneath the lowest of the rails between the stanchions and kept rolling until he was in the deep shadow of the yacht's superstructure. There was no sign of movement anywhere. Gunn rose to his feet and paused, gradually getting his breath under control. He pulled in all the rope and then concealed it amongst the pipes of an air-conditioning unit.

He bent down, opened his pack and removed a number of the PE charges with detonators and timers; these, he put into the zipped pockets of his flying suit. He removed the Browning and returned it to its holster on his ankle, inside the flying suit. His first priority was to destroy the yacht's communications so that no information could be sent back to Hong Kong. All the yacht's aerials were grouped together in an aerofoil arch at the stern of the yacht, which resembled those on the rear end of racing cars. Gunn made his way aft until he reached the metal-runged ladder, which led up to the aerials. He climbed the ladder and in less than two minutes had placed the charges. He returned to his pack on the starboard side of the yacht and removed the homing beacon, which HMS Swordfish was using to track the yacht and concealed it in a life raft canister. Gunn climbed the companionway to the sun deck and made his way for'ard towards the communications room. This had to be close to the bridge and he found it by following the electrical conduits carrying the aerial cables.

Outside the closed steel door was a guard, armed with a Kalashnikov sub-machine gun. Gunn removed the Stirling from around his neck, switched the change lever from 'safe' to 'single shot' and with little more noise than that of the mechanism re-cocking, the

9mm bullet struck the guard in the head and toppled him off his chair. Gunn moved quickly to the door and opened it. The communications officer was sitting facing the door, surrounded on every wall with the very latest in high-tech communications equipment. He rose to his feet as Gunn entered the room and his mouth opened just in time to take the second 9mm bullet, which threw him back against a wall of dials and switches. As soon as the guard had been dragged into the communications room, Gunn placed the charges, glanced at his watch and then set the timers. He closed the door behind him and went for'ard to the bridge.

*

The Governor's personal secretary, Martin Holmes, interrupted the dinner party at Government House and informed the Governor that he was wanted on the phone. The Governor excused himself to his guests - this dinner party had been the last thing he wanted, but he had been advised to try and maintain a facade of normality - and went to the 'box'. He picked up the phone; it was Major General Rogers, the CBF. 'Yes Patrick, is there any news?' he asked.

'Yes there is and it's both good and bad. The good news is that Swordfish has reported that Gunn is aboard Middle Kingdom,' started the General.

'What about the CIA man. . . ?'

'I'm coming to that Sir; both of their parachutes were sabotaged and failed to open. . . .'

'Well, how in God's name are they alive?'

'We don't know the details, but can only assume that both he and Barnes came down with the container parachute. Barnes was injured in the drop and has a dislocated shoulder. He's in the sick bay aboard Swordfish and is still under sedation after the ship's surgeon put his left arm back in place. Once he's conscious, we should get more details. The bad news, Sir, is that we have a very highly placed informer here in Hong Kong, who had access to the plan within minutes of us setting it all up this morning. Oh yes, we've also just had a report from the Marine Police that the C130 which flew Gunn and Barnes out to YS' yacht crashed into the sea some twenty miles to the east. The initial report is that it was brought down by an explosion. It appears that all the crew except one survived. I've arranged with Group-Captain Carmichael for a Wessex to be sent out to the boat, which picked up the survivors, so that they can be brought back quickly for a debriefing. That's about it, Sir, for the moment,' the CBF finished his report.

'What I don't understand, Patrick, is if this informer knew that we intended to send Gunn and Barnes to the yacht, then he also knew that we had ignored the threats in the tape. Why didn't he contact us to stop the plan being put into action? Do you think he has carried out his threat to kill Miss Wyngarde?' asked the distraught Governor, wondering how he was going to break this news to his wife.

'I think we've got the answers to both those questions, Sir. If he had told us that he knew of the plan, it's just possible that we could identify him; indeed, that is one card up our sleeve. He thinks that Gunn and Barnes are dead and therefore there is no need to implement the threat to the hostages.'

'How can you be sure, Patrick?'

'I can't, Sir.'

'Do you think we should pull Gunn out?' The CBF had expected this question and had delayed his phone call until the Swordfish had confirmed that Gunn had left the sea-raider and was out of touch with the patrol craft.

'I'm afraid it's too late for that, Sir, the charges will have been set and until Gunn contacts Swordfish, there's nothing we can do.'

'Thank you, Patrick; so we've no alternative, but to rely on that young man.'

'That's about it, Sir.'

'Very well; thank you for keeping me informed, Patrick. Goodbye,' and the Governor replaced the phone and reluctantly made his way back to the dinner party.

*

The early evening news announced that the centre of typhoon Pamela was on a direct track for Hong Kong. The speed over the sea was still 12 knots and the periphery winds and seas were expected to reach Hong Kong by mid day on Saturday. The container port was almost clear of all ships, as were all the anchorages. The Yorktown was still anchored in the Eastern Anchorage and marine engineers had been taken out to her to assist with the repairs to the engines. The senior engineer was from the Swedish company of Astra Nova; the other two engineers were from the Hong Kong United Dockyard and all three of them were led down to the engine room by a less than hospitable captain.

Extra diesel pumps had been lifted on board to pump out the engine room and these were now holding their own against the ingress of seawater. One glance at the scene, which surrounded him in the engine room, was enough to tell the Astra Nova engineer that the Yorktown was long overdue a major overhaul and refit – if not scrapping. Heavily corroded and leaking saltwater piping, bodged repairs to steam pipes and fuel lines and filth, dirt and grease were everywhere. He inspected the boilers, port and starboard, one of which had failed completely and the other was about to follow suit. He found a hairline crack in one of the two gearboxes and the uneven wear at the various glands and stuffings on both propeller shafts indicated that they were out of true. After returning on deck, he unclipped the radio from his belt and called the harbourmaster. As soon as he received a reply, the Astra Nova engineer asked for the Hong Kong Salvage and Literage Company to send out two tugs to bring the Liberian registered Yorktown into the dockyard for a major refit. If nothing else it was vital to get her out of harm's way until the typhoon had passed. The captain of the Yorktown had shown considerable agitation at this decision and was protesting strongly at being taken in tow and the possibility of salvage being claimed by the Harbour Authorities. He was given reassurance on the latter point, but the engineer made a mental note to speak to a colleague of his in Customs and Excise. He considered that it might be worth a thorough inspection of the ship's cargo as the captain's anxiety to get to sea in the face of such appalling conditions was highly suspicious. When he had glanced at the cargo manifest prior to his inspection of the engine room, there was nothing listed there to cause any anxiety. Yes, he thought as the dockyard work boat took him back, as soon as he returned to the office he would give his colleague in HM Customs and Excise a ring and meet him for lunch. The two squat, twin funnelled tugs appeared from the dockyard, soon had lines aboard the Yorktown and started the tow westwards across Kowloon Bay to the dockyard.

*

Gunn could hear the sound of voices coming from the starboard wing of the bridge. Two men were silhouetted against the night sky and the glow of their cigarettes was reflected off the bulkhead. Again, using the single shot on the Stirling, Gunn shot them both. One of them had been holding a glass or a mug and this fell to the deck and smashed. There was an exclamation from inside the bridge as Gunn entered it from the aft companionway. There were two men on the bridge; one was the coxswain, who was standing in front of the small wheel, which was operating by itself under the control of the autopilot. The other, Gunn assumed, was the officer of the watch who was just moving towards the starboard side of the bridge to investigate the noise on the wing. Neither had noticed Gunn and both men died without ever knowing who or what had dispatched them. The coxswain fell forward on the wheel, which tripped the autopilot; this in its turn tripped an alarm, which sounded in the captain's cabin. Raoul Bueno was having supper on his own when the alarm sounded. He swore, wiping his mouth with the back of his hand and went up

174

the short companionway which led from his cabin to the bridge. Reaching it, he found the place deserted and was instantly alert, cursing for not bringing his gun which was still in his cabin. Gunn had just removed the coxswain, when he was interrupted by the arrival of Bueno on the bridge. He swung round, bringing up the barrel of his sub-machine gun as he did so, but Bueno was well practised in this form of fighting. He moved with astonishing speed for his bulk, kicking out with his foot as he moved. His kick struck the bulbous silencer of the Stirling, deflecting the bullet into the main wireless transmitter causing a vivid white flash and a shower of sparks. Bueno's kick followed through and struck Gunn just below the heart, driving all the breath out of him. Bueno was off balance. Dragging air into his lungs, Gunn grasped his ankle and launched himself backwards, using the leg as a lever and twisting it hard as he did so. Bueno crashed into the engine control console with a force that should have put him into the sick bay for forty-eight hours, but he was back on his feet in an instant and was quicker than Gunn who was still sucking in great lungfulls of air. Gunn had rolled over and was reaching for the sub-machine gun. Bueno beat him to it and scooped it up and fired in one continuous movement, squeezing the trigger and expecting to get a long burst of automatic fire. The Stirling fired one round which went well wide of Gunn and hit the autopilot, causing the yacht to veer wildly to port. This threw Bueno off balance and he crashed to the deck again, fumbling with the unfamiliar weapon as he tried to find the change lever and move it to automatic. Gunn hurled himself towards the aft end of the bridge, putting the metal chart table between himself and Bueno. With a curse of satisfaction, Bueno found the lever and moved it from single shot to automatic and stood in a crouch with the sub-machine gun held out low and central to identify his target. The Browning's first bullet hit him in the chest, throwing the Stirling out of his hands and the second one hit him centrally between the eyes spreading the back of his head onto the bridge's 'clear view' glass. The whole bridge was suddenly flooded in fluorescent light, momentarily blinding Gunn.

'Put that automatic down, Mr Gunn and stand up very slowly,' YS warned him.

*

Dan Grant climbed down the ladder over the stern of American Pie and into the dinghy. He pulled the recoil starter on the outboard and then pushed in the choke. The shopping party was due any minute and he was keen to avoid any anxiety to his guests after their experiences with typhoons and pirates. If they didn't see the yacht in the place where they had left it, there was always the possibility of

175

panic setting in before they looked carefully up and down the beach. He took the dinghy over the shallows in the middle of the cove and headed towards the beach at a point opposite their previous anchorage. Once there, Dan beached the dinghy and walked nimbly through the red hot sand to the shade of the first line of coconut palms. Here, he sat in the shade on a fallen trunk and broke the top off a can of Budweiser beer.

The shore party was only about twenty minutes late and when they arrived at the beach to be met by Dan Grant, were all excited about a story which they had picked up in the village of a wreck lying only a few hundred metres off the shore. It seemed from the accounts which the villagers had given them, that it was an American warship which had been sunk by the Japanese in the last war.

After Dan Grant had asked one or two questions and had been assured that his guests knew exactly where the wreck was lying, he readily agreed to a diving expedition on the following day. Whilst Dan ferried the first group back to the yacht, the others strolled along the surf line in the direction of the southern anchorage. Once they were all aboard, Amy disappeared to the galley with all the shopping to start preparing the evening meal, while the men brought out the scuba gear in preparation for the diving expedition on the next day.

*

'Thank you Mr Gunn,' said YS smoothly, as Gunn laid the Browning down on the deck. He was still blinded by the glare of the fluorescent light. A member of the crew was now standing in front of the wheel and Middle Kingdom seemed to be back under control. 'Stand up slowly and turn with your back towards us. My bosun will then search you. Please don't offer him the opportunity of getting his revenge; you see, Mr Gunn, you've just killed the coxswain who was his brother.' Gunn did as instructed and saw out of the corner of his eye a stocky character of mixed Asian origin come forward to search him. The diving knife was removed, but after a thorough search nothing else was found. He grunted something unintelligible to YS.

'You will now leave the bridge by the door over there,' and YS indicated the door through which Gunn had reached the bridge only a few minutes before. 'My crew are waiting at the foot of the ladder, Mr Gunn, so please don't do anything foolish.' Gunn did as ordered and as he ducked his head to go through the door of the bridge, the bosun drove the barrel of an automatic into his kidney, making him stumble and then fall to the bottom of the steps. It was obvious that the bosun was hoping for some form of retaliation from Gunn, but he dragged himself to his feet and asked, 'which way now?'

A grunt and a kick propelled him aft and into YS' private suite, to the dining room where Mandy was seated. A chair was pointed out and once he was seated, Gunn was tied firmly to it. The bosun was then dismissed and YS sat in front of Gunn. He placed a small Mauser automatic on the table just in front of him. 'Now, Mr Gunn, you have proved to be not only a great nuisance to me, but also very resourceful. I have no intention of wasting time on any crude form of interrogation as there are far easier ways of finding out just how much you think you know,' and YS turned to his daughter. 'Please go and get your little box of tricks, my dear,' Mandy rose from the table without a word and left the room. 'You realise that this puts your friend Miss Wyngarde and the Governor's children in a most precarious position. The phone call that I am about to make to Hong Kong will no doubt bring Miss Wyngarde's life to an early and abrupt end.'

Gunn couldn't see a clock anywhere, but was sure that the timers which he had set must be due to detonate the charges any second. Had they been found? Possibly, but there hadn't been much time. Mandy returned to the room carrying a small black case, which she set down on the table. YS pressed a button under the table and two of the crew appeared at the door and then on a signal from YS came and stood behind Gunn's chair. Mandy opened the case and removed a syringe, needle and glass phial. She took a small saw blade and used it to weaken the neck of the phial after which, with an expert flick of her finger, she removed the glass top. The needle was slotted onto the syringe and then inserted into the phial. Mandy rose from her place at the table and came round and stood beside Gunn who was immediately grasped from behind. Because the two men were unable to role up the sleeve of the flying suit, the zipper was undone and the suit pulled over his shoulders. Mandy came round to his left side, depressed the plunger on the syringe to remove any air and then after swabbing the skin on his arm, inserted the needle.

YS stood up; 'I shall look forward to our little talk, Mr Gunn, but for the time being it will have to wait. The drug which Mandy has just injected into you is extremely effective but does take rather a long time to achieve maximum effect, so I will see you tomorrow,' and with those words he turned and headed for his conference room. Mandy withdrew the needle and the two men released their hold on Gunn. Just as YS reached the door, the yacht was rocked by an explosion, quickly followed by another. YS stopped and turned; 'your work Mr Gunn?'

Gunn couldn't reply as his tongue felt as though it was a large sponge, filling the whole of his mouth. The door into the dining room

177

burst open and the bosun appeared and spoke rapidly to YS. Gunn was fast losing consciousness, but heard YS. 'It would seem, Mr Gunn, that we have no communication with anyone.' He then spoke to the two men behind Gunn. 'Take him down to cabin eight.' YS left the dining room followed by the bosun. The two crewmen picked up Gunn and carried him to the cabins on the deck below. He was placed on a large double bed and then they left, turning out the lights and locking the door. The two men returned to the dining room and handed the keys to Mandy, who was still sitting at the table. They both left the room without a word. Apart from the throb of the engines and the occasional shout from on deck, the ship was quiet. Mandy picked up the syringe and then with a smile, packed it into the case and left the dining room.

CHAPTER 16

The cargo manifest, which the Astra Nova engineer had seen, itemised the contents of each of the Yorktown's four holds. The ship had arrived in Hong Kong with a cargo of food and clothing, donated by charity, for the Vietnamese refugee camps. The captain of the Yorktown had no cargo to load in Hong Kong and so had put the word around in all the usual haunts of Kwai Chung that his ship was available for charter or a cargo, or both. It was three days later that he had been contacted by a shipping agent to inform him that there was a cargo available to be shipped to Pattaya in Thailand. The cargo was tractor engines and the captain was informed that the representative of the company handling the shipment would be coming out to the Yorktown's anchorage. The man had arrived in a sampan while the cargo was being transferred from the barges which had been towed out to the Yorktown from the cargo handling basin at Shek Tong Tsui on the Island.

The captain had invited the man down to his cabin where the contract was signed. He was then informed that if the cargo was not delivered to exactly the correct anchorage off Pattaya, at exactly the specified time on the right date, he could dismiss any plans he might have for taking advantage of any pension plan. After the man's departure, the captain and his first officer had gone down to the number four hold which was immediately for'ard of the bridge. The hold was fully loaded and deserted by the rest of the crew who were now working aft from the for'ard hold, closing the hatches and lashing tarpaulins over them. The two of them had opened one of the wooden packing cases to find that it contained exactly what it said on the manifest; namely, two tractor engines in each packing case. The first officer had gone to the engine room and reappeared with a tool kit and had set about removing the cylinder head of one of the diesel engines. This had taken some time and when the head was finally removed, all that was revealed was a row of four piston heads. Puzzled, the first officer was just about to replace the cylinder head when the captain had turned the flywheel. The wheel spun freely, but none of the pistons moved. 'Curious,' the first officer had muttered and then had lifted out all four pistons, which were not connected to a crankshaft. All that could be seen at the bottom of the cylinders was oil. Once again the first officer had left the hold, but this time he had gone to the officers' wardroom where there was a fake coal fire and a brass scuttle with a poker and a pair of tongs. He returned to the hold with the tongs and inserted them into one of the cylinders and down into the oil. When he pulled them out, clamped in the brass claws was a tightly sealed polythene bag. Ten minutes later, there were thirty of these bags. The first officer took a notebook from his pocket and started to do some calculations after the seal on one packet had been broken to reveal the fine, white powder inside. He had then turned to the captain; 'we've just loaded between three and five tons of pure, refined heroin.'

That had all been three days ago and before the collapse of the port boiler in the engine room. The Yorktown had been towed to the stand-by berth outside the dry dock, which was in the process of being flooded so that the vessel which had just completed repairs could be towed out. The ship's chief engineer had been summoned to the captain's cabin. When he arrived, still in grease-covered overalls, he found the first officer and the captain poring over a chart of the South China Sea. The Sicilian captain looked up as the engineer entered the cabin. 'Can the diesel pumps which the harbour authority put on board keep the engine room dry?' he asked.

'Well, they should be able to until the ship is taken into dry dock,' was the reply.

'No; what I mean, is how long would they last if, say, we were forced to put to sea?'

'Oh, I'm not sure, Captain; two or three days, possibly a little longer; why?'

Ignoring the question, the captain asked, 'and the starboard boiler; can you make that raise enough pressure to drive the shafts and if you can, what speed would it give us?'

The Korean engineer was now well aware that the captain and the first officer were planning to avoid taking the Yorktown into the dry dock. He knew, as did most of the crew, that there was no financing to cover the cost of a major engine overhaul and that once this was discovered, the ship would be confiscated and disposed of to the highest bidder to cover the dockyard costs. He would once again be out of a job and with very little prospect of finding another. 'Now that we have the diesels pumping the bilges, there's a chance that the starboard boiler would hold pressure for about 24 hours; perhaps more, probably less. With luck, I could get about 12 to 15 knots; certainly no more. Where are you planning to go, Captain?' the engineer finally asked.

'Just over four hundred miles; d'you think she'd make it?'

180

'She might; is it worth it?'

'It is; you'll be able to buy your own engines at the end of this trip.'

'When do you want the engines ready?'

'We'll slip out at 0100 hours tomorrow morning.'

'That's cutting it a bit fine; the typhoon is due on Saturday.'

'The typhoon isn't due until after mid day. We will be well clear by then. Can you manage it?'

'Aye, aye, Sir,' and the engineer gave a mockingly formal salute and left the cabin. When the door had closed, the captain spoke to the first officer.

'What d'you reckon its worth?'

'I'm no expert, Captain, but its street value must be worth well over half a billion dollars - US, of course!'

'Right; plot a course for Baguio on the north island of Luzon. We will make contact with the leader of the Communist rebels who bought that arms shipment off us some years ago when they were trying to remove Aquino. What's his name. . . ?'

'Cordoba.'

'That's right; do we still have the radio contact procedure?'

'Yes, I've got that.'

'Good; get the crew together and tell them what's going to happen,' and with that, the captain of Yorktown had dismissed his first officer.

*

Gunn awoke to find himself in complete darkness. It took a few minutes to bring all the recent events into focus as he shook off the effects of the drug. How was it that he felt no effects from it? If he had been injected with YS' patent cocktail, why hadn't it scrambled his mind? His mouth was a little dry, but other than that he had suffered no more discomfort than the restriction of his cramped legs and arms, which were suffering from the bosun's enthusiastic knot tying. He was lying on his back on a double bed, and presumed that it must be the early hours of Friday unless Mandy's injection had knocked him out for twenty-four hours. Gunn carefully eased himself over to the side of the bed and then swung his legs down to the floor and sat up. The effort made him feel slightly dizzy and he closed his eyes until his head cleared and then opened them again. He immediately shut his eyes, believing that the drug he'd been given really had taken effect or that he was dreaming. Gunn slowly opened his eyes, which had now gained their night vision and the person standing beside his bed was no dream or drug-induced illusion. Mandy stood beside his bed as naked as the day she was born, except for a thin gold necklace, which

181

extended to the cleavage between her firm and perfectly shaped breasts. Still not convinced of the reality of the situation, John Gunn tried to get up from the bed, but his legs had gone numb from the loss of circulation and would not bear his weight. Mandy took two steps towards him until the nipples of her breasts touched his forehead. He could smell the most tantalising scent from her skin as she reached over him and untied his wrists. He could feel her hard and prominent nipples as they brushed against the stubble of his unshaven face. Having untied his wrists, she bent down and started to untie the rope around his ankles which positioned her neatly rounded buttocks, with slim legs slightly spread, right in front of him. She was warm and moist and as his hand gently stroked her, he felt a shiver of sensuality pass through her body like an electric current. Holding his hand into her groin, Mandy stood up and pushed Gunn back onto the bed. Quickly, and still without a word, she removed his clothes while kneeling astride him. The circulation was now returning to Gunn's legs and the pain it produced blended with and heightened the eroticism of the silken-skinned beauty whose head was buried between his legs. Still without a word, she turned, placed him inside her and thrust herself down on him in a frenzy of aroused passion until, with a gasp, she sank down onto his chest, burying her head and mane of black hair on his shoulder.

The first grey streaks of dawn had started to lend form and shape to the cabin, as the light filtered through the curtains drawn over the portholes, before Mandy rose from the bed and wrapped a cotton kimono around herself. She had told Gunn that the drug she was meant to have injected would have kept him unconscious until eight that morning when she was required to give him another injection. The combination of the two drugs produced a remarkable effect on the human brain, but very few, if any, survived the treatment. She had told Gunn that it was her father's intention to leave the yacht that morning, using one of the two helicopters, and that he was going to Manila to catch the China Airlines flight to Shenzen. Gunn had asked her what the purpose of this visit was but she explained that all she knew was that there was a rendezvous for the yacht to the south of Pinghai on Monday. Her father had left the task of questioning Gunn to the bosun.

'Why are you telling me all this, Mandy?' Gunn had asked her as she lay with her head on his chest after yet another bout of love making. She had told him that she was aware that a plan was being prepared to do something to prevent the hand over of Hong Kong to China. Her father had never ceased making plans since the day their family had been decimated by the Chinese Communists and she also knew that her father was working very closely with another person in Hong Kong. She had only become aware of the scale of the conspiracy when her father had told her, on leaving Hong Kong, that she would never see the place again. No, she didn't know the person in Hong Kong, when Gunn asked her, but she was sure that it was a man, that he was very highly placed with the government or police, but again, had no idea if he was Chinese or European.

She had loosely retied his hands and feet, and told Gunn that she would return with a member of the crew on the next visit at eight o'clock. By then the yacht would be fairly close to land and it seemed to her that this would be the best time to make his escape. Bearing in mind that Mandy's visit might have been contrived by YS to find out how much he knew. Gunn made no mention of the patrol craft, but agreed to go along with Mandy's suggestion. If this had been one of YS' schemes to prise information out of him, there had been nothing contrived about his daughter's enthusiasm for the task. The cabin door closed softly behind Mandy and was re-locked.

Gunn got off the bed and removed the rope from his wrists and feet. He did a thorough inspection of the cabin and then glanced at his watch. It was now twenty past six; an hour and forty minutes to go. He returned to the bed, replaced the rope and waited. He was woken by the sound of the gas-turbine engine on the helicopter starting up. Gunn eased his hand out of the loosely tied rope and looked at his watch. It was two or three minutes to eight. Right on cue, he heard a key turn in the lock; the door opened and Mandy appeared escorted by the bosun. Gunn feigned unconsciousness while Mandy came round to the left side of the bed and placed the black case containing the hypodermic syringe on the bedside table. The bosun had taken a cursory glance at Gunn and was now looking out of the porthole on the right side of the bed. At this moment Mandy dropped the glass phial, cursed and spoke to the bosun who grunted in response and walked round the bed. She pointed to where the phial had rolled under the bed. Gunn had heard all this and seen the move of the bosun through partially closed eyes. Mandy's ploy - if it was one - would place the bosun ideally for him to deliver a fatal blow to the bosun's neck as he bent down to retrieve the phial. The bosun dropped to his knees and bent down. Gunn swung over, both hands coming free from the loose rope and raised, locked together, to deliver the blow, but there was no need. As Gunn's hands started to come down in a hammer blow, the bosun collapsed to the floor without a sound, a needle-sharp knife protruding from the spinal cord in the back of his neck.

The sound of the helicopter engine increased in pitch as Mandy led Gunn to the cabin door. It was now some ten hours that Gunn had been on Middle Kingdom and it was imperative that he took steps to make the yacht go slower. The maximum speed of HMS Swordfish was twenty-five knots and he had no idea how long the patrol craft could maintain that speed. Mandy took Gunn to her father's suite where he found the sub-machine gun, his Browning and the diving knife. All attention on the yacht was concentrated on the departure of the helicopter. Gunn advised her to stay in her room until he returned, and then left YS' suite and went down the companionway on the starboard side of the yacht to the place where he had concealed the pack containing the charges. The pack was still hidden under the canvas cover of one of the four motor boats and Gunn removed the last three charges and then made his way to the starboard companionway, which led down to the engine room.

He swung both of the locking levers on the watertight door and walked onto the catwalk surrounding the engines. It was unfortunate that the duty engineer was checking a control panel on the starboard side and saw Gunn as soon as he came through the door. The man threw himself underneath the metal catwalk where Gunn was unable to shoot at him and started for'ard, weaving in and out of the machinery towards the engine control room and the telephone which would alert the bridge and the rest of the yacht's crew. At the for'ard bulkhead, the man had to leave the protection of the catwalk to get into the engine control room. He was exactly half way to the door when the burst from Gunn's Stirling stitched a diagonal row of scarlet holes from the left side of his waistline to his right shoulder. Not waiting to see where the engineer's companion was, Gunn ran towards the stern of the compartment, where he had previously discovered the yacht's steering flat. He opened the watertight door and went into the darkened compartment. It took him a few seconds to find the light switch and then the cramped area was flooded with light.

Large hydraulic pistons were mounted on quadrants, which, in their turn were connected to the two rudder-posts. Slightly for'ard of this mechanism was the emergency steering gear which could be locked into the steering quadrants and the rudders then were turned using a lever and ratchet system. Gunn placed a charge on each of the hydraulic pistons and one on the emergency steering gear. He squeezed the detonators into the PE and then set the timers for fifteen seconds. He moved round to the port side of the compartment where he had left the unconscious steward only two nights previously and opened the door. The engineer's companion had been waiting for him to emerge from the closed starboard door and swung round, firing a wildly inaccurate shot at Gunn, which ricocheted off the metal piping and struck Gunn in the right arm, wrenching it off the trigger of the sub machine gun.

Gunn dropped to the surface of the catwalk as another bullet struck the handrail. He hadn't lost any movement in his right hand although he could feel the hot wetness of the blood from the wound. He swung the bulbous-ended silencer towards the engineer and squeezed the trigger at exactly the same moment as the charges in the steering flat exploded. The explosion ripped the starboard watertight door off its hinges and hurled it out into the engine room, carrying the engineer with it. The port door was open and the shock waves of the explosion dissipated out and up from the aperture leaving Gunn, face down on the catwalk, unscathed. The position of the charges and the subsequent explosion locked both rudders with four degrees of port helm. Middle Kingdom was still travelling at twenty-five knots and the sudden application of port helm caused the yacht to heel sharply to starboard.

On the helicopter pad, just aft of the swimming pool, YS had climbed into the rear seat of the helicopter and fastened the strap across his lap. The pilot brought the engine revs up and gave the rotor blades their aerofoil angle with the collective stick. The island of Luzon lay to starboard and only five miles away on the port quarter was the anchorage selected by Bueno for Middle Kingdom to wait until the RV off the coast of China in three days. At the instant that the skids of the helicopter left the pad, the explosion ripped open the stern of the yacht and she heeled over to starboard. The pad caught the port skid of the helicopter and tipped the machine over to the right. The pilot was caught completely by surprise and reacted too slowly to save himself, the machine or his passenger. The helicopter side-slipped to the right, the landing skid hooked in the guard rail and in a matter of split seconds it had cart-wheeled over the side of the yacht and disappeared into the boiling wake.

Middle Kingdom was barely five miles from a line of razor-toothed rocks and was racing straight for them. The duty crew on the bridge fought to regain control of the yacht, but there was no response from the steering and none from the crew in the engine room. The second helicopter was dragged out of its hangar, rotors locked into position and the second pilot started up the gas-turbine. Two members of the crew rushed to join him, both carrying Kalashnikov sub-machine guns. The rotors of the helicopter were engaged and quickly built up speed; another member of the crew climbed on board the helicopter. Middle Kingdom was now only two hundred yards

185

from the first of the rocks. The bridge watch appeared on the boat deck, took one look over the bow and threw themselves over the side where they were immediately sucked under the hull and then spewed out through the water jet propulsion system. Nothing could possibly save Middle Kingdom now as the yacht surged towards the rocks, bent on self-destruction.

*

The Governor's Security Committee had met that morning at 8 am in the EXCO Conference Room. There were six men in the room; The Governor, his private secretary, CBF, the Chief Fire Officer, the Commissioner of Police and Robin Masefield, who had now been appointed Chief Secretary, but was attending the meeting with the dual responsibilities of Head of the Civil Service and the Secretary for Security. The Commissioner of Police gave his report on the progress towards identification of the hostages' location. His men, in fact, had made no progress at all, except to eliminate a handful of places from the odd million or so where they could have been held captive.

When he had finished, it was CBF's turn to give the meeting an account of the operation to board Middle Kingdom. This he did, repeating much of what he had told the Governor the previous evening. The only fresh information to the Governor's ears was the news that HMS Swordfish had reported that the homing beacon was still working and that they were now eleven miles astern of the yacht which was at Latitude 13° 50′ North and Longitude 122° 20′ West. 'Where's that in layman's language, Patrick?' the Governor asked.

General Patrick Rogers got up and walked to the wall map which covered the Western Pacific, South China Sea and Indian Ocean. Using a slim, chrome plated pointer, he placed the tip just to the east of the island of Luzon. 'Here, Sir,' he said.

'And what's that island to the west of the position you've just pointed out?' The General removed a pair of reading glasses from his pocket and studied the map closely.

'Catanduanes Island, Sir.'

The red light came on over the door and the Governor's private secretary left the table and went out of the room. He returned in a matter of seconds and went round the table to the Commissioner of Police. Martin Holmes spoke quietly to him and Sir Peter Aldridge, after an apology to the Governor, left the room.

'Not more bad news?' sighed the Governor, as Martin Holmes resumed his seat at the table.

'Yes, I'm afraid, sir, it is; there has been an attempt to murder Mr McBain, the Assistant Commissioner of Police. Sir Peter will have the details when he returns shortly. The Head of Serious Crimes is briefing him in the ante-room now.'

'Wasn't he due to fly back to UK with his family this weekend?' asked Robin Masefield. Before anyone in the room could comment on that question, the door opened and Sir Peter Aldridge returned. He went straight to his seat and turned to the Governor.

'I really don't know what significance this has on the present situation, Sir, but it appears that an attempt has been made to kill my Assistant Commissioner and his entire family,' began the CP and then paused at the various exclamations from around the table.

'Go on, Peter,' prompted the Governor.

'Very briefly then; Charles McBain failed to appear at the emergency briefing for me at seven this morning and there was no answer from his phone. His deputy conducted the briefing while a car was sent to his flat. When the officer arrived at the flat there was no answer and he was about to go and speak to a neighbour when he realised that there was a strong smell of gas which appeared to be seeping out from McBain's flat. Fortunately, he was able to get the passkeys quickly from the apartment security staff and went into the flat. The main gas pipe had been severed and it took the officer three trips before he was able to find the tap and turn off the supply. He threw open all the windows and then sent the security guard down to ring for an ambulance and the Serious Crimes Squad. McBain, his wife and both his boys were unconscious in their bedrooms and are now at the Matilda Hospital. McBain regained consciousness first and had no idea what had happened,' the CP concluded.

'Has McBain been involved in this present crisis?' asked the CBF.

'He's been in charge of all the searches we've been conducting,' replied the CP.

'Is it possible to deduce from that, Peter,' interjected the Governor, 'that he may have been getting close to a discovery of some sort?'

'It's possible, I suppose,' answered the CP slowly, 'but the man is still in a state of shock and was finding it difficult to think coherently.'

'Yes, of course.'

'Why did the officer who discovered the incident send the security guard to phone from his desk down at the entrance?' asked Robin Masefield.

Patiently, the CP turned to the new Chief Secretary and explained, 'when a flat is full of gas the slightest spark can blow the whole place to smithereens. Even the minute current in a telephone has been known to ignite a gas leak, Robin.'

Robin Masefield was unperturbed. 'Thank you, Sir Peter; please correct me if I misunderstood your briefing of the sequence of events leading to the discovery of the McBain family. You told us that when McBain failed to appear at seven, someone phoned his flat; just once or perhaps twice?' There was absolute silence in the room.

'As I recall, certainly once and possibly twice,' was the CP's cautious reply.

'Thank you, Sir Peter. . . .'

'Is there a point to these questions, Robin?' interjected the Governor.

'Yes, there is, Sir. Sir Peter, I'm no electronic engineer, but I have always understood that current is generated in a telephone by an incoming call which activates the bell. If, as you say, one or possibly two or more calls were made to McBain's flat only a matter of minutes before the officer went to the flat, why wasn't the gas ignited and why wasn't the phone answered by their amah?'

'That's a very good question, Robin. I suppose because either the telephone didn't cause a spark or the gas concentration was too weak to ignite. The officer said there was no amah in the servant's room at the back of the flat,' answered the CP.

'That's exactly as I understand it. So how long, Sir Peter, with your experience, would it take gas from a severed pipe to build up to an explosive concentration in a flat with all doors and windows shut, as is the case in all flats at this time of year when the air-conditioning is on?'

'That's difficult to say, Robin; you see. . . .'

'But I do want you to say, Peter,' insisted the Governor quietly and very firmly.

'Yes, of course Sir; let me see . . . in a flat of that size . . . and I understand that the bedroom doors were shut. The gas would have to fill the kitchen, the hall and the living room . . . oh, no more than an hour to an hour and a half,' was the CP's estimate.

'So, Robin; the point of your line of enquiry please,' requested the Governor, turning to his Chief Secretary.

'One last question, if I may Sir; how long was it from the first phone call to McBain's flat until the police officer arrived there?'

'Let me see . . . twenty five minutes . . . half an hour at the outside,' replied the CP.

'Sir,' and Robin Masefield turned to the Governor. 'I have very little experience in these matters, but it would seem to me that the murderer broke into the flat less than an hour before the police arrived. I would suggest that is most unlikely since the majority of us are up by six in the morning. Either that or the gas pipe was severed after the first or second phone calls. Did McBain know of the plan to board Middle Kingdom?'

'Yes, he's my right hand man . . .' the CP stammered.

'Then I suggest that we should consider a police guard on McBain,' Robin Masefield said. There was complete silence once more and then the CP rose and left the room. The door had barely closed before it reopened and Sir Peter Aldridge returned to the room.

'Charles McBain discharged himself from the Matilda Hospital eighteen minutes ago.'

*

American Pie left her anchorage in the southern cove of the bay at 6 am. They had all been keen to make an early start so that they would be over the wreck in time for breakfast. Dan had set up his GPS with great care that morning, even to the extent of doing a resection with his hand-bearing compass to position the yacht to the nearest metre before he fed the latitude and longitude into the computer. He picked three way points and American Pie was now approaching the second of these which would then give them the bearing and distance to the wreck. The GPS bleeped at Dan to tell him that he was over the way-point and he swung the yacht to port onto the new bearing. It was now just after seven and the smell of frying bacon and hot coffee drifting from the galley had whetted everyone's appetite. At 0731 hrs the GPS bleeped again and Dan Grant put the yacht astern and signalled to the boat boys to let go the anchor. The wind, what little there was of it, was from the north-west and American Pie swung round to lie to the anchor, pointing towards the blue-hued shape of Luzon. All the diving gear was brought up on deck and the canvas cover was removed from the air-compressor amidships. The wreck was supposed to be lying in twenty metres of water so they would need plenty of air bottles to allow for decompression on the way up from that depth. The plan was to have breakfast, then pause to digest it and start diving at nine o'clock.

Dan was just finishing his eggs and bacon - he would be staying on deck while his guests dived - when he was nudged by one of the young Japanese men who was pointing with his other hand. 'Looks as though we might be going to have company,' he remarked with a broad grin. Dan cursed silently to himself; he should have spotted that boat, particularly after the incident in the south. He got up from the table and collected his binoculars from the wheelhouse. With relief, he saw that she was an extremely smart yacht, probably the largest he'd seen for some years and going at some speed too, he thought to himself as he trained the glasses on her. He handed the glasses to his guests and excused himself saying that he was off to the heads. He caught the anxious look on Amy's face and gave an imperceptible shake of his head as he went below. In the engine room he opened the

189

two weapon compartments and removed the same quantity of ammunition and weapons as he had for the previous encounter and placed them ready for use on the workbench. Dan then returned to the cockpit and rejoined his guests.

The yacht was almost abeam of them and about five miles out to sea, Dan estimated. The sighting of the yacht, gleaming white in the low, morning sun had temporarily banished all interest in the forthcoming dive and Dan's guests were chatting excitedly in their own language. Because the wind was blowing from the yacht towards American Pie, the sound of the explosion carried clearly across the sea, preceded by the vivid flash from the stern. Dan Grant was holding the binoculars and exclaimed, 'Jesus Christ! That explosion has just thrown the yacht's chopper over the side. Pedro! Salvador! Get the anchor up fast,' and with that he handed the binoculars to one of his charter guests and switched on the heaters for the diesel engines. Both engines started immediately and Dan Grant left them running at 1000 revs to get them ready for instant use. He moved to the binnacle and bent down and sighted over the top of it to get a rough bearing to the position where the helicopter had disappeared into the sea.

'Is that anchor clear yet?' Dan shouted at his boys.

'Can you give us help with the engines, Skipper?' Salvador shouted back. Dan cursed himself for forgetting to do that; he brought the revs down and engaged both engines for a few seconds, which gave American Pie headway and took the strain off the chain. The winch brought the chain rattling over the bow roller and into the chain locker.

'Clear! Skipper,' came the shout from the bow. Dan engaged the engines and set them at 1500 revs, which would give the boat a speed of 12 knots.

'Look!' came the exclamation from one of the guests, 'she's going to crash into the rocks!' Dan looked to his left and gasped. The yacht was barely a mile away and was heading straight for the barrier of rocks, which protected their anchorage in the southern cove and where, but for this diving expedition, American Pie would now be anchored. On the aft deck of the yacht, he could now see another helicopter with the rotors turning.

'Salvador! Godammit! Take the wheel for a bit and keep her on a bearing of 290°,' Dan ordered as he stepped to one side and braced himself against the wheelhouse while he steadied the binoculars on the yacht. 'What's going on?' he half muttered; he had just seen two men climb into the helicopter carrying weapons. He then saw two of the crew dive over the side of the yacht and another member of the crew, also armed, climb into the helicopter. A fourth man ran towards the helicopter only to be cut down by a burst of fire from an automatic weapon from inside the machine. 'Pedro!' Dan shouted.

'Yes, Skipper,' came the calm and quiet response right beside Dan Grant.

'Sorry son, didn't see you there. Take the men and bring the weapons into the wheelhouse. Got that?'

'Aye, aye, Skipper,' the boy replied, grinning from ear to ear and disappeared with the four Japanese men.

'Amy dear, could you and the other ladies go below. I've no idea what's going on. but those men are armed and I don't want any of us to be caught in the crossfire.'

'You will take care, Dan, won't you.'

'Don't worry honey, I don't aim to become involved in this battle, unless it's to protect you and our guests,' Dan assured his wife unconvincingly as Pedro and the four Japanese men started loading the weapons.

CHAPTER 17

Gunn reached the boat deck on the port side of the yacht just as the helicopter, with YS as passenger, was hurled over the starboard side. On the port bow was the line of rocks with surf breaking over the jagged edges protruding from the sea. Above him was a fever of activity as the second helicopter was made ready for flight on the aft helicopter LP. The track on which Middle Kingdom was jammed led unerringly towards the line of rocks and it appeared that no attempt was being made to reduce speed or alter course. He had sent Mandy to her cabin to keep her out of the line of fire, but now he had to get her out before the yacht was eviscerated on the rocks.

Gunn ran up the companionway to the sun deck, narrowly avoiding two of the crew, armed with Kalashnikovs, who were running towards the helicopter, whose rotors were beginning to turn. Neither of the men paid any attention to him, so intent were they on reaching the helicopter before it took off. Gunn went straight to Mandy's cabin where he found her lying beside her dressing table bleeding from a wound on the side of her head. She said that she had fallen as the yacht healed and had struck her head on the edge of the dressing table. Gunn picked her up and carried her out of the owner's suite onto the sundeck. In front of him, a member of the crew, carrying what looked like an M16 rifle, was running for the helicopter, which was about to lift off from the LP. Twenty yards from the machine, he was cut to ribbons by a long burst of automatic fire from the helicopter as its skids left the deck and it staggered into the air. A glance over his shoulder revealed the breaking surf on the rocks, less than a hundred metres away. Gunn had no idea what the effect of the impact would be when the yacht struck the rocks, but it was bound to be disastrous. On his left was the swimming pool; without a second's further thought, he carried Mandy to the edge of the pool, laid her down and then jumped in, helping her in after him and then held her at the aft end of the pool in about five feet of water.

Under the sea, the rocks formed a ramp of razor like blades. Middle Kingdom's raked bow rode up this ramp which ripped out the 'entrails' of the yacht as neatly as a knife gutting a fish. The impetus of the yacht carried it over the rocks and into the cove on the other side where it started to sink rapidly.

As the yacht struck the rocks, the water in the pool was thrown forward against the for'ard end and then washed back aft, carrying Gunn and Mandy with it. The noise was deafening as metal crumpled, pressurised pipes burst, structures were ripped off their mountings and pieces of equipment were hurled forwards as the yacht's speed was reduced from twenty five knots to zero in less than a hundred metres. Battered and grazed by the impact, Gunn helped Mandy out of the pool, climbed out after her and then led her down the boat deck and towards the stern. The deck was already awash; all four motor boats had broken free of their lashings. The two for'ard boats had been crushed against a metal bulkhead, but the two aft ones had been thrown against the yacht's fenders which had been stowed in front of them and both boats appeared to be undamaged. Gunn pulled the canvas cover off the boat on the port side and then helped Mandy into the aft-facing seats behind the driver's seat. The sea was now over his knees and the boat was nearly afloat. Middle Kingdom was foundering rapidly and unless Gunn timed it correctly, both he and Mandy would be pinned under the superstructure and carried down with the yacht in its final plunge.

The motor boat swung clear of the debris around it and Gunn pushed it over the yacht's rail, now some six or more inches under water. With a final heave he pushed the boat away and jumped in. Gunn climbed into the front left seat behind the wheel and then, to his dismay was confronted with a key-start ignition. He looked into the stern of the boat and saw that there was an emergency paddle stowed on the starboard side. He climbed through the gap in the seats and pulled the paddle from its stowage. A great burst of trapped air helped to push them away from the yacht, but the stern had now disappeared and the vortex caused by the sinking yacht dragged the boat back. Desperately, Gunn leant over the side and paddled, first on one side of the motor boat and then on the other. Little by little, he forced the boat away from the yacht. The flesh wound from the bullet in his right arm had reopened and the blood ran out from under the cuff of the flying suit and onto the paddle making him lose his grip. The for'ard part of the yacht disappeared and for a few moments the sea boiled as trapped air escaped and then there was silence. Gunn dropped the paddle in the stern of the boat and returned to the driver's seat. He bent down under the boat's dashboard and found the heavily insulated ignition wiring. He ripped this out, just as the momentary silence was broken by the reappearance of the helicopter, which dived towards the boat. It roared over the top of them, while Gunn feverishly tried to remove the insulation from the wires with his diving knife. As the helicopter banked and climbed, a burst of fire

193

raised a line of gouts of water, which only missed the boat by the smallest of margins. Gunn quickly checked that the combined gear and throttle lever was out of gear and gave the inboard engine about a quarter throttle. He was holding four wires in his hand; all with the same colour code. He touched two of them together; a shower of sparks, nothing from the engine and the helicopter had banked, turned and was now making its next attacking run. Gunn discarded one of the wires and touched the next one to the first wire. Nothing; it was dead. The helicopter engine was rising to a crescendo. The third wire; the engine fired and died; again the blood on his hand made the wire slip - the engine fired and ran; the hammering beat of the helicopter's rotors was pounding the thin, humid air. Lever into neutral and then slammed fully forward; the water boiled behind the motor boat, the stern dug into the sea and it shot forward, throwing Mandy into the stern. The gouts of water from the long burst of fire from the Kalashnikov traced a line across the sea in the wake of the motor boat. Gunn hung onto the wheel as the boat raced across the calm water of the sheltered cove and then out into the open sea.

*

On the bridge of HMS Swordfish, Lt Commander Nick Swift lowered his binoculars and walked over to the chart table where his navigating officer, Lieutenant Mike Spears, was making a plot on the chart. Swordfish was a shade over ten miles astern of Middle Kingdom and would have been a great deal further astern if it hadn't been for Nick Swift's decision to cut inside the course taken by the yacht. He had made the decision for two reasons; twenty-five knots was Swordfish's maximum speed and could not be maintained indefinitely without blowing up the engines, and he wanted to keep the patrol craft as close to the coast as possible to hide its radar signature amongst the land clutter. This had given the navigating officer the very difficult task of plotting a course for Swordfish through all the shoals and shallows round the north and east coast of Luzon while the ship was travelling at its maximum speed. Mike Spears had done an excellent job, but had now been on the bridge for nearly ten hours and the strain was beginning to show. The signal from the beacon had given Middle Kingdom's exact position throughout the night and morning and then quite suddenly, the cessation of the Doppler Shift on the signal, indicated that the yacht had stopped dead.

'What d'you make of that, Mike?' Nick Swift asked his navigating officer.

194

'Malfunction of the beacon, Sir,' was the prompt and confident response. 'Those electronics 'gizmos' are unreliable and erratic.'

'I'm not so sure,' Nick Swift murmured, almost to himself. 'From the moment it was switched on last night, it's pin-pointed the yacht's position with considerable accuracy.'

'That's the trouble, Sir, with these gadgets. One comes to rely on them and then they invariably let you down.'

Mike Spears was a young, self-assured and ambitious officer, who had done all the right things - in his opinion - throughout his short career in the Royal Navy. He therefore couldn't understand his appointment as navigating officer to one of these 'toy boats' in the Hong Kong Squadron - as he had been heard to refer to the patrol craft in the wardroom at HMS Tamar – the naval headquarters in Hong Kong. His entire life revolved around four things; navigation, seamanship skills, the furtherance of his career and his model train set in the attic of his parents' house, near Petersfield in Hampshire. Almost without exception, his peers in the same year at the Britannia Royal Naval College at Dartmouth and in the Squadron, considered him to be the most insufferable bore. However, he was highly competent at his job and was respected by his Captain and the crew of Swordfish for that ability.

Nick Swift was an experienced officer and the ribbon of the Distinguished Service Cross beside his Gulf War ribbon and the General Service Medal were but an indication of his ability and courage. He had only been a relative youngster of twenty two in 1991 when an explosion in the engine room of the Type 42 Destroyer in which he was serving threatened the lives of all the engineering ratings. The DSC was for his conspicuous gallantry in attempting to rescue his sailors with little or no regard for his own safety. The previous evening, when Spears had navigated the ship so accurately to the rendezvous with the two SAS characters, Nick Swift had decided to give his navigating officer the benefit of the doubt in his annual confidential report, which he was currently drafting for the Commander of the Squadron. Now, he had doubts again. There had to be another reason for the behaviour of the beacon; namely the one which the beacon was trying to tell them. The yacht had stopped. 'Let's, for a moment, assume that the beacon is working; what would our plotting equipment indicate?' Nick asked the young officer.

'That's very straightforward, Sir,' was the instant reply. 'It's indicating that the yacht ran into a rock and stopped dead.'

'Good, that's exactly as I read it. Now, the exact location of the yacht.' Mike Spears could barely keep the insinuation of nonsense out of the tone of his voice, which did not escape either his Captain or the duty watch.

'Here Sir, off the west coast of Catanduanes Island.'

'How far from our present position,' and Nick glanced up to see that the ship's speed was being maintained.

'Approximately. . . .'

'No, not approximately, Mike; exactly.' The navigating officer went crimson with embarrassment and anger which was not helped by a stifled snigger from the for'ard part of the bridge. He placed his dividers on the chart and then moved them to the latitude scale.

'Seven miles, two cables, Sir,' and here the over-emphasised 'Sir' didn't escape his Captain.

'Thank you, Mike,' and then to the bridge watch, 'give me the engine room please. Who's the duty watch engineer?'

'CPO Burns, Sir,' came from the coxswain.

'Engine room,' responded the voice from the tannoy speaker.

'Burns, it's the Captain here; I'm about to ask you for maximum revolutions and when I say that I mean it. I don't give a damn if the engines fall out of the ship, I want every fraction of shaft-horse-power that you can give me. This order will be recorded in the log and you will be exonerated from blame for any damage caused to the engines as a result of my order; understood?'

'Yes Sir, ready when you are.'

'Thank you Burns. Give me maximum revolutions now,' and then turning to the duty watch, 'new course! Steer 135°. Officer of the watch! Close the ship up to action stations. Watch that beacon like a hawk, Mike; I'm going below to get ready for action stations and to check on our American friend. Oh yes; please get the duty watch officer to warn all ships on channel 16 that we are going to the rescue of the yacht Middle Kingdom and get a signal back to Tamar to clear this all through the Philippine Consulate. Don't want to cause an international incident, do we,' and with that remark Nick Swift left the bridge.

*

American Pie was just under a mile from the spot where Middle Kingdom had driven herself onto the rocks. The sight and sound of the ship's destruction had left everyone speechless. They had watched the helicopter lurch precariously into the air just before the impact with the rocks and had seen it swing back towards the yacht and had heard the firing, but they were unable to see what was happening on the other side of the rocks.

Salvador grabbed Dan Grant's arm and pointed. There were two pairs of binoculars on the boat and Dan was determined not to miss anything so that he could make the right decision should the need arise. His charter guests were passing the other pair around like the witches' eye in Grimm's fairy tales. Dan looked to his left where Salvador was pointing. From around the headland of the cove where they had been anchored only a few hours previously, came a motor boat. Even as they watched, the helicopter came into view as it banked low round the headland and then straightened up for another attacking run on the motor boat.

'That guy in the boat doesn't stand a chance. Now how the hell do we tell who are the good guys and who are the bad guys?

Dan saw the puff of smoke from the helicopter as someone opened fire. At exactly the same moment the motor boat swerved hard to port and headed directly for American Pie. The bullets from the helicopter sprayed harmlessly across the sea. 'Inside everyone!' Dan ordered and was obeyed instantly. The helicopter had turned and was straightening for another run. Still the boat came straight for American Pie. Dan Grant went into the wheelhouse and brought out his Armalite and the pump-action 12 gauge shot gun. Twenty metres from American Pie's port quarter the driver of the motor boat threw the throttle into neutral and a young woman dived over the side of the boat. He shouted, 'take care of her, please!' which was almost drowned by the roar of the engine as the throttle was slammed forward and the motor boat disappeared under the bow of the yacht and out into the open sea. Once again the helicopter changed direction and banked towards the motor boat, its skids only feet above the surface of the sea.

Pedro had dived into the sea and he and Salvador were now helping a young Chinese girl up the diving ladder, which had been rigged in preparation for the dive to the wreck. Amy appeared with a towel and the girl was led below. In the saloon, Mandy was propped up on the settee and given a glass of brandy.

'Can you speak English, honey,' Amy asked gently. Mandy nodded, took a sip from her glass and put it down on the table.

'Please help John, if you can,' and she turned to Dan, 'otherwise they'll kill him.'

'Fine honey,' this was Dan, 'but can you tell us quickly who you are, who is John and what the sainted hell is going on?'

'Sshh Dan!' came from Amy.

'No, he's right, I must be quick,' Mandy interrupted. 'The men trying to kill John work for my father who owned that yacht,' and she made a vague gesture in the direction of the cove. 'They're all Triad members and hired gunmen; please help John,' this was added as the sound of automatic fire reached down into the saloon.

'I'll buy that; never could resist a pretty face.'

'Take care,' followed Dan as he went up on deck, collecting his two anti-tank missiles as he went through the wheelhouse.

*

With relief Gunn saw someone dive into the sea to help Mandy aboard the yacht. That was all the time he had to think of Mandy's well-being as yet another burst of fire strafed across the water towards him; a handful of rounds thumped into the stern part of the boat, but Gunn had no time to inspect the damage, he just prayed that nothing in the engine installation had been hit. It was only seconds before the reek of petrol reached his nostrils; one unlucky round from the Kalashnikovs could now turn the boat into his funeral pyre. He spun the wheel hard to starboard bringing the boat round in a 'U' turn. As the boat went through the turn, he saw another ship approaching the scene. He was unable to identify it at first glance, so he swung the boat hard to port, again thwarting the helicopter pilot's attempt to position his machine for the men in the back to get an aimed burst at the motor boat. As his boat pointed out to sea again, Gunn stood up to get a better view; it was HMS Swordfish.

*

Lt Commander Nick Swift was sitting in the Captain's chair on the starboard side of the bridge. Beside him was Doyle Barnes with his left arm in a sling. The engineer had achieved revolutions for thirty knots, which Swordfish had sustained for the thirteen and a half minutes that it had taken them to reach Middle Kingdom. 'Coxswain! Revolutions for fifteen knots,' Nick ordered, bringing his patrol craft down from something in excess of full speed to a fast manoeuvring speed. His binoculars and those of Doyle Barnes were trained on the motor boat and helicopter.

'That's John in the boat, Sir,' Doyle said turning to Nick Swift. 'He doesn't stand much of a chance against those bastards in the chopper.'

The Captain picked up the microphone from the hook by his head. 'Gun crew and air defence machine-gunners; your target is the helicopter, I say again, your target is the helicopter; weapons free! weapons free!' The OTO Melara 76mm gun immediately trained and laid on the helicopter. On either side of the bridge were twin 7.62mm General Purpose Machine Guns in SCAT air defence mounts. Each of the gunners cocked the two weapons in front of him and the number two on each weapon mount made sure the belted ammunition was free to run.

The Captain turned to the gunnery officer; 'set the gun to minimum rate David, please.'

'Minimum rate, aye, aye Sir,' was immediately repeated and then, 'minimum rate set, Sir.' The gunnery officer was extremely proud of the Italian OTO Melara gun. It had proved to be one of the most successful of all guns of its type in the Western Navies and was capable of firing a 12 pound shell some 16 kilometres at a rate of up to 85 rounds a minute. This was to be the first time that he had ever used it in action - other than on prescribed naval gunnery ranges - and he was determined to prove to his colleagues the effectiveness of the gun.

The helicopter had just climbed and turned as the motor boat avoided it with another 'U' turn. The pilot was taking it down in yet another dive on a crossing course from left to right on the patrol craft's bow. Thump! Thump! Thump! Three rounds left the gun; the range was 1000 metres, so it was difficult to separate the detonation from the firing. Both twin-mounted machine guns opened fire and the one-in-five tracer arched its deadly necklace towards the helicopter.

So intent was the pilot on positioning his machine to get a killing shot at Gunn in the boat that he hadn't even noticed the arrival of HMS Swordfish on the scene. It was only a tight left turn to allow the weapons behind him to get a crossing shot at the boat that saved him. The three shells exploded fifty metres to his right. The machine rocked in the blast and a gasp from his observer, seated on his right, and the blood splattered on the perspex dome, told him that the hunter had now become the hunted. A glance to his left revealed the warship; to his right was the yacht. The only way to escape from the warship's guns was to fly over the land and if he could position his machine so that the yacht was in the direct line of fire, the warship's guns would be unable to shoot. Brilliant, the pilot congratulated himself on his cunning. His self-congratulations were only mildly diminished when he saw that one of his passengers in the rear seats was hanging forward in his straps, the whole of the right side of his body shredded by the impact of the white-hot tungsten spheres from the exploding shells. The helicopter dived towards American Pie.

*

The arrival of HMS Swordfish had brought a cheer from Dan Grant's guests and his boat boys. The helicopter was now nearly a mile further out to sea than American Pie. They all saw the helicopter turn to chase the motor boat, which was immediately followed by the explosion of the three shells and the flicker of the rounds from the machine guns. American Pie was not under way and Dan had let her drift in the light north-easterly breeze.

The helicopter banked and turned towards the yacht, apparently ignoring the motor boat. 'Goddammit! He's coming for us,' exclaimed Dan. 'Get ready men,' he warned and then he realised what the pilot was doing. The machine had come right down to sea level and was aimed straight at the yacht. Any round from the warship would be bound to hit or come dangerously close to the yacht, thus making the warship impotent. 'Get behind the wheelhouse all of you. Open fire only after you see the missile leave this launcher,' and he patted the tube. 'Aim over the top of the helicopter; all understood?' The four heads nodded. 'Right, move it!' and the four Japanese and the two boat boys quickly sheltered behind the wheelhouse.

American Pie was lying with her stern towards the helicopter. Dan Grant squatted down on the deck and pushed the missile launch tube through the spokes of the large ship's wheel to provide some concealment and so that the pilot would have no warning of the reception he was about to get. The skids of the helicopter were no more than six feet above the sea and the distance was 500 metres and closing fast. Dan placed the cross wires of the sight right in the centre of the helicopter's perspex dome and squeezed the trigger. The missile leapt from the tube to the accompaniment of a fusillade of fire from the wheelhouse.

A bullet from the Armalite of one of the Japanese guests killed the pilot a split-second before he took evasive action, having seen the missile fired from the yacht. The missile struck and the helicopter erupted in a fireball plunging into the sea only fifty metres astern of American Pie. Bits and pieces from it flew all round the yacht. In less than twenty seconds the remains of the machine had disappeared and only one or two pieces of fabric were left floating on the sea.

*

'That yacht's got a better weapon system than us,' laughed Nick Swift, as the men on the bridge watched in amazement at the destruction of the helicopter. 'All engines stop, secure from action stations, David,' this was to the first officer, 'please go and help Mr Gunn aboard.' The motor boat was approaching the warship; it was down by the stern and even as they watched from the bridge a wave broke over the stern and the engine spluttered and stopped. Gunn glanced over his shoulder to the stern of the boat. The bullets, which had hit the boat extended in a line across the seat on which Mandy had been slumped moments earlier, through the hull of the boat and into the fuel tank. He eased himself up onto the seat and as the boat slipped below the surface, he swam clear. Swordfish had gone astern and was now stationary only twenty metres away. Gunn swum to the ladder which had been rigged on the port side and climbed wearily up to the deck, where he was helped by Doyle's one good arm and the first officer.

HMS Swordfish headed for American Pie, which had anchored once again. Down in the sick bay, Gunn was given a change of clothing and the flesh would in his right arm was strapped up. He returned to the bridge as Swordfish went astern just fifty metres from the yacht. The sea-raider was lowered in the davits and brought round to a small companionway, which had been rigged on the starboard side of the ship. Gunn went down the steps and boarded the RIB, which ferried him across to the diving ladder on American Pie. Dan Grant was waiting for him and helped him up to the deck where the two men shook hands. Gunn was then introduced to Amy and the guests and then, unable to wait any longer, Mandy appeared from the wheelhouse and threw her arms around Gunn's waist and hugged him.

'I can't say thank you enough for your help,' Gunn said to Dan Grant. I only wish I could stay a little longer and get to know you all, but unfortunately the sinking of that yacht has made my job even more difficult. Many thanks for taking care of Mandy; I've got to take her to HMS Swordfish.' Once again, Gunn shook all the hands, was kissed by Amy Grant - to her husband's surprise - and then climbed down the ladder into the inflatable. He helped Mandy into the boat and they crossed the short distance to the warship. Once on board, Mandy was taken to the sick bay, while Gunn stood on the bridge wing and waved farewell to Dan and Amy Grant and their charter guests.

'We've both been told to report back to Hong Kong immediately,' Doyle Barnes told Gunn as he came into the bridge. 'It seems they've got some lead and want to match it with anything you might have learned from the young Chinese lady,' Doyle continued with a broad grin. Gunn smiled.

'Very little, I'm afraid Doyle and her father's dead. Incidentally, she,' and here Gunn indicated with a slight movement of his head in the direction of the sick bay, 'doesn't know about her father yet. She thinks he's on his way to Manila. I'll have to break the news to her shortly. Tell me, how are we to 'report back immediately' to Hong Kong?'

'Come down to the sick bay, John, and I'll give you your travel itinerary, courtesy of the US Seventh Fleet!'

CHAPTER 18

The Royal Observatory's predication that Typhoon Pamela would increase speed during the night had proved to be correct. By 1000 hours on Friday morning the centre of the typhoon was 350 miles to the south of Hong Kong and already the periphery winds were beginning to be felt in the territory. The sky had become overcast with only the occasional glimpse of a watery sun. The east and west anchorages of Victoria Harbour were clear of ships and the patrol craft that wasn't on deployment had been taken out to its typhoon buoy in the harbour.

At Kai Tak Airport scheduled flights were still arriving and leaving, but all incoming aircraft were being warned of the increasing velocity of wind-sheer on the runway and some pilots had already chosen to divert to Taipei. Those aircraft which were unserviceable and could not be positioned inside hangars, were being anchored to the dispersal apron with inch and a half diameter wire hawsers which were shackled into steel ring bolts recessed into the concrete.

The District Administrative Officers and the police had succeeded in persuading large numbers of the occupants of the squatter shanty villages in the New Territories to leave their tin and cardboard shelters. In the area of Tuen Mun at Castle Peak, there were some disused factory buildings and over the last three days these had been made ready to house squatters and those who might have to be evacuated during the typhoon. This work had been carried out by the Architectural Services Department of the Hong Kong Government and the Gurkha Engineers, who were conveniently placed in their barracks just to the east of Tuen Mun.

The Gurkha Engineers had been stretched to the limit of both their resources and manpower. All the fences surrounding the refugee camps had had to be strengthened to ensure that they didn't collapse during the typhoon and release the pathetic occupants. The only ships to be seen in the harbour and surrounding waters were Ramp Powered Lighters of the Gurkha Transport Regiment - capable of transporting one 55 ton tank or any combination of vehicles, stores and men - and the Marine Police. The helicopters of the RAF, the Army Air Corps and the Honk Kong Auxilliary Air Force were constantly patrolling the whole area of the territory to ensure that the

202

typhoon warning had been received and acted upon. Armoured cars of the Police Tactical Unit were moved up to the border fence to assist the Hampshire Fusiliers and the Gurkhas in their task of keeping illegal immigrants out of Hong Kong. The typhoon would offer an ideal opportunity for the IIs - even these wretched souls had to have an abbreviation for their collective misery - to try and cross the border fence. They were prepared to take on the fury of a full blown typhoon or the sharks in Deep Bay in the west and Mirs Bay in the east in their desperation to reach Hong Kong and escape the oppressive and reactionary Communist regime of China.

There was one factor, which the Royal Observatory had not been able to predict; that year, El Nino, the warm current from the coast of Chile, had produced another anti-cyclone to the north-east of Taiwan. The pressure in this was no lower than 990 millibars, but the strong northerly winds it produced had met up with the hurricane force winds of Typhoon Pamela coming from the south. In recent years, this conflict of weather systems had been rarely recorded until the 1979 Fastnet Race. On that occasion, two conflicting weather systems had met in the Celtic Sea to the south of Ireland and produced crossing seas with waves of frightening proportions. The resultant toll on yachts and lives had been a national disaster, but the witches' cauldron of that particularly unpleasant weather system hadn't included one ingredient in its recipe, which was about to be hurled at Hong Kong; Typhoon Pamela.

On the popular beaches of the south coast of the Island and on the surrounding islands, the owners of the many beach cafés and restaurants did their routine preparation for a typhoon which usually never appeared. The streets were a little less choked with traffic for a Friday, but other than that the casual observer would have noticed nothing different in the frenetic life of Hong Kong. Three hundred miles to the south of the territory, the surface of the sea was being squeezed between conflicting winds which piled up the water into colossal waves and then drove them together to form mountainous seas of sunami proportions.

*

Gunn and Doyle Barnes entered the sick bay where they found the ship's surgeon dressing the cut and bruising on Mandy's forehead.

'I'll leave the three of you alone,' the naval surgeon smiled, clearing away a stainless steel bowl of instruments and medications. 'Please don't talk too long as this young lady is suffering from mild concussion and ought to be asleep. Let me know when you're finished and I'll clean up that wound on your arm.' Mandy was sitting on the examination couch which was to be her bunk while she was on board.

John and Doyle squeezed into the minute sick bay and closed the door behind them

'Right Doyle,' Gunn spoke as soon as the door closed, 'you kick off with the arrangements for our return to Hong Kong and then we'll all pool what information we have to see if it helps us nearer a solution to what Mandy's father has been up to.'

'OK John, so this is what happens. The Seventh Fleet is six hundred miles to the north-east of us. The nuclear powered aircraft carrier, USS Abraham Lincoln, is making maximum speed towards us and this patrol craft is likewise making maximum speed towards the Seventh Fleet. At the appropriate moment, Abraham Lincoln, will fly off an SH 3D - that's a Sea King in British Naval terminology - which will take us back to the carrier. On the carrier we'll transfer to two of the Tomcats which will fly us back to Hong Kong. Now the Sea King's got a maximum range of something like 750 miles, so the pick up won't be for about four hours. We should be back in Hong Kong by 2000 hours tonight.'

'Fine; now Mandy, before we get chased away by the ship's surgeon, is there anything at all that you can remember about your father's plans?'

'I'll try, John; my father said that he was flying to Manila and from there to Shenzen Airport. He will arrive at Shenzen at about 1830 this evening. I know that because I looked up the flight schedules for him. Middle Kingdom had a rendezvous with my father on Monday, somewhere to the south of Pinghai. I think I've told you everything else.'

'Can you think of any place, any building, house or whatever, either in Hong Kong or China where your father might have been going?' Gunn asked.

'I'm sorry John, my head aches and I'm not thinking very clearly,' Mandy apologised, touching the swollen contusion on the right of her forehead.

'No, Mandy you're doing fine and we must leave you to get some sleep. C'mon Doyle; it might help if we all got some sleep while we wait for this chopper; I'm shattered,' and Gunn opened the door of the sick bay.

'I had plenty of sleep last night, John, so I'm OK, but you go ahead,' replied Doyle as he ducked his head to go through the door.

'Wait a minute, John,' Mandy called as he turned to leave the sick bay. 'My father has used a house for business trips to China when he doesn't want the authorities to know that he has entered the country. It's in a town called Shui.'

'Where's that, Mandy?'

'Oh, it's about fifteen miles from Daya Wan.'

'Daya Wan?'

'Yes, John,' Mandy said sleepily, 'a gweilo would call it Daya Bay.'

*

The Governor's Security Committee had been scheduled to meet at 1415 hours that Friday afternoon. From 1400 to 1415, the handful of key senior men on the Emergency Committee had met to brief the Governor who had opened the meeting by asking the Commissioner of Police to update them on all the activities of his Assistant Commissioner.

'We've got every man I can spare and a few I can't, Sir, looking for Charles McBain. He's vanished; I've just returned from the hospital where I've been talking to his wife Aileen. She has no idea what this is all about. The hospital pathology laboratory has analysed the contents of her's and her children's stomachs; all had traces of barbiturates. So it would seem that all three of them were given some form of drug at bedtime, which would prevent them from waking early and noticing the escaping gas. My scenes of crime officers agree completely with the theory put forward by Robin for which I must again thank him. The significance behind all this is anybody's guess at the moment. McBain was either involved in the plot like all the others and wanted to ensure that he didn't become a suspect, by making himself the target of an attempted murder, or it was done for a totally different reason.'

'May I interrupt, sir,' asked Robin Masefield.

'Please do, Robin, particularly if you are about to help us with another clear-headed, analytical observation,' the Governor replied.

'You told us, Sir, that in your discussions with this British agent, Gunn, you discussed the activities of his partner from the CIA, a Mr Barnes.'

'I did indeed, Robin; tell me what it is that we've all missed this time?' asked the Governor with a certain irony in his tone.

'You said that Mr Barnes had been overpowered at Henshaw's house by men working for YS and taken to some building on the Peak.'

'I did.'

'You also made particular mention that Mr Barnes, while bound and blindfolded, had heard the voice of what appeared to be the man in charge of this . . . er . . . conspiracy, for want of a better word. . . .'

'Of course, why. . . .'

'Please, Sir, let me finish.'

205

'Sorry Robin, go on,' apologised the Governor who had already seen the point of his Chief Secretary's questions.

'I believe that I'm right when I say that Mr Barnes made special mention of this man's clear, accentless English?' and Robin Masefield's voice rose in a questioning tone.

'Correct.'

'Then I've two points to suggest; the first is that Charles McBain, even though he's Scottish, speaks in accentless English and secondly, if Sir Peter was able to lay his hands on a recording of McBain talking, we could play this back to Mr Barnes. Although that doesn't help us find McBain, it might confirm his leading role in the conspiracy with YS.'

'Who is now dead,' came from Major General Patrick Rogers.

'Sorry, Patrick, I don't quite follow,' said the Governor.

'We've just had a signal from Swordfish, Sir. YS and the entire crew of Middle Kingdom are all dead and the yacht itself has been sunk. Gunn escaped with YS' daughter who has been able to give some information, but not a great deal.'

'Good God! What sort of a man is this. He survived a drop without a parachute and then kills the entire crew of that yacht and sinks it. I'm glad he's on our side. Sorry, Patrick, you were saying,' and for the first time in the last forty eight hours, the Governor of Hong Kong believed that there was a glimmer of hope of saving the territory and the hostages.

'The US Seventh Fleet is going to help us get both Gunn and Barnes back here in double quick time, so that we can all compare the bits of information which we do have and see where that leads us,' explained the CBF.

'Will you want me to speak to the US Consul, Patrick?'

'In due course, Sir, but this is all being routed through CINCLANT to the US Seventh Fleet, so both London and Washington are fully in the picture.' The Governor turned to the Commissioner of Police.

'Do you, Peter, by any remote good fortune, have a recording of your Assistant Commissioner's voice?'

'I do indeed, Sir. McBain,' those around the table noticed how the first name had now been dropped, 'gave the address at Burns' Night last January in the Central Headquarters Police Officers' Mess. That address is always recorded and I'll get it dug out immediately.'

'Excellent, at last we seem to be holding some cards, but perhaps not yet a winning hand. When will those two men get back to Hong Kong, Patrick?' asked the Governor.

'At about 2000 hours tonight, Sir.'

*

The USS Abraham Lincoln had arrived with the Pacific Fleet to replace the USS Nimitz, which was due for a refit and the replacement of the uranium core in the nuclear reactors. Each of the carriers carried some ninety aircraft, which constituted a more powerful airforce than the majority of national air forces around the world.

The top speed of these huge ships was undisclosed, but was well in excess of thirty knots. The closing speed of Abraham Lincoln and Swordfish was fifty knots and the computers aboard the carrier gave the lift-off time for the Sea King so that it would meet the patrol craft just inside the limit of its return endurance.

On the bridge of Swordfish, Doyle Barnes was standing beside the Captain. John Gunn was down in the Captain's cabin, fast asleep, as was Mandy in the sick bay. The duty signaller came onto the bridge. 'From Abraham Lincoln, Sir; signal reads; SH despatched at 1350 hrs. ETA Swordfish 1610 hrs. Maximum range prevents provision of full in-flight entertainment. Exclamation.'

'Thank you signaller,' acknowledged Nick Swift and then turned to Doyle. 'Why don't you go and get you head down; we'll have you ready in plenty of time for the arrival of the chopper.'

'Thanks, I think I'll do just that. Mind if I use your wardroom, Sir.'

'No, please use the duty watch officer's bunk. David, show Mr Barnes to your cabin, please, and get my steward to give Mr Gunn some dry clothing,' and Doyle's head had no sooner touched the pillow than it seemed that he was being shaken awake.

'Time to get up, Doyle;' Gunn said as his friend's eyes opened. 'The Sea King will be here in about fifteen minutes. See you up on the bridge.'

'Thanks, John.' Doyle said, swinging his legs down from the bunk. 'See you in a couple of minutes.'

The Sea King appeared on the radar eight minutes later. The duty watch officer picked up the microphone. 'Helicopter detail stand to, aft deck!' echoed over the tannoy system. Four men appeared on the aft deck, one with signalling batons, two in fire fighting gear and carrying extinguishers and the fourth one carrying an eight foot metal rod with heavily insulated handles and a cable at one end. This was screwed onto the ship's metal decking to discharge the static electricity generated by the rotor.

The helicopter came into view, very shortly followed by the noise of the turbines and rotor blades. Swordfish immediately slowed to eight knots and after saying their farewells to the Captain and duty watch, Gunn and Doyle Barnes went to the aft deck to wait for the arrival of the Sea King. Swordfish was turned into the wind and the helicopter swung round the stern and came into a hover above the aft deck. The wire appeared from the hoist and was lowered towards the deck; six or so feet above the deck it was hooked by the metal rod and its static charge grounded. At the end of the wire was a loop and Doyle went forward and slipped this over his head and then under his arms. The crewman working the hoist winched him clear of the deck and up into the helicopter. Gunn followed and as soon as he was aboard, the door was slid shut and the helicopter banked hard to port and with nose down was soon up to its maximum speed of 130 mph on its way back to Abraham Lincoln. Both of them were given headsets with attached boom mikes and as soon as they were strapped in, were welcomed by their pilot, who gave a very passable imitation of an airline pilot's patter and then to their amazement coffee was produced by the crewman. Gunn turned to Doyle Barnes and depressed the pressle switch. 'That's what I call service!'

'That's only the start, John,' Doyle laughed, 'you wait 'til they bring out the broads tucked away in that flight deck.'

'Hey, what've we got back there?' came over the headsets from the pilot. 'A real pair of jokers; weren't allowed to ask who our passengers would be back on the ship, but you must have some clout if you can get Abe Lincoln turned around to come and play taxi for you.' A few minutes later the pilot came back to join them for a coffee and a chat before he was summoned back by his co-pilot for the run in to the carrier.

From a distance, they saw the USS Abraham Lincoln which looked like a toy ship lit by the setting sun, but as the Sea King made its approach, the sheer size of the carrier beggared description. The helicopter made its landing on the angled flight deck and was immediately surrounded by flight deck crew. Before Gunn and Barnes stepped out of the helicopter, the deck sank beneath them and they went down to the next deck level where they were told to take off their clothes and were made to dress in the 'G' suits ready for their flight in the Tomcat. As soon as they had been checked, they were driven for'ard to another lift which rose up to the flight deck beside the two steam catapults where the Tomcats were waiting with engines running.

Gunn was led over to the fighter on the starboard side and then strapped into his seat. The mechanism of the ejector seat was explained and he was told what not to touch. As soon as everything was connected, the flight deck crew moved away and the canopy closed. The pilot spoke to the flight control and then the General Electric F110 engines built up power until the whole aircraft shook. Something like a sledge hammer hit Gunn in the back as the Tomcat rocketed off the catapult and the pilot slammed the throttle through the gate into reheat. The pressurised 'G' suit kept Gunn's blood roughly in the right parts of his body as the fighter streaked into the sky above the setting sun.

Turning his head with considerable difficulty, Gunn saw the navigation lights and mid-fuselage strobe of the other Tomcat in their five o'clock position slightly behind and to the right.

Gunn's headset clicked and then his pilot spoke; 'I'm Jack Belman. Can't say I'm used to this passenger bit, but you and your friend are welcome to this service. Anyway, you'll have to wait until we get to Hong Kong before you get served with the martinis, but I can tell you that we're flying now at just a shade over 50,000 feet and we'll be coming in on the main runway at Kai Tak in twenty eight minutes. You all right?' this was added as an afterthought as Gunn hadn't spoken up to that point.

'Yes thanks, I'm fine and taking off from that carrier must surely come close to being the second best sensation in the world,' Gunn replied. 'My name's John Gunn and in the other Tomcat is Doyle Barnes, a fellow countryman of yours.'

'Is that right? Hell, is that the Barnes who was with 82nd Airborne?'

'That's the one.'

'Goddam, but that's the strangest coincidence. We were both at college together and you know what?' John felt that a response was required, so he obliged.

'No, what's that?'

'I married his sister Tracy. Got two kids now, Jack Junior and Jane.'

'I've met Tracy, Jack, when I first bumped into Doyle about four years ago on an exchange at Fort Benning. Give her my best wishes when you next write or see her.'

'Is that so? Nice to have you aboard John,' and then Jack was speaking to flight control on Abraham Lincoln after which he flicked to Kai Tak's frequency. Jack told Gunn that he was starting the approach to Kai Tak and all other aircraft had either been stacked or had chosen to divert. The Tomcat rolled to starboard, fell out of the sky and plummeted earthwards until the flare out over Lantau Island. The wing geometry changed for the approach and the two fighters landed together. It was just before eight in the evening and the darkness masked their arrival and any consternation, which it might have caused. The two Tomcats were taken to a relatively deserted part of the dispersal area where tankers were waiting to refuel them. Gunn saw from the cockpit that there was a car waiting for them. Jack brought the Tomcat to a halt and the canopy opened. Steps were placed alongside the fuselage and two, RAF ground crew, who had been sent down from RAF Sek Kong for this task, released Gunn and Barnes from their seats. In a minibus was a change of clothes for both of them and the pressure suits were returned to the Tomcats. John told Doyle that his brother in law had just flown him and so he nipped up the steps and spoke to Jack Belman for a moment before they were both whisked away to Government House.

*

The members of the Security Committee were seated in the Governor's private lounge. Hamish Walker had proved to be one of the first casualties of the crisis facing the Government and Security Forces of Hong Kong. He had been unable to stay off the whisky and so had been relieved of his position as Head of the Fire Services and locked in a room at a private clinic to be dried out. The door opened and Gunn and Barnes came into the room. The Governor stood up immediately and led the two men over to two armchairs.

'Mr Barnes, the first thing we want to do is to get you to listen to a tape and then we want to know of every scrap of information you have both gleaned so that we can, hopefully, shed some light on this conspiracy. My private secretary is going to put a blindfold over your eyes, Mr Barnes, as that might assist the experiment,' the Governor explained. Martin Holmes placed the blindfold over Doyle's eyes and then walked over to a stack of hi-fi equipment and depressed the play button of the tape deck. It was only after a half dozen words that Doyle ripped off the blindfold. 'That's the guy! Not a shadow of doubt; who is he?'

'That's Charles McBain, the Assistant Commissioner of Police, who would seem to be the key figure behind this entire conspiracy,' the Governor replied.

*

The security guards on the gates of the Hong Kong United Dockyards were confronted with some twenty drunken sailors. They eventually discovered that they all came from the Yorktown and so were escorted back to their ship. The guards returned to the security office taking the duty guard with them, who had been patrolling the area where the ship was berthed. There seemed to be no point in guarding the ship against the possibility of it being removed when not one of the crew, including the captain of the vessel was capable of walking up the companionway unassisted, let alone slip a ship from its moorings.

A soon as the security guards had disappeared, the play-acting ceased and the crew of Yorktown set about the tasks which each of them had been allocated. The engineer reported to the captain and told him that the starboard boiler was holding pressure and the diesel pumps were able to keep pace with the seepage into the bilges. The berth occupied by Yorktown pointed directly out into Hung Hom Bay, which meant that the ship merely had to go astern to get clear. If the berth had involved any manoeuvring by the ship, with the assistance of tugs, then the Yorktown captain's scheme would have been impossible. The wind was blowing force six from the north, which would assist the task of slipping from the berth. A signal had been sent to Cordoba and the RV in Baguio had been arranged. The captain and the first officer had decided to open the sea-cocks and scuttle the ship as soon as the heroin had been unloaded.

The bosun led a party of ten men down onto the dockside and a pair of men went to each of the warps and springs, holding Yorktown into the berth. Each pair was equipped with a torch and a series of signals had been arranged with the deck party, which was responsible for taking in the mooring lines. The bowline and spring would be the last to go as they would be holding the weight of the ship against the northerly wind. They had agreed at the planning stage that it would be too risky to use radios as there was always the chance that the harbour authority would pick up their messages.

The first two lines were slipped and the first officer relayed the torch signal to the captain who was standing beside the man on the wheel. He was holding the microphone, which would keep him in contact with his engine room. 'Dead slow astern,' was the order. The old, pitted propellers started to rotate. This was the crucial moment when someone might spot what was happening, but there was no one around and now that there was rain in the wind, none of the dockyard security staff were over anxious to stick their heads outside. The captain of the Yorktown noticed the rain with pleasure as this would help to mask the departure of his ship.

The propellers started to give the ship stern way and the lines went slack. This was the moment for which the shore party had been waiting. The remaining three lines were cast off, light signals given and then the bosun and his men rushed for the lowered companionway. The rusted steel side of the Yorktown was now moving along the dockside. The men scrambled onto the steps as the gap between ship and dock gradually widened. The last man only just made it and had to be pulled onto the bottom step by two of the crew. They all scampered up the companionway to the deck and then swung it inboard using one of the loading derricks. The Yorktown

211

was now half-way clear of the berth and showing no navigation lights. The first officer and the captain exchanged glances; it was going to work. A flashing signal from the bow told them that the bow would soon be clear and to stop going astern. 'Both engines half ahead,' the captain said into the microphone and then to the helmsman, 'fifteen degrees, starboard wheel.'

'Fifteen degrees of starboard wheel it is, Sir,' came the reply from the man on his left. The captain turned and looked at him to see if the man was making fun of him as no one had repeated orders on this ship for as long as the captain could remember, but he appeared to be in earnest. Slowly the stern way came off the ship and the bows started to swing to starboard. The lights on the end of the runway in Kowloon Bay came into view and then the red-lit buoys marking the prohibited zone beyond the runway. The bow of Yorktown was slowly coming round and the speed was now up to eight knots. 'Wheel amidships, helmsman,' the captain ordered and it was repeated as the wheel spun to port and then centred. The bow of the ship came round a couple of more points and then steadied. There was the Lei Yue Mun Channel and the open sea beyond. They'd made it. The captain and first officer shook hands. In a few hours they would be well clear of the typhoon and on their way to a fortune from the sale of the drugs and tractor engines.

CHAPTER 19

'Robin, I'd like you to chair this meeting in your capacity as Secretary for Security,' the Governor turned towards his new Chief Secretary, 'and see what we can achieve by a really thorough debrief of Mr Gunn and Mr Barnes.'

'Very well, Sir; perhaps you would start, Mr Gunn, by telling us what information you've gleaned.'

'Yes, of course; these are the facts; the guesswork comes later,' Gunn began immediately without any formalities. 'In February of this year, the body of a Chinese man who had died from a massive overdose of radiation was washed up on Ping Chau. He'd been employed on the construction site of the Daya Bay Power station, but had been sacked some six months before his death for stealing material from the site. The subsequent investigation was unable to find anything amiss at the nuclear power station and no radioactive material was missing. It was very shortly after this that MI6 discovered the extent to which its activities in Hong Kong had been penetrated, which was followed by the death, after torture, of the MI6 agent here. The MI6 agent was killed by YS' men. YS' loathing of the Communist Chinese is common knowledge, as are the attempts he has made - some of which have been successful - to destroy the current regime of the People's Republic of China by means of economic bankruptcy. He recruited five men into his organisation, to ensure that he had all the information he needed to wage his private war against the PRC. We all know who these men were, but his informers also included Peter Causland's daughter, Sadie, who had been engaged to the MI6 agent. She was killed by mistake in the assassination attempt, which was supposed to eliminate me,' Gunn added as he took a sip of coffee which had been handed round by Martin Holmes.

'We believe that Middle Kingdom was used to transport radioactive material. We think YS has probably gone to the town of Shui in Shenzen Province and that he had arranged an RV with his yacht on Monday off the coast of the Pinghai peninsular,' the telephone in the lounge rang and Martin Holmes answered it.

'Excuse me interrupting, Mr Gunn,' the private secretary apologised. 'That s the call for which you were waiting, Sir,' Martin

Holmes spoke to the Governor. 'It's the MD of Asia Light and Power to tell us that the opening ceremony of the Daya Bay Nuclear Power Station is to go ahead as planned for 10 am on Monday. The Chinese consider that the typhoon will have blown itself out before then and have no intention of adjusting their schedule.'

'Will President Jiang Zemin and all his retinue still be going?' the Governor asked.

'Yes Sir; and then coming to Hong Kong for the handover ceremony. You know that he is a personal friend of the Chairman of Asia Light and Power,' the secretary replied.

'I'm so sorry, Mr Gunn, would you continue please,' the Governor said.

'Having heard the context of that telephone conversation, I believe I can now tell you where the bomb is and when it will be detonated - and, possibly, where the hostages are. The Daya Bay Power Station is the bomb and the nuclear explosion will occur when the Head of the Chinese Communist Party arrives to open it. The hostages are probably in the house at Shui and, I have no doubt, will be used to prevent anyone interfering with McBain's plan to destroy the territory of Hong Kong rather than see it given to the Communist Chinese.'

'How are you so sure . . .' started the Governor.

'Daya Bay has already been inspected by international experts and scientists from the UN Atomic Energy Authority . . .' the CBF interrupted.

'Gentlemen, please let me finsih,' Gunn stopped them both. 'The experts found nothing at Daya Bay because there was nothing to find. That's exactly what he wanted to happen; the nuclear power station was inspected and cleared. He knew that it was to be opened by the Chinese President. That was something, which I didn't until a couple of minutes ago. Both YS and McBain saw the ideal opportunity of removing a large proportion of the old guard of the Communist hierarchy and preventing them getting their hands on Hong Kong. The other fact, which confirms Daya Bay as the target is something that was said by Balmain as he was dying and which made no sense to me until now. I was trying to get him to tell me where the bomb was. He said it wasn't a bomb it would be 'like Cher' . . . and he died before he could complete the word.

'Well, what does it mean?' asked a rather irritated CBF and was then silenced by a wave from the Governor.

'Go on, Mr Gunn,' encouraged the Governor ignoring the pink-faced discomfort of the General.

'What he was trying to say, I believe,' Gunn continued, 'was "like Chernobyl".'

Between ten that Friday night and four on Saturday morning, the depression centred to the north-east of Taiwan moved towards Japan. The northerly winds it had produced over Hong Kong backed to the east and then south-east, which released the huge seas to the south of Hong Kong. These towering waves now swept towards the territory; in their vanguard was a sunami wave of huge proportions, measuring over sixty feet from trough to crest.

At 3.38am, this wave was identified on the radar of the meteorological station on Waglan Island. The duty operator noticed the solid line of what appeared to be clutter or a set fault, register at the bottom edge of the screen. He adjusted the controls, but the line moved steadily up the screen as it headed for Hong Kong at the speed of an express train. He scratched his head and went to the duty officer in the next room, who was unplugging a boiling electric kettle to make some tea. They both returned to the radar VDU, the duty officer carrying his cup of tea. He stood in front of the screen for a matter of seconds and then, to the amazement of the radar officer, the cup of tea fell from his hands as he rushed to the phone in his office. The warning reached the Royal Observatory when the tidal wave was twenty miles to the south of the islands of Hong Kong and approaching the land at a speed of 80mph.

At 4.18am the tidal wave and the tidal surge behind it struck the southernmost islands of Hong Kong, from Tai A Chau in the west to Waglan Island in the east and surged up the Pearl River estuary towards Guangzhou.

Within half-an-hour, 18,500 people had perished in Hong Kong, Macau and Guandong Province in Southern China. In the east, the met' station on Waglan Island disappeared, as did all the houses and restaurants on the beaches of Po Toi Island. In the west, the Vietnamese refugee camp on Tai A Chau was swept from the island with total loss of life of the entire camp. The great wall of water roared into Repulse Bay, sweeping all the yachts from the club on Middle Island and hurling them onto the terrace in front of the Repulse Bay Hotel. In Deep Water Bay, the expensive sea-front houses were washed away, as was the Golf Club, and the carnage in Aberdeen harbour was beyond description. The Jumbo and Palace floating restaurants were capsized and sunk and the fishing boats, which provided both a home and livelihood to more than two and a half thousand Chinese, ended up as a mass of smashed timber strewn on the surface of the water. Stanley Village and Shek O Village vanished completely as did many cars and sections of the southern coast road. The wave went north through the east and west Lamma Channel and destroyed all the fish farms and the restaurants in Picnic Bay. It funnelled through the Lei Yue Mun Gap increasing its height to nearly seventy feet in the confined space and then dispersed into Kowloon Bay, swamping the Airport. The water level in the harbour rose by fifteen feet, flooding the reclamation areas, ripping the Star Ferries from their moorings and damaging or sinking the majority of yachts at the Royal Hong Kong Yacht Club Marina. The tidal surge then receded, dragging its devastation and debris with it. The morning barely dawned, so dark had the skies become and the wind now howled over the territory, increasing in strength by the minute. The scene of devastation, which awaited everyone as they awoke left the majority in shock. Many were quite unable to cope with the enormity of the disaster, which had struck in the night. Even by 6am the wind speed was over 100 mph and rising; Pamela had struck, like the shock wave of a nuclear explosion, six hours earlier than predicted.

*

The Yorktown had staggered the seven miles to the entrance of the Lei Yue Mun Gap and then the starboard boiler had exploded, killing two of the engine room crew instantly. The southerly wind funnelling through the narrows started to drive the cargo ship back into Kowloon Bay and towards the airport runway. The captain thought there still might be a chance of hi-jacking the cargo and so once again he sent out a May Day call. The harbour authorities couldn't believe that anyone would have been so stupid and warrants for the arrest of the captain and his entire crew were issued while the two ocean-going tugs made ready to tow the Yorktown back into the docks. The distress call from Yorktown was timed at 0348hrs and the tugs left their berths at a minute before 4am to drag the wretched cargo ship out of harm's way before the full fury of the typhoon struck. The ship was drifting stern first towards the runway which jutted 2000 metres out into Kowloon Bay. The wind was now howling through the rigging and derricks, driving the rain in great sheets across the harbour. The captain and first officer were both drinking brandy on the bridge while they waited for the tugs to arrive. The first officer was looking for'ard through the bridge clear screen and he was the first to see the wave. His brain couldn't grasp what his eyes told him and his jaw dropped. The captain turned to follow the direction of the look of horror on his face at the exact moment the wave struck. Yorktown was picked up like a toy, hurled across Kowloon Bay and driven to the sea bed on top of the cross-harbour tunnel.

All three of the cross-harbour tunnels had been built using the same technology. The tunnel was constructed in sections in the form

216

of huge concrete caissons. A ditch was dredged in the seabed and the caissons were floated out and then sunk in the appropriate position. When all the caissons were joined up, they were pumped free of water and then the inside if the tunnel was completed. The tunnels were only partially under the seabed and quite a quarter of the caisson was above it. It was the top of these caissons which was struck by the cargo ship rammed down by thousands more tons of tidal wave. The casing of the tunnel was split asunder like a sledge-hammer hitting a glass bottle and the sea engulfed the four-lane road tunnel. Mercifully, there wasn't much traffic at that hour in the morning, but what there was vanished under thousands of tons of sea water and was then spewed out at either end, such was the force of the in-rush of water. Both of the tugs survived; they were dumped by the wave, two hundred metres inshore, in the industrial site near the Hung Hom Power Station.

*

By 8am, Pamela struck with its full force. Those trees, which were not ripped out of the soil, bent until they touched the ground, stripped of every vestige of branch and foliage. The air was full of debris hurtling in every direction and all of it lethal to human and animal life; a matchbox travelling at over 160 mph was as lethal as a bullet. Torrential rain bucketed out of the sky and roads and fields in the New Territories were soon flooded by raging torrents of brown water. Squatter shacks perched precariously on the sides of hills were swept away and houses with tiled roofs were stripped bare in the first few minutes of the onslaught. Rescue work was impossible as no one could survive in such conditions. The 400,000 volt pylon lines were dragged to the ground under the weight of wind and rain, bringing the pylons down with them which plunged the whole of Hong Kong into semi-darkness. In those flats, which didn't have typhoon shutters, the pressure of the wind burst the windows and inundated the rooms with water, turning the lift shafts and stairwells into cascading waterfalls. The skyscraper blocks in Central could be seen swaying in the hammering gusts of the hurricane force winds, which ripped pieces off some buildings and then slammed them into others. This smashed all the glass which then sent shards with razor-sharp edges slicing through the air, ripping tyres and bodywork of cars and buses left in the open and cutting to shreds everything which they struck.

At the airport, those aircraft, which had survived the swamping from the tidal wave, were ripped clear of the wire hawsers and thrown across the tarmac like paper darts. On the border, a number of illegal immigrants had tried to use the typhoon to conceal their escape bid with disastrous consequences and not one had survived to break through the fence. The police and the army had been given strict orders to remain within the relative safety of buildings or armoured cars until further notice. Most of the senior police and military commanders had agreed that any illegal immigrant who made it across the border in these conditions probably deserved to be allowed into Hong Kong.

All the roads and streets were deserted as the wind still increased in ferocity and mountainous seas hammered against any exposed shoreline of the territory. In nearly every circumstance, the emergency services were totally powerless to do anything to rescue anyone or save life. One TV channel was kept clear of all programmes so that emergency messages could be received by those places, which either had emergency generators, batteries or were still receiving power. Battery operated TV sets came into their own as did all equipment which did not rely on mains power. Hong Kong was at a complete standstill and its inhabitants cowered under the onslaught of the devastating effects of Pamela.

*

The conference at Government House had finished just before midnight. Gunn and Doyle Barnes had been given bedrooms and the others had returned home before the full force of the typhoon had struck. Whatever plan was made, nothing could be done until the worst of the typhoon had passed. The Auxiliary Airforce had confirmed that one of its helicopters had taken off on Friday with three stretcher cases under the supervision of the Assistant Commissioner of Police. The order to apprehend McBain had been received forty minutes too late. The pilot of the helicopter had been forced to land the machine in the New Territories, had been removed at gunpoint and then knocked unconscious. The helicopter had taken off, presumably piloted by McBain, and had headed northwards according to eye-witness accounts. The pilot had made his way back to Kowloon and had reported the incident to the head of the Auxiliary Airforce. The information had reached the Governor during his conference with his Security Committee at Government House. The Governor had decided to meet again with Gunn and Barnes at seven in the morning. Robin Masefield had elected to stay the night at Government House so that he could be present when the planning started again at 7am.

Gunn was roused from his comfortable bed at 6.30am. He showered and went down to the dining room where breakfast was laid. Both the Governor and the Chief Secretary were already there and in a few moments he was told of the devastation caused during the night. Government House was using its diesel generator. The Chief Secretary had had less than an hour's sleep throughout the night as he monitored all the reports coming in from the emergency services.

'I dread to think what the death toll is going to be, let alone all of those who've been injured,' the Governor said as he concluded his briefing of the damage done by the typhoon. 'Can the Royal Observatory predict how long it will be before the typhoon moves inland and dissipates its energy,' Gunn asked as he helped himself to some scrambled eggs and bacon from the sideboard. Robin Masefield replied. 'The emergency services will be able to start rescue work between four and six this evening is the prediction. They say that anyone going out before then is a guaranteed casualty.'

'Have you been able to get in touch with the Government of the PRC, or is that still being cleared through London?' Gunn asked. Doyle appeared at this point and was brought up to date by the Chief Secretary. He then walked over to the long windows which had shutters closed over them. 'Was there no warning of this tidal wave?' he asked turning away from the window.

'There was, but it came too late and of course it struck at the worst possible time, when everyone was asleep. Had it struck during the day, then the death toll would still have been high, but nothing like the figure I'm afraid we'll discover when the clear-up starts,' the Governor replied. Doyle helped himself to coffee and toast and sat at the table.

'Your signal went to London at 1 am and we were promised a reply before eight this morning. It's very difficult to judge the reaction of the PRC to this. Relations have been strained for some considerable time now, which hasn't been helped by all this disagreement over the Basic Law,' Robin Masefield sighed.

Gunn turned to the Governor; 'do you think the Chinese will allow us to come and help them, or would that be seen as a loss of face.'

'Mr Gunn, I wish I could answer that; in their present frame of mind where the 'open door' has been very firmly closed again, I hold out little hope of their agreement to our assistance. How would you get there in these conditions anyway?'

'Doyle and I discussed that together last night, or early this morning, I rather lost track of time last night,' Gunn replied and then continued. 'There's only one vehicle in the territory that has any hope at all of getting through this,' and he waved his hand towards the shuttered windows, 'and that's one of the police armoured Saracens. They weigh about fifteen tons and the drive goes to all six wheels.

God knows what sort of debris will be lying all over the roads. From the border at Sha Tau Kok, the road hugs the coast for about 12 or 13 miles and then goes into the hills, which rise to nearly 2,500 feet before the road drops down to Daya Bay. I don't suppose the distance is more than forty miles, but in these conditions it could take anything from ten hours to two days. Did you manage to find out who is available at the nuclear power station to give detailed advice on the construction of the reactors and all the safety mechanisms?'

'Yes,' this was Robin Masefield, 'we spoke to Asia Light and Power and all the experts are there for the opening ceremony when the fourth and last reactor will come on line. The chief technical adviser throughout the building of the power station has been a Mr Fellowes - Jeremy Fellowes, I think - who is there now. He is both a nuclear physicist and engineer and has been responsible for the design and construction of five other high-pressure, water-cooled reactors of this type. What do you think McBain is going to do?'

'My guess,' answered Gunn, 'is probably less accurate than many of you who knew him in more recent years. My parents knew his parents and both him and Aileen. I think everyone in Hong Kong knew of his dedication to this small lump of granite on the southern tip of China and the service his family has given since it arrived here in the middle of the last century is well documented in the history of the Colony. His obsession with this part of the world and the betrayal he felt when the Joint Declaration was signed would seem to have unbalanced his mind, if that's the right expression. YS gave him the unlimited financial resources he needed to do this and, of course, the muscle to intimidate and murder. He doesn't know for certain that YS is dead, although his absence at the safe house in Shui will probably make McBain suspect the worst. I think that McBain will take the hostages to the Daya Bay Power Station - remember that he's got a helicopter up there somewhere - and from there he'll hold all of us off by threatening to kill Candy and the Governor's children. Once the process of the melt-down - I seem to remember that's what it was called at Chernobyl - in the fourth reactor is irreversible, he will disappear in his helicopter, up wind, to the non-existent RV with Middle Kingdom off the coast of Pinghai. What do you think, Doyle?'

'I don't know this man, I only heard him, but believe me, Sir,' and here Doyle spoke to the Governor, 'I'm sure he'll do as he says. While he might have lost his marbles, he's as cold as ice and the thought of killing one or more million people won't bother him. John's right; he'll do it and we'd better believe that. The only alternative that I'd add to what John has said is that if the Chinks refuse to co-operate, then we ought to have a plan to go in covertly to neutralise this guy McBain,

220

free the hostages and prevent them switching on this fourth reactor. If that turns out to be the only option and it's agreed to by Washington and London - wouldn't be surprised if Russia is consulted as well - then we've got about 26 hours to plan and execute such an operation. We don't have much time.'

'And what do you estimate, Mr Barnes, are the chances of us rescuing Miss Wyngarde and my children as part of this operation?' asked the Governor.

'Less than 50/50, I regret, Sir.'

'Thank you for being so blunt; I suspect that what you really mean, Mr Barnes, is considerably less than 50/50.' Martin Holmes came into the dining room. 'The Prime Minister is on the line, Sir.'

'Well, we shall know very shortly what's to be done,' and the Governor left the room.

'How's that left arm of yours?' Gunn asked Doyle. It was no longer in a sling. 'It's usable John; a bit stiff now and then, but it's my left arm, not the one I shoot with.'

'Would you be up to the journey to Daya Bay?'

'No problem; can I suggest that we take two of those armoured cars if we do that journey; increases the odds in our favour.'

'Agreed,' Gunn replied as the Governor returned to the dining room. He appeared to be bowed down with the responsibility, which he was shouldering and it was immediately obvious to all of them in the room that the conversation with the Prime Minister had certainly not contained good news. The Governor spoke standing up, reading from some notes, which he had made of the conversation.

'The Government of the People's Republic of China has refused any assistance for what it considers is entirely an internal matter. The information about the suspected sabotage to the fourth reactor is considered to be an imperialist attempt to discredit the ability of the Chinese to develop the peaceful use of nuclear power and if there is such a person as McBain, then the PLA will deal with him.' The Governor paused at that stage and sat at the breakfast table. 'There's a bit more, but that's the essence of the Chinese reply to our offer of assistance. What that really means is that they have suffered loss of face and will now rush around in a frenzy of uncoordinated activity, arresting and killing people with exactly the same finesse and restraint which they showed in Tianenmen Square. It also means that the chances of seeing my children alive again are about nil and the chances of McBain's plot succeeding have just risen to at least 60/40 in his favour. Now what the Prime . . .' but once again his private secretary interrupted.

'There's a call for you from China, Sir,' said Martin Holmes.

221

'Can you put the call on the loudspeaker system in the study, Martin?' the Governor asked.

'Yes, Sir; that's no problem.'

'Well then, I suggest that you do that and all of us can listen to this call as it might save a great deal of time,' and the Governor was followed by the four men into the study.

'This is the Governor speaking.'

'My name's Jeremy Fellowes; I'm the . . .'

'Yes, Mr Fellowes, I know who you are. Please tell me what is happening at Daya Bay.'

'Sir, I have been directed to read you this message and can say nothing more than that. The nuclear power station has been taken over by a group of eight men led by a man called McBain. A number of hostages have been taken, in addition to your children and Mr Wyngarde's daughter who will be killed if there is any interference by the PLA or anyone else. Provided that there is no interference, your children, Sir, and Miss Wyngarde will be released on Monday, unharmed, at a location, which will be notified to you in due course. Any attempt to prevent the meltdown of the fourth reactor will result in the death of the hostages. McBain has all the hostages under armed guard in the main control room,' and at this point Fellowes coughed, 'I'll repeat that; we are all in the main control room, from which the entire operation of the power station can be controlled. I have been told to tell you, by McBain, that I have seen the modifications which have been done to reactor number four and you must believe me, Sir, that when those fuel rods are lowered into the core, Chernobyl will seem like a damp squib in comparison. You are to proceed with the evacuation of the territory if you so wish. The . . .' but the connection was broken. There was complete silence in the study, which was broken by Gunn.

'Is there an expert in Hong Kong on the design of the Daya Bay Power Station, particularly the security aspects of the site?'

'Yes there is; Graham Freeman of Euro-Pacific. He worked closely with Fellowes on the design of the entire power station. He's our man,' and then the Chief Secretary saw Gunn's face, 'in spite of the way he chooses to conduct his private life.'

'Are there any police armoured cars on the Island?' Gunn asked.

'Yes,' Robin Masefield answered immediately, 'they're kept at Central Police Headquarters.'

'May I suggest that we start by sending one of the armoured cars to Freeman's flat to pick him up. He should then be taken to his office at Euro-Pacific - or wherever the drawings and plans are kept - and

222

then brought here. This should be cleared with Peter Wyngarde who should be brought here as well.'

'What do you think can be done?' the Governor asked. It was Doyle who replied.

'That guy, Fellowes, is a brave man, Sir Charles; you heard him stop and then repeat the phrase 'main control room' with the emphasis on the word 'main'.'

'Yes, we all did, but I'm afraid I missed the significance of that.'

'Robin, here, has just told us that Fellowes and Freeman worked together on the design of the nuclear power station. Fellowes knows that Freeman is in Hong Kong. There is something about this main control room that Fellowes wants us to find out from Freeman. That's how I read it, sir,' Doyle replied.

'Can you arrange that, Robin, please,' the Governor turned to his Chief Secretary.

'Martin's gone to phone him and warn him to stand-by to be collected from his flat,' Robin Masefield told the Governor and then turned to John Gunn. 'Time is short; what else will you need.'

'We'll need two police armoured cars with drivers,' Gunn started and then the Governor interrupted.

'I think I'd better be told what you have in mind before we go any further,' the Governor said quietly, 'as I have to brief the Prime Minister. I was about to say before we received that second phone call, that the Prime Minister directed me to come back with a course of action within the hour. The Governments of the UK and the United States would support some form of covert intervention provided that it was carried out by Gunn and Barnes. The use of British military personnel is ruled out, but nothing was said about equipment,' the Governor added.

'Before we get down to the detail of a plan, let me see if there's anything else required,' the Chief Secretary interjected.

'Very well, Robin,' agreed the Governor. Robin Masefield turned to Gunn.

'What else do you need?'

'I think that CBF and the CP should be brought here; could the CBF bring with him an intelligence officer who knows the deployment of the PLA units on the border. I need to know exact location, strength, equipment and vehicles. In addition to more ammunition for our own personal weapons, I'd like two SA80 assault rifles, fitted with image-intensification scopes.' The Chief Secretary was making notes. 'Ten stun grenades and ten high-explosive grenades,' and Gunn turned to Doyle, 'what else will we need, Doyle?'

'Helmets with visors, driving goggles, a couple of your bullet proof jackets might come in handy and some strong gloves,' Doyle answered and continued. 'How do we get across that harbour? The cross-harbour road tunnel is smashed, the Causeway Bay Tunnel's flooded and there's no power for the Mass Transit Railway. I can't say that I fancy taking a ride in a sampan across the harbour.'

'That's no problem; you will use one of the diesel maintenance cars on the MTR. I'll arrange for the armoured cars to be taken to the Tsim Sha Tsui entrance to the MTR and you can pick them up there,' the Chief Secretary answered and then turned to the Governor. 'If you'll excuse me, Sir, I need to get on with this. I expect you'll want to contact London and tell the Prime Minister that a covert entry to China is planned, but conforms exactly with the guide-lines laid down by London and Washington.'

'Yes, Robin, I'll do that,' and the Governor and his private secretary returned to the study.

'What d'you reckon on our chances, Johnny?' Doyle asked as he walked to the sideboard and filled up his coffee cup.

'About a hundred-to-one against, I'd say.'

CHAPTER 20

The Governor gave the outline of the plan to the Prime Minister and received conditional approval subject to the detailed plan being submitted before midday. Sir Peter Aldridge, the Commissioner of Police, was the first to arrive at Government House and gave a grim description of the damage and destruction, which he had seen on his way from his house on the Peak. He was followed twenty minutes later by Major General Patrick Rogers who arrived with a nondescript-looking man who transpired to be a fluent speaker of Chinese and the current expert on the deployment, tactics and composition of the PLA. Gunn and Doyle disappeared into the 'box' with the intelligence expert who was carrying maps and a briefcase full of satellite and aerial photos. A quarter of an hour later, Graham Freeman arrived, accompanied by Peter Wyngarde. Both of them went into the 'box'. For the next hour, the five men poured over the maps and photos while outside the typhoon increased in intensity and fury as the eye of the hurricane force winds approached Hong Kong. While Freeman was briefing Gunn and Doyle Barnes on the Daya Bay Power Station and the plan was beginning to take shape, the Governor and his Security Committee were briefed by the Chief Secretary on the measures which would be required to clear up the destruction caused by the typhoon and how this would affect the handover ceremonies. Shortly after nine, Gunn left the study and told the Governor that he and Doyle were ready to brief the Committee on their plan. A valuable Stubbs oil painting was removed from the wall in the dining room and was replaced by a large map of Hong Kong and Southern China. Other paintings were taken down and replaced with plans and drawings of the power station. John Gunn had made a selection of a number of the photos, which he placed on the table. Once this was complete, the Governor and the other members of the Committee took their seats.

'Sir,' Gunn turned to the Governor, 'Doyle and I have decided not to present this plan to you in military terminology as there's only one other person on your Committee who is a soldier. We'll follow the military sequence of giving orders, because it is entirely logical. Martin Holmes has photocopied my notes and is now typing them so that they can be sent by secure fax to London. I'll start by covering the situation, which faces us; here we'll deal with McBain, the power station, the Chinese and the PLA and how we predict that McBain and the Chinese will behave. In a sequence of orders for a military operation, I'd then discuss our own forces; I see no point in that as you are all well aware of our own forces and what they do or do not have. After that we'll cover the aim of this plan and how we intend to carry it out. At the end there'll be some timings, communication and administrative points.'

'Thank you, Mr Gunn, I'm most grateful for that, please continue,' said the Governor.

'Very well, Sir, I'll start by explaining the significance of the emphasis which Fellowes placed on the main control room at Daya Bay. It appears that ever since the disastrous melt-down at Chernobyl, which was caused by a handful of scientists and engineers carrying out an unauthorised experiment, the International Atomic Energy Authority agreed on a number of measures to try and prevent the recurrence of such an incident. It was decided that all nuclear power stations should have a duty security team, which would keep an eye on everything which happened in the power station. At Daya Bay, everything and every function is controlled from the main control room; this also includes all the security aspects of the power station. What the majority, if not all, of the people who work in nuclear power stations do not know, is that all the functions of the main control room are monitored and can be over-ridden in another control room. Not only that, but there are hidden cameras in the main control room which scan every corner and crevice and send the pictures to the security control room. Fellowes' message to us indicates that McBain does not know about this.'

'But surely McBain will just kill one or more of the hostages if he realises, as he's bound to, that somehow his control of the reactor is being over-ridden,' interrupted the CBF.

'Questions and comments at the end please, Patrick. I don't want any more interruptions. Go on, Mr Gunn, please,' the Governor said to Gunn without even turning to look at the CBF, who was once again puce after the second rebuke from the Governor.

'The significance of the security control room,' Gunn continued, 'is the ability of those in that room to see exactly what is happening in the main control room, where McBain is holding the hostages. Underneath the main control room is a space of eighteen inches which carries all the mass of electrical, electronic and fibre-optic cabling, not to forget a bit of humble plumbing as well. This under-floor space can be entered from outside the main control room as well as from inside it. Any part of the floor in that room,' and here Doyle used one of the

Governor's snooker cues to point out the room on one of the plans on the wall, 'can be removed to gain access to the cabling space. It can be opened just as easily from underneath as from on top. I have gone into some detail, Sir, as we see this as the key factor. It not only gives us a chance of taking McBain by surprise and preventing the insertion of the fuel rods into number four reactor, but it gives us a very reasonable chance of saving the hostages.' The Governor nodded his appreciation. 'Perhaps we could now leave that aspect and talk about the other problem we face; the Chinese, and the PLA in particular,' Gunn continued and then added, 'Doyle Barnes will deal with this aspect of the plan,' and Doyle handed the cue to Gunn while he checked his notes.

'The PLA has a number of units, not only along the border, but also along the route, which we intend to take. These are large regiments which contain all their own intrinsic vehicles, artillery, armour and logistic support, in addition to their farms and workshops. In the area of the border, the units are in company size locations - that's approximately 200 men, rather larger than the British or American equivalent. With the exception of their soft-skinned vehicles, the majority of the PLA equipment is Russian, or Russian design and of the fifties or sixties vintage. A British Saracen armoured car would be about as unnoticeable as a hippopotamus in a duck pond. We have abandoned the plan to use the Saracens and take them across the Border. The only way we have any chance of getting to Daya Bay is as soldiers of the PLA.' The intake of breath around the room was audible. 'John's Chinese is nearly fluent and mine is enough to order a beer. We have decided that we must use both the darkness of tonight and the typhoon to cover our crossing into China and once there, we will be travelling in a BMP - this is a tracked, amphibious Russian armoured personnel carrier which has a turret-mounted, smooth-bore gun and anti-tank missile launcher. This will be 'borrowed' from the PLA unit to the north of Sha Tau Kok. I'll now hand back to John, who'll take you through the aim of this plan and how we're going to execute it,' and Doyle took the snooker cue and moved over to the map.

'Now the aim of this operation,' and Gunn looked straight at the Governor; 'is to neutralise McBain and thereby prevent the melt-down of the fourth reactor and secure the release of the hostages.' Gunn paused for a couple of seconds while the significance of that statement sank in. The Governor had realised from the moment that his children had been kidnapped, that their safe return was subordinate to the prevention of nuclear fallout over South China and Hong Kong. Peter Wyngarde's face registered the misery of his realisation that Candy' safety was a secondary consideration in such high stakes. 'Now in general outline, this is how we intend to carry out this operation. From Government House we'll go in a police armoured car to the Harcourt Road MTR Station, where we will board a diesel maintenance car. That will take us to Tsim Sha Tsui Station in Kowloon, where we'll be met by another armoured car, which will have our equipment, rations and weapons. From there we go to the Police base at Sha Tau Kok and then turn left - or west - along the border fence. Two hundred and fifty metres from that left turn is Gate Number Two, which is opened each day to allow farmers to come across from China to farm their land. As we reach that gate, the emergency power for the border fence lighting will be switched off for five minutes. Doyle and I will leave the armoured car and carrying our equipment in backpacks will cross the border into China. From there we make our way along this road - being pointed out by Doyle - to the PLA base - here. We will remove a BMP from this base and use it to drive along this road' - again Doyle traced the route on the map with the point of the snooker cue - 'which will take us through the Shenzen Border fence and over the pass in these hills to Daya Bay. Once we reach the power station we'll neutralise McBain and rescue the hostages. We have a number of alternatives for the return trip, which rather depend on the level of success of the operation; I will, therefore leave out any detail in this part of the plan. No one else will cross the border into China other than Doyle and myself.' After this, Gunn and Barnes covered further detail on radios, equipment, timing, routes, weapons and so on. At the end Gunn turned to the Governor, 'that completes our plan, Sir. Doyle and I will answer any questions we can, but we do still have Freeman and Major Charlesworth, the intelligence officer, who have been waiting in your private lounge and who could join us now if anyone would like to direct specific questions at them.'

'Thank you, Mr Gunn and Mr Barnes; Robin, can you go and get the two gentlemen from my lounge to come and join us and the rest of us can have a couple of minutes to collect our thoughts. On your way out, Robin, you might ask the staff to arrange some more coffee,' the Governor added. The two men in the lounge came into the dining room and the Governor's wife followed them to supervise the coffee. Then came question time, which continued until eleven thirty. 'Wouldn't it be better to send John and Doyle in as British Soldiers rather than spies,' asked Peter Wyngarde.

'I think I'll answer that one if I may,' interrupted the Governor. 'I accept your sentiments entirely, Peter, and agree with them. The reason that the Prime Minister was so adamant that no British

Serviceman would cross the border is because the Chinese would be given the perfect opportunity to portray this as an armed incursion into Chinese territory. They could then retaliate by marching into Hong Kong after throwing the Joint Declaration out of the window and taking it by force with no regard to all the safeguards we have negotiated for the Territory and its population. If Gunn and Barnes are captured, then they will be dealt with as spies, God help them, and with typical diplomatic hypocrisy, we can deny all knowledge of their existence.

'Doyle and I have thought of a cover for our trip into China, Sir, if you approve. We were going to suggest that Peter Wyngarde hires us as private detectives or mercenaries. A readily traceable payment or photograph of money changing hands might prove of help if this whole thing turns into a can of worms,' Gunn added.

'I'm sure that something along those lines would be wise. Robin, can you arrange that. Now gentlemen,' the Governor went on, 'it's time I contacted the Prime Minister. It seems that no one can come up with a better plan than has just been put to us, so I have decided to accept it and wish them both Godspeed.' The Governor paused for a couple of moments and then rose from his chair at the dining room table and went into the study.

There were two police armoured cars outside Government House waiting to take people back to their homes. Throughout the entire briefing, Graham Freeman said not a word to Gunn, or to anyone, unless he'd been invited to explain something. Gunn spoke with the Chief Secretary who then spoke to the Commissioner of Police. With so much at stake on the success of this operation, not the slightest risk of a leak could be risked. Graham Freeman was a security risk and it was agreed that he should be detained in 'protective custody' until the operation was over - one way or another. Just as he was about to leave Government House, the Commissioner of Police stopped him and explained that he would be spending the next 48 hours at Central Police Headquarters. Gunn and Doyle spent a further hour studying the aerial and satellite photos and then both of them went to their rooms to try and get some sleep for what could well be the last time in the next two days.

*

The eye of the typhoon went over Hong Kong at 1415 hours that Saturday afternoon and brought with it an eerie stillness which lasted for almost eighteen minutes and then with terrifying suddenness, the raging winds struck again from 180° in the opposite direction. Some structures, which had just managed to withstand the constant hammering in one direction, crumpled and collapsed when they were violently stressed in the opposite direction. The seas broke into a smother of white foam and the air was filled with stinging salt spray and spume. Millions of gallons of torrential water spewed out of the catchment ditches into the reservoirs, which were already full after a very wet rainy season. The road over the highest hill in the territory, Tai Mo Shan, which had been built by the Royal Engineers and appropriately named Route Twisk, was a cascade of water in both directions. In the south it discharged tons of water into the high-rise flats of the Kowloon suburb of Tsuen Wan and in the north it did the same to the houses and military married quarters in the village of Sek Kong. The same happened on the roads circling the Peak and at least one parked or broken-down car had been swept over the side and a thousand feet down to the Mid-levels. The Royal Observatory was still predicting a drop in the wind speed at approximately 1600 hours and the winds at manageable strength by midday on Sunday.

*

Gunn and Doyle Barnes were woken at six that evening and both given a nourishing meal. The police armoured car arrived at 6.45 and the Governor and his wife came to the front door to see them off. Nothing was said because the noise by the front door was deafening. The armoured car had backed right up to the front door and the two men climbed into the back and closed the heavy steel doors. The engine roared and they moved off. It was impossible to think let alone speak as the wind howled round the vehicle. It was constantly struck by every conceivable object, which added to the cacophony. Gunn and Barnes could see nothing as the armoured car gingerly made its way over piles of debris on its way to the MTR station. It took nearly forty minutes to cover the 1500 metres from Government House to the station. This was about the same time that it would take in rush hour, Gunn thought, as the machine came to a halt and the vehicle commander came down inside from the turret and with sign language made it clear that it was time for them to go. Both of them had been given police riot helmets with visors to protect their faces from being cut to ribbons. The driver had positioned the armoured car in a sheltered place by the steps leading down to the MTR. Gunn and Barnes were roped together like climbers and fought their way the few paces across the pavement to the MTR entrance and then down the steps. Once down in the MTR, the noise subsided and when they reached the platform, the diesel car was waiting for them. The journey to Tsim Sha Tsui took eight minutes and the two men made their way up the steps from the station as none of the escalators was working. When they reached street-level, they found another armoured car,

230

which had been reversed right inside the MTR entrance. Again they climbed in, the doors were closed and the vehicle set off. Laid out on the seats on both sides of the vehicle was all the equipment for which they had asked and the first half hour of the journey was spent checking all of this thoroughly and then packing it into the back-packs. The journey to Sha Tau Kok was a nightmare. The twenty mile drive lasted for two hours and fifty minutes and was only made bearable by the fact that some thoughtful soul had put a box of sandwiches, some coffee and a couple of cans of beer in the back for them. They arrived at the T-junction at Sha Tau Kok just before eleven. The vehicle commander came down from the turret and pointed to their position on the map. Gunn and Doyle put on their helmets and gloves after slinging the packs onto their backs. The SA80 riffles were wrapped in waterproof bags and strapped to the packs. There was no point in trying to use them as weapons as it was impossible to see anything to shoot. Both men preferred to have their hand guns strapped in shoulder holsters on the outside of the waterproof jackets they were wearing and both carried divers' knives strapped to their calves. The armoured car came to a halt. The vehicle commander held his hand out with the thumb down. They waited, sweating in their bulky clothes and the close humidity of the armoured car. The thumb went up; they opened the doors and looked out into blackness so impenetrable that the men felt they could touch it. Pieces of vegetation and debris struck them. It had been planned that the armoured car would point itself at the gate before all the lights were switched off. Once again the two of them were roped together, Gunn leading. He felt his way along the side of the armoured car and then groped forward, head and body bowed into the wind. Underneath the visor of the helmet both men were wearing goggles. It took a few moments for their eyes to become accustomed to the darkness, even though the light in the back of the Saracen had been a red night-vision one. Gunn found the gate by walking straight into it. It was on rollers and slid open. Both men went through and then Doyle closed it behind him. They crawled down the slope to what used to be a stream and the bridge over it. The stream was a tumbling mass of floodwater and the bridge was already awash. They pulled themselves over the bridge and tripped, staggered and crawled into the patchy undergrowth on the outskirts of the village of Sha Tau Kok. The border lights came on again. The two men looked back, heads down to protect themselves from the never-ceasing hail of missiles which struck them all over their bodies. The lighted border seemed as though it was a thousand miles away, in another world. Gunn turned away and forced himself forward into China.

231

There was water everywhere; it poured off the roofs of houses, swirled down the narrow streets and where it was unable to flow away, collected in deep lakes of floodwater. Nothing seemed to bear any resemblance to the maps and diagrams, which Gunn had memorised in the study at Government House. Of human or animal life there wasn't a sign other than up-ended animal carcasses floating on the surface of the floodwater. Using a luminous compass, which was strapped to his left wrist, Gunn made desperately slow and laborious progress through the welter of water, mud and airborne debris. If the two of them hadn't been roped together the operation would have finished in the first quarter of a mile, as both men constantly lost their footing and would have been swept away but for the rope. It took them an hour to skirt round the village and find the road, which headed north out of it. Fortunately, the road ran along the shore line and the torrent of water flowing down from the 3000 foot peak to the north of Sha Tau Kok was able to escape over it into the sea. Progress was painfully slow and exhausting as the two men battled to stay upright against the battering from the wind and rain. The mile and a half to the left turn into the PLA barracks took another two hours; for a large part of the route they could do no more than crawl on hands and knees when they were exposed to the full fury of the wind. It was virtually impossible to plan a concealed approach towards the barracks, as any progress was a matter of trying to survive. The wind appeared to be coming from the east, off the sea and was driving the two men towards the PLA camp, but also masking their approach, had there been anyone looking. At the gate to the camp, there was no sign of life. Not a light showed anywhere and the gates hung from their hinges, hammering back and forth in the fierce gusts of wind. There was a guardroom, of sorts - it had been one until the typhoon had ripped off its roof. A large proportion of the metal-roofed buildings had collapsed and every now and then, a piece of the corrugated iron would break off and fly through the air destroying everything in its path like the sword of a huge and invisible giant. It seemed as though the camp had been abandoned. Gunn made his way forward from building to building, where both of them would pause in any shelter available, there appeared to be some construction in the centre of the camp, which the photographs had shown as a parade square. Slowly, yard by yard they staggered towards it. They were only ten yards away, when Gunn realised what he was looking at. The PLA had done exactly what the British units in the New Territories did when the number eight typhoon signal was hoisted. All the vehicles were removed from the steel and 'wriggly-tin' garages and driven into the centre of the parade-square. There was an exact science in the way that all the vehicles were parked, each one no more than a couple of inches from the other and resembling an interlocking pattern of the wood blocks on a parquet floor. This technique had proved to be highly successful and with previous typhoons, like Rose and Hope, most of the vehicles had survived without so much as a scratch, whereas all the garages had crumpled and collapsed.

What was even more pleasing, as Gunn led Doyle Barnes towards this mass of metal, was that the PLA had very sensibly positioned their armoured vehicles on the periphery of the 'box' to bear the brunt of the typhoon. There was no possible way of telling, which of the BMPs might be unlocked, which would have a full tank of fuel and so on. Gunn went up to the nearest one and with Doyle's help, opened the door in the reverse sheer at the back of the tracked armoured personnel carrier. They both climbed in to the cramped rear compartment which had been designed to take a section of ten Russian dwarfs - or so went the joke. The NATO armies had had their first chance of seeing the interior of these machines after they had been captured by the Israelis in the Six Day War. Doyle Barnes closed the door and the relative diminution of noise was blissful. Gunn removed his helmet and goggles and backpack with considerable difficulty in the confined space in the back of the BMP and then switched on his torch for the first time since they'd left Government House. There was absolutely no possibility of them being seen or overheard even though the conversation was carried on in a volume only just below that of a shout.

'Doyle, I suggest that we examine this BMP and see if it can be started and has any fuel. If we produce a big fat zero, then we'll work our way round the edge of this square of vehicles until we find a suitable BMP. If we fail, then we've got to find their fuel pumps. I can never remember, are these things diesel or petrol?

'The ones we have back in the States are all diesel, but for all I know, the Chinks run these on rice wine. Let me take a look,' and Doyle crawled forward to the driving position on the front left side of the APC. The controls were in the same position and the switches appeared to be the same as the captured BMP he'd seen, but he was unable to read the Chinese characters. It was rare to find Russian military equipment that used a lockable ignition and the BMP was no exception to this. In the centre of the instrument panel between the two steering levers were two knurled plastic twist switches. The one on the left controlled the lights: head - dip and high beam - side, convoy and spotlight. The switch on the right was the ignition. Above the switches were four dials; two large ones on either side and two small ones, one above the other in between them. The left-hand dial showed the engine revolutions and the right indicated the road speed. In the centre, the top dial recorded coolant temperature and engine oil temperature and the bottom one, fuel. Doyle switched on the ignition and was rewarded with an ignition light and a diesel cylinder head heating element light. 'It's diesel,' he shouted over his shoulder to Gunn, 'and the fuel tank's empty. After this is over, I'll see that the driver of this APC is shot for negligence,' Doyle added in frustration. He switched off and after various contortions, wriggled back to where Gunn was. 'Right, you go left and I'll go right. Come back to this BMP as soon as you find one that's got enough fuel to get us to Daya Bay,' Gunn said as he replaced his helmet and gloves. Doyle opened the door and the two of them climbed out. The first one Gunn tried produced no ignition light, which ruled that out. The next two both had empty fuel tanks so he returned to the original BMP where Doyle was waiting for him inside. As soon as Gunn opened the door, Doyle held up his thumb and handed John Gunn his pack. They left the BMP and turned left towards the second APC away. They climbed inside, dumped their packs again and Doyle went forward to the driver's seat followed by Gunn, who stood up in the APC commander's position. They removed their helmets and replaced them with the thick Russian leather helmets, which incorporated headphones and a boom mike. Gunn put on his goggles and undid the two securing levers on the commander's hatch and opened it with considerable difficulty against the force of the wind. Doyle switched on the ignition and the power to the APC'S communication system. The headphones hummed and then Doyle spoke on the intercom. 'OK John, if you're ready, let's get this show on the road. I can see virtually nothing out of the driving periscope when the seat's lowered and I'm certain I won't be able to drive with the hatch open, so it looks as though you're the eyes of this machine.'

'Right, Doyle; start up and reverse straight back using no stick,' Gunn acknowledged.

'Roger to that, here goes,' and Doyle turned the ignition switch to pre-heat, paused for ten seconds and twisted it to the start position. The big diesel turned over, fired and rumbled into life.

'Tell me when you're ready.'

'Give it a minute or so to warm up the oil in the transmission. I'm getting ready now; OK, let's go, John.'

'Roger, reverse!' The engine revs increased and the BMP moved slowly backwards from its slot amongst all the other vehicles. As soon as the front was clear, Gunn ordered, 'left stick!' and Doyle eased back on the left steering tiller. This, in turn, opened a valve releasing hydraulic fluid to the brake pads on two over-sized disc brakes on the differential drive on the left track and locked it. The right track kept turning in reverse and swung the BMP round. 'Halt! Forward, right stick, 'Gunn ordered and the APC trundled slowly forward towards the gate of the camp. John discovered that by raising the armoured steel hatch to the vertical position and locking it, he could then rotate it so that it provided a shield from the rain and missile-laden wind. With only his head above the hatch opening, he found he now had a reasonable view into the pitch black howling maw of the night. Yard by yard, the APC rumbled towards the gates, or where Gunn hoped the gates were. He saw what was left of them when the BMP was less than five yards from them. The left gate had been ripped from its hinges and lay on the concrete in the gateway. The other gate still slammed back and forth. Gunn spoke to Doyle and the BMP eased over to the left and went over the obstruction, avoiding the guillotine action of the right-hand gate. If anyone had seen them or had been alerted, Gunn would have been none the wiser as his sight and hearing were overwhelmed by the volume of noise. The BMP crept down the road to the 'T' junction at walking pace and then Doyle turned left onto the main road leading out of Sha Tau Kok. He looked at his watch; it was nearly twenty past two. 'OK, let's have some lights and get going,' Gunn said. The lights came on.

'Tell me which is better; low or high beam,' Doyle said, switching the lights from one to the other setting.

'Low beam's better'; the APC changed up through the automatic box and the tracks bit into the tarmac as Gunn guided it along the road towards Daya Bay.

CHAPTER 21

Gradually the swirling clouds of drugged unconsciousness began to clear as Candy struggled out of what had seemed to be an interminable nightmare. It was a nightmare filled with faces, which appeared and then receded; prolonged silence followed by distorted sounds and movement, but now she found herself creeping back to consciousness and sanity. Reality was even more confusing than her nightmares. Where was she? What was this extraordinary room with all its gadgetry? Then she tried to move, but discovered that although her legs were free, her wrists were tied together. Candy's vision began to focus more clearly and she realised that there were others around her in the same predicament. What had happened to her? The effort of concentration hurt, but the effects of the drug were beginning to wear off and slowly her brain began to put everything into perspective from the jumbled confusion of a surrealist painting.

She could remember returning to her flat on the Wednesday night after the party on the yacht and the shooting in Picnic Bay, but nothing after that. She was convinced that somewhere in the confusion of her nightmare there had been an aeroplane or helicopter, but none of it made any sense. Who were these people with her? And what were all these people dressed in white coats and overalls doing?

'Ah, Miss Wyngarde, I see that you have decided to join us at last. Can you hear me?' A nod confirmed that she could. 'Good; my name's Charles McBain. We have met before, but I'm sure you won't remember me. I was the Assistant Commissioner of Police in Hong Kong. You are in the control room of the Daya Bay Nuclear Power Station, together with the Governor of Hong Kong's children. The other people - over there,' and McBain pointed, 'are members of the duty staff of this control room. You and they will remain here until my plans are complete and your presence will ensure that no one is foolish enough to interfere. Once I have finished here, you and the Governor's children will be released. I regret to inform you that Gunn and his CIA friend, Doyle Barnes, are both dead. . . .' McBain's voice continued and Candy wondered if she'd slipped back into her nightmare, but unfortunately, it was all only too real.

'Can I have a drink of water?' she interrupted McBain.

236

McBain paused and turned to one of his men and spoke in Chinese. The man left the room and then reappeared with a plastic cup filled with water. The chilled water helped enormously and Candy sat up. Again McBain spoke and the same man came forward and removed the leather thong, which had bound her wrists together. She rubbed them to restore the circulation and to give herself time to collect her thoughts before speaking to McBain. 'I haven't got things straight yet. I can remember you . . . it's Charles McBain, isn't it?' a nod and slight bow confirmed that she was correct. 'If you're a policeman, why are all of us sitting here with our hands tied? What's happening here at . . . where are we again?'

'Daya Bay.'

'Daya Bay; that's in China. Why are we here?'

'I am here because I'm going to destroy Hong Kong rather than let the Chinese Communists have it. You're here as insurance to prevent anyone interfering with my plans.'

'Why?'

'In 1984, Britain signed away Hong Kong to the Chinese. Hong Kong is my country. My family has been here since 1843. They toiled, sweated and died for Hong Kong and my uncle was tortured to death by the Japanese in the last war when he was fighting with hundreds of others to save the colony for Britain. Hong Kong was never a part of the treaty with China; that was only the New Territories. The Chinese aren't entitled to it nor to Kowloon and especially not the Communists, so they aren't going to get it. I'm going to destroy it.'

'How are you going to do that?'

'In thirty-six hours, the Chinese President will arrive here to open this power station. Just before he arrives, I will insert the fuel rods into the core of the fourth reactor. The fuel rods are made of weapon grade uranium, which will cause nuclear fission at a far greater temperature than that for which the reactor is designed. The great heat will cause the safety shutdown devices to operate automatically. These devices have been modified. Instead of inserting control rods, additional fuel rods will be inserted causing the fission to accelerate. The coolant will merely circulate back to its reservoir. Meltdown will take place within four minutes, by which time I will be well on my way from here.'

'But you'll kill thousands, millions of people . . . the majority will be those in Hong Kong . . . the country your family has served for 150 years. It's a monstrous crime you're committing, as bad as the Nazi holocaust . . .' but McBain was no longer listening. The Governor's children were beginning to regain consciousness and their hands had been untied. McBain turned towards them.

'If either you or they attempt to escape or interfere, my men will immediately shoot one of the other hostages. Is that understood?'

'Yes,' Candy replied. 'Is there a toilet of any sort here which I'd be allowed to use?' Again, McBain spoke to the man who had produced the water and she was escorted from the control room.

*

The route which Gunn had selected offered a good road for the first four miles to Yantian and then little more than a rough track which followed the coastline of Mirs Bay, through the Shenzen border fence at Tai Mui Sha and on to Xiantanling. At that point, it was only two and a half miles to the north of Ping Chau Island. The track then turned east, inland, on the Dapeng Peninsula, round the foot of the 1800foot Qiushui Ling range of hills to the town of Wangmu. Two miles to the east of Wangmu, the map showed a left turn which ran north past the lake of Damali Shuiku and over the Qiushui Hills to the town of Aotou and the Daya Bay Power Station.

Their increase in speed was short-lived as torrents of water were flowing down the ravines and gullies of the 3000 foot peak of Wutong Shan to the left of the road. The culverts were unable to cope with the flood and the road, in places, was under a metre's depth of water. They passed slowly through the small village of Shajingtou, which had been flattened by the typhoon. Gunn caught a glimpse of a light coming from the ruins of a building, but other than that there were no signs of life. Dead cattle floated past and on two occasions the tracks of the BMP lost contact with the road as the depth of water lifted it clear of the ground. Most of the trees had been blown down and the boats, which belonged to this fishing village had been swept ashore and pounded to matchwood. The wind was still in the east and driving in over the sea. Although this filled the air with salt-laden spray, it had the advantage of carrying no broken foliage or debris and driving along the coast road was rather similar to steering a boat through a hurricane force wind.

They reached the bridge over the river to the west of the town of Yantian just before three in the morning which meant that they were going no faster than someone jogging. Gunn and Doyle had hoped to get into the hills to the north of Wangmu before it was daylight, but at this rate they were unlikely to cover more than ten miles before dawn. They had been faced with the problem of pressing on as fast as possible and risk being spotted or moving under the cover of darkness and risk some form of disastrous PLA assault on the power station. The decision had been taken in favour of pressing on regardless, in the hope that no one would be interested in stopping

238

them in such appalling weather conditions. Now that Gunn saw how long it was going to take, there was no alternative but to press on.

Gunn strained his eyes to see the bridge. It didn't exist and neither did the majority of the town of Yantian. The river had burst its banks much further back up the valley to the north-west and had engulfed the town. Gunn told Doyle to stop and then he lowered himself down into the BMP and switched on the interior light. He studied the map; there was no way round. The main road ran up the valley beside the river and so that would be under even deeper water. They had to get to the other side of the town to find their route along the coast.

'What chance of the water propulsion units on this BMP working, Doyle?' Gunn said into the intercom.

'Everything else works; are we about to test the swimming capability of this machine?'

'We've no choice.'

'You know that these thing float nine-tenths submerged.'

'Yes; the pictures I saw weren't too encouraging, but that was supposed to be with a full load of soldiers. I'm hoping that with just the two of us it might ride a bit higher.'

'Me to; well, your propulsion units work. Now if we're going in, I'd better raise the bow-wash plate and I'm keeping the hatch open for a quick exit.'

'OK, give me a call when you're ready.' On the front of the BMP was a steel plate which was raised and lowered by hydraulic pistons which pushed the water to each side - like the bow of a boat - rather than allow it to wash over the front of the BMP and into the driver's hatch. The plate was raised and then Doyle wound up his seat so that his head now protruded from the driver's hatch.

'Ready to roll,' came from Doyle over the intercom.

'Right Doyle; I'm going to head you in the direction of half-left so that we try and prevent ourselves from being washed out to sea. As soon as we're afloat, give the propulsion units plenty of revs; there's a hell of a current running. Right, let's go!' The BMP moved forward and the lights flicked up to high beam. They only moved forward ten yards before the tracks came clear and Doyle transferred the drive to the propulsion units. Gunn hoped that they would be able to cross the flood to the north-west of the town which would bring them to the higher ground. The BMP was crabbing along in the right direction and fortunately for both of the men it was riding with eighteen inches of freeboard. Had it been fully laden, then the turbulent floodwater would have burst over the top of the APC and sent it to the bottom. The headlights picked out some lampposts leaning at an angle under the pressure of the water, which provided some form of guide as to where the road was beneath them. Gunn could see lights in the second storey windows of some houses and as they were swept past, he saw families huddled round paraffin lamps. The ground floor of every house was under water and anything not made of bricks and mortar had been swept out to sea.

The lights picked out the edge of the floodwater and at the same moment he felt the jolt as the tracks grounded. Doyle transferred the drive and the BMP climbed out of the water like some prehistoric monster onto the high ground to the north of the town. Gunn directed him to the right and they followed the contour of the ground until they picked up the route on the east side of the town.

At Tai Mui Sha, the Shenzen border fence had been swept away, the checkpoint on the road was under water and there wasn't a sign of anyone. They eventually reached Xiantanling shortly after 8.30 as a very late and heavily overcast dawn started to break. Apart from the occasional light and the glimpse of the people in Yantian, they hadn't seen a soul. The area around Xiantanling was all paddy and was now a huge lake which stretched for 2,500 metres up the valley to the north-east. Somewhere under the water was their road and once again Doyle switched the drive of the amphibious APC and they set off inland towards the town of Wangmu. There was high ground on both sides of them, which offered a modicum of protection from the wind and rain.

The BMP came out of the water and crossed over a low saddle joining the Qiushui Hills to the north with some lower hills to the south. Visibility had improved marginally and Gunn stopped the BMP at the crest of the saddle, which gave them a view overlooking the town of Wangmu and the plains surrounding it. There was no town. Gunn dropped down into the APC and studied the map. Seven rivers fed into the plains from the Qiushui Hills which enclosed the low ground like a horseshoe; the open end of the shoe was the large river estuary in the south. Two of the rivers flowed into the Damali Shuiku Lake. In the middle of the agricultural plain was a small area of high ground, which rose to 250 feet. Gunn climbed back into his hatch. The town of Wangmu had disappeared. The only feature, which he could identify was the island of high ground in the new bay which had been formed by the floodwater of the typhoon. 'Wangmu has disappeared, Doyle. I'm just going to get out of the BMP and take a compass bearing,' and Gunn unplugged his intercom and climbed back inside the vehicle and then out of the door at the back of it. Doyle raised himself up so that he could keep an eye on him and saw, with relief, that Gunn had tied the rope round his waist. Gunn moved away from the APC to avoid distortion of the compass bearing and then returned. Once he was in and reconnected to the intercom he spoke to Doyle; 'can you see that saddle in the range of hills over there with the peak of much higher ground to the right?

'Yes,' Doyle said slowly as he looked in the direction Gunn was pointing.

'That's where I reckon that the road goes into the hills. That's your landmark for the next stage of our voyage. You feeling alright or would you like me to take a spell at driving?'

'No thanks, I'm fine at the moment. Let's get off this bare-arsed bit of ground and into the water and when we get to the other side we'll swap over and have a bite to eat,' Doyle suggested and eased both of the tillers forward. The BMP rolled down the track and into the water.

The wind had whipped the water into a steep chop and as the BMP was not designed for these sea conditions, quite a few of the waves broke over the top of the vehicle. Fortunately, both John and Doyle were jammed in the hatch opening, rather like corks in a bottle, so very little water entered the APC. They reached the north shore of the flooded plain and climbed out onto the rising ground of the Qiushui Hills. Doyle picked up the track 150 yards to their right and turned the BMP towards it. Once on the track, the APC swung to the left and followed it into the hills. 'We might be able to find a sheltered spot on the other side of the ridge. We'll stop anyway, shortly, have some food and I'll give you a spell at the wheel,' Gunn said to Doyle on the intercom. Once over the ridge, the track swung to the west across the face of the hill range. There was a vertical rock face on their left and a sheer drop of 500 feet on the outside of the track to what was usually, no doubt, a stream, but which was now a raging torrent of floodwater. The track followed the corrugated sides of the pass and on the inside of the second of these bends, Doyle pulled the BMP right up close to the rock face and switched off the engine. They closed both the hatches and crawled into the back of the APC. 'How much further is there to go?' Doyle asked when he had removed his leather helmet.

'About eight miles from the foot of this pass,' John replied, looking at the map and then at his watch. 'A quarter to ten; 24 hours until that madman starts a melt-down in the fourth reactor.' They were in a well-sheltered spot, but both of them had noticed that the wind had lost some of its ferocity. 'We must keep going, John; the wind is easing and that means that the Chinks will be on the move,' Doyle said, unwrapping a bar of chocolate and then replacing his helmet. Gunn went forward into the driver's seat and started the engine. There was a click in the headphones. 'All set?'

'Ready.'

'Let's go then.' Gunn let off the tiller brakes and pulled the BMP out into the centre of the track as water and stones poured down the face of the rock. Even though it was approaching midday, it was still no lighter than the brief period of dusk in these latitudes. Gunn steered the BMP round the first of the hairpin bends and then dragged back on both tillers. The track was totally blocked by a landslide. A waterlogged mass of mud, rocks and stones had broken away and oozed down the steep gully where a re-entrant carved back into the rock face. It went over the track and then spilled over the edge and down into the torrent below. The track was completely blocked and some of the rocks being pushed by the mass of mud were larger than the BMP.

'What the hell do we do now?'

'Wait a second,' and Gunn unplugged his intercom and climbed out onto the top of the BMP, where he could get a better view of the oozing mass of mud and rock. He then climbed off the BMP and went into the back of it where he looked at his map. There were two other routes; both meant going back 15 miles in the wrong direction before the first alternative route struck off to the east through the Pi Chia Shan range of hills. There was no guarantee that they would not find a similar landslide on that pass. The second alternative was to use the main road and go via Shui to the north of Daya Bay. Either route would add a minimum of eight hours, and probably more, to their journey. The main road would be highly risky and in only a few hours would be full of traffic and if the other route through the pass was also blocked, it would be just so much wasted time. That left only two alternatives; turn round and take the main road or try and drive across the landslide. Gunn got out of the BMP and walked towards it. There was no doubt about the easing of the typhoon and the rain now only came in flurries rather than in a steady driving torrent. The mass of fluid mud and rock seemed to be alive and looked like some giant, carbuncled boa constrictor slithering down the gully and over the road. Gunn walked over to the edge of the road where it plunged in a sheer drop at this point into the roaring floodwater below. He turned as Doyle came up to inspect the obstacle. 'You're not thinking what I think you're thinking are you?' Doyle shouted after glancing at the drop over the side of the road.

'That depends on what you think I'm thinking,' Gunn shouted back.

'I was afraid of that. If we go over - there,' and he indicated with a jerk of his head, 'then 'boom!'' and Doyle made the shape of a mushroom cloud.

'If we go back, Doyle, we'll be too late. The PLA will be there and McBain will set off the meltdown, shoot all the hostages and escape in his helicopter. He'll be able to fly that thing if conditions improve at the present rate. We may even be too late already and that means to me that there's no alternative; I've already wasted five minutes thinking about it,' Gunn said, turning back to the BMP.

'Right, how did you plan to take on this sonofabitch?'

'Pick my moment when the big rocks leave a gap and then keep the front pointing into the rock face as I drive across.'

'Can't think of a better plan; let's go,' and Doyle climbed up onto the BMP and lowered himself into the commander's hatch. Gunn settled himself into the driver's seat and gunned the engine. Now he had to choose the right moment. Two large rocks, the size of a car, rolled end over end and then plunged into the gorge below. Now! Gunn released the tillers and stamped on the accelerator holding the pre-selector in low. The BMP lurched forward and reared up onto the twenty metre wide river of mud and rock. The tracks bit into the slimy surface, helped by the large quantity of stone and rock. Five metres; the tracks spun, unable to grip anything in the mud and the front of the BMP began to swing away from the rock face. The right track gripped and spun the front back and the BMP lurched forward again for a couple of yards. 'Look out, John!' came Doyle's warning in the headphones, but Gunn had already seen the huge rock break away from the side and topple into the landslide. Like a slow motion picture it swung round and pushed the front of the BMP away from the rock face towards the edge of the road. The BMP moved towards the edge as Gunn whipped the selector lever into reverse and then stamped on the accelerator. The front of the APC eased slowly forward until it hung over the side of the road, the reversed tracks seeming to have no hold on the mud. Gunn gave each of the tillers a slight tweak in turn, just to wiggle the BMP in the hope of the tracks biting. He was nearly level with the sheer drop over the side. The landslide was at its shallowest at the edge and the tracks gripped. First a metre and then two, the BMP moved back from the brink. The huge rock, which had pushed the BMP round, hung for an instant on the brink and then spun end over end into the water below. Once the momentum had started the BMP moved back towards the rock-face. Now came the crucial time to turn and change gear. Gunn pulled on the right tiller, the BMP spun, he pushed the selector into low and slammed his foot back on the accelerator. The tracks bit on the rock and stones and the BMP rushed forward over the far side of the landslide and nearly cannoned into the rock face. Gunn drove on for fifty metres and then stopped.

'Perhaps you'd like to have a bash at that, Doyle. Can't say I did it very professionally and I wondered if you'd like to show me how it's done,' Gunn suggested as he wiped the sweat off his hands.

'Not bad for a first attempt. Remind me to give my support from the spectator benches if we come to another of those . . .' and the rest of Doyle's comment was drowned in the roar of the diesel as Gunn moved off.

Visibility was improving all the time as Pamela moved into the landmass of Southern China and its ferocious destructive power was dissipated. The track on which they were driving wound down the northern side of the Qiushui Ling Hills and then across the western curve of Dumbell Bay to the Pi Chia Shan Hills. The floodwater was beginning to subside and in the villages of His Hsiang and Hsiao Kuei, tragic little groups of people waded through the subsiding water in search of lost possessions. As Gunn drove the BMP through the second village, which lay at the foot of the last ridge of hills before Daya Bay, he saw that it was only a few minutes before five o'clock. The sky was already beginning to darken again and within and hour it would be night. The BMP came up to the crest of the ridge and Gunn stopped it. Below them, some three miles away, was the town of Aotou and to the east of it the unmistakable shape of the Nuclear Power Station. Gunn leaned back into the interior of the BMP and grabbed his binoculars. He climbed out of the driver's seat and onto the top of the BMP. Barnes had his glasses pointed at the power station. Gunn swung his glasses from the power station, westwards along the road to the town and then to the junction of the track which they had used and the main road south from Shui. The main road to Shui climbed steadily towards the north and Gunn followed it with his glasses until it disappeared in the hills. He lowered the glasses and wiped the lenses and then raised them to his eyes again.

'Doyle, see what you make of this,' Gunn said. Doyle lowered his glasses and noted the direction in which Gunn's binoculars were pointing.

'Follow the line of the road running north out of Aotou towards Shui. Just before it disappears behind those hills, where there seems to be some form of greener vegetation than the surrounding land.'

'I've got it . . . wait; well spotted Johnny. Looks like we're running out of time. Come on, I'll take the wheel and we'd better get to the power station in double quick time.' Doyle jumped down into the driver's seat and Gunn took over the commander's position. A burst of black diesel smoke poured out of the BMP's stack as it dipped over the crest of the ridge and headed down the hill towards the Daya Bay

Power Station. Six miles away to the north, a long column of T62 tanks was on a converging course with the BMP.

*

The Governor's Security Committee was scheduled to meet at 1600 hours on the Sunday to discuss the measures which were being taken to deal with the destruction caused by Typhoon Pamela. In the same way as he had done previously, the Governor had asked the key members of his Committee to arrive half an hour before the main meeting to listen to a briefing on the even more serious crisis facing Hong Kong. Once the eye of the typhoon had passed over the territory, the force of the wind had gradually dropped and was now little more than gale force strength. Power had been restored to the majority of the Island, but most of the New Territories was still without any electricity while teams of engineers struggled to repair the damaged pylons and lines.

The population had been warned to stay off the streets to allow the emergency services to cope with the search for the dead and injured and start the long process of clearing away the debris of collapsed buildings. All the hospitals were filled to capacity, including the temporary Army Field Hospital which had been set up to cope with the remaining British Forces prior to the handover. Hamish Walker, the Chief Fire Officer, had been replaced by his Deputy, Peter Cheung. He now sat on the left of the table next to the Commissioner of Police, opposite the Secretary for Security and the Commander British Forces. The Governor took his seat at the head of the table and turned to the Secretary for Security; 'Robin, can you please bring us up to date on the Daya Bay operation.'

'Right Sir,' Robin Masefield started. You will recall, gentlemen, that John Gunn asked us to provide him with an EPIRB - that's the acronym for 'emergency position indicating radio beacon' - it's used to keep track of yachts on ocean races and to assist in Search and Rescue. This was the only gadget, which was immediately available and we acquired it from the Royal Hong Kong Yacht Club. Communication specialists from the US Consulate re-tuned the EPIRB to the frequency of the US Early Bird satellite system and gave us the frequency to receive the relayed signals from the gadget carried by the two men. They switched it on as soon as they got into the vehicle at Tsim Sha Tsui and it has given their position with great accuracy ever since. It has taken them nearly twenty-four hours to get to Daya Bay, but they are now within two miles of the power station. That, gentlemen, is the good news,' and Robin Masefield paused to take a sip from the glass of water in front of him. 'Now for the bad news'.

The Chinese Ambassador in London has presented a note to the Prime Minister. This informs both the UK and the USA - the same communiqué was delivered to the White House - that any attempt to interfere at the Daya Bay Nuclear Power Station would be considered as armed aggression against the People's Republic of China. Any such act of aggression would be outside the conditions agreed at the Joint Declaration in 1984 and would, therefore, in the opinion of the Government of the PRC, nullify that agreement. The Government of the PRC believes that it would achieve a clear majority vote in the UN. This would be achieved despite the veto of the permanent members of the Security Council and would approve retaliatory measures against the Government of Hong Kong and the United Kingdom, with the aim of protecting the Chinese ethnic majority of a country which would shortly revert to its rightful ownership. And now, gentlemen, we come to the worst part of the communiqué,' Robin Masefield paused and turned a page of his notes. 'The forces of the People's Liberation Army have been despatched to the Daya Bay Nuclear Power Station and are expected to arrive there by nightfall tonight. If they discover that there has been any attempt to interfere with the safe generation of electricity from nuclear fission, then those responsible will be punished with the utmost severity. If hostages are being held captive, every attempt will be made to free them. It must be clearly understood that the Government of the PRC would place the safety of the people of China and Hong Kong at a higher priority than investigating the information passed by the capitalist governments of the UK and USA. That, gentlemen, is the end of the communiqué. As you all know, we have no means of communicating with our two men until they reach the Security Control Room, when they will try to contact us by telephone.'

'Thank you, Robin. Are there any questions or comments from anyone before we call in my Security Committee to see how we are coping with the trail of destruction left by the typhoon.' There was silence around the table. 'Very well, gentlemen, we've no choice but to stand by the course of action we chose. I can only add that the governments of the UK, USA and Hong Kong will have to deny all knowledge of Gunn and Barnes. Any investigation by the press will reveal that both men were hired by Peter Wyngarde to rescue his daughter. Now, Martin, please show in the other members of the Security Committee.

CHAPTER 22

The streets of the town of Aotou had suffered as badly as the coastal places through which Gunn had driven. The main street was blocked by collapsed buildings, which required a detour to get back on the road to the power station. It was now completely dark and as soon as the BMP emerged from the rubble and mud, which had filled the larger part of the ground floors of all the houses in the town, Doyle switched the lights to low beam and then finally to side only.

'In about two hundred metres, Doyle, the road swings to the left away from the sea to avoid an outcrop of rock. The power station is about 200 metres beyond that bend and the road is open with no cover, if you remember what Freeman said. Put the side lights out now and I'll tell you when to stop.'

'OK, got all that,' Doyle acknowledged as the speed of the BMP came right down and it trundled slowly forward at little more than walking pace.

'That'll do fine. Grab your rifle and scope and we'll go and have a look at the gate security and who's guarding the entrance to the power station.' Doyle joined Gunn and they both walked forward round the high ground, which concealed them from the power station. As they came round the rock outcrop, they had a clear view to the perimeter fence and main entrance of the power station whose plans had been explained in every detail by Graham Freeman. In the centre of the two-lane entry and exit roads was a small square building, which controlled access to the power station. On both sides, there were large sliding gates, which were worked from a control panel in the building. The lights in the building were on and both gates were shut.

'McBain must have some of his men in that building to give him warning of the approach of anyone. Use the scope and see if you can spot any guards patrolling the area between our position and the fence. I'll take the left of the gate you take the right,' Gunn suggested. There were floodlights all round the perimeter fence and all of these were working despite the typhoon. It was the area between the floodlit fence and where they were crouching, which was in pitch darkness by comparison and in which Gunn was particularly interested. Speed was essential to stay ahead of the PLA, but it was equally important not to throw caution to the winds and ruin the operation by stumbling over a guard who would alert McBain.

'Yes,' murmured Doyle, 'there's a guy my side and he's armed, what about you?'

'Nothing yet . . . got him. He's just lit a cigarette. Yes, he's armed as well. Right we'll deal with those now as agreed.' From a zip pocket, both men removed large silencers, which they screwed onto the SA 80s. 'On the count of three . . . one, two, three,' and there was a noise like a stifled cough as both weapons fired together. The sentries fell to the ground without a sound. 'Right, Doyle, you go back to the BMP and start up. I've got all my kit here in the pack. Remember if there's an explosion in the guardroom, go like hell for the gates and smash them off the hinges. If all is quiet and you see the right hand gate open, come forward at a steady pace,' and the two men separated; Doyle to return to the BMP and Gunn to head in the direction of the building in the perimeter fence. At the edge of the lighted strip of ground surrounding the fence, he stopped and raised his binoculars. There were two men in the room. The fence was made of expanded, galvanised wire and there was no indication that McBain had put an electric current through it. John Gunn ran the last twenty yards and then crouched below the guard's field of vision. He removed the bolt-cutters from his pack and unfolded the handles. The long handles gave him such leverage that the jaws of the cutters went through the wire as though it were string. He cut a vertical line from the ground for three feet and then horizontally for eighteen inches at the top and bottom. He folded the wire back and squeezed through the fence bringing his pack through afterwards and then bent the wire back into position. The guardroom contained three men, not two. There was one man seated with his back to the wall. Gunn had been unable to see him. He switched the change lever on his rifle from single shot to automatic. He checked his Browning, the knife on his calf and the grenades in the pack. Crouching low he went under the sill of the window and round to the back of the guardroom. Very carefully, he tried the door. It was not locked. He raised his foot and slammed it forward, bursting open the door and firing at the same time. The man to die first was the one by the telephone, the other two, split seconds later. The door made the only noise as it hit a table behind it. Gunn removed the magazine and replaced it with a full one and then operated the switch to open the gate. It would now only be a matter of minutes, at the most, before McBain realised that something was wrong, as he was bound to have arranged for a report from the gate at regular intervals.

The BMP appeared in the floodlit strip as it trundled towards the gate. Doyle stopped it outside the guardroom. Gunn closed the gate behind him having tidied up the interior of the guard room and propped the men up around the table. He climbed up onto the BMP after handing his pack up to Doyle.

'Happy with the route?'

'Yeah, I think so. Hold on,' and the BMP moved off towards the power station. The security control room was reached from an entrance at the back of the power station, for which there was a thoroughly practical reason. If the operators of the main control room noticed a group of people whom they never saw inside the power station, then it would not be long before they became aware of being under some form of surveillance. Those who did shifts in the security control room had timings, which never coincided with the arrival or departure of those working in the main control room.

As Doyle drove the BMP round the power station, Gunn noted the helicopter LP and hangar, in which he hoped to find the red and white helicopter of the Hong Kong Auxiliary Airforce. Round the back of the station, Doyle found a place to conceal the BMP and then the two men slung their packs and walked to an entrance indicated in Chinese characters for 'Maintenance Staff Only.' Inside the entrance was a lift, exactly as described to them in the study at Government House. They took the lift to the fourth floor and the door opened onto a long corridor, which went the full length of the reactor halls and gave maintenance staff access to each of the reactors. At the end of the corridor was a large notice in black and yellow with the international warning sign for radioactivity. 'What does that say?' Doyle asked.

'Dangerous levels of radioactivity. No admittance unless wearing protective clothing,' Gunn replied. 'We're here,' and he pushed open the door. They were in a small vestibule, which had suits of protective clothing hanging from pegs on the wall. The door on the other side of the 'dressing room' was locked. They had been told that it was always kept locked, but they would find a telephone on the right of the door, which could be used to communicate with those people inside the security control room. Gunn picked up the phone from its cradle and pressed the button below it. No answer; he pressed again; someone had lifted the phone on the other side of the door. 'Wai,' came a cautious 'hello' from the other side of the door. Gunn spoke in Chinese.

'We have come to rescue you and the hostages in the main control room. Will you please open the door quickly as there is very little time. If the door is not opened by the time I count to three, at the end of this conversation, then we will use explosives on it. So if you have decided not to open the door, please stand well away from it so that no one is hurt. I'm going to start counting . . . one, two,' and the door opened. Gunn and Barnes went into the room, which had two men and a woman in it. They looked terrified and the appearance of John and Doyle did nothing to dispel their terror. Doyle Barnes had gone straight to the TV monitor screens. Gunn spoke to the three Chinese technicians.

'Please understand that you are in no danger from us. We have been sent here to rescue you. Have you used these?' asked Gunn as he saw the row of three telephones. 'Have you spoken with anyone in your Government?'

'We have tried, but the typhoon must have destroyed the lines to Beijing as we cannot get through,' was the reply from the eldest of the three Chinese.

'May I try your phone, please?' Gunn asked. Freeman had explained that all the telephone lines were in underground cabling up to the town, but then were carried on poles above the ground to Beijing. The line to Hong Kong was direct by a cable under the sea. A courteous gesture was made in the direction of the phones and Gunn walked over to them and picked the one up indicated by the senior technician.

*

The Governor's Security Committee had departed after briefing him on everything that was being done to deal with the injured first and the damaged property second. Power would be restored to the New Territories before ten that night and flights in and out of Kai Tak would start as six the following morning. The Government's PR Director, who was on the Committee, had asked the Governor to visit some of the hospitals, to which the latter had readily agreed. They all left except the principal members of the Committee.

'Martin,' the Governor said, 'serve some drinks please. I think we could all do with one. I certainly could. Would you get me a malt, please.' Martin Holmes closed the outer door and walked to the drinks cabinet, but stopped half way as the phone rang. 'That's OK, I'll take it, you do the drinks,' the Governor said, as he picked up the phone. 'Hello, this is the Governor speaking,' and then he said nothing for about a minute before replying quietly, 'yes I've got all that, thank you so much for keeping me informed,' and he replaced the instrument and glanced at his watch. Martin Holmes placed the malt whisky in front of the Governor.

'Everything alright, Sir?' he asked. It was a trite query when everything couldn't possibly be worse, but the Governor knew it was meant well.

'Yes, I hope so,' and then he looked up at all the enquiring faces around him. 'That was Mr Gunn. Within the next few minutes he and Mr Barnes will attempt to rescue the hostages,' and he took a sip of his whiskey. 'He wants us to implement CRACKER JACK. Can you deal with that Patrick, please?'

'Yes, of course, sir. Did Gunn give a time?'

'Yes he did; CRACKER JACK to be effective in forty minutes; that was exactly a minute and a half ago.'

'Right, Sir.' CBF picked up the phone and the code word was passed to the operations room in the Joint Headquarters.

*

Gunn replaced the phone and joined Doyle at the TV monitors. The hidden cameras gave them complete coverage of the entire control room. The duty shift was all seated on a line of chairs by the wall furthest away from the reactor control console. There were two white-coated technicians standing by the controls of the nuclear reactors and it had to be assumed that these two had been bought by YS and had given McBain and his handful of gunmen an entry into the power station. Besides McBain and the two technicians, there were three other men, all of whom were armed. Right in the centre of the control room were three chairs on which Candy and the Governor's two children were seated. Gunn removed the drawing from the waterproof folder in his pack and spread it out on the metal surface beside the monitors. He looked at the position of all the hostages and then turned to Doyle. 'Right, strip off and let's get on with it. The PLA can only be a few minutes behind us and McBain's going to find out any second that he's lost the guys on the gate.' They both removed their waterproof clothing and then wearing only their black flying suits, they replaced the packs, handguns and knives, picked up the assault rifles and started for the door. Gunn turned back, apologised to the security control staff and then picked up the three telephones and removed the plugs from their sockets. They went back to the lift and down to the first floor. As the lift stopped, both men raised their rifles. The doors opened, but there was no one outside the main control room. At the foot of the wall along the corridor were panels with twist screws securing them in position. John Gunn had memorised the calculations he had made a few minutes earlier and now walked along the corridor to the fifth panel. He put the telephones down, took off his pack and removed two stun grenades, which he put in his thigh pockets. He checked the SA80 and strapped a second magazine to the one in the rifle. He pulled his Browning out of the holster, removed the magazine, checked it and then replaced it.

'OK,' he said to Doyle, who raised his thumb. Gunn took the knife out of its sheath and undid the screws securing the panel. Once it was off, he switched on his torch, and placed his pack just inside the opening from where the panel had been removed. He disappeared on his back into the aperture and pulled himself along, counting the floor panels as he went. He stopped, controlled his breathing and then very gently pushed up the edge of the floor panel above his head. 'Damn,' he muttered, and moved over to his right and did the same again. Spot on! He was right beside Candy's feet with the three hostages between him and McBain's men. Gunn lifted the other side of the panel. McBain was holding a phone and appeared to be getting no reply to his call. Time had run out. Gunn removed the stun grenades from his pocket and placed them on his chest. He pulled the pin on the first one, lifted the edge of the floor panel and then slid the whole panel open about four inches. He took the grenade and rolled it under Candy's chair towards McBain's men. The other one he rolled towards McBain, who had his back to it as he used the phone. Gunn blocked his ears; a two-second delay was followed by an ear-splitting explosion and then by another. Gunn hauled himself through the opening in the floor and round the edge of Candy's chair. All three gunmen were on their knees and died that way as the burst of fire from the SA80 ripped into them. Gunn heard a single shot and then a burst of fire behind him. He swung round. Doyle was crouched on the floor with the two technicians dead in front of him. Of McBain there was no sign. 'You OK, Doyle?'

'Just a flesh wound; really only a graze,' and he took his hand away from his side, which was covered in blood. John pulled down the top of the flying suit and saw the wound. The bullet had scored across one of his ribs, which would be extremely painful. He pulled out his knife and after removing the overalls of one of the dead technicians, he cut it and then tore a long strip off it. He cut off another strip and folded this into a pad and then bound it tightly against Doyle's side.

'How's that?'

'Painful, but I'll live.'

'Did you see where McBain went?'

'Yes; he went through that door,' and Doyle pointed, 'but watch it; he's armed.'

'You OK to look after Candy and the Governor's children?'

'Yes, I'm fine.'

'Right; I'll deal with McBain and you get this lot down to the chopper.' He then turned to Jeremy Fellowes who was still recovering from the blast of the stun grenades. 'Will you be able to repair McBain's handiwork before the opening ceremony tomorrow?'

'I think so,' Fellowes replied. 'It will take a couple of hours to replace the fuel and control rods and check out all the safety mechanisms. We will start work immediately.'

'Fine; just let me deal with McBain and then you can start. When the PLA arrives, say nothing of our presence here,' Gunn added and then turned back to Doyle. 'You know the deal; if I don't appear before the PLA tanks arrive, you get the hell out of here and implement CRACKER JACK,' and he headed for the door. Gunn pushed the door open, which immediately attracted a burst of automatic fire from the direction of the lift. He held his rifle round the side of the door and sprayed half a magazine and then came out into the corridor. It was empty but the lights on the lift showed it moving up to the fourth floor. Gunn pulled his pack out of the aperture in the wall and removed three magazines and two grenades. He went up the stairs, which surrounded the lift shaft until he got to the third floor. There, he paused long enough to press the button to summon the lift. When it arrived he leant in and pressed the button for the fourth floor and then ran up the stairs. Once again the opening door was greeted with a hail of bullets which Gunn returned from the stairwell and was just in time to see McBain disappear through the door at the other end of the corridor. The door was for maintenance access to the number four reactor.

John Gunn ran down the corridor and paused at the door; it opened inwards. He swung it open and stood back. Nothing; the door opened onto a steel platform which ran all round the reactor hall. There was no sign of McBain. Half right from Gunn was a steel ladder. Even as Gunn saw it, the barrel of a sub-machine gun appeared over the top of the ladder. Gunn fired; the burst hit the barrel of the sub-machine gun and hurled it out of McBain's grasp. He moved quickly across to the top of the ladder, but McBain was already on the platform below. Gunn couldn't get a shot at him, but if he moved out onto the ladder he would make a perfect target for the man below him who might well have a handgun.

There were two large 'I' beams, which stretched from one side of the hall to the other about ten feet above Gunn and passed over the reactor core. Travelling on these two beams was a powerful gantry crane, somewhat similar to the one, which Gunn had seen in Middle Kingdom. He presumed that this crane was used for removing fuel rods and heavy plant associated with the reactor and its turbines. Stretching from the crane motor to the platform on which Gunn was standing was the control cable; this was wound round a drum and at the end was a remote switch unit, which operated the crane. John Gunn picked up the unit and switched on the power. After a few false starts he got the hang of the controls and the crane moved along the two beams towards his side of the hall, but stopped well short. Another button on the control unit brought the hook and its pulleys down until they were hanging some fifteen feet or so below the level of the platform. Gunn then moved the crane back along the beams, stopped it and brought it back again. The large hook built up a pendulum movement until it was swinging up to the rail on the platform. Gunn slung the rifle over his head and one shoulder and tied the loop of the control cable round his waist. The hook swung right over the rail and Gunn jumped. He caught hold of the thick, greased metal cable and stood on the block and pulley of the crane's hook. He swung back towards the reactor and at the same time, a bullet ricocheted off the gantry above him. McBain was now using a handgun. Gunn pressed the button to lower the hook and turned the rheostat fully to the right for maximum speed. Even as he started to descend to the floor of the reactor hall, Gunn heard the clattering of McBain's shoes on the metal rungs of the ladder as he raced down to retrieve the sub-machine gun.

Gunn stopped the hook at the lip of the concrete well, into which the reactor core was sunk. As he climbed off the hook and disentangled himself from the electric control cable, he saw McBain dash from the base of the steps to another set which led down into the well surrounding the reactor. Gunn assumed that he'd seen where the gun had fallen and this proved to be correct, for no sooner had McBain reached the bottom of the steps, another twenty feet below John Gunn, than he scooped up the sub-machine gun and fired. The burst was wildly inaccurate, but Gunn retreated behind a metal control panel, from where he could see McBain without exposing too much of himself to offer an easy target. McBain had moved round the circular well and was examining a set of large, red-handled valves. Gunn noticed that he had just crossed over a section of the well floor, which was covered by a metal grid. Above this, were four, eighteen-inch diameter pipes which ended just above the metal grid. All four pipes were painted red. Beside them was a warning notice in Chinese. Gunn couldn't read the characters because the angle was wrong. He moved to another cluster of piping, which provided cover from McBain's gun and read the notice. It announced that the four pipes were the emergency high-pressure steam dump pipes and must not be activated if anyone was in the reactor well. John Gunn moved back to the control panel and saw that McBain was about to turn one of the

254

valves down in the well, which had to be part of the sabotaged mechanism to initiate the reactor melt-down.

On the control panel were four red switches with safety caps over them. They were the dump valve switches. Gunn flicked back the covers of switches one to three. He placed his palm against all three switches and pushed them over. He fell back behind the control panel as strident alarm bells rang and a wave of searing heat swept out from the reactor well as the turbines in the other three reactor halls discharged the super-heated, pressurised steam which had been driving them. The noise was deafening and Gunn groped with his hand until he found the switches and pushed them from open to closed, The noise and billowing clouds of steam subsided. Gunn crawled out from the panel and moved cautiously towards the edge of the well. There was nothing left of McBain except a peculiar-shaped metal object which had once been a sub-machine gun. The intense heat of the steam had rendered flesh, muscle and bone to a porridge consistency and flushed what had once been a human through the metal grid in the floor of the well. Gunn went down the steps to the well, keeping his hands well clear of anything metal. He hooked up the trigger-guard of the sub-machine gun on the barrel of his rifle and went back to the ground floor of the reactor hall. He heard shouts from the platform, which he'd left minutes before. Keeping out of sight of whoever was now on the platform, Gunn left the hall and went out into the night.

*

Commander George Gresham had been captain of the USS Los Angeles, a nuclear-powered, hunter-killer submarine with the Seventh Fleet, for eighteen months. The current deployment had been a particularly uneventful one. Twenty-four hours previously, he had received orders to proceed to a position of 22° 30' North, 117° 10' West and await further instructions. He passed the information to his navigator who immediately asked for confirmation of the position. The captain confirmed it. 'What's your problem, Pete?' he queried.

The navigator marked the position on the chart .

'That's only just in international waters off the coast of China,' he replied. 'Depth?' asked the captain.

'120 feet, but the area is littered with islands and according to the chart,' he bent lower to read the notice to mariners, 'uncharted wrecks.'

'Well let's hope we don't add to their number. Revolutions for twenty knots. Sonar!'

'Sir!'

'We're going in close to the Chinese coast. What sort of stuff have the Chinks got in this area?'

'Where are we headed, Sir?'

'Thirty-five miles to the east of Hong Kong; just inside international waters.'

'That'll be the South China Fleet then. Nothing inshore except their patrol boats. Twin screw, petrol - they're fast, nearly thirty knots, but only armed with a 20mm cannon and machine guns; no depth charges, no sonar capability.'

'Thanks, Murphy.' The submarine had arrived at the location and had then waited on the seabed for 24 hours.

'Signal from Abraham Lincoln, Sir.' The Captain read it. 'Ask the first officer to come to my cabin please,' and George Gresham left the control room.

'Come in, Frank,' the first officer came into the cabin and sat down. 'This is a covert operation which is a joint one between us and the Brits. Both our countries have got a man in China and we've got to get them out before the Chinks start World War Three. They could either fly off in a chopper, which it's thought only has enough fuel for a few minutes flight, or they may try to get off by boat. If the chopper comes it will land on the aft hull. Have a party ready to anchor it to the casing. The pilot's our guy, but he's Army and a bit rusty and he's never flown the type of chopper before. . . .'

'Jesus Christ . . .' came from the first officer.

'Yes, we could do with His help as well,' the Captain continued as though nothing had been said. 'Once we've got everyone on board - oh, yes Frank, nearly forgot, there are these two guys, a broad and two teenage children.'

'Any animals, Sir?'

'Not this time, Pete, but I'll see what I can do next time. Any problems, oh, and before you ask; yes, they can have my cabin. We transfer them to a British Navy patrol boat just inside Hong Kong waters.'

'The chopper, Sir?'

'We dump it. Give the order to surface.'

*

Deafened and confused, Candy and the Governor's children were lead out of the power station and across to the hangar by the helicopter pad. The door was bolted, but soon gave way to Barnes' bolt cutter. The RHKAAF helicopter was the only machine in the hangar. Despite their confusion, the three of them helped Doyle to push the machine out of the hangar and onto the pad. Lights

256

appeared round the bend in the road and the wind carried the unmistakable sound of tank engines and tracks. Doyle hurried the three of them into the back of the helicopter and strapped them in. He climbed into the left-hand seat and shone his torch on the instrument panel. He switched on the power and started the turbines. They'd been right back in Hong Kong; the machine which McBain had commandeered had only been half full and now had less than ten minutes' fuel - just enough to get him to Pinghai. The turbine engine heat rose, as did the revs. The lights of the tanks were now at the gates of the perimeter fence. Where the hell was John? Doyle released the rotors, which quickly gathered speed. The tanks were through the gate and moving to surround the power station. 'Come on, come on!' Doyle coaxed the helicopter. The needles came into the green sectors. There was no sign of Gunn. They'd been spotted by the leading tank. The gun swung towards them. Doyle pulled the chopper off the ground and headed into the darkness followed by a necklace of tracer rounds, which passed under the machine. Doyle banked the helicopter round the back of the power station and then up over the top of it and down again where none of the tanks could bring either their main or sub-calibre armament to bear.

*

As Gunn emerged from the reactor hall, he saw the helicopter take off and swing in an arc towards the back of the power station; he also saw the tanks. To his right was the fire escape which led all the way down from the fourth floor corridor. He ran towards this and raced up the steps. When he got to the top, he ignored the fire door into the corridor and climbed up the framework of the metal fire escape onto the flat roof of the reactor hall. He removed the torch from his pack as he heard the helicopter. It appeared above the domes in the reactor hall roof. Gunn aimed the torch at the cab and flashed it. The machine swung round and then Gunn turned the torch on himself and held it steady. The chopper came forward towards him and planted one skid with its two, small rubber wheels, on the edge of the roof. Gunn ran forward, ducked under the blades and climbed onto the skid. The helicopter lifted off, circled for altitude over the centre of the power station and then with nose down flew out into Daya Bay. Gunn climbed in and slammed the door shut. He did up the lap-strap, but left the shoulder straps and then quickly pulled the headset over his head. 'Thanks, do the same for you if I could fly these damn things. Has this machine got a landing light?' John asked.
  'Yes, right here,' and Doyle indicated a switch.
  'How much fuel?'

'Not much more than vapour in the tank, John. We don't get a second try at this one.'

'Right, I'll start flashing the letter 'A' now.' The signal was answered immediately by a very powerful aldis lamp and lights appeared below them illuminating the deck of a very large submarine. 'Here goes,' muttered Doyle over the intercom. Gunn glanced over his shoulder for the first time to see three very frightened faces. The helicopter sank towards the sea and levelled out over the hull of the submarine. The turbine started to lose power.

'Just two seconds more,' Doyle coaxed. The skids hit the casing, chains were thrown round them and pulled tight as Doyle killed the turbines. The rotors slowed and Doyle slammed on the brakes ignoring the fact that the revs were still too high. The blades juddered to a halt and the doors were wrenched open. The three in the back of the machine were helped out and lowered down an aft hatch.

'Make it quick, everyone. We're about to have company,' and Gunn and Barnes quickly followed the others down the hatch. 'Cast off the chains,' carried down the hatch and then that clanged shut as the high-pressure air forced water into the ballast tanks and the submarine sank below the surface. The red and white helicopter floated for thirty seconds and then followed the submarine under the waves. A minute later, a Chinese patrol boat arrived at the spot, but by then the USS Los Angeles was at flank speed in international waters and on her way to Hong Kong.

CHAPTER 23

The six men were still sitting in the Executive Council Room at Government Office. The phone had rung three times since the call from Gunn and each time all of the men in the room started. All three calls had concerned the mopping-up process after the typhoon and the preparation for the handover of the Territory to China. The phone rang again and the subdued conversation ceased. Martin Holmes picked it up, listened, thanked the caller and then replaced the instrument. The disappointment in the room was tangible. Martin turned from the phone and spoke to the Governor. 'Sir, your children are safe, as is Miss Wyngarde. McBain is dead and no trace is left of him for the Chinese to find. There has been no confrontation with the PLA and there will be no meltdown of the fourth reactor. They are all on their way back in an RAF Wessex and should be at Government House in about eight minutes,' but Martin Holmes was talking to an empty room.

*

At the bar, a handful of people chatted as wine, aperitifs and cocktails were sipped. Gunn and Candy were thoroughly enjoying the ambience of the restaurant and the excellent food and wine. Gunn had ordered moules mariniéres and pepper steak and Candy had settled for smoked salmon and steak tartare. This had been washed down with a chilled '86 Chablis followed by a very pleasant bottle of St Emilion with the steak.

Hong Kong was slowly recovering from the typhoon. The waiter approached their table. 'I'm sorry to disturb you M'sieur, Mme'selle, but there's a call for you,' and with that he produced a cordless phone and handed it to Gunn.

'John Gunn.'

'Hello John, it's Simon here. Are you having a good dinner? I hope I shan't spoil it. Can you catch the Cathay Pacific flight tomorrow evening. I've taken the liberty of booking you on it.'

'Yes, I suppose so. What for, Simon?'

'The director would like to speak to you. He wishes to make your employment full time.'

'That's all very well, but what about Euro-Pacific?'

'The director's already spoken with your boss; the latter has given his blessing. If you agree and can tie up any loose ends, I'll see you at Heathrow the day after tomorrow.'

'Yes, OK; I'll be there. I've one loose end to tie up.' Gunn smiled as he ended the call, took the black rose from its vase and dropped it neatly down Candy's cleavage.

ALSO BY BRIAN NICHOLSON FEATURING JOHN GUNN

AL SAMAK ....is about intrigue, treachery, conspiracy, revenge and violence. It's a story of the flawed and bungled political manoeuvring in the UN before the invasion of Iraq by coalition forces in March 2003. It's the story of Russia's fight to protect its embryo democracy against plotting by die-hard communists. It's the story of Iraq's struggle to achieve a WMD capability to prevent the invasion. It's the story of the desperate measures taken by the intelligence agencies of the coalition to prevent a nuclear holocaust in the Middle East.

It's John Gunn's second assignment with the British Intelligence Directorate, but above all, it's a story.... a story of 21st Century political intrigue and weapons of mass destruction, but this story started as long ago as the 7th Century, as a storm-lashed papyrus raft broke up in the Arabian Sea......but is it a story?....you decide.

ASHANTI GOLD

An investigation into the disappearance of an ineffective operative, from the now-defunct Secret Intelligence Service at the British High Commission in Accra, reveals a conspiracy to overthrow the governments of the majority of countries in West Africa by subversion, terrorism and tribal civil war.

The cruelty and corruption of the 18th century Portugese, Dutch and British slave-traders who raped West Africa of its human and mineral resources, is easily surpassed by that of 21st Century, power-hungry, West African exiles, ruthless arms dealers, diplomats and politicians on both sides of the Atlantic who are involved in the conspiracy.

Governments can be brought down by subversion, terrorism and civil war. Terrorists need weapons which must be bought with money....lots of it. Gold is money......and in Ghana is the richest gold mine in the world at Sawaba in the Ashanti Region where nuggets as big as walnuts can be illegally panned from the Ofin River and then sold to dealers abroad......just as was done during the 18th Century slave trade.

John Gunn is sent on this assignment by the British Intelligence Directorate while still recovering from a gunshot wound received on his previous assignment.

FIRE DRAGON

The slaughter of half a million Communists by Indonesia's President in the 1950s is a weeping sore for Arief Sulitsono (Alias Dr Ramano Rusman) the illegitimate son of Aidit- the Communist leader - who is determined to return Indonesia to a Communist Dictatorship. He realises that he can do nothing against the power of the USA unless he and other developing countries of NAM possess nuclear weapons. He therefore enters into a conspiracy with the North Koreans to help them avoid US interference with their nuclear weapons programme.

Fortuitously, he stumbles on the enormous treasure amassed by Admiral Yamamoto and hidden in the islands off Irian Jaya and uses this unlimited funding to build a rocket launch site on Waigeo Island on the Equator. From this rocket launch site he plans to place the North Korean nuclear warheads in geo-stationary orbit out of reach of IAEA inspection and US satellite surveillance and available to any country resisting US interference.

Rusman's plan unravels because there are other clues to Yamamoto's treasure and his launch site is being built on the most likely epicentre of a cataclysmic earthquake. This is John Gunn's fourth assignment with the British Intelligence Directorate which leads to a confrontation with man-eating dragons in 'the ring of fire'.

THE AUTHOR

Brian Nicholson's life has been almost as exciting and eventful as that of John Gunn. Apart from flying, sailing, scuba-diving, skiing, renovating classic cars and being a talented artist and writer, he has led an unusually exciting and successful life as a soldier. This has varied from active service to negotiator extraordinary in Beijing to rescue the 1984 Anglo/Sino Joint Declaration on the future of Hong Kong. As the personal Military Adviser to Ghana's Flt Lt Jerry Rawlings, he assisted in the planning of the military intervention in Liberia in 1991. As the Defence Attaché in Jakarta, his highly successful expedition to unlock the mystery of what happened to the ill-fated, WW2 Australian commando raid - Operation Rimau - on Japanese shipping in Singapore received wide press coverage at the time.

His first book, 'GWEILO' focuses on a conspiracy to prevent the return of Hong Kong to China. His second book, 'AL SAMAK' is about Saddam Hussein's efforts to obtain WMDs to prevent the invasion of Iraq by the coalition forces in 2003. The third book 'ASHANTI GOLD' uses his exciting exploits in West Africa as a colourful background to a novel that focuses on the famine, chaos and corruption in the African Continent. The author's fourth novel 'FIRE DRAGON' uses material from his experience as a Defence Attaché in Jakarta, where he travelled extensively from the remote areas of Sumatra, Kalimantan and Irian Jaya to the troubled Island of East Timor. This provided an ideal backdrop for a North Korean/Indonesian conspiracy to develop a nuclear weapon and the means of delivering it.

He is now writing his fifth novel featuring John Gunn while he continues to sail, play golf, ski and restore classic cars.

PHOTOGRAPH OF AUTHOR

ISBN 142513356-8

9 781425 133566